CW00524067

SHADOW
FALLS

SHADOW FALLS

WENDY DRANFIELD

bookouture

Published by Bookouture in 2021

An imprint of Storyfire Ltd.
Carmelite House
50 Victoria Embankment
London EC4Y 0DZ

www.bookouture.com

ISBN: 978-1-80019-132-7
eBook ISBN: 978-1-80019-131-0

For my husband

PROLOGUE

January 2000—Austin, Texas

"Nathaniel Monroe, I'm arresting you on suspicion of murder. You have the right to remain silent. Anything you say can be used against you in court. You have the right to talk to a lawyer for advice before we ask you any questions…"

Nate zones out. He can't listen to this cop arresting him when the woman he loves is dead on the ground at their feet. He forces himself to look down at Stacey. Her eyes are staring but unseeing. Her long hair is matted in a red puddle, and under the harsh fluorescent light, he can make out blood spatter on the garage wall, clinging on amongst the DIY tools. Her body is still here, but everything that makes her Stacey is long gone.

His head swims; she'll never say his name again, she'll never kiss him and tell him she can't wait to get married. She'll never infuriate him again.

"… If you decide to answer questions now, without a lawyer present, you have the right to stop answering at any time. You understand?"

Nate slowly turns to look at the black, uniformed officer who has cuffed his bloodstained hands together. They're probably the same age, around twenty-one, but because of the body on the floor, their lives will play out completely differently. "This isn't happening."

The cop raises his eyebrows and nods to Stacey's lifeless body. "Actually, it already happened."

He spins Nate around and, in what feels like slow motion, pushes him out of the garage, past the crime-scene technicians and the cop securing the scene with yellow tape, and out to the waiting police cruiser.

It's dark outside, but the flashing red and blue lights are a painful contrast, and brighter than Nate expected. He feels a migraine starting behind his eyes. He looks beyond the car. There's already a crowd of Stacey's neighbors standing around, shivering in the cold, misty night. The cruiser's flashing lights reflect the horror on their faces. Some are wearing bathrobes over pajamas, with their arms crossed tight and their eyes eager.

One man is standing a little distance away, behind the others. The town's parish priest and Stacey's uncle, Father Jack Connor. He's watching Nate with a sanctimonious look on his face.

What's left of Nate's faith dissolves as he realizes what Father Connor has done.

CHAPTER ONE

June 2019—Malibu, California

Madison Harper yanks her sneakers off and lies back on the creaky motel bed, exhausted. She's just finished the morning shift as pot-washer and waitress at Big Bob's Diner. Since her release from prison back home in Colorado, it's how she's made her money. But she can't do it anymore. Today is the day she's finally going to give in and ask for help, and it goes against every instinct in her aching body.

This motel is supposed to be a halfway house for recently released prisoners, but it's more like an extended version of prison. She's been here just over seven months so far, which is longer than she's allowed. She's been told by Leonard, the creepy building manager, that if she's not out by next week, she'll be thrown out. He's always been uneasy around her and she thinks it has something to do with him finding out what she used to do for a living. He's not exactly running this motel legitimately.

She sighs as she sits forward and slips her shoes back on. This place is meant for the kind of people she used to arrest, not for a cop. Or an ex-cop, which is how she's now considered, causing a ball of anger to swell in her chest. She was so proud to be a detective that it's particularly painful to be in her new situation. As a recently released convicted murderer with only the worst employers willing to give her a job, life can't get much worse, so she refuses to stay a day longer.

She stands up, ignoring the squeak of the bed and the pain in her feet, and looks out of the motel's grimy window. There are three provocatively dressed hookers on the street opposite, all gossiping and looking at each other's phones. She'd guess they're proudly sharing photos of their kids. She once worked alongside women like this; when she was assigned to work undercover for the vice squad. What surprised her most during that time wasn't that women were willing to put their lives at risk to earn money; it was the love they had for the kids who were conceived through violent assaults. It humbled her to see how strong they were in the face of their adversity, and she called on those memories more than once while she was locked up with power-hungry male guards.

Whilst working for vice, Madison helped catch some of the worst pimps in Colorado. Now she's living amongst pimps and their girls, only a few weeks away from needing to sell her own body in order to survive.

One of the girls, Patty, notices her and waves enthusiastically. Madison waves back. She brought some leftover breakfast food home from work that Patty's kids can have for lunch if they reheat it. If Big Bob had caught her, she would've been fired on the spot. He might even have called the cops on her for stealing. She laughs at the irony, whilst blinking back the angry tears behind her eyes.

She turns away from the window as Patty gets into a john's car. The time has come. It has to be now. She grabs a handful of coins from her purse and heads out to the payphone on the street corner.

CHAPTER TWO

Nate Monroe struggles through a flashback from the worst time in his life. He feels the stomach bile creeping up into his throat and swallows to keep his breakfast down.

The room service is getting worse in this hotel, but it's still a million times better than prison food. He stands up and slides the tray that holds greasy eggs and half-eaten toast outside his room, then closes the door on the smell. Sipping a black coffee, he walks to the window.

It's another sunny day in California. He got so little sunshine while incarcerated on death row in Texas that for years he craved living somewhere like this. Somewhere with energetic young people hanging out on bright sandy beaches, and a never-ending ocean view. Now he's here, it feels bittersweet. The sun burns his fragile skin quicker than it used to, he has few friends, and instead of working hard to become a priest, he works as an unlicensed private investigator, helping those the police ignore.

Sometimes the idea of leaving his hotel room cripples him with panic. After spending seventeen years in a ten-by-six-foot prison cell, the outside world can seem too vast, too bright and too dangerous.

He watches from afar as an athletic surfer flirts unsuccessfully with a cute brunette. The sky is clear and blue with no clouds in sight. It's mid morning and already hot. The seagulls are huddled together in the shade of the lifeguard tower, waiting for lunchtime. Nate knows from his daily beach gazing that once the tourists start eating their picnics on the sand, that's when the gulls will feast. For now, they're conserving their energy.

His cell phone rings. He walks to the nightstand and pulls the phone off its charger. He tries to ignore what's left of the white powder next to his wallet. He doesn't want to spend yet another day feeling ashamed of himself.

"Nate Monroe."

"Hi, my name's Madison Harper and I need your help."

This is how all of his phone calls start. There's no family calling to check up on how he is, no girlfriend to ask him out on a date. Just desperate people needing his help. He takes a seat on the bed and pulls out a legal pad and a pen from under the pile of true-crime paperbacks on the floor.

"What's the problem?" he asks.

"I can't tell you over the phone. I'd like it if we could meet in person."

He's intrigued. The woman has a warm voice and speaks eloquently. Not his usual clientele. "I'm in Malibu. You know it?"

"I know it," she says. "You're staying at the Majestic Hotel near Zuma Beach. I've done my research on you, Mr. Monroe, and there's a reason I want your help in particular."

He's alarmed that she knows where he's currently staying. He tries to live off-grid so the police never screw him over again. He immediately suspects she's a cop. "Listen, Ms. Harper, I don't want to get involved with any police business. I don't—and won't—ever work with the police."

"I'm not a cop. Would you meet me at the Mango Bar at noon? I'm not trying to waste your time."

He thinks about it. He's just finished an emotionally draining cold-case investigation that resulted in his client finding out his missing wife was dead and had been for nine years, so he was hoping for a few days' reprieve before moving on to another case. Thanks to the wrongful-conviction payout he eventually received after his release, he's not in this game for the money. He's got enough to last him a lifetime of modest living if he doesn't blow it all on, well, blow. His payout might not make up for losing his fiancée and seventeen years of his life, but it's better than being executed.

Even though he doesn't need the money, he decided to become a private investigator for a reason: he is driven to solve mysteries that no one else dares to or cares to, like someone special once did for him. Fixing other people's problems stops him dwelling on his own. Besides, it's not like he has anything else to do with his time; he never got the chance to finish college so he's not qualified for anything.

"Fine," he says. "I'll be there at noon."

"Thanks. I appreciate it."

His watch tells him he has an hour to get ready.

CHAPTER THREE

Nate deliberately arrives at the bar ten minutes late so he can scope out the parking lot for anyone who might be here as backup for Madison Harper. He may have been out of prison for almost two years now, but he still watches his back and suspects he always will.

Walking through the near-empty bar that smells strongly of vodka, he's grateful that alcohol has never been an issue for him. He can take it or leave it, unlike most ex-prisoners. Since his release, Nate's medicine of choice is cocaine, but even that he can control. Most days.

He spots a solitary woman outside on the veranda overlooking the ocean. She has straight shoulder-length blonde hair and is sitting upright with crossed arms leaning on the table. She's on edge. She looks like a cop in her skinny jeans and smart—if somewhat crumpled—white shirt, and he'd bet she's armed. He has a few seconds to consider backing out in case this is some kind of trap to put him back inside, but she turns to look for him and spots him immediately.

She smiles. It's a nervous smile. Not something he'd expect from a serving detective. It's only that smile that pushes him forward onto the veranda.

"Ms. Harper?" he says.

She stands up and shakes his hand. "Please, call me Madison. I hate that word, *Ms*. Makes me feel old." She smiles brightly at him and points to the chair opposite her.

He smiles back, but he's not fooled by her attempt to set him at ease. It's a standard police tactic and gives him reason to believe she was lying when she told him she wasn't a cop.

He sits opposite her, placing his legal pad and pen on the table next to the menu. He knows using a notepad ages him, even though he's only thirty-nine, but he missed the digital revolution whilst inside, and although he's learning to upgrade, he still feels more comfortable relying on good old-fashioned pen and paper in these situations. No one can hack a notepad, and when you burn a sheet of paper, no IT guy in the world can retrieve its contents.

The waitress is straight on them. "What can I get you guys? Today's special is lemon shrimp."

"I'll just have a black coffee," says Nate. He looks at Madison.

"I'll have a beer, thanks."

"Sure thing." The waitress takes their menus away, probably disappointed she's not in store for a larger tip.

"So, what kind of help do you need?" Nate asks, getting straight to business.

Madison looks over her shoulder like she's expecting some kind of drugs bust. "Confidential help. Is everything I tell you confidential?"

"Sure. But I'm not a lawyer, so if I'm subpoenaed to testify about you, I will. I'd really rather not be subpoenaed in the first place, though. Are you in that kind of trouble?"

She looks him in the eye for the first time. Her eyes are almost the color of the ocean. Her frown creases her face into sharp little wrinkles. He'd guess she's only a few years younger than him, maybe in her mid to late thirties, but she looks exhausted. On closer inspection, he realizes she has the grey tint to her skin that only a prison stay can produce. He knows it well.

"I just got out of prison," she says, as though she's read his mind. "I served six years of a ten-year sentence for voluntary manslaughter."

Nate's surprised, but he doesn't react. He pulls his legal pad in front of him and starts taking notes. "Who were you convicted of killing?"

"A man I worked with." She hesitates for a second and moves her cutlery around. "A cop."

He looks up as he drops his pen. His gut tells him to leave right now. "Sorry, Ms. Harper, but like I said on the phone, I don't work with cops. I wish you well."

He gathers his things to leave.

CHAPTER FOUR

The pretty young waitress brings their drinks over and looks confused as Nate gathers his things. Madison reaches for his arm.

"Please, Mr. Monroe? Just give me a few minutes of your time and I'll explain. If you don't like what you hear, you can leave." She's trying not to sound desperate, but she recognizes pity in his eyes.

The waitress realizes she's interrupting something and excuses herself. Nate slowly sits back down and looks out at the ocean. He appears to be enjoying the cool breeze on his face, but he looks like he'd rather be down there playing volleyball with the locals than sitting up here with a disgraced cop.

Madison leans forward. "I didn't do it, Mr. Monroe. I was framed. I served the sentence but now I'm out, I want to find whoever did this to me. I can't have this conviction hanging over me for the rest of my life. I need to get it overturned."

He appears to think about it, sighs, and then takes a sip of his coffee. "You know, when it comes to the legal system, I used to believe there was no smoke without fire, but I'm not that naïve anymore." He sits up straight. "I'll probably regret this, but tell me more. Where did the victim die?"

She tries not to get too excited that he's willing to hear her out. "Colorado, my home state."

He raises his eyebrows, probably thinking she's a long way from home. "Why would someone frame you if you were a cop?"

She takes a sip of her beer. She's ordered an alcoholic drink for courage. She's not used to asking for help. "That's why I called you."

He remains silent. Unconvinced.

"I chose you because I'd seen your story in the news after your release," she continues. "In prison we all watched your case closely. You were the famous 'killer priest'."

Nate winces. Understandably, he must hate the name the media gave him, but it was inevitable. She'd read he was on track to becoming a Catholic priest, and although he hadn't been ordained yet, that didn't stop the press running with it as soon as they found out about his religious background.

She leans forward. "Your happy ending gave us all hope of having our own, less serious convictions overturned. I'd seen that you were framed too and I thought you'd understand what I've been through. What it's like to serve someone else's sentence."

He meets her eyes and she hopes he understands her need to be exonerated. "Was I wrong?"

Nate turns away and looks out at the ocean again.

She can't stop talking. "I know you served seventeen years on death row for your fiancée's murder. You've been in my position, but worse. You're one of the few people who knows how it feels to lose your life because of someone else's vendetta."

She stops there because she notices his hands have started shaking slightly and beads of sweat have popped up on his forehead.

"Who do you think it might have been?" he asks. "Did you have any enemies, or piss anyone off? Or were you in the middle of a break-up?"

It's her turn to look away. The ocean is glistening in the sunshine. "No. I was single at the time. It had been almost three years since I'd split from my girlfriend."

"Okay." He picks up his pen and writes something down. "Why did you split? Was she mad at you for something?"

She looks at him, unsure whether to trust him yet. "We split because I have a soft spot for men."

He doesn't react. "Was she angry enough to murder a police officer and frame you for it?"

Madison shakes her head. "No. She'd already met someone else by the time I moved out. She visited me in prison during the first couple of years, to make sure I wasn't completely alone. It wasn't her."

Nate's pen moves fast. "What's her name?"

"Stephanie Garcia. But she's not a suspect, Nate."

He still writes her name on his pad. "What did you do on the force?"

"I had just been promoted to detective. It was my fifth year as a cop but my first week in my new role. I was arrested for murder on my thirtieth birthday."

"When were you released?"

"Last November; seven months ago. I came out with no money and no job prospects so I had to spend time finding crappy housing and an even crappier job before I could start looking into who framed me. I can't do it on my own because people won't talk to me."

"What people?" he asks.

"My co-workers." She pauses, before adding, "The rest of my police department."

He drops his pen again, realizing what she's insinuating. "Are you saying you think this was an *inside* job? Someone on the force framed you?"

She takes another long slug of her beer and then smiles at him. "That's exactly what I'm saying."

He leans back in his chair and shakes his head. "Shit. I can't take on a whole police department."

Her heart sinks.

CHAPTER FIVE

Madison has never chased after a guy in her life, but desperate times call for desperate measures. She almost trips on a chair as she runs across the veranda and into the parking lot, ignoring the stares from the waiting staff. Nate is already opening his car door when she reaches him.

"Nate? That's not the only reason I called you today." She has to catch her breath. Any fitness she once had has disappeared after spending six years confined to a cell. It doesn't help that she took up smoking to pass the time.

The PI puts his sunglasses on and leans against his car.

"You mean there's *more*?"

"Yes. I want to work for you. As an investigator."

He laughs, and she wants to punch him for not taking her seriously. She's had enough of that from other people. "I'm serious."

He shields his eyes from the bright sunlight and she has to cover her own. Even sunglasses aren't enough on a day like this. She notices something around his neck, peeking out from under his T-shirt. It looks like black rosary beads. Her eyes drift down to his defined chest, and she can just make out the outline of a cross under the fabric. She's surprised he has any faith left after the horror of what he's experienced.

"I work alone," he says. "I have trust issues. I'm sure you understand."

"Of course. Issues I share. I don't mean I want to work on my own case, but I can pick up unrelated investigations. No employer worth working for will hire me with this manslaughter conviction on my record, and I need money to survive. I was a good cop and I believe I can help you with your cases."

He laughs again.

"If you laugh at me one more time, I'll punch you." She crosses her arms, getting angrier by the minute.

"Look. I'm not laughing at you. I'm laughing at how my day is going. I'm seriously not on the lookout for a business partner, I'm sorry. Why don't you set up on your own?"

Madison rolls her eyes. "Because, like I said, I don't have any money."

He reaches in his pocket for his phone and gives it a quick glance. "The client pays your expenses, so all you really need is a case. You can get that by setting yourself up with a website and a business number. Your phone will probably ring within twenty-four hours. The majority of cases are cheating partners, but you can more or less charge what you want. You'll need a license too, if you want to do everything above board." He stops to think about what he's just said. "Actually, I couldn't get a license, even with my conviction being overturned, so I doubt you'd be granted one. You'd have to be upfront with any clients about that, unless you want to end up back inside."

"See! These are the kind of things I could be learning from you," she says. "Let me at least help you with your next case—like a trial period." She avoids the word "probation" for obvious reasons. "Or give me all the menial jobs, so you can focus on the big-ticket cases. If I'm a pain in the ass, you can let me go after. But I'll still want you to work on my case, either way."

He appears to be thinking about it. "I assume you're on parole. What are your conditions?"

She takes a deep breath. "Basically, I just need to stay out of trouble. No arrests and no drugs. My parole officer surprised me with a few random drug tests after my release, but not anymore. She could see I wasn't a troublemaker. As long as I call her once a month for the foreseeable future, I'm all good."

Nate nods, then smiles. "You just told me you're broke; how are you going to pay me to work on your case?"

She smiles back. "That's the beauty of it. My wages will go directly to you. So in essence, I'd be working for free. Well, obviously I'll need you to cover some of my living expenses, but I live cheaply. I don't need anything fancy. Not since prison, anyway."

He pauses, which gives her hope. But then he gets into his car. Before he closes the door, he looks at her. "Let me think about it."

She takes a deep breath as she watches him pull out of the parking lot. She doesn't want to get her hopes up, but right now, Nate Monroe is the only chance she's got of ever getting her son back.

CHAPTER SIX

The office of Dr. Pamela Jarvis

Dr. Jarvis takes a sip of her coffee and grimaces. She's out of sugar, but she needs to stay alert today and knows this will be the first of many strong coffees for her. Last night was horrendous. Knowing what she had to do today meant she didn't sleep at all. It's a good job she's single, as she would have been kicked out of bed with all the tossing and turning she was doing. And thank God for under-eye concealer.

Moving a pile of paperwork from her office chair, she sits behind her oak desk in preparation for reading a client's journal. A while ago now she suggested this client keep a stream-of-consciousness account of what she's feeling, to help her cope with the aftermath of the accidental death of two of her children last year. Pamela was concerned with the way her client was internalizing her pain, and she thought this might help to release some of it.

She opens the journal and reads the first couple of pages, written a year ago:

It's been one month since the accident. I worry where my thoughts take me lately. Did they die because of me? Is it something I did whilst raising my children that caused this? Or were they always destined to only reach three years and five years old? If so, I wish I'd been told sooner. I would never have had them. I've learned the bitter lesson that it's not better to have loved and lost than never to have loved. That's a lie manufactured to make people feel better. I know now with great, searing clarity that it's better never to have loved in the first place.

It is no comfort to me that they died together. No comfort that my husband has stayed with me when I'm told most couples who lose a child split up. How can there be any kind of comfort after what we've been through? It should've been all of us. That would have been kinder.

I often wonder if forgiveness is real or just a concept we pay lip service to because it's expected of us. They say nothing can ever prepare you for losing a child, but what about losing two? As horrific as it is to never be able to hold your children again, to never be able to tell them you love them and miss them, the look of pity in people's eyes when they see me now is almost as bad. The doctors, the nurses, the police, the neighbors, the parents at school. It's a look that gives away their thoughts: "I'm so glad it wasn't my children."

I don't blame them for it. God knows I'd like to be one of them. The question now is whether to live this life of pretense or whether to end the pain and die. At this moment I could go either way.

She takes a deep breath and closes the journal. She hadn't realized quite how close her client was to giving up last year. As a therapist, missing the signs is unforgivable.

CHAPTER SEVEN

Nate has driven to the dog beach. He sits in his usual spot in the shade of the afternoon sun whilst slathering sunscreen all over his face and arms and watching other people's dogs splash around in the ocean. He had a chocolate Labrador as a kid and has had a soft spot for dogs ever since. In his experience, they're more trustworthy than people. All animals are. He thinks of the cat they had on death row, brought in once a week by a well-meaning charity to try to reduce the inmates' suffering. He was black with a white chest and his owner called him Oreo. That cat spent more time with Nate than anyone else and he always wondered why. He liked to think it was because he was the only innocent person on the unit, but he knows that probably wasn't it.

He checks his phone out of habit: no messages. He doesn't have a new case to work on yet so he doesn't see how he could take Madison on as an investigator. At the moment the majority of his jobs come through his friend Rex Hartley. Mainly because Rex is a sucker for a sob story and listens to whoever is willing to confide in him. Rex is one of the good guys and has helped Nate acclimatize to life on the outside, like an unofficial therapist. He's an ex-convict himself and Nate met him through Kristen, the woman who helped get his conviction overturned.

He'd give anything to be able to speak to Kristen again, to show her how all her hard work paid off in the end and to greet her without the handcuffs and prison-issue white uniform. But after more than two years of no contact or sightings, he has to assume she's dead, and probably because of him.

He sometimes wonders whether that's why he became a PI: to find Kristen. He shakes his head as if he's spoken the thought aloud. He's kidding himself. He knows the real reason. He became an investigator to find Stacey's uncle. That was something else the police screwed up: they let Father Jack Connor get away with murder. Nate won't be doing that.

He enjoys the sun on his face as he watches a game of beach volleyball and the pack of dogs excitedly trying to join in. He thinks about Madison Harper again. If she's telling the truth, she's right to want to find out who framed her. She appeared genuine. And Nate knows a guilty person wouldn't want someone looking into their conviction *after* they've been released from prison. They'd want to move on with their life and forget it ever happened. Madison obviously wants to clear her name.

If he's honest with himself, he'd love to take the case. He'd love the chance to nail a bent cop, assuming it was someone from her police department, but his gut instinct warns him that getting involved with the police would put him at risk. Whilst inside, he vowed never to set foot in a police station voluntarily. He knows he couldn't serve more time. Sin or no sin, he would take the easy way out if they ever tried to make him go back there.

His cell phone rings and Rex's name appears. Nate smiles as he answers the call. "How're you doing, Rex? I was actually just thinking about you."

"I'm not bad, my friend. How about you? Are you living it up in Vegas with your millions yet?" Rex laughs heartily. "I keep expecting you to tell me you've squandered it all on broads and booze."

Rex is a big man, in height and size, with a deep, booming voice that's intimidating to the right people. But Nate knows he's a softie inside. He lives on an old ranch in San Diego with a herd of stray animals: dogs, cats, horses, snakes, geckos. He takes anyone in. Anyone except cops, that is, because he hates cops even more than Nate does.

"I'm waiting for you to come with me," Nate says.

"I wish! Who would feed the animals?"

Nate laughs.

"Anyway, this is a business call," says Rex. "I've been contacted by a friend of a friend who knows this woman whose granddaughter went missing two weeks ago. She was at a summer camp called Camp Fearless in Shadow Falls. That's in the Wildwood National Forest, north of the state. You know it?"

"Can't say I do."

"Well, according to Google Maps, it's about a twelve-hour drive from Malibu and in the middle of nowhere. Anyway, the grandmother says the police have been useless—go figure—and she suspects foul play. The girl hasn't been spotted since her disappearance, so she wants to hire an investigator. You interested?"

"I don't know. How old's the girl?"

"Twelve. Name's Jennifer Lucas. Grandmother's called Esme and she talks with an old-money accent. I called to find out a bit more about it and she said she'd like to keep it all on the down-low. Doesn't want the police knowing that she's going around them. Sounds like just your thing."

Nate thinks about it. He's ready to move on from Malibu and he doesn't have anything else to work on right now, unless he takes Madison's cold case. He's not sure about her yet. "Do we have any idea how the police investigation went?"

"Yeah, the grandmother said they're working on the assumption that Jenny ran away. There's no body and no sign of foul play at the summer camp. Staff have been background-checked: no registered sex offenders on the payroll. She said she'd prefer to discuss the rest in person, like they all do. She and the girl's parents live in Santa Barbara."

Nate would assume it was a runaway case too if the rich grandmother hadn't asked for help. It's unusual for people with money to go against the police. He's intrigued, and as he watches a huge black Newfoundland running toward him, completely soaked with sea water, he decides to take the case.

"Okay, send me her details. I'll contact her."

"That's my boy!" says Rex. "I should start charging commission for all the work I bring you."

"Or you could leave the safety of your ranch for once in your life and help me work the cases. We'd be like Cagney and Lacey."

Rex laughs. "My hair's too short for that."

Nate smiles, then asks the question he's asked a hundred times before. "Any leads on Father Connor or Kristen?"

Rex sighs down the line and answers the same way he always does. "You'll know as soon as I hear anything, Nate."

It was Rex who had managed to get an illegal copy of the police report into Stacey's death. He found a witness statement from a neighbor saying they thought they saw Father Connor leaving the crime scene just minutes before Nate showed up and found Stacey's body. Nate was fifteen years into his capital murder sentence and just two years away from his final execution date at the time Rex discovered it. It had apparently been ignored by the police and prosecution so Rex gave it to Kristen for her to act on. Up until that point he'd had an increasingly bad feeling about Stacey's uncle, but he hadn't wanted to believe he'd actually murdered her.

Once Rex told him what was in the police report, he knew for sure. He just didn't know *why* Stacey's deeply religious uncle would do that to his beautiful niece and then frame Nate for it by planting the bloody hammer in his car seconds after Nate's arrival at the house.

He's disappointed that there are still no leads on Father Connor, but he's hopeful that he'll come face to face with him one day. He ends the call and stands up, but he's too late to miss the spray from the dog shaking himself dry. "Come on! Give me a break," he says.

The dog barks at him, excited to get a reaction. Nate hears a woman laugh behind him and turns. He recognizes the redhead who's looking at him.

CHAPTER EIGHT

The next morning, Madison packs what few belongings she owns. Nate wouldn't answer her calls last night and she's worried he's going to move on to the next job and forget about her. She looks around the small room that has served as her home for the last seven months. The bedcovers are threadbare, the carpet is covered in stains and the soft furnishings are filthy. She's leaving here today and never returning. And if she ever makes it back into law enforcement, which she's determined to do, she'd love to come back and arrest Leonard for pimping out the women who have kept her company.

She pulls the cheap Glock pistol she bought on the street out from under her mattress. She doesn't intend to go back to Colorado unarmed, so a gun was one of the essential items she spent her first month's wages on. She slips it into her purse, picks up her holdall and opens the door. Without looking back, she walks to Patty's door and knocks. Marcus, Patty's oldest son, opens it, rubbing his eyes as if he's been asleep.

"Hey, sweetie," she whispers. She looks over his shoulder and can see Patty is in bed with the babies. "Is your mom still asleep?"

Marcus nods.

"Would you do me a favor and give her this when she wakes up?" She hands him a parcel of leftovers and a sealed envelope. On the front is a brief note: *I'm sorry it's not more. Take care. M x*

He looks up at her. "Are you leaving?"

She nods, not trusting herself to speak. Marcus is nine years old and similar to her own son in many ways.

"Wait here." He turns away from the door and puts the leftovers down on the coffee table, then runs to his side of the double bed. He squats down and picks something up. When he hands the item to her, he turns shy. "On TV, cops always wear aviators. I found these and saved them for you."

She looks at the mirrored sunglasses and knows he didn't find them; they're branded and new-looking. But she's touched he would steal them for her. She kneels down for a hug, enjoying the warm embrace. "Thank you. I love them. Just please don't get caught. Remember what I told you about prison?"

He nods.

As he waves goodbye and closes the door, Madison turns her back on the motel for the last time. She fights back tears behind her new sunglasses as she begins the three-mile walk to Nate's hotel.

With her feet aching in her worn sneakers, she's sweating and pissed off as she reaches the Majestic Hotel, which is surrounded by palm trees and overlooking the beach. She can't help feeling envious of Nate. He might have had it worse in prison, but he's living better than her now he's out.

As she turns the corner into the parking lot, she sees him carrying bags to a metallic-grey Jeep Grand Cherokee. She's about to approach him when an attractive redhead appears. Madison waits behind a palm tree as she watches the woman wrap her arms around Nate's neck.

"I'm never going to see you again, am I?" she says.

Nate pulls her in closer by her waist. "Never say never." They kiss. "If I'm ever back in Malibu, I'll call you."

"You better." She smiles at him and Madison jumps as a cab appears behind her.

Just before the redhead gets in the back, Nate calls out, "Say hi to Blake for me."

She laughs whilst shaking her head. "You're *so* bad."

It's only as the cab drives away that Nate notices Madison walking toward him. She finishes her cigarette and removes her sunglasses.

He watches her as she checks out the Jeep. "It's one of the few luxuries I afforded myself once I received my payout. I figured it would be comfortable enough to sleep in if I ever had to go on the run. Not that I should have to, but you never know what life has in store." He laughs. "It's smaller than my prison cell, but more comfortable, and with much better air quality."

Madison crouches to look through the car's tinted windows and then gestures to his bags on the ground near the trunk. "Going somewhere?"

"What are you doing here, Madison?" he asks, noticing her own stuffed holdall.

"Call me Maddie. You didn't return my calls last night." She stands up straight. "You're leaving, aren't you? Moving on to the next town, the next job."

He nods. "I am. I was going to call you before I left this morning to let you know that I'm happy to look into your case, but I realized I didn't have your cell number. Did you use a pay phone to contact me? It came up as number withheld."

She smiles and then turns away before he can see her tears. Her heart starts beating faster as she realizes what his help could mean. If he finds out who framed her, she could be exonerated and back on the force within months. Earning again. Living again. She could find her son and tell him she's not a murderer. She could wipe the slate clean.

While she struggles to contain her emotions, he gives her a minute to compose herself by checking he's brought all his belongings from the hotel room.

With a shaky voice, she asks, "What persuaded you?"

He throws his bags in the trunk and closes it. "If you were framed by a cop, we could really nail the assholes. We could take down a whole department. Because these things don't happen in isolation; a bent cop needs cover, which means someone else knows what they did to you. They could do it again. Hell, it was six or seven years ago now, so they probably *have* done it again. I don't like that, Madison. That kind of thing keeps me awake at night."

She nods, more relieved than he'll ever know. He's trusting that she's innocent.

"But for now, I've been called out on another case, so I can't go to Colorado with you just yet. I'm sure you'd agree your cold case isn't as urgent as a missing child." He turns to get in his car. "I'm not sure how long I'll be gone, but if you give me your cell number, I'll contact you when I've wrapped that up."

"No."

He turns back to look at her.

She's shaking her head. "No. It's taken me almost seven years to find help. I'm sticking with you so you don't forget about me."

"What do you mean?"

She feels desperate. He can't make her wait any longer. She steps toward him. "Let me come with you. I can help you with your other case. I can do the admin, invoicing, driving, whatever! I have nothing here, Nate. I have nothing anywhere."

He looks up at the blue sky, as if he's enjoying the warm sun on his face.

It's agonizing for her to be reliant on a complete stranger to sort out her problems. "I travel light." She picks up her holdall and nods to it. "And I'm not a big talker. You won't even know I'm there."

"Is that seriously all you own?" he asks.

She watches as he realizes it was a stupid question. He would have left prison the same way as her; with nothing but the crappy street clothes they give you and fifty dollars from the state. If he hadn't received compensation, he wouldn't be in the position he's in now. She just has to hope he remembers how that feels. "Please,

Nate. Just give me a chance. You never know, we might even get along." She attempts a hopeful smile.

He looks as if he's seriously considering it, but then says, "You don't even know where I'm going."

She shrugs her shoulders. "Like I said, I have nothing keeping me here, so I don't care where you're going. All I know is you're stuck with me until you solve my case."

He takes a deep breath, then motions to the car. "Okay, get in. But don't make me regret this."

She jogs around to the passenger side before he can change his mind. After buckling her seat belt, she gives him a thumbs-up through the windscreen.

Nate shakes his head, but she thinks he's probably happier than he's letting on. The world is a lonely place for ex-convicts. They need to stick together.

CHAPTER NINE

Madison watches the beach disappear in the rear-view mirror. She can't believe her luck. It's been so long since anyone said yes to her that she's worried Nate will change his mind before they've even left Malibu. She tries to stay quiet so he forgets she's there. Sinking back into the comfortable leather seat, she thinks about Owen, her son.

He was ten years old when she was arrested. He would've celebrated his seventeenth birthday this month. Owen was a summer baby and had the blond hair to match. Her chest aches whenever she thinks of him. She needs to find him. She needs to explain where she went and why, but not until she's been exonerated, because he needs to know he's been fed lies about her for the last seven years.

"Did you move here straight after your release, Maddie?" asks Nate.

"I came here to find you. I don't live anywhere at the moment."

He takes his eyes off the road for a minute. "How did you track me down?"

She thinks there's no harm in telling him. "Through one of those websites dedicated to murderers. It constantly updates with who's been convicted, sentenced, released or…" She tails off.

"Or put to death?" he says.

She nods. "Yeah. Someone had updated your profile to say you'd been spotted living in San Francisco recently and you were working as a PI, then someone else said they'd heard you'd moved on to Malibu. It wasn't hard to find you down here. I used to be a cop, remember."

He looks a little annoyed. "I've been trying to keep a low profile."

"Not hard enough, obviously. If I could find you, any cop or federal agent could. You need to travel under a different name."

He's silent for a few miles and she's desperate to ask him about his experience. She's intrigued by the fact that he was almost a priest but gave it all up at the last minute for a woman. She knows he was convicted of murdering his fiancée, and that he was just months away from taking that final walk to the death chamber when he was finally exonerated. That's got to change a person; knowing the day you're going to die. What must be even worse is knowing you're being killed for something you didn't do, while the real killer is free. She'll be surprised if she doesn't discover somewhere along their journey that he has a temper. Anyone would be angry and vengeful after spending almost two decades on death row.

Even so, she's not afraid of him. Having been a cop, she knows how to protect herself, but so far, he appears to be anything but angry. Still, she won't ask him anything about his case until they know each other better. Clearing her name and finding Owen is her priority.

"I thought about it," he says, finally. "I thought about changing my name once I'd been released. But I didn't want to give up my identity after everything else they'd already taken from me. I don't know, call me stupid, I guess."

She looks over at him. "I understand. I feel the same way. We shouldn't be ashamed of who we are. We haven't done anything wrong."

He nods, and she can tell his mind is taking him backwards, to prison, so she changes the subject.

"So, where are we going?"

He laughs. "I can't believe you've only just asked that." He punches a zip code into his sat nav and takes a right turn. "First, we're going to Santa Barbara. Should only take an hour depending on the traffic. I've been asked to investigate the disappearance of a twelve-year-old girl, and that's where her family lives. She was at a summer camp north of the state when she disappeared. The cops think she's just a runaway, but the grandmother's adamant she wouldn't do that."

Madison rolls her eyes. "That's what they all say."

"I'll bet, but this feels different to me. The grandmother doesn't trust the investigating cops, so you can see why it appealed to me." He smiles at her.

She likes his smile. Apart from being a bit weathered around the edges, he's handsome. He has a thick head of sun-kissed light brown hair, and attractive blue eyes. He's tanned, probably taking any opportunity to sit in the sun since his release, like her, although she'd bet he's obsessed with sunscreen, if her own experience of increased UV sensitivity is anything to go by. She knows from the news reports that he's thirty-nine years old. He hasn't let himself go, unlike most ex-prisoners. He still shaves, and he dresses smartly. His jeans and T-shirt look like surf wear, but she'd guess they're designer. She did a lot of digging into Nate Monroe and she knows all about his three-million-dollar payout. He was one of the lucky ones, and she's happy for him. She doesn't expect that to ever happen to her; her life just doesn't work that way, never has.

"By the way," she says. "Don't call me Maddie. I prefer Madison. I'm not a teenager."

He looks surprised. "But you said…"

"I know, because the sad fact is that men prefer helping vulnerable young girls rather than thirty-six-year-old women. I guess I just used some persuasive powers by making myself seem vulnerable when I needed your help. Sorry. I once worked vice, so I learned a few tricks."

He shakes his head and looks back at the road. "This is exactly why I hate cops."

She turns away from him and smiles.

*

When they stop at a gas station forty minutes later, Madison buys them both coffees. Thanks to months of waiting tables and smiling prettily for tips, she has enough money to last her four or five months—if she sticks to the essentials. But she wants to show Nate she's not here for a free ride. Paying for coffee is a small gesture, but it's all she can afford to do right now. Nate might be helping her, but she's still got to look after what little she has. And she has her pride.

"Here you go." She places his coffee in front of him. They're taking a break on some old patio chairs outside the gas station. "Did you want milk with that?"

"You sound like a waitress," he says.

She bristles. "What's wrong with waitresses?"

"Nothing, it was a joke." He looks up at her.

She lets it slide and takes a seat next to him. It's been a while since she's spent this long with anyone, so she knows she's lost her sense of humor. She looks at her pack of cigarettes, but she only has one left. She's trying to cut down, and drops the pack on the table. "Who's our client? The grandmother or the girl's parents?"

"Grandmother. I spoke to her last night, but she was pretty guarded. We're going to see her at her son's house. He and his wife know she's contacted an investigator, but they're not happy about it, apparently."

"Why not?"

Nate takes a sip of his coffee and grimaces. "This is bad." He places it back on the plastic table. "Because her son thinks their daughter ran away, and his wife is so devastated by the whole thing that she doesn't want any more officials coming to her house and searching the girl's bedroom. She's finding it hard to cope with her disappearance, so we have to tread carefully."

"Probably a good thing you have a woman with you then. It sounds like she's sick of men in suits." She tries the coffee. He's right, it is bad. Even so, she can't pour it away. She worked an hour clearing tables to pay for it. That's what she does now that every penny counts: she adds up the cost of everything she spends versus how long it took her to make it. It's depressing, but when you spend all your free time alone, there's not much else to do to pass the time.

"The grandmother told me she was using a burner phone," says Nate. "Can you believe she knows about things like that?"

Madison is surprised. "Good. That was sensible if she thinks the cops could be listening to them. Maybe the detectives working the case are hiding something. She must have her suspicions about them if she's hired a PI."

Nate appears to think about it. "You know, it never ceases to shock me how many cops are bent. I know there are excellent officers out there too, but it just feels that things are taking a turn for the worse. Especially lately."

"Well, when the politicians get away with murder, what do you expect?" Madison says. "But we're not all bad; just fallible like everyone else."

Nate looks at her for a moment. "You don't seem like a cop. Did you enjoy it?"

She nods. "I loved my job. I'd finally got the promotion I had worked hard for. I had everything I ever wanted."

Nate glances away. "We'll get it back for you."

She looks down at her coffee. "Some things you can't get back."

CHAPTER TEN

November 2000—Austin, Texas

After almost ten months in jail awaiting trial, Nate thought things couldn't get any worse. After all, the daily confrontations, weekly beatings and random threats of rape were pretty horrific. Add to that the slop they call food, the sweltering conditions in the cells and the complete lack of comfort, and he'd be forgiven for assuming that. But when his trial begins, he realizes he's been naïve. Everything before the trial now feels like high-school drama. Things are about to get much worse.

Midway through the trial, Nate takes the stand, very much against his attorney's advice. He's adamant he wants to speak up for himself, to make the jury see he's not a killer and that he genuinely loved Stacey.

A deathly silence ripples through the courtroom as everyone stops whispering. All eyes are on Nate. His lawyer asks him the opening question they discussed beforehand.

"Nathaniel. Could you please give us an insight into your life with Stacey Connor?"

Nate's mouth is dry but his hands are shaking too much to risk taking a sip of the water in front of him. He looks at the mic as he speaks, unable to meet anyone's eyes just yet.

"Stacey and I met at eighteen, just after I moved to Austin from my home state of Kansas. I came here to study philosophy at the University of Texas with a view to eventually becoming ordained as a priest. We were introduced by her uncle, the Reverend Jack

Connor, or Father Connor, as he prefers to be called." He tries not to grit his teeth as he says the man's name. "I was spending a lot of time at my new local church in between classes and Father Connor was the priest. He took the time to explain what the role of a priest involves and he introduced me to the community. I thought he'd taken me under his wing at the time, but…" He stops, not wanting to go there just yet.

"Anyway, I pretty much fell in love with Stacey from the get-go. She was kind enough to let me hang out with her during church services because she knew her uncle was helping me. It seemed to me that she didn't have many friends of her own. When I found out she lived just a block over from me, with her mom and uncle, we started walking home together after mass. Until Father Connor found out and put a stop to it."

He looks up. A shake of his lawyer's head reminds him he's not supposed to bad-mouth Stacey's uncle. It will make him look resentful, apparently, which could be used as a motive for murder by the prosecution.

"When her uncle introduced us, he obviously didn't think we'd hit it off so well, but we soon became inseparable. Clichéd, but true. I developed feelings for her that confused me. She met my dad; she was the first girl I'd ever introduced him to, because I'd never had a girlfriend before. Until I met Stacey, I'd never wanted anyone that way, so it was never an issue. We spent a lot of time with her mom, Deborah, just watching movies and eating dinner together. Father Connor spent nearly all his time at the church, so it felt like she was lonely."

He has to avoid the impulse to look over at Stacey's mom to check for her reaction. Does she even care that he is in this position? That her brother did this to all of them? He hasn't been able to shake the feeling that Father Connor killed Stacey, but he has no way of proving it. Would Deborah let him get away with it if he had? He feels his eyes wandering in her direction, so he pulls them back to the mic.

He'd lose it if she was staring back at him with cold, impassive eyes. He needs to believe she genuinely cared for him once.

"Pretty much everything we did had to be under the watchful gaze of Stacey's mom and uncle, as they're incredibly religious." This time he doesn't look at the lawyer for his reaction. He's just telling the truth, and if the jury can't handle that, then too bad. "I mean, I know I was becoming a priest, but they really took their devotion to the next level."

He sneaks a look at the jury; two women have disapproving looks on their faces, as if he shouldn't be criticizing other people's religious beliefs. Most Texans are incredibly conservative, so Nate's been told to tread carefully while his life is in their hands.

"Anyway, once I'd fallen in love with Stacey, and she with me, I battled with my decision to become a priest. I mean, I spent months arguing with myself about whether I should give up a woman I loved for a career I'd always wanted. Normally I would've turned to my parish priest for counsel, but I couldn't, because that was Stacey's uncle and his behavior toward me had turned from friendly to icy once he saw how Stacey felt about me. He must've been under the illusion she'd never leave home and marry, because he hated the idea of us being together. Eventually, after battling my feelings, I chose Stacey over the priesthood."

His lawyer jumps in, pre-empting the kind of questions Nate will get in the cross-examination from the prosecution. "Didn't that leave you a little resentful? That you'd never get to fulfill your ambitions because of"—he turns to the jury with an apologetic but pre-rehearsed smile—"the attractions of a woman? Did you not see her as a temptress, trying to lure you away from God? I mean," another rehearsed smile at the ladies, "wasn't she Eve with the ultimate apple?"

Nate watches as one of the women on the jury smiles back at the lawyer, almost flirting with her eyes. Clearly not all jurors are smart to the tactics of attorneys.

The lawyer turns back to Nate. "Because let's face it, you'd wanted to be a priest since you were thirteen years old. You were studying philosophy specifically for that career, and you'd spent your teenage years heavily involved in the work of your local parish. How come you were able to give up on that dream so quickly, and all for a woman you'd only known for a couple of years?"

Nate shakes his head and looks at the jury one by one. They return hard, unreadable stares. They've been told repeatedly by the prosecution and the media that Nate was found with his dead fiancée at his feet and her blood on his hands. They're bound to be biased; anyone would be. He just has to hope they have a grain of intelligence between them and realize that he was covered in her blood because he'd tried to save her.

"Not at all. I felt I didn't have a life without Stacey, so I didn't consider it a sacrifice to give up that dream. I'd have done anything for her. I'm nothing without her." He feels a lump in his throat that threatens to choke him, so he takes a few seconds to compose himself.

"In your opinion, Nathaniel, what kind of woman was Stacey?"

Nate hears Father Connor making disapproving sounds from the seats behind the prosecution, which attracts the jurors' attention. He knows Father Connor hates hearing anyone talk about his family, because he can't edit what they say. He doesn't want anything to reflect poorly on him.

"Stacey was the funniest person I ever met. We were always laughing. She had a positive outlook on life but a cynicism that was refreshing for someone living in such a strict household."

"Could you explain that?" asks his lawyer.

"Her uncle limited what Stacey was exposed to, in TV, films, books, life experiences. But she was still worldly. It's hard to explain. She trusted people on one hand, but was cynical about them on the other. It's like she knew that most people's lives were all for show on the surface, and mostly fucked up underneath, no matter how much they prayed."

There's a ripple of disapproval from the jury at his use of the f-word but he continues regardless. "What I mean is that Stacey knew that no one was perfect, despite how well their front lawn was cut or how many times they attended church on a Sunday. Behind closed doors everyone has their problems and everyone tries to pretend otherwise."

"And what were your problems?" asks his lawyer. "In your relationship?"

Nate hesitates. He knows the jury aren't going to like this. "I didn't consider it a problem because I loved her, but Stacey was an alcoholic."

Father Connor jumps up and shouts, "How dare you!"

The jurors look shocked, and Nate can't tell whether that's because they didn't know a woman from a religious family could be an alcoholic, or because of her uncle's outburst. Regardless, Judge Kemper takes control.

"Silence in court or we'll adjourn until tomorrow. Father Connor, with respect, this is your only warning: compose yourself or leave my courtroom."

Father Connor remains standing but faces the judge. "I'm sorry, Your Honor, but that's my niece he's slandering and she can't answer for herself so I have to." He sits down with a thud and dabs his eyes with a tissue.

Stacey's mother is crying now. Nate is regretful that he had to disclose Stacey's secret in such a public forum, but Deborah and Father Connor both knew about her drinking and turned a blind eye. Until it got worse and they started blaming it on Nate.

Nate's attorney waits for Judge Kemper to give him a nod to continue. Then he asks, "When did you first realize Stacey was an alcoholic?"

Nate shifts uncomfortably in the wooden chair. He feels like he's betraying her but he vowed to tell the truth. "She already liked to drink socially when I first met her, despite being underage. But during the weeks leading up to her death she was drinking every day and it was hitting her harder."

"Did you ever discuss it with her?"

He nods. "She knew she needed to cut back. But the week before she died, she told me she'd found out something upsetting and she needed to take the edge off."

There's silence in the courtroom now. Everyone is listening intently.

His lawyer asks, "Did she disclose what she'd found out?"

Nate looks at his hands. "No. She was planning to tell me on the night of her death. We'd arranged to go out for dinner, just the two of us. She told me over the phone a few days before that she'd been wrestling with the discovery on her own and she wasn't sure whether to tell anyone. For some reason she was nervous about how I'd react."

His lawyer glances at the jurors and then back at Nate. "What did you think she was going to tell you?"

Nate laughs nervously. "I was convinced she was going to break up with me."

"Why is that? Were you hiding something from her?"

"No, I wasn't." Nate glances at Deborah, then at her brother. "But she was arguing with her mom and uncle so much that I thought she'd figured I wasn't worth the effort. Even then, I didn't believe she would really want to split up with me. I thought maybe she just wanted an easier life. I don't know, the whole situation was so confusing to me."

"Confusing enough for you to lash out and kill her?"

He tenses. "Of course not. I loved her. If she wanted to split up with me, I would have turned back to the Church and continued my path to becoming ordained. I'm not a violent person and you'll never find anyone in my life who will testify otherwise." He looks at Father Connor, who's playing the grieving uncle role to perfection. "No honest person, that is."

CHAPTER ELEVEN

It's just after lunchtime when Nate and Madison reach Santa Barbara and locate the Lucas residence. It's a big contemporary Spanish-style home, which looks pretty new. Nate pulls up to the intercom at the double-gated entrance. He gets out of the Jeep into the intense midday heat and pushes the button. When he announces himself, the gates open and the house reveals itself behind an impressively landscaped front garden. He can tell this family has money. Not that it will be much comfort to them while their daughter is missing.

He pulls into the private driveway.

"I'll let you do the talking," says Madison as they approach the entrance.

The door opens as soon as they reach it and a tall, slim woman with stylish grey hair greets them. "I'm Esme Lucas, Jenny's grandmother. Thank you for meeting with us, Mr. Monroe." After a quick shake of his hand, she gives Madison a critical glance.

"This is Madison, who will be assisting me."

He realizes just in time that he probably shouldn't mention Madison's last name in case anyone googles her. That would be bad for business. His name is bad enough and has already put some people off hiring him. It took a full year after his release before his wrongful conviction was wiped from his record. Before his compensation payout, he tried to get housing and a job, but the conviction showed up on background checks, which meant he was always turned down. He resorted to carrying newspaper clippings about his exoneration. He still keeps them in his wallet in case he's ever arrested for something he didn't do.

"Come on in." Esme leads them to an immaculate open-plan living room. It has large windows giving panoramic views of the distant ocean over countless treetops.

"You have an amazing view," says Madison. "And a lovely home."

"It isn't my house. My son and his wife live here with Jenny."

Jennifer Lucas. The missing girl. Nate hears hushed voices before two adults appear from another room. The man is tall and slightly overweight, with sandy hair. He walks up to Nate with a frown on his face, but extends his hand in greeting. "Hi. Grant Lucas. And this is my wife, Anna."

Anna is also tall, but slimmer than her husband. She has long red hair, tied back. She heads straight to the couch without making eye contact. She's carrying a box of tissues and is wrapped in a grey cashmere shawl, even though it's hot outside.

Nate shakes Grant's hand. "Nate Monroe. Pleased to meet you. Can we take a seat?"

"Sure."

While Jenny's parents sit opposite Nate and Madison, the grandmother stands. Nate can tell she's struggling to stay still, fussing with her clothes and hair instead.

Grant takes control. "I know my mother asked you here, but I don't want to waste your time or her money. The police are working on the assumption that Jenny has run away for a while, so I don't really see how you can help if they, with all their resources, have been unable to find her."

Nate chooses his words carefully. "Two weeks is a long time for a twelve-year-old to be missing. Did she have any reason to run away?"

"Well, no," says Grant. "But do kids ever have a reason? It's probably just a phase she's going through. You know, because she's about to hit puberty. She's been a little more moody than usual. Like all kids, she spends most of her time on her phone."

Madison clears her throat. "Mr. Lucas, happy children do not run away from home. Whether their emotional turmoil is real or imaginary, they're running away from something. I know, because I was a cop. I spent a lot of time with runaways."

Anna Lucas wipes the tears from her eyes. "But she has a good home here. There's no reason for this."

Nate watches Grant place his hand on his wife's arm. She instantly stops crying.

"What name does she usually go by?" asks Madison. "Does she prefer Jenny or Jennifer?"

"Her teachers call her Jennifer," says Grant, "but we tend to call her Jenny, which she recently told me she's outgrown. She said it makes her sound like a little kid."

"What about a nickname?" Madison looks at Anna. "Anything you call her in private?"

Anna shakes her head, but Esme speaks up. "Grant started calling her Curly, because her beautiful blonde hair is poker straight. It stuck, and now I use it sometimes because it makes her giggle. She wouldn't like anyone at school to call her that, though. She tries to act cool around school friends."

"They grow up too fast," says Anna, shaking her head.

"Why don't you tell me how it happened?" says Nate, retrieving his legal pad to take notes. "How she disappeared." He watches the father's face closely.

Grant takes a deep breath. "I dropped her off at Camp Fearless during the first week of June. She spent a week there with very little communication with us, so we assumed she was enjoying herself too much to think of home. We were actually relieved that she was happy!" He rubs his forehead, clearly struggling to contain his emotions.

"You said she has her own cell phone?" asks Madison.

"Yes, but it was left on the bed in her cabin, switched off. Probably so we couldn't track her through the app we put on there."

Nate doesn't know much about tracking apps, but he makes a note to look into them. "Is that normal these days? To track your children?"

Grant looks confused by the question, and Nate is reminded how much he missed whilst in prison.

"Well all the parents I know use one. The police told us that on the day she disappeared, she'd participated in normal camp activities, ending with a swim in the lake with her new friends. That's the Black Moon Lake, and it's right next to the camp, only a few feet away from her cabin. Her friends went back to the cabin without her, but they said Jenny was definitely out of the water when they left, and getting dressed. No one saw what happened next. All her clothes were gone from the lakeside and nothing was missing from her cabin apart from her backpack. We don't know what was in it."

Madison leans in. "Did none of her bunk mates notice she was missing?"

"Sure they did. But according to the detective in charge, they assumed she'd decided to sleep by the campfire. She'd done it before, saying she liked to watch the stars."

Nate shares a look with Madison, and he'd bet they're thinking the same thing: sleeping alone at the campfire, Jenny was easy prey for a potential child abductor. "What time did the others leave her at the lake?" he asks.

"Nine o'clock; just before sunset."

He wonders what safety protocols are in place at a summer camp, and how they keep track of so many kids. "Did staff do a head count before lights-out?"

Grant shakes his head. "Not that night. Apparently the guy who was supposed to just plain forgot. Which means it wasn't until the next morning that anyone raised the alarm. One of Jenny's friends noticed she wasn't in bed when they were getting up in the morning, so when she wasn't out by the campfire either, she alerted the counselors at breakfast. The counselors searched for her, convinced they'd find her themselves or that she'd just turn up. I think they wanted to avoid negative publicity, so they didn't call the police until lunchtime, when it was clear she was missing."

Grant looks at his mother. "I still think I should sue the ass off of them for that."

Esme doesn't respond.

He turns back to Nate. "The police say they've found nothing suggesting abduction. She just vanished."

Esme groans as if she's in pain. "I can't deal with this." She puts a tissue to her mouth and gulps back tears. "I call the detective every single day, but he's stopped taking my calls and never returns them. That's why I hired you. I don't think he's even still looking for her!"

"Of course he is, Esme," says Anna. "You need to let him do his job uninterrupted. What's the point of him calling to tell us there's no news? It's a waste of his time. You're just distracting him."

Esme looks bereft. "I can't help it." She turns to Nate. "Have you got people to help you search for her, Mr. Monroe?"

"That's not really how it works with a private investigator," he says. "We have other means of tracking people down and we look into the background of everyone at the scene of the disappearance. Can I ask what you both do for a living?"

Grant seems surprised by the question. "I'm a financial adviser and Anna is a teaching assistant at a nearby elementary school. We've been married for fourteen years."

"Does Jenny have any siblings?"

He shakes his head.

"Was she happy to go to summer camp?" asks Madison. "Has she been before?"

Anna looks at her. "It was her first time and she was looking forward to it. She doesn't have many friends at school because she's… shy. So we thought it would help her to open up. Camp is meant to teach children social skills and enrich their lives."

"Is she on the autism spectrum?" Madison presses.

Nate stops writing and looks up at the parents. He wouldn't have thought of asking that.

Anna looks like she's going to cry again, but she shakes her head. "No. She's just a sensitive girl. It's not her fault. Some kids are just like that. She'll blossom eventually, I know it." She covers her mouth.

Nate takes a deep breath. It's good that she's not given up hope of seeing her daughter again. Hope will give her strength. Sensing how difficult it is for them to rehash their daughter's disappearance, he decides it's time to wrap things up. "Okay, I'll need the name of the local police department, and the detective who's investigating the case. Here's my email address and cell number." He stands up and hands Esme his business card. "Please email me anything of importance: where Jenny might have run away to, who she liked to hang out with, or anything the police have told you so far that you haven't told us."

"Will you be visiting the summer camp?" asks Esme.

"Absolutely. We'll head up there next and I'll keep you updated."

"We really hope she's just attention-seeking." Grant stands up. "Do either of you have kids of your own?"

Nate shakes his head, but he notices Madison doesn't respond.

"Well," says Grant, "twelve-year-olds are at that experimental stage where they're testing boundaries and people's patience. I heard the term 'tweenager' recently and laughed, because it describes her perfectly. She's battling between wanting to stay Daddy's little girl and wanting to be cool in the eyes of her school friends. So let's hope she's just camping out in the forest on her own adventure, and existing by stealing supplies from the campsite. I have every faith she'll reappear with her tail between her legs."

Nate is a little surprised by his attitude. Most parents would assume the worst for their missing daughter. Grant is probably putting on a brave face for his wife and mother, and it's understandable that he wouldn't want to entertain the thought that his daughter could be with a child abductor. But Nate is pretty sure that if Jenny was just camping in the woods, the police would've found her by now.

"Before we go, can we look in her bedroom?" he asks.

Anna looks up, shocked. "Why?"

"Just to get a feel for what she's into." He doesn't tell them the real reason, of course. He has to check whether the girl is, or ever has been, lying in there dead; and whether there's anything of interest to be found, like posters indicating a dark obsession with death, or a diary that could explain where she might be.

He would rather Jenny had run away than been abducted, and a kid's bedroom holds vital clues about their personality that you won't get from a parent's perception of them.

CHAPTER TWELVE

Grant and Anna share a look, but Grant reluctantly agrees. "Mom, would you show them upstairs?"

Anna remains seated, pulling her wrap tighter around her shoulders.

Nate follows as Esme leads the way, clearly glad to be of some use. "She's a quiet girl, but she does ever so well at school, especially in biology. She wants to be a doctor. She's a bit of a tomboy and isn't into dresses or Barbies. Here are some photos of her."

All the way up the stairs are family portraits showing Grant, Anna and Jenny. Nate takes his cell phone out. "Can I snap a photo of her to save you giving me one of these?"

Esme nods, but looks upset. "She loves her father, you know. Before she started acting a little more like a teenager, they would spend so much time together. She's definitely a daddy's girl. Grant taught her to fish last summer, and they enjoy sitting on the beach together with their fishing rods."

Nate takes photos of two of the portraits, which look as if they were taken a couple of years apart. In the first, Jenny is almost angelic-looking, with her porcelain skin, blonde hair and winning smile. She's wearing a white summer dress with yellow sandals and must be about nine or ten. She's standing next to Grant, but Nate can't see an obvious resemblance to her father.

"She's pretty," says Madison behind him.

"She is," says Esme. "So photogenic."

In the second portrait, Jenny's a little taller, and tanned, her hair now a slightly darker shade of blonde. She's staring at the camera with a combative look in her eyes, and Nate can see what they mean about her change in attitude. He supposes it's inevitable as kids near their teens, but she doesn't look as happy as in the earlier photo. Her smile is strained. Both parents seem oblivious to her mood as they smile for the camera. Jenny is skinny for her age and her clothes look designer. Grant is resting one hand on her shoulder. Anna has a hand on her other shoulder.

He can tell these shots were professionally done. The photographer has succeeded in making them appear like a wholesome American family. It's only when you look closer that you see how much Jenny would rather be anywhere else.

Esme notices him inspecting the photo. "She was in a bad mood that day, poor thing. Probably her hormones starting to kick in. It's rare that she's not smiling or giggling about something."

"Does she have any distinguishing marks?" asks Madison. "A mole, or a birthmark?"

Esme nods. "I forgot to tell the detective this—perhaps Anna did—but she has a long, straight scar down her left forearm from an accident she had when she was younger."

When they reach the spacious hallway upstairs, Nate glances around. It looks like anyone else's house, with neutral walls and wooden floors, and a large potted plant on the landing. It's extremely clean and tidy, almost like it was prepared for their visit. There are seven closed doors, suggesting five bedrooms and two bathrooms. It's a large house for just three people.

"Do you live here?" he asks Esme.

"No, I live a couple of miles away." She lowers her voice. "I'd like you to send your invoices to me. Here are my contact details."

She hands Nate a piece of paper with her full name, address, email and cell number on.

"As I'm the one paying for your services, I'd like to be the primary contact for any updates you have." She stops and looks at them both. "I'm just trying to minimize the distress to my son and daughter-in-law. I'm sure you understand."

They both nod, and Esme opens the door to Jenny's room. It's just as tidy as everywhere else. It's a large room with wooden floors and another panoramic view of the hills and ocean. There are posters on the walls depicting the anatomy of the human body, complete with medical terminology and an explanation of the different bodily functions. There is even a full-sized plastic skeleton in the corner, though it's wearing a pink cowboy hat from some cheap beachside store. Nate picks up a notebook from the small desk under the window. Algebra. He flicks through it, but it only contains equations and doodles. Jenny's noticeboard is showcasing some heart-warming paintings, mostly of her family. They seem a little young for a twelve-year-old girl, and he imagines they'll soon be replaced by posters of boy bands. Her bed is made up, ready for her return.

As Nate looks around, Madison quizzes Esme.

"What kind of things is Jenny interested in at the moment? Does she have any favorite books or TV shows?"

Esme grimaces. "Oh well, now there's a topic! She used to love reading Young Adult novels, but Grant recently found a horror novel in her backpack. Can you imagine that!"

Nate laughs. He loves a good horror novel. "Let me guess. Stephen King?"

Esme looks surprised. "Yes. How did you know that? It had a murderous clown on the front. Why on earth would a twelve-year-old girl want to read something like that? It would give me nightmares."

Madison smiles. "Trust me, you don't need to worry about Jenny enjoying books like that. It's perfectly natural for teenagers to want to read about death. It sounds gruesome, but they're just trying to scare themselves. I read all sorts when I was her age."

Esme looks unconvinced.

"How would you describe Jenny's personality?" asks Madison.

"I'd say she's different to other girls her age." Esme pauses and takes a deep breath. "She's so shy and quiet in front of outsiders, but in the house she puts on these fabulous productions where she plays all the characters. She'll see a TV show or a movie that sparks her imagination, and she'll adapt it slightly and then invite us to watch it in the living room." She laughs as she wipes tears from her watery eyes. "When I watch her flip perfectly between the different characters, I can't help but marvel at how she can portray so many different people just by changing the intonation of her voice, or her mannerisms. I told her more than once that she could be a movie star one day."

Madison is smiling at Esme's memory. "Did that appeal to her?"

"At first, but then she decided that she wouldn't be able to handle the critics. She said that if she was singled out for a poor performance, or if the movie flopped, she'd blame herself. Unfortunately, she does have a thin skin. But that's something that will improve as she matures. I'm in my sixties and I don't give a hoot what people think of me anymore." Esme attempts a laugh, but it comes out as a sob.

Nate feels for her. He tries to change the subject. "It's tidy in here for a kid's room."

"I tidied it when she left for camp," says Anna.

They all turn around. Nate hadn't heard her join them.

"It's the only opportunity I've had for a while to give it a proper clean." She leans against the door frame. "My husband might sound sure of himself, but we really don't know where Jennifer could be. He's trying to pretend everything is okay because he's worried about Esme's health."

They all look at Esme, who appears almost ashamed at being a bother.

"Being outnumbered by three women, he likes to take care of us and perhaps underestimates our ability to cope. Don't judge him as uncaring or delusional. Knowing he can't help his daughter is hard on him, so he's pretending he isn't too worried yet. As you don't have children, you won't know how it feels when your child goes missing." Anna pauses. "I'm not going to lie: Jennifer can be challenging at times, and if she *has* run away just to get some attention, I'll find it hard to forgive the pain she's caused. Perhaps she's figured out she'll be in trouble for that, and that's why she's staying away. But whatever she's done, I still want her home. It's unbearable not knowing where she is. Please find her as soon as possible." She breaks down and covers her face.

Esme hugs her tight whilst holding back her own tears, and Nate notices that even Madison is struggling to remain composed. He takes that as their cue to leave. He indicates to Madison and they make their way downstairs, where Grant lets them out.

"I'll be in touch," Nate says, shaking his hand. "Call me if you hear from Jenny or the police."

"We will."

Nate senses exhaustion coming from Grant, and realizes how much this family are suffering.

CHAPTER THIRTEEN

When they leave the Lucas house, Madison opens the trunk of Nate's car to get her bottled water. She leans against the car as she drinks. "I can't take this heat."

Nate slips his shades on. "It's beautiful. You don't like summer?"

She looks up at the house and realizes they're being watched by Esme from the front window. "I think we'd better leave."

Nate follows her gaze and they hear the sound of the electric gates opening behind them.

Once they're on the road, the coastal breeze through the windows feels good on her face.

"What did you make of the family?" asks Nate.

She thinks about it. "Esme's a little high-strung and the parents are standoffish, but most families are when their kids go missing. They don't know who to trust and it's not like they get a manual on how to react. Some families court the media, others hide in their shock. The husband was somewhat domineering over his wife and I sense the grandmother knows more than she's letting on. We need to secure her confidence so she's honest with us sooner rather than later."

"Okay," says Nate. "Maybe Grant's a control freak and Jenny ran away to escape her dad. I know my room didn't look that tidy when I was a kid."

Madison smiles, remembering how messy Owen's bedroom was. She misses tidying up after him. She misses everything about him and realizes she might not even recognize him the next time they meet. Before she can dwell on it, she pushes him from her thoughts. "If Jenny vanished from the lakeside after swimming, it could mean that she fell into the lake by accident after everyone left, in which case she drowned. But the fact she might have slept alone at the campfire is worrying, because it would have been easy for someone to grab her. I guess until we get there we won't know what the campsite is like and how accessible it is to outsiders. If she was abducted by someone, they had a good head start, with about fifteen hours between when Jenny was last seen and when the cops were called." She shakes her head. "And that was two weeks ago. They could be anywhere by now."

"If she's in the lake, wouldn't her body have emerged before now?" asks Nate.

She nods. "I'm pretty sure the police would've sent divers down to look for her body, but lakes are difficult to search. There's usually a lot of debris down there: fallen branches, discarded garbage and dead animals. Her body could be trapped under something."

"What about her missing backpack?"

"That could've just been stolen by one of the other kids, or maybe it was never with her. We're relying on the memories of children, remember."

Nate focuses on the road signs.

"Have you ever been here before?" she asks.

"No. I don't know any of California well." When he gets onto the correct exit, he seems to relax. "I think the best chance we've got of knowing what happened is to speak to the staff and the kids who were there that night. With a little luck, the other parents didn't pull their kids out of camp after her disappearance. Someone must've seen something. Kids don't just vanish without a trace."

Madison looks at him. "I can tell you've never been a cop."

He smiles. "Thanks. That's a huge compliment."

"I didn't mean it to be." She lets the dig slide. "You're being naïve, Nate. People vanish without a trace every day. If the police didn't find Jennifer Lucas, it's unlikely we will, unless we get lucky.

We need to investigate a potential motive for her disappearance first of all."

Nate takes his eyes off the road and glances at her. "You're already convinced she was abducted?"

She nods. "If there's no body at the scene, she's probably been taken."

He thinks about it. "Are tracking apps on cell phones really a thing?"

She smiles. He's so out of touch. "Sure. I'd use one if..." She stops herself. "But I know from working with detectives in the past that these app companies do *not* like giving out users' data. Just like the social media giants don't like giving police access to people's accounts, even when the user's life is at risk. It's disgusting, if you ask me, and hopefully that'll change at some point, as I believe it could save lives by helping us find missing kids quicker. But in Jennifer Lucas's case, her dad said her cell phone was found switched off in her cabin, so it's unlikely to yield anything important about her current location. It would be interesting to read her text messages, though, and to see if she's got any social media accounts."

"Surely she's too young for those?"

Madison rolls her eyes. "Not really, Grandpa! Sure, there's a minimum age, but all the kids are doing it. Most parents don't even vet their accounts. How do you think pedophiles get away with grooming kids online?"

Nate shakes his head.

She types the zip code of the summer camp into the sat nav. "Shit, it's an eleven-hour drive. I'm glad you've got A/C in this thing."

"We can stop for breaks along the way. Why don't you find us a motel to stay at when we get there?"

She calculates what time they're likely to reach Shadow Falls. "If we stop for breaks, we're not going to arrive until about three in the morning, and if we hit traffic, it could be even later. It's not worth wasting money on a motel room for less than half a night."

He looks over at her and she can tell he's trying to figure her out. "Money's that bad?"

"What do you think?"

He doesn't smile and she knows it's because he's been there. She can only imagine how it felt for him to be handed a substantial payout. The relief must've been immense.

"I'm not asking for money," she clarifies. "I just don't want to waste mine on a room for a couple of hours' sleep. I'll sleep in the car, or stay awake. I can find you a room, though?"

He looks back at the road. "I think you're right. Let's see what time we get there before we think about sleeping. Maybe we can head straight into camp and see who's around. We can always catch up on sleep tomorrow night. You could even grab a couple of hours while I drive if you like."

Madison's grateful he doesn't make a big deal out of her trying to save money. She's only known him for twenty-four hours, but she already feels comfortable. Which makes her feel bad for misleading him about what happened with her own case.

CHAPTER FOURTEEN

Nate decides to take route 101 all the way to San Jose. By the time they get there, it's seven o'clock and the sun is starting to ease behind the sparse white clouds, but the day's humidity is going nowhere. Even though the A/C in his car is second to none, he's ready for a break. When they encounter delays leaving San Jose, he decides to stop for something to eat.

"Let me treat you to dinner," he says, pulling into the parking lot of a large steakhouse. He can feel his stomach rumbling as he leads them into the restaurant, where a young waitress greets them with a tired smile.

"Hi, how are you? Table for two?"

"Please."

"Follow me." The waitress hunts for a spare table. She seats them near the window and takes their drinks order. "Be right back."

"I used to serve food to pay my way through college, but I was terrible at it," says Nate after she leaves. "I once spilt a whole plate of spaghetti down a man's back. Turned out he was in a criminal motorcycle gang, so I sure knew how to find trouble."

Madison laughs. She has a nice laugh but he'd bet she doesn't do it very often anymore.

"Yeah, waitressing is my new life," she says. "I've been surprised by how variable the tips can be. If I show a little cleavage to the right customer, I can afford to buy the good cheese instead of the processed crap."

He smiles sadly. That must feel like quite a comedown for a detective, but he admires her determination to do what she needs to in order to survive.

Once they've ordered their food, Nate glances at the TV above them. He recognizes a photo of Jennifer Lucas on the screen. "Look."

Madison follows his gaze.

The shot turns to an outside broadcast. The reporter is standing in front of a sign for Camp Fearless. "Jennifer Lucas, the young girl who vanished from this summer camp two weeks ago, is still missing, and locals fear time is running out for the twelve-year-old from Santa Barbara."

They run video of a middle-aged woman standing in her front doorway. "I'm too scared to let my kids play out on the front lawn in case whoever took that poor girl comes back for more. They should have found her by now. It's scary."

A second, older local appears. Nate assumes he's a neighbor of the woman, keen to offer his ten cents. "I think she was grabbed by a sex offender. I'd bet she's dead in a ditch by now. If the cops ever find out who took her, they should string him up by his—"

The footage cuts back to the reporter, carefully edited. "The Trinity Creek Police Department have asked anyone who may have information about the whereabouts of Jennifer Lucas to contact them as soon as possible. Jennifer's parents have put up a twenty-five-thousand-dollar reward for any information that leads to the safe return of their daughter."

The piece ends with another photo of Jennifer, one Nate hasn't seen. She's sitting on a pony and patiently smiling at the camera.

Madison turns back to face him. "I hope her parents didn't watch that. They don't need to know the locals are writing their daughter off as dead."

Nate nods. "They didn't mention the reward to us."

"Probably because it's not produced results so far. Although I'd bet the local PD have taken some bogus calls from people trying to claim it."

The waitress returns with their food, and as Nate digs in, he decides it's time to start delving deeper into Madison's story. "I googled you before I decided whether to take your case."

She doesn't look surprised. "That was the logical thing to do. I obviously did my research on you too. I'm surprised it didn't put you off helping me, though."

He chews his steak. It's not great, but the lattice fries are deliciously salty, with a coating of paprika. "So you're from a small town in south Colorado. Is that where you served your sentence?"

"Yeah. They tried to get me out of the state so they could forget about what they did to me, but I ended up in La Vista Correctional Facility, north of the state."

That sounds about right to him. The police like to cover up their corruption. "How was prison life for you?"

She puts her knife and fork down and takes a sip of her beer. "It was probably a hell of a lot better than your experience on death row. Some of the women were decent, but most of them were nasty. There were a lot of messed-up relationships going on, and if one of them thought you'd looked at their bitch the wrong way, you'd know about it. I have a bone in my arm that will never sit straight again."

She pulls her shirt sleeve up and he winces at the deformed angle. "What was their reaction to you being a former cop?"

She looks out the window. "The decent women I mentioned stuck to me like glue, because they were convinced I could help them get their sentences overturned when I got out. They actually thought I'd be straight back on the police force and able to reopen their cases. Can you believe that? As if my manslaughter conviction would be overlooked. It was soul-destroying that after everything they'd gone through, they still believed the judicial system would come right for them in the end." She shrugs. "As for the guilty inmates, well, they were obviously inside because they were caught by cops, so they took every opportunity to show me how angry they were at that." She pauses. "I spent a lot of time in the prison infirmary during my first year. Until I realized the only way I'd get out alive was to fight back."

Nate is confused. "How did you get released four years early if you were fighting back?"

She picks up a French fry and dips it in some sweet chili sauce. "Most of the correctional officers were easily bought. Nothing went on my record inside. I made promises I had no intention of ever keeping, plus I paid them with what little I had. But then…"

He lets her trail off, because he knows not to expect everything from her in one go. It's hard to put the prison experience into words. He's surprised when she continues.

"Halfway through my sentence, a new guard started: Troy Dunn. He was a mean son of a bitch. He liked to work out, but his legs looked like they belonged to someone else because he was so top-heavy. Once he found out I was a cop, he targeted me because he knew he could gain respect from the other inmates if he got to me for them." She drops the fry back onto her plate and looks Nate in the eye. "He raped me eight times in all. But that's only a third of the times he came for me, so I can't complain. Plus, he had a small dick, so it's not like he did much damage."

Nate takes a deep breath and pushes his plate away. "Jesus, Madison." He notices an older couple sitting in the booth next to them. They're staring at her with their mouths open. He knows how they feel.

She looked detached as she spoke, a coping mechanism no doubt. He doesn't ask if she reported the assaults. He wouldn't have if that had ever happened to him—and if he'd been in general population, it would have. One of the only perks of being on death row is the rapists can't get to you. Not unless your sentence is commuted to life in prison, in which case you're thrown in with the sharks. Nate witnessed inmates kill themselves after being told they were leaving death row to go into general population. He was prepared to do the same thing. Some people aren't cut out for prison life and he has no shame in admitting he's one of them. In a fucked-up way, he felt lucky to be on death row instead.

"Is the guard on your list?" he asks.

She looks surprised. Then she smiles. "You have a list too?"

"Of course. All wronged people do, don't they?"

She looks down at her hands. "Yeah. Have you managed to get anyone from your list yet?"

He nods. "Did you notice the woman you passed at the hotel in Malibu this morning?"

She smiles. "You mean the stunning redhead with the model's body? It would be hard not to, she was gorgeous."

"She's the wife of Blake Diaz."

Madison looks confused. "So, what, you're having an affair?"

He shakes his head. "No. Detective Blake Diaz was a friend of Stacey's uncle, and he helped the son of a bitch get away with framing me. The way I figure it: he screwed me over, so I screwed his wife. Many times."

She laughs, clearly delighted. "You went to Malibu just to get back at Diaz?"

He nods. "He moved there from Austin while I was on death row. Once I was released, I knew I needed to do something to the asshole, but I'm not a violent person, so when I spotted how hot his wife was, I 'accidentally' bumped into her in the grocery store. We got talking and I found out she hated him almost as much as I did. He slaps her around so she's on the verge of divorcing him, but she wanted to do something to really piss him off before she disappears. I told her who I was and why I was mad at him, and she practically dragged me into bed."

"Oh, I bet you put up a fight."

He can tell she's teasing him. "As you saw for yourself, she's hard to resist. But I was completely upfront with my motives and she was enjoying it as much as me. So now I feel like I got the asshole back, because when he finds out she slept with me of all people, he'll know I won. It's juvenile, but when you spend seventeen years on death row, you take whatever satisfaction you can against the people who put you there."

She nods. "I know exactly what you mean. One day I'll get Troy Dunn for what he did to me, but he's second on a long list."

Nate chews a lattice fry. "Who's first?"

She downs the rest of her beer before standing up, signaling it's time to get back on the road. "That's what you need to find out."

CHAPTER FIFTEEN

It's dark when they finally reach the Wildwood National Forest. Nate looks at the clock: it's just after two in the morning and Madison is asleep in the passenger seat next to him. When he approaches a motel, he swings the Jeep into a dark parking spot, away from the road. If it were just him, he'd get a room, but he understands Madison's financial constraints. He's not sure what their situation is yet, and doesn't know whether to treat her as an employee, a client or a new friend. The long journey up here has resulted in him overthinking things and he's ready for a break. As he's not tired yet, he decides to take a walk around the outside of the motel to stretch his legs.

Since being incarcerated, he's been an insomniac. Before, as a busy young man with lots going on, he'd slept eight hours straight every night without fail. Now, he's lucky if he gets three hours a night. It's probably aged him, but he's getting used to it.

As he walks past the reception, he looks in. There's a small lamp giving the room an orange glow, but the check-in desk is empty. The night clerk is probably asleep or watching TV in the office behind. That's good, because it means he and Madison can probably get away with parking here for a while. He grabs a couple of sodas and chocolate bars from the vending machine outside and then heads to a picnic table near the motel's drained swimming pool. He picks a spot where he can still see the car. It's not that he thinks Madison would steal it—after all, she needs his help—but motels don't have a bad reputation for nothing, and someone else could.

Satisfied he's in a good spot, he pulls out a bag of coke from the hidden lining in his sneakers and cuts it up, making sure no one's watching from one of the few windows overlooking where he's sitting. All the drapes are closed.

Father Connor has been playing on his mind all day, threatening to overwhelm him. Maybe because Madison's experience of being framed is bringing up old resentments. Whatever it is, he needs to be able to focus on the here and now. Knowing what helps when he feels this way, he takes a twenty from his wallet and uses it to snort what he needs. The effect is immediate: a fast buzz that makes him feel better. More confident, even. His doubts about taking Madison on as an employee vanish. He feels sure he can find Jennifer Lucas, too. He wipes his nose and puts everything away, rubbing a small amount of white powder off the table.

He looks up at the sky and watches the lights of a plane. It's a clear night and the stars are out. After fifteen minutes of enjoying the buzz, he can already feel it receding. He's managed to reduce his coke intake a lot in the last few months so that he feels in control. Despite his body craving another line, he ignores it. He knows it'll pass soon enough.

When he pulls out his cell phone, he finds an email from Esme Lucas giving him the details of the local cop assigned to the case: Detective Ted Morgan from Trinity Creek Police Department. They passed Trinity Creek about twenty miles back, so the department must have jurisdiction over more than one town. Nate has no intention of contacting Detective Morgan before he's done some investigating of his own. In fact, the longer the police are ignorant of his presence, the better for him and probably for the missing girl.

Just then, he hears someone approach, and it's not Madison. It's a slim woman wearing nothing but a bra and jeans. One of the doors behind her is open, with a weak light spilling out.

"Hey, you." She takes a seat next to him. "Do you have a light?" She balances a spliff between her full painted lips.

"I don't smoke, sorry."

She leans in and puts her hand on his knee. "I can keep you company if you like?"

Nate's not naïve; he knows this woman charges by the hour for her company. As someone who never got to sleep with his fiancée and was then incarcerated for so long, he can't pretend he's never been tempted by a prostitute. Once he was released, he thought a lot about using one to experience sex for the first time, just to get it over with. But most sex workers are controlled by pimps, and the thought of helping a sleazy guy like that profit from a woman put him off. Instead he let nature take its course, and it wasn't long before he attracted the attention of a hotel receptionist. She taught him a lot.

He smiles at the stranger and shakes his head. "Thanks, but not tonight." He opens his wallet and slips her a fifty-dollar bill. "Have a meal on me, though."

Her smile slips and he gets a glimpse of the woman behind the facade. "Thanks, man. My baby needs diapers."

She gets up and walks away, and he finds himself hoping she uses it for those diapers and not for drugs.

"I'm in room twelve if you change your mind." She doesn't look back as she says it.

Nate glances at his cell phone again and sees he has another email. This one makes him tense before he even opens it. It's from Stacey's uncle. No one else would know that, as he's not stupid enough to use his real name, but Nate recognizes the fake email address. This isn't the first time Father Connor has been in touch using a pseudonym, and Nate has no idea how he obtained his email address, which is less than two years old. Clearly the asshole has done some digging of his own. He checks the Jeep is still okay and then opens the email.

Every day you live you are closer to your seat in hell. My beautiful niece died because of you and God will never let you near her again.

I pray every night that you will meet the devil, and soon. Do the world a favor and go to your grave. Stop chasing me. You will never find me, Nathaniel. I have God on my side.

Nate shakes his head, puts his cell phone on the picnic table and closes his eyes. He rubs his temples instead of throwing his phone against a wall. That man is deluded. He knows the hatred the priest has for him is misdirected self-loathing, so it means nothing. What angers him is the fact that he won't accept responsibility for Stacey's murder. Nate is certain they'd be happily married right now with a couple of teenage kids if it weren't for Father Connor. He gives in to his craving and prepares another line of coke.

CHAPTER SIXTEEN

"What are you doing?"

Nate jumps as Madison approaches him. She thought she saw him lean down to the table on her way over here, but there's nothing there when she reaches him. She's been around a lot of drug addicts in her time and she doesn't think Nate is one.

He looks over at her. "Just checking emails. I thought I'd let you sleep."

"Aren't you tired?"

He turns his phone over so she can't see the screen. "No. Here, I got us some snacks."

She sits next to him at the picnic table and together they watch the sun slowly rise.

"I would've killed for this experience a few years ago, when it felt like I'd never see the sun again," says Nate.

"Just think," she says. "One day that sun will rise on a morning when it's all over for both of us."

He looks at her, his face bathed in an orange glow. "What do you mean?"

She pulls out a pack of cigarettes and a lighter. After taking a long, satisfying drag, she looks at him. "Well, one day I'll have my answers and I'll be able to pick up my life from where it was halted seven years ago. And one day you'll find that priest and see him behind bars. It will be over. We just have to get through these tough years in between. We've both been through worse, so I know we can do it."

He looks away and appears to watch the sparse traffic pass on the highway; just delivery trucks, mainly. "How did you know I was looking for him?"

She leans in. "Because we're both being driven by revenge. Despite what the Bible says, there's nothing wrong with that. It's what got me through my incarceration."

Is that relief she sees in his face? It's probably not often he gets to talk about what's been keeping him alive.

"He killed his own niece, Madison. What kind of man can do that and not take responsibility?"

She shakes her head and opens a can of soda with her free hand. "From what I've read of your case, it sounds to me like he was a control freak and he used the Bible to suit his own ends. Once he realized he couldn't keep Stacey at home with him and his subservient sister, he saw how little control he actually had, for which he blamed you."

Nate nods. "He's convinced he has God on his side, and unfortunately, he might be right."

"What do you mean?"

He hesitates before responding. "Once I was released, my lawyers told me not to bother chasing after him. They said that even if I caught him and he was finally charged with Stacey's murder, no jury would convict a priest with a whole congregation willing to testify about what a good man he is, especially not when I make a better suspect. Apparently they wouldn't want to believe a man of God was capable of it."

"But you were training to be a priest, so how come they convicted you?"

"Because the prosecution made out I was evil. They said I swapped God for sex. That I'd been turned by the devil and I willingly let him in. They only just stopped short of calling me a devil worshipper. They even said I'd used my belief in God as a ruse to get close to Stacey and ruin her. But the crazy thing is that Stacey and I never had sex during the two years we knew each other. We were both virgins when she was killed. We were trying to abide by the Bible we both believed in."

Madison is surprised, then angry. "You've got to give it to them." She shakes her head in disgust as she stubs her finished cigarette out on the table. "Prosecutors should be writers, seeing as the majority of their cases are built on fiction."

Nate continues. "The police now have evidence to prove Father Connor killed Stacey, but my lawyers said it's more than likely any jury would overlook it because he's been an upstanding member of the community and has given his life to serving Jesus and helping those less fortunate than himself. They thought the best I could hope for—if we ever found him—was an involuntarily manslaughter charge and a suspended sentence. How fucked up is that?"

He's getting angrier the more he talks about it, and she can tell his old resentments are coming to the surface.

"As much as it pains me to say it, Nate, they're probably right. His defense team would sure as hell try to pick strongly religious jurors."

"That's not difficult in Texas. You know, if he got off based on his religious beliefs that would be worse than never finding him in the first place. Because he doesn't even believe in God. He can't do or he wouldn't have committed murder. His supposed faith is just a mask to hide the evil inside him."

"I agree. And at least while he's on the run he's looking over his shoulder, waiting for you to appear. That kind of life will grind him down and ruin any chance he has of moving on. He'll never be able to relax. He'll never be able to forget what he did to Stacey." She hesitates. "So where does all this leave you? Do you still believe in God?"

He turns away, looking at the sunrise.

"I don't know. It's complicated."

She feels sorry for him. It's clear that Father Connor didn't just steal Nate's life. He stole his faith too. She watches as he feels for the rosary beads around his neck. She'd bet there's a story behind those beads, as he seems to use them for comfort.

He turns to face her, looking like he wants to confess something.

"When I find him… Madison, I want you to know I won't be turning him over to the police."

She immediately realizes what he's implying, and a feeling of dread creeps through her. As someone who wants to return to the force, she can't condone murder and she can't be a part of it. But she does want to see justice for Nate and his dead fiancée. "That would put you right back on death row," she says.

He smiles at her. "Only if they find his body."

She finds herself smiling back at him, and is surprised at her own reaction.

CHAPTER SEVENTEEN

November 2000—Austin, Texas

The day of the verdict comes as a relief to Nate. He's sick of being paraded in front of the jury every day. He's also fed up of listening to the lies Stacey's uncle tells about him: about how Stacey had never even tried a drop of alcohol until she met Nate. That is completely untrue, and Father Connor knows it.

Nate's also worried about his own father and the impact all this is having on him. Every day his dad loyally sits behind him and the defense team. His hands are permanently folded to hide the trembling and a look of weary contempt remains in place for the prosecutors, but listening to all the lies told about his son is clearly difficult for him. Nate's siblings refused to attend the trial, already condemning him, so he relies on his dad's support to get him through the long, frustrating days.

It's only when Nate looks at Stacey's mom that he feels anything other than horror and fear. Instead, he feels anger and disappointment. Deborah won't make eye contact with him. A slim, meek woman at the best of times, she appears even slimmer by the end of the trial. She's been dominated and overshadowed by her older brother the whole time Nate has known them. Publicly she'd agree with his outdated sermons, but in private she was different. She would make dinner for Stacey and Nate at the beginning of their friendship, during his first year at the University of Texas. She welcomed him with open arms and sat on the couch watching comedies with them at the weekend. She appeared to like him, or so he thought.

When she took the stand and made up multiple stories about how she'd witnessed Nate hitting her daughter, he knew then that she was never religious. If she was, she wouldn't have lied under oath. Just like her brother, Deborah was living the worst possible lie: pretending to be an upstanding, law-abiding member of the community whilst breaking every rule in the Bible whenever it suited her.

When Nate had proposed to Stacey on her twentieth birthday, she'd wanted to keep their engagement a secret. She knew her uncle would ruin it somehow. They'd told Deborah, but she shared Stacey's pessimism.

"We want you to settle down with someone who shares our religion," she'd told her daughter. "Someone who isn't an atheist. No offense, Nathaniel."

"I'm not an atheist, Deborah. I changed my mind about becoming a priest, but not about God. My faith is real," he'd said, frustrated that he had to keep explaining this. He had hoped Deborah would be glad for them since she could see how happy they were together.

"It's up to me who I marry, Mom," said Stacey. "I love Nate and no one will ever compare to him in my eyes. You'll both realize that eventually."

Deborah had smiled at them, but it was a sad smile. One that showed no hope for their plans.

As he watches the jury file in from outside, Nate wonders whether that was the moment he should have walked out of their lives. To stop the madness that was about to happen.

CHAPTER EIGHTEEN

After an early breakfast at a local diner, Madison is feeling anxious. She's craving another cigarette—hell, a pack of them—but she's only recently managed to reduce the twenty-a-day habit she picked up in prison.

She's worried about what Nate told her. She's worried about the implications for her. Will his showdown with Father Connor happen in her presence? Will she have to testify against him? Will she be responsible for putting him back on death row? It's not even just what he's planning. What he told her has made her think about the consequences of looking into her own case. What exactly is she planning to do when she finds out who framed her? What if she doesn't get exonerated? Would she kill for revenge?

She tries not to think that far ahead. One thing at a time. It's a relief to have this new case to work on. It will buy her time while she figures things out in her head.

To relieve some of her anxiety, she decides to get a few things clear between her and Nate before they reach the summer camp and begin their investigation.

"So, what's the deal here?" she asks. "Am I officially working for you now? I don't mean to be presumptuous, but allowing you to pay for my meals is making me uncomfortable." She pushes away her plate of half-eaten eggs and wipes her mouth with a napkin. "It would be different if I was on your payroll and it was considered expenses."

Nate smiles and finishes his coffee. He pushes his cup away and leans back on the diner's leather bench. "Tell me if this works for you. I'm happy to cover basic living expenses—hotel rooms, food, gas, et cetera—and any expenses that come up as a result of our investigations, but you don't get a percentage on top of that until you find a case of your own. Consider the Jennifer Lucas case a training session for you to learn how investigators do things differently to cops, because we *are* different and a lot of people are more willing to open up to someone without a police badge. Then, assuming we're still getting along okay, we can split the cases between us so we're not stuck together all the time. How does that sound?"

She doesn't even have to think about it; it's the best job opportunity she's likely to find until she can get her conviction overturned. "Deal."

It means she can keep her own money safe for other things. She doesn't agree that people are more willing to trust PIs than cops, though. After all, PIs get paid more and are usually motivated solely by money. She's yet to figure out what motivates Nate, considering money isn't an issue. "Do I get a uniform?" She grins.

He laughs, surprised. "If you want a uniform, we need to come up with a name for my new business so I can get it stitched on."

"I'll have a think about that." She downs the rest of her coffee and they head out to the car.

As Nate pulls away from the diner, he says, "There's a brand-new cell phone in the glove box if you need it."

She looks at him. "Is it a burner phone?"

He nods. "I always like to have a spare lying around. Just in case."

She retrieves it from the glove box and switches it on. It's cheap, but it'll do. "Thanks." She hasn't had a phone since her release from prison. It was a luxury she just couldn't afford. All her research and personal affairs have been done using the local library's PC, so she's looking forward to having internet access again.

"The cell number is on the box." He points to it.

She tears off the piece of cardboard with her new number on and asks Nate for his. Once she's saved it, she enters a few others that she remembers by heart. Whether or not they're still valid remains to be seen.

Nate switches the radio on low while he drives, but the signal is weak out here in the forest, so he quickly turns it off.

It's not long before they come across a road sign for Camp Fearless. It's practically the only business in Shadow Falls, apart from a small Main Street they drive through on the way, and a gas station. Having grown up in small-town Colorado, Madison feels at home in towns like this.

"Did you grow up in Texas?" she asks.

"No. I'm from Kansas originally. I actually picked Texas for its university, rather than its infamous death row." He smiles. "I hated it there until I met Stacey. She changed my life in many ways."

He doesn't volunteer any more details, so she doesn't ask. They drive through the dense forest made up of countless redwood trees. Madison opens her window and sticks her head out, trying to see the tops of the trees, but they stretch upwards as far as city skyscrapers and she can't crane her neck back far enough. "Amazing."

"Check those out." Nate points to a herd of deer running through the trees off to the left.

She watches them in awe, taking in their beautiful chestnut color.

"I'd bet there are bears here too," he says.

She'd be less excited to see a bear.

After about ten minutes of admiring the incredible forest that serves as a long, secluded driveway, they spot some wooden signposts for the campsite buildings and parking lot. Nate pulls into a parking space—there are plenty to choose from—and they leave the cool interior of the car to step into the already rising humidity.

Madison follows him to the camp's entrance. There is a large archway made out of dead wood with the camp's name engraved and painted across the top. She finds it kind of eerie. Partly because it looks like it was made by kids, like some sort of pet cemetery, and partly because someone has scratched out the "less" part of Fearless, making it Camp Fear instead. Other than that, the location looks idyllic in the morning's summer sunshine. It's a large wooded area with cabins covered in bunting and noticeboards showcasing all the activities going on. The birdsong is strangely relaxing.

There's a large campfire area to the left and picnic tables off to the right, near the lake, which has some small boats tied to the jetty. Madison can hear the sound of kids enjoying themselves out in the wild. It strikes her as having a business-as-usual feel, as if a child going missing is perfectly normal in these parts.

She never attended summer camp—she didn't have that type of childhood—but she can see the appeal for kids. As an adult—or maybe just because she was a cop—this place looks almost too idyllic. The perfect place for something bad to happen.

The sound of children's laughter makes her think of her son. Did Owen get to attend summer camp while she was locked up? She pushes away the thought that she might never know.

A group of children run out from the woods and over to the largest cabin. They all have painted animal faces, and a tired-looking young woman dressed in a purple T-shirt and white shorts jogs behind them.

"Don't forget to wash your hands first!" she yells.

While Nate stops to look around and take it all in, Madison turns toward the lake, where Jenny was last seen alive. What seems to be a new makeshift fence blocks off the wooden jetty. Maybe the staff have cordoned it off in case any other kids go missing. If so, someone in charge clearly believes she drowned. The lake isn't as vast as Madison was expecting. If the local PD sent divers down, it's likely they would've found Jenny's body if it had been in there. In her experience that means the girl was abducted. Which also means that everyone here is a potential suspect.

The glare of the sunshine bouncing off the lake is giving her a headache, even with her new sunglasses on, and she remembers why she's never been a fan of summer. She hates having to wear bug repellent and sunscreen, and the high temperatures drive her insane. It would sound crazy to most people, but Madison would much rather be wrapped up against a harsh winter. She waves away a persistent bug that's trying to bite her, and then watches a woman approach them.

The woman looks mad.

CHAPTER NINETEEN

"Who are you and what are you doing here?" says someone behind Nate. Then the tone of voice changes abruptly. "Oh, wait. Are you Billy's parents?"

Nate spins around and looks at the small woman. She has a strained smile on her face and is shielding her eyes from the sun with her left hand. She is carrying a clipboard close to her chest.

"No, I'm Nate Monroe and this is Madison, my associate. We're here to look into the disappearance of Jennifer Lucas."

The woman's smile quickly fades and she immediately folds both arms over the clipboard. "Oh. Jeez, what now? Haven't we told you everything already?"

"We're not police, ma'am. We're here on behalf of Jenny's family. They've asked us to look a little closer into her disappearance. I'm sure you can understand they'll do anything to find their daughter."

She still looks annoyed, but she stares past Nate's shoulder toward the lake. "She's down there, I just know it."

He follows her gaze.

"Can we have your name?" asks Madison.

The woman looks at her. "I'm Donna Gleeson, camp director. I'm the one who called the police when we realized Jenny was missing. I reacted as quickly as I could. There really wasn't much else I could do."

Just then a car pulls up and a young couple get out and rush over to them. "Are you Donna? Is Billy ready?" asks the woman.

Donna's smile is back. "Yes, just head into the office. Kat will sort you out. I really wish you weren't taking him home early, though. He was doing so well and he loves it here."

The couple glance at Nate and Madison and whisper something to Donna.

"That was an unfortunate accident," she says in response. "Billy has coped very well. We hope to see him again next summer."

"Did your son know Jenny Lucas well?" asks Nate.

Billy's dad shoots him a look of contempt. "What's it to you?"

Donna shoos Billy's parents away in the direction of the main office before turning back to Nate.

"Please don't cause any more problems for us. We've already lost nine children early over this. Once news got out to the parents that a child had gone missing, they started panicking and taking their kids home. I managed to talk some of them out of it, but they're still coming to collect the children early and demanding refunds for the time they'll miss. I think some of the older kids are scaring the younger ones with stories of monsters in the woods. It's making them want to go home."

Nate feels for her. Negative publicity can kill a business like this.

"Sounds to me like you're more interested in profits than a child's life."

They both turn to look at Madison. Nate was worried this might happen. Once a cop, always a cop. He steps in before Donna can explode, which, judging by how red her face has gone, she's not far off.

"Can we talk somewhere in private?" he asks her. "I want to get the details straight, because so far I've only heard what happened through third parties."

Donna nods.

"Madison, would you take a look around while I talk to the director?" He's assuming she'll realize he wants her to scope the place out and talk to any willing kids before Donna censors them.

Madison agrees. "I need to find a bathroom anyway."

Donna points past the main office. "You'll find the cafeteria back there too. You'll have to pay for your food and drinks; we can't afford to offer charity to strangers."

"No problem."

Donna leads Nate to the office. They pass Billy and his parents, who are returning to their car with his belongings, looks of relief on their faces. They got their child back. The Lucas family weren't so lucky.

Nate considers what Donna said about stories of monsters in the woods, and wonders where those stories originated from. Perhaps there was a sighting of a stranger wandering around and, like Chinese whispers, it's grown into a campfire ghost story.

When they enter the office, Nate sees four boys being scolded by a young woman.

"If one of you hits this ball into a window again, we'll have to tell your parents to come and collect you early. Is that clear?"

The boys, who all look around twelve, stare hard at the ground and say in unison, "Yes, Kat."

"Glad that's clear. I know you think I'm being a b-i-t-c-h, but this is for your own good. I'm teaching you how to be responsible members of the community. You'll thank me one day. At least your girlfriends will."

The boys don't respond.

"Right, you can go. But remember, next time I'll be calling your parents and telling them what little shits you've been."

Nate has to hide his smile as he watches the boys file out of the cabin looking shamefaced.

"Kat's a hard taskmaster," says Donna, "but the boys seem to love her no matter how much she yells at them."

Nate wonders if it has anything to do with her large breasts, which are barely contained by a thin, low-cut T-shirt. Then he wonders if the boys are getting into trouble on purpose.

Donna turns to Kat. "This is Nate Monroe."

Kat gives him a wide smile and looks him up and down. "Hey, Nate. Are you one of the parents?"

"No, he's not. Don't you worry yourself about who he is. You just arrange for that glass panel to get fixed."

Nate flashes Kat an apologetic smile as he follows Donna into the back office.

"She's like a dog on heat, that one. Wouldn't surprise me if she's already been knocked up by one of the other counselors. Would you like a water?"

Nate raises his eyebrows, surprised at Donna's comment. "Sure."

It's hot in here. There's only one small window, and it's closed. Probably because of the bugs constantly tapping at it, trying to get in. Donna's desk is overflowing with paperwork.

As they both sit down, Nate pulls out his legal pad. "Could you tell me in your own words what happened from the minute you were alerted that something was wrong."

Donna takes a deep breath and rolls her eyes at the same time. "I never knew I'd have to repeat this so many times. I should've recorded it onto my cell phone the first time I was asked. It sure would've saved me some bother."

Nate smiles patiently.

"It was Jessica Conway who told me that Jenny wasn't in her bed when the Bunk 5 girls woke up that morning."

"What time was that?"

"Seven. We have a trumpeter—just one of the kids—who raises the alarm for everyone to wake up and get ready to start the day. Breakfast is served between seven thirty and eight thirty. I rushed straight over to their bunk and spoke to the rest of the girls."

"How many kids to a bunk?" asks Nate.

"Eight. Jenny's bed was messy, so it was hard to tell whether she'd slept in it. The children don't tend to make their beds, no matter how much we scold them. They rarely wash either, but that's another story. I asked them when was the last time any of them had seen her. Two of the girls—Jessica and Lizzie—said they'd been with her at the lake after supper, before lights out. They said they'd all swum out to the water slide, had a few goes and then come back in. They wanted to cool off because it had been a particularly sticky day and they'd all participated in a softball game that afternoon."

"What time was that?"

"Around nine o'clock. Jessica and Lizzie raced each other back to their bunk once they were dressed, and they swear they left Jenny drying herself off. None of her clothes were by the lake, so she must have finished dressing before…"

"What about her towel?"

Donna sighs. "The police asked that too. Her towel was gone too. It wasn't in her bunk and it wasn't in the laundry room."

Nate writes this down. "Do we know what color it was?"

"The girls think it was blue-and-white-striped, but I believe the parents said they hadn't packed a towel for her that matches that description. We found a pink towel in her belongings, but it was bone dry and folded."

"And what was she wearing?"

Donna hunts among the pieces of paper on her desk. When she finds what she is looking for, she reads from a list. "Navy shorts, a white polo shirt, a red sweater and Converse sneakers. Her bathing suit was a black one-piece. Her backpack was red."

Nate takes a drink from his water bottle while he thinks. Now he knows what items to look for while he and Madison are walking around the place. "Have there been any sightings of strangers in the camp? Any of the kids reported concerns?"

Donna shakes her head. "None at all, Mr. Monroe. The monster stories are just that: stories. And we have a strict curfew in place now: everyone has to be in their cabin by ten o'clock, even the staff."

He'd be surprised if the staff abide by that. "One theory I'm considering is that Jenny might have got lost in the forest. Perhaps she intended to run away but hadn't meant to stay away long. Do you teach the kids any survival skills?"

"Of course. During their first week we concentrate on swimming lessons first and foremost, because of the lake. But we also have compulsory lessons to teach survival skills. All the children will know to stay in one place if they get lost, and what not to eat in case it's poisonous. They know that if they get separated from the rest of us, they need to be smart and wait for us to find them."

Nate makes notes. "And I assume the woods were searched by the police?"

"Yes, they had about twenty volunteers plus a team of police officers looking for her on the day we called them. They were only out there for five hours, which obviously isn't enough time to search the whole forest, but I guess a child wouldn't get much further than that on foot. They searched the lake too, that evening."

"I see. But nothing was found?"

"Not that I've been told."

"Are there locks on the children's cabins?" he asks.

"Of course not. We can't lock them in, Mr. Monroe! What if they need the bathroom, or there's a fire? But we have other security measures in place."

"Such as?"

"We have a security guard."

He's surprised. "I'm glad to hear it. Can I meet him? I'd like to ask him a few questions."

Donna smiles. "He won't answer you, but yes, you can meet him. He's a dog."

Nate almost laughs. Is that their idea of security? "A dog?"

She nods. "He's an ex-police dog. His police handler died in the line of duty. The camp director before me rescued him from a kill shelter just before he was due to be euthanized. When she quit to move away, she left Brody behind. He's part of the camp, not a house pet. He doesn't have much time for me and you can certainly tell he was a police dog, because he's always restless and alert."

Nate feels for him. All dogs mourn the loss of their owners, and he would expect K9s to be no different. The fact that Brody's story mimics his own—being so close to being killed by the state and then rescued at the last minute—isn't lost on him. "What breed is he?"

She makes a thinking face. "Now let me get this right. He's a German shepherd–husky mix. Gorgeous to look at, but he's got way too much energy for me. I'm more of a cat person. He loves patrolling the camp, but he's not that keen on the kids."

"Really? I thought all dogs loved kids."

"From what I can tell, he finds them too noisy, and he hates being hugged by the younger children. They tend to grab rather than stroke. But he's good with them and just walks away when he's finding them too much. No one can ever tell what he's thinking, but he's not a happy dog, that much is obvious. In fact, the only time he looks like he's enjoying himself is when he's chasing a stranger or patrolling the grounds."

Police work is obviously in his blood. Nate would bet he was bred from another K9. "How old is he?"

"When I started working here, I was told he was three. So he'd be four now. To be honest, he's a pain in the ass. He's very vocal and keeps me awake some nights with his nocturnal howling. He likes to roam the woods like a free spirit. Kat thinks he's looking for his cop dad, but she's a little whimsical."

Nate wonders whether the dog saw anything the night Jenny disappeared. "How come Brody didn't greet me and my colleague when we arrived?"

"He's probably watching you from afar. If he ever thinks someone's in danger, he just appears out of nowhere. Trust me, if he thought you were a threat, you'd be on the ground right now."

Nate smiles. He likes the sound of Brody.

CHAPTER TWENTY

The office of Dr. Pamela Jarvis

Pamela is afraid to read on. Afraid to learn of any other warning signs she might have missed from her client. Walking to her office window instead, she looks out at the parking lot and wishes she could just get in her car and drive away. She checks her watch: it's still early. She knows she has to read the whole journal, but she'd rather be anywhere else but here. There are voices outside her office, enquiring after her. They're probably wondering why she hasn't joined the morning meeting. She told Stephen, her clerical support, to hold all calls and visitors, because she can't be interrupted until she's finished.

With a deep breath and a feeling of dread building in her chest, she heads back to her desk and starts reading the next entry.

It's been nine months since the accident that killed my babies and nothing is better at home. My therapist keeps telling me over and over that things will improve. That I'm expecting too much too soon. That time heals all wounds. She knows all the cheap dime-store platitudes, but they mean nothing in real life. She listens to me with a concerned look on her face, but she doesn't hear me. She thinks I'm too emotional, still reeling from grief, but that's because she doesn't see the side of my abuser that I see. No one does.

Dr. Jarvis just thinks we all need to get used to our new normal since the deaths of Susie and Thomas. But she doesn't see the violent outbursts I'm being subjected to; the changes in behavior when no one else is around. I can't help wondering whether it's my fault. Did I cause this to happen? I'm terrified, but I can't make anyone see what's really happening at home, so it's better to just write it down. But if my abuser finds this, it would end badly for me. The only way out is to beat them to it.

Pamela is stunned. She had no idea this woman was experiencing violence at home. She had never disclosed that in any of their sessions together. She tries to think whether her client ever turned up to appointments with bruises, and is ashamed to admit she can't remember. Not that they would be visible anyway. If her abuser was cunning, as they so often are, he would have avoided her face as it would have raised too many questions.

With shaking hands, she reaches for her coffee cup, but it's empty. She looks at her drinks cabinet, and for the first time in her life, she considers pouring a bourbon before lunchtime.

CHAPTER TWENTY-ONE

Madison feels a little conspicuous as she wanders around the summer camp. But interestingly, no one questions her presence—none of the counselors or the children—indicating the security is beyond lax here.

She wipes away the sweat forming at her hairline and wishes she could have a shower and change her clothes, but that will have to wait.

Knowing that Nate could be a while with the director, she approaches one of the wooden cabins and looks through the window. It's empty, so she sticks her head in the door. She immediately flinches as the smell of young boys hits her nose. She used to coach her son's baseball team for a year or so and she remembers that odor of sweaty socks and damp towels well. She looks around the cabin without going in. It's so messy it looks like a Tasmanian devil has swept through; with sports equipment all over the place, unmade beds, and clothes bundled up on the floor. She's surprised the staff don't insist on the kids keeping the cabins tidy. Then again, with it smelling so ripe, maybe they never venture inside.

Memories of Owen and his friends threaten to flood back, so she leaves and walks around the rear of the cabin. It's close to the woods. She looks over her shoulder. All the cabins are close to the woods except for the two that serve as an office and a cafeteria.

She walks into the dense forest, where it immediately feels cooler. The thick canopy is keeping the sun out. It smells of damp soil and wet grass in here, almost like it's got its own microclimate. The deeper she goes, the more she realizes a child couldn't survive in here for long. There's no way Jennifer Lucas is hiding. Even if that was her original intent, she would have come back by now, hungry and desperate for sunshine and fresh air. She wonders if the rest of the forest is like this. Perhaps Jennifer walked far enough to come across a clearing or a walking trail.

A huge black beetle the size of a cockroach scurries across her shoe. Creeped out, she kicks it off with her other foot. No. If the girl voluntarily ran off, the bugs alone would have brought her back to civilization.

Voices behind her make her turn and walk back to the camp. She follows the sound of the children's delighted screams and comes across a game of soccer. It looks like it's boys against girls; they're wearing either red or blue jerseys.

She approaches a bench and sits next to a young boy. She doesn't know if it's watching the kids play soccer, or being outdoors on a sunny day with the smell of freshly cut grass, but she feels like she could be at one of Owen's games, waiting to cheer him on as he waves to her from his position. Her heart aches with a mixture of regret and anger.

"Hi. Are you a new counselor?" says the boy. With red hair, freckles and a bright red nose, he's going to burn in today's sunshine. She instinctively picks up one of the baseball caps discarded on the ground near the spare sports equipment and places it on his head.

"No, I'm just visiting. I'm Madison."

"I'm Scotty. I'm injured so I have to sit this one out."

He pulls his sock down and she can see a bandage around his ankle. The swelling and purple bruising spreads further than the bandage.

"Ouch. I bet that hurt."

"Nah. Well, a little. I didn't cry, though. My friend did it by accident. Do you want some lemonade? I made it myself."

She smiles at him. He's probably a year younger than Owen was when she was arrested. "Sure."

He limps over to the cooler box and pulls out a jug and plastic cup. When he hands her the cup, she can see three tiny flies floating on top of the lemonade, but he watches for her reaction so she drinks it down regardless.

It actually tastes good: sweet and cool. "That was amazing. Well done! I think you could bottle that and sell it in Walmart."

"Thanks!" He grins at her and goes back to watching the game.

Madison tries hard not to think about Owen.

CHAPTER TWENTY-TWO

Nate leaves Donna's oppressive office with her permission to look around camp and get a feel for the place, under the strict proviso that he doesn't hassle any staff or children. He can question them but not "interrogate" them, as Donna doesn't want more angry parents to deal with. He gets the impression she won't be returning to manage this place for a second year and he can understand that. Losing a kid on her watch isn't going to help her career and has probably dented her confidence.

He steps out into a cool breeze. Most of the cabins are shaded by a canopy of large trees, so it's not unbearable under here. The smell of freshly cut grass has him wondering whose job it is to mow all this, then a swarm of bloodthirsty mosquitoes attack him, making him slap his neck and arms. He wipes away the dead insects and wonders where Madison has got to. Something tells him to walk over to the lake before he looks for her, to check out the area where Jenny was last spotted. He notices the jetty is protected by a barrier and a warning sign to avoid the area when alone.

Stepping up to the edge, he can see the grass is worn away here, no doubt from the happy feet of many kids launching themselves into the cool, glistening water. It's something that appeals to him right now. Without the shade to protect him, the intense sunshine burns his neck. A swarm of flies buzz around his ears and he curses himself for not buying some bug repellent. Something green—a tennis ball—is bobbing in the water, so he leans in to retrieve it. A dog barks behind him. He spins around.

A handsome wolf-like creature is looking at him with his huge ears pointing forwards. He's big. His coloring is an interesting mix of creams and browns, and he has intense brown eyes. Nate can definitely see characteristics from both breeds in him.

"Hey, boy. You must be Brody."

The animal barks again. If Nate were afraid of dogs, he'd probably walk away right now, trying his best not to run. Instead, he kneels down and holds out his hand. The dog doesn't move, but his tail starts thudding the ground, and Nate thinks his expression softens slightly.

"Come on, Brody. I'd like to meet you."

Brody gives him one more look before launching at him. Nate knows he needs to hold his ground, and not just because he's close to the edge of the lake. The dog runs up to him and sniffs his face, with his front paws digging into his thighs. He's so heavy he knocks Nate over, so he sits on the ground and lets Brody sniff his hands. Brody surprises him by resting across his legs, pinning him down.

"Jesus Christ, you're heavy."

Brody barks as if to confirm it, and Nate wonders why Donna made out he was unfriendly. The dog is enjoying having his thick fur coat ruffled as they both watch Madison appear. The closer she gets, the more alert Brody becomes. He sits up and then stands in front of Nate. Madison stops a few feet away.

"Who's this?" she asks.

"Hold out your hand and crouch down. He's friendly."

She doesn't look so sure, but she does it. Brody sniffs her hand and then, not finding anything of interest, immediately turns his attention back to Nate.

"You want this, don't you?" Nate holds up the tennis ball, and the dog drops onto his front legs, ass in the air, tail wagging energetically just like any regular pet.

Nate gets up and throws the ball as far as he can, but the dog just watches it. He doesn't run for it. "Fetch!"

Brody looks at him like he wants to chase the ball but for some reason he won't.

"He's not earned it yet," says a male voice.

Nate looks behind Madison and sees a tall young man with ginger hair, probably in his early twenties, approaching them. "He was a working dog so he has to earn his ball."

Madison nods. "Of course. The ball is the reward for a job well done. Do you know what he was trained to find? I assume it was drugs."

The stranger looks down at Brody and pats his head. Brody turns away, unimpressed, and sits next to Nate.

"Bodies, actually. He's a cadaver dog. That's what the shelter was told when the cop's wife handed him in. She didn't like the idea of keeping her dead husband's cadaver dog, apparently, and I can't say I blame her."

Nate looks at Brody. The dog has been through a lot: losing his owner, discarded by his family and out of the job he was bred for. He has nothing to do but roam the woods every day. Nate can already feel himself falling for him and wonders whether anyone's put him to use in the woods to look for Jenny's body. He stands up and holds his hand out to the man. "I'm Nate Monroe."

"Josh Sanders. I work here. I've been a camp counselor for a few summers."

He turns to Madison, who introduces herself.

"You're looking for Jenny Lucas, aren't you?" says Josh.

"We are," Nate confirms. "The family have asked for our help."

"We have a spare cabin if you'd like to stay here for a few days. We've lost that many kids early that we've made the remainder bunk together, which leaves us one spare. You'd have to share, but there are plenty of empty beds to choose from."

Nate looks over at Madison to see what she thinks.

"Fine by me," she says. "The less travelling back and forth we have to do, the more time we'll have to find Jenny."

"Great," says Josh. He turns around and points past the office. "It's the farthest cabin over there. I'll make sure there are clean sheets and towels for you. Want me to take you there now?"

"Not yet," says Madison. "First, we'd like to check out Jenny's cabin. I understand it's number 5. Is that correct?"

Nate notices Josh hesitate. Perhaps he's wondering if Donna will be mad at him for letting them enter one of the kids' cabins.

He nods. "Her bed was the one closest to the door."

"Thanks."

Nate follows Madison. He looks back at Brody as they walk away. The dog doesn't follow them; eventually he gets up and runs in the opposite direction, toward the woods, leaving the discarded tennis ball untouched.

When they walk into the cabin, Nate is surprised to see there are no children inside. He's overcome by a strong smell of perfume, hairspray and sweaty socks, all mixed together to form a sickly-sweet aroma.

Jenny's bed stands out, as it's the only one with no sheets on it.

"If she was nearest the door, she'd be the easiest to grab," says Madison.

"But she didn't sleep in here that night. Didn't Grant say her friends thought she had chosen to sleep by the campfire?"

Madison gives him a look. "*If* we believe her friends. Remember, we only have the statements of young kids to go by. We need to be open to the idea that they could be covering up for themselves, or maybe for their favorite camp counselor."

Nate would never have considered a child could have any involvement in Jennifer's disappearance. He pulls open the drawer of the nightstand, but it's empty.

Madison has no luck with the tall locker on the other side of the bed. "The contents have either been released to her parents or they're still being held as evidence."

He walks around the rest of the cabin. It looks like a bomb has gone off, with clothes everywhere, toiletries covering every shelf and nightstand, and home-made bunting wrapped around lights and bedheads. In comparison, Jenny's small area looks like no one has ever stayed there. He starts to feel as if she's out of their reach. As if the task of finding her is too difficult. The thought of letting Esme down fills him with dread.

"Come on," says Madison. "Let's mix with the kids and see what we can find out."

He's relieved to follow her out into the fresh air.

CHAPTER TWENTY-THREE

Madison pulls opens the wooden door to the cabin that houses the cafeteria and walks in. The smell of hot dogs and fried onions is strong and makes her stomach growl.

"Want a coffee?" asks Nate.

"Please. Grab me something to eat too. A hot dog would be good."

He nods. "You find us somewhere to sit."

Madison scans the rows of noisy, animated kids and spots a young girl sitting on her own, picking at some tomato pasta. She's about Jenny's age. Every now and then she glances up at a table of older girls, who are giggling together, but they don't invite her over.

"Hi, I'm Madison. Do you mind if my friend and I join you?"

The girl looks up at her and smiles. "Sure."

Madison notices her braces. "I had those when I was your age. They suck, don't they?"

The girl nods and touches them self-consciously. "I'm having them taken off before school starts. I can't wait."

The sad look on her face makes Madison feel sorry for her. It's hard being that age. She remembers the struggle of trying to get good grades and please her mother whilst also trying to fit in with her peers, some of whom could be mean like the giggling girls. She wonders what kind of worries Jenny had in her young life and whether these girls made them worse. Or perhaps she was one of them. She wipes some crumbs off the table and rests her chin in her hand. "What's your name?"

"Becky."

Nate joins them and passes Madison a fully loaded hot dog and a coffee.

"This is Nate," she says.

He smiles at Becky. "Hi."

Becky blushes. Probably not enough for Nate to notice, but Madison does. "Did you get to know Jenny Lucas while she was here?" She takes a bite of her dog. The onions taste amazing but the mustard squirts everywhere.

"I wasn't in her bunk but I knew who she was. Do you know what happened to her?"

Madison shakes her head and uses a napkin to wipe her mouth. "Not yet."

Becky looks teary. "I wanted to go home when she vanished, but my parents are abroad on holiday so I couldn't."

Madison doesn't want to upset the girl further. "Don't worry, we'll find her."

Becky goes back to picking at her pasta.

Madison finishes her hot dog and spots a suited man walk in. He scans the room and then eyeballs her. She nudges Nate, who looks up and watches the guy approach their table.

"Let me guess," says Nate, wiping ketchup from his fingers. "Detective Morgan from Trinity Creek PD?"

The man doesn't show any surprise. "How did you guess?"

Nate smirks. "I can spot a cop a mile off. I'm Nate. This is Madison."

Madison looks at Morgan. He's probably a little older than her, with dark hair and a tan. He must be hot in his navy suit.

"The camp director tells me you're looking into the disappearance of Jennifer Lucas," he says. "Is that right?"

Nate pushes his plate away and Madison can feel the hostility oozing off him. "News travels fast around here. Is that a problem?"

She notices the cafeteria has gone quiet and all eyes are on them.

"It's only a problem if you give the family false hope," says Morgan.

"Why would we do that?" she asks.

He ignores her. "Which family member hired you?"

She and Nate share a look, and then both stand up without replying, collecting their dirty dishes. She manages to down some coffee. "We'll catch you later, Becky."

The girl smiles and immediately glances at the table of mean girls to see if they noticed she has adults talking to her.

Morgan looks irritated. "Can we discuss this outside?"

They stack their dishes on the cleaning bench and follow him outside, into the sunshine.

He looks around. "I hope you've been warned about the crazy dog that lives here. Damn thing near took my face off last time I was here. It's just a matter of time before it bites one of the kids." He slides his sunglasses on and takes a seat at a picnic table.

Madison sits opposite him with Nate next to her. For some reason Morgan looks only at Nate as he talks. It irritates her.

"Donna tells me you're private investigators, working for Jennifer's family. Are you both licensed? Because I'd like to record your details."

Nate shakes his head. "Unlicensed. The family were aware of that before they hired us."

He looks dubious, like they're lying just so he can't get their details. "That's fine and all, but this is an open case for my police department and I don't want anyone messing it up. You're free to ask questions and look into things, but I'd appreciate it if you'd work with me, not against me."

That gives Madison hope that he's not an asshole. She sees surprise on Nate's face. "Are you saying you want us to keep you in the loop with anything we find?" she asks.

"Yes. I'm happy to cooperate with you if you don't fuck things up."

Nate's shaking his head. "I don't work with cops. I'm being paid by Esme Lucas, so she's the only person I'll be updating. You've had two weeks to find her granddaughter. What have you been doing?"

Morgan stares hard at him.

Madison speaks up before they come to blows. "Let's not be hasty, Nate." She turns to face Morgan. "Detective, I'm a former police officer and I know what a pain in the ass PIs can be. But I agree with you, there's nothing wrong with us all sharing information. After all, we're here to find Jenny, not to score points." She looks back at Nate, who looks away. Then she turns back to the cop. "Let me give you my number so we can stay in touch."

He retrieves his cell phone and she takes it from him. She pulls out the piece of cardboard with her new cell number on and enters it as he watches.

"Why don't you work with cops?" he asks Nate. "What have you got against us?"

Nate laughs. "Let's just say I've yet to meet a good one."

"Hey! What about me?" Madison hands the phone back to Morgan. "Send me a message so I have your number."

He sends her a text. "What's your last name, Madison?"

She freezes, unsure whether to tell him. She could really do without him googling her to try to figure out where she used to work.

Nate speaks up for her. "You don't need to know our last names. We're not the ones being investigated here."

Morgan sighs, giving the impression he's running out of patience. "Listen, I'm happy to tell you what we've done so far." He looks around, making sure no kids are listening in, but he needn't bother: it's eerily quiet. Madison's pretty sure that everyone left on the campsite is eating lunch in the cabin behind them.

"We've done a background check on everyone working here. Apart from some minor misdemeanors, there's no one of interest. We've searched the woods and the lake and found nothing. Not even Jennifer's backpack or an item of clothing. Which means one thing."

"She was abducted," says Madison.

"Exactly. Shadow Falls is small, and my department has jurisdiction over five towns altogether. I've checked for registered sex offenders nearby and only found two that aren't currently serving time. They both have credible alibis and even let us search their homes without a warrant, so they're not suspects in Jenny's disappearance."

"So it could've been someone who was driving through and looking for easy prey?" says Nate.

"Probably. They don't get many truck drivers through here as it's off the beaten track, but it's not unheard of for sex offenders to stalk summer camps. With only so many staff to go around, there are always going to be easy pickings for people like that. If that's what happened here, there's small hope of finding the girl or her abductor; they'll be long gone."

"So why did you tell the family she probably ran away?" Madison asks.

Morgan leans back with a confused look on his face. "I never told them that. A twelve-year-old girl wouldn't get far if she ran away from here. These woods stretch for miles into the Six Rivers National Forest, and there are no busy highways nearby where she could've hitched a ride."

Madison glances at Nate.

"The grandmother told us you thought she's likely to be a runaway," he says.

Morgan slowly shakes his head. "No. At the beginning of my investigation I did say it was one of the possibilities I would look into, but once we realized she hadn't taken anything with her other than the clothes she was wearing and her backpack and towel, I didn't think that was a credible theory. Maybe the grandmother misunderstood. She was hysterical on some occasions. She still calls me five times a day."

Madison nods. "Parents and relatives tend to hear what they want to hear. It's understandable. God knows I'd rather cling onto the hope that my child had run away than consider he's with a sexual predator. So, this case is still open with your department then?"

"Of course," says Morgan. "But the trail's gone cold so there's not much we can do at the moment. I'm keeping an eye on other missing child cases from around the state. Who knows? Maybe I'll find a link one day and nail the bastard who took her. But I don't expect to find Jennifer Lucas alive. Obviously I haven't said that to her family, so don't quote me."

"We saw on the news that there's a substantial reward," Madison says. "Are the parents covering that?"

He nods. "They are."

"Could money be a motive for kidnap?"

"I don't think so, but I guess anything's possible. There have been no ransom requests so far."

"What about her cell phone; did you find anything of interest on there?" She can feel Nate staring at her.

"We're still pulling the data." Morgan looks amused. "I can imagine you were a good cop. Why did you quit?"

She's taken aback. Is it wrong to feel flattered that another cop appreciates her?

"Are there any other missing children around here?" asks Nate, probably buying her time to come up with a cover story.

"Not in Shadow Falls, no. There's actually never been a child homicide or abduction recorded in this town, which is something in itself. There is an open missing person's case—an adult—but it's completely unrelated."

"Did the amber alert generate any leads?" asks Madison.

Morgan looks annoyed now. "I didn't issue an amber alert."

Her mouth falls open. "What? You're kidding, right?"

"No. I had to make a judgment call, and based on the lack of evidence to suggest she was abducted, I decided against it."

Morgan stands up. "If you find anything, don't keep it to yourselves. Despite the odds against it, I want that child home with her family. Preferably alive."

He's distracted by Josh, the camp counselor they met earlier, who smiles at them as he walks past with another male counselor. The doors behind them open and a bunch of kids start piling out, running in various directions and shouting as they go.

"Thanks for your time." Detective Morgan nods at them both and heads back toward his car.

Madison has no doubt mistakes have been made here, not just the length of time it took Donna to call the police, but the way Morgan has investigated so far. As she watches him walk away, she wonders how long it will be before he tries to figure out who she and Nate are. She worries that her conviction might get her kicked out of Shadow Falls, making it harder to find Jennifer Lucas.

CHAPTER TWENTY-FOUR

November 2000—Austin, Texas

As the foreman prepares to read the verdict to the packed courtroom, Nate is pulled upwards by the arm. His lawyer is trying to make him stand, but Nate's legs are shaking hard. His knees don't feel strong enough to hold him and he doesn't want to risk causing a scene. He stays where he is.

"I'll only ask one more time," says Judge Kemper, with impatience written all over her face. "Will the defendant please rise."

"Yes, Your Honor." His lawyer pulls him again, harder this time. "Come on, buddy," he whispers. "I've got you."

Nate stands but leans forward onto his knuckles on the tabletop. He can't even look at the jury to try to gauge their verdict. He blesses himself and recites a silent prayer. Stacey's uncle might have made out he was the devil, but he does still have faith. Whether that will last long after today he doesn't know.

He always believed in the American judicial system until he was arrested. Since then, his eyes have been opened and he has no doubt at all that he's about to be found guilty of murder. The only doubt is whether he'll be convicted of capital murder, which carries the possibility of being sentenced to death. He doesn't know if the prosecution managed to poison the jury into believing that he'd gone to the Connors' home with the intention of raping Stacey before killing her, but whether it's capital murder or just plain murder—life in prison or the death sentence—it's all inconsequential. Stacey is still dead.

He's been hearing her lately. She whispers to him in the dark after lights-out. He enjoys hearing her voice again, but only until he remembers she's not real. Prison can send a person crazy in ways not possible on the outside.

He takes a deep breath. He's spent three long weeks in this small, windowless courtroom and he's ready to get out of here for good, but he'd take it over a prison cell any day. He looks around him. Everyone is leaning forward, waiting with bated breath to find out whether this trainee priest is a killer in the eyes of his peers.

He looks directly at Judge Kemper, who spends an infuriating amount of time shuffling papers, as if she's stopped proceedings merely in order to tidy her bench. Then she stands up, stretches her back and sits down again, adjusting the cushion behind her. Nate can't help wondering if she's enjoying all the media attention this case has brought her. One of his cellmates told him that judges in Texas are all corrupt, and that they get paid a bonus for every murder conviction they secure, and more for capital murders. Nate doesn't believe that, but the look of contempt Kemper wears whenever she glances in his direction makes him glad the final verdict isn't up to her.

The judge takes a sip of her hot drink and looks around the courtroom, nodding at several court officials as if checking it's okay to proceed. Then she looks directly at Nate.

"I will have no emotional outbursts in my courtroom." She stares hard for a few seconds before turning to the foreman. "Please read the jury's verdict loud and clear."

The older white male—Juror 11—stands. He looks nervous. His hairline is wet, as if sweat is threatening to roll down his forehead, and his glasses are gradually sliding off his nose. He doesn't make eye contact with Nate, instead preferring to stare hard at the sheet of paper he's holding. It's then that Nate knows for sure.

"We the jury find the defendant Nathaniel Monroe…" He pauses. All the other jurors are looking at Nate with unrepentant stares. "… guilty of capital murder."

There are some gasps behind him but definitely more cheers. Nate exhales everything he's holding onto as he realizes those four words have ended his life.

"Thank you to the jurors for taking your job seriously and acting professionally throughout the trial," says Judge Kemper. "We will begin the sentencing phase after an hour's recess."

The courtroom buzzes into action, with jurors being led out of one door and the spectators out of another. Nate doesn't even look around at his father. He doesn't want to see the disappointment on his face. He wants to collapse into his seat, but he's being handcuffed again.

His lawyer pats him on the back. "Don't worry, we'll start the appeal immediately. The judge was hostile from the beginning and that would've swayed the jurors. Leave it to me."

But Nate doesn't hold out much hope.

CHAPTER TWENTY-FIVE

Suddenly Brody bursts out from the woods, heading straight for Detective Morgan. Nate watches from the picnic bench with a widening smile on his face as the detective spots the dog and starts running toward his car, clearly scared for his life. He drives off faster than necessary, leaving a cloud of dust behind.

Nate notices Madison watching his reaction.

"I know you have an ax to grind, but you can't blame all cops for what happened to you, Nate."

He turns to her, surprised. "Why not?"

"Because Detective Morgan hasn't done anything to you. He'll be working under a lot of pressure to find Jennifer Lucas, so he probably doesn't need you acting like a petulant teenager. We're lucky he even offered to work with us. He could order us out of here if he wanted to."

Nate's annoyed. He's wondering if Madison is always going to be loyal to anyone with a badge, and if so, where does that leave him when he finally catches up with Stacey's uncle? Will she arrest him herself? He realizes he needs to be a little more cautious around her.

"Fair enough. I'll give the guy a break. Once he's proved himself."

She rolls her eyes at him and looks at her cell phone.

Brody is barking after Morgan's car.

"Brody," shouts Nate. "Come here."

The dog stops in his tracks and turns around to face him. Nate follows his command with a whistle, and Brody bounds over to him alarmingly fast. He skids to a halt next to Nate and gives him his paw.

"What do you want, boy? You hungry?" Nate would swear the dog can understand him, as two lines of drool start leaking out of the sides of his mouth.

"He doesn't eat normal dog food, by the way."

Nate looks up at Josh, who is carrying a stack of child-size orange life jackets. "No? What does he eat then?"

"Whatever we eat. The cafeteria women leave two bowls out all day for food and water and just keep topping them up with the kids' leftovers. He seems happy enough with that."

Nate is surprised. He looks behind him and spots two empty silver bowls. "Does no one actually look after him?"

Josh shakes his head. "Not really. He can look after himself. I'm not sure anyone here likes him, to be honest with you. He isn't like a pet or anything. He just does his own thing. Kids want to play with animals, but Brody doesn't like that. He's a lone wolf."

Nate looks down at Brody and rubs his back. "We'll get you something to eat, don't you worry." The dog has intelligent eyes and probably can look after himself, but the fact that he's letting Nate touch him suggests he does want company sometimes. Doesn't everyone?

Madison stands up. "Can we ask you some questions about the night Jennifer Lucas disappeared?"

"Not right now," says Josh. "Sorry, I'm busy. I've got a small sailboat class planned. The kids are about to earn their merit badges. Maybe I'll catch you tonight in the staff bar."

"There's a bar here?" she asks.

"Of course. How else would we get through the long days?" He smiles and walks away just as a group of kids catch up to him.

Nate notices that one boy stays close to Josh, holding onto his arm. He'd be surprised if the kids didn't get attached to the staff here. But that could lead to trouble.

He goes inside to find some food for Brody. A teenage girl points him in the direction of the slop bowl, where everyone scrapes their leftovers.

"Seriously? You don't have anything better for him?"

"Sometimes I give him sausages, but the kitchen is closing. Sorry."

Nate picks up the whole bowl and takes it outside to where Brody's sitting next to Madison.

"Here you go, boy. Eat as much as you want."

Without hesitation, Brody buries his face in the bowl, tail wagging the whole time.

"I don't like him," says Madison, nodding in the direction Josh went.

"Why not?"

"He has an annoying swagger that suggests he thinks he's clever. He works at a summer camp, for God's sake. What's he got to be so cocky about?"

Nate thinks about it. "You think he's a potential suspect?"

She pats Brody's hind. "I think he's the most likely suspect so far. He's the only member of staff who keeps talking to us unprompted, he clearly knew the missing girl, and he always has an annoying smirk on his face. I'd like to look into his alibi."

Nate isn't so sure. "We haven't been here long enough to come to that kind of conclusion. You need to keep an open mind."

She looks unimpressed. "In my experience the most obvious suspects are obvious for a reason: because they're hiding something."

Nate shakes his head and holds back his annoyance. "That's exactly the kind of thinking that got me convicted of Stacey's murder." He'd like to walk away from her right now. He knew he'd find it tough working with an ex-cop, and if this is how she really thinks, he might have to drop her sooner rather than later.

"One of the kids told me earlier that Josh's girlfriend works in the front office," she says. "Let's at least pay her a visit and see what she has to say about the night Jenny went missing."

Nate knows it's the next logical step seeing as they can't talk to Josh himself right now. "Okay, fine." He leaves Brody eating. As they head to the office, he thinks of Kat. "I bet I know exactly who Josh is screwing."

CHAPTER TWENTY-SIX

Madison follows Nate into the main office, but there's no one there. She looks around the wooden cabin, which is large but messy. There are children's paintings pinned on the walls and sports equipment heaped in piles in every corner. It smells of sweat and it's hot in here. They clearly don't have any A/C, and for some unimaginable reason the windows are closed. It makes her wonder what it's going to be like trying to sleep in one of these cabins tonight. She hears a woman talking in the room off to the left.

"Sounds like she's on the phone," says Nate.

"Hello?" yells Madison.

A young brunette in a pair of short denim cut-offs and a plaid shirt barely buttoned up over a low-cut T-shirt walks out of a room behind the front desk. Her nails are painted black and she's wearing about fifteen necklaces. She wipes her nose and looks a little alarmed. She can't be older than eighteen, despite the make-up desperately trying to suggest otherwise. She's been using. Madison would recognize that nose wipe anywhere.

"Hey, Nate," says the girl, looking past her. "What can I do for you?"

Madison glances over her shoulder at Nate, who just smiles. She turns back to the girl. "What's your name?"

"Kat. I work here."

"Hey, Kat. Nate and I wanted to ask a few questions about the night Jennifer Lucas disappeared. Were you working that night?"

The girl looks down and starts busying herself with some loose papers on the front desk. "It was my night off. I was in the counselors' cabin with my boyfriend."

"Who's your boyfriend?" asks Nate.

She still doesn't look up. "Josh. We watched YouTube for a few hours before falling asleep."

Madison gives Nate a look to suggest that if Josh's alibi hangs on this girl covering for him, he's still a potential suspect. Nate appears to know what she's thinking.

"Were there any other staff in the cabin with you?" he asks.

The girl thinks about it but keeps tidying the desk. "Shelley was there for a while. But then she snuck into town with the others. We're not supposed to leave the camp at night but sometimes we need a break, you know? Me and Josh were alone when we went to sleep."

"What did you watch on YouTube?" Madison asks.

Kat finally looks up at them. Is that panic behind her eyes?

"Just some horror movies. You can check my phone if you don't believe me. The detective already did. I've only just got it back from him."

Madison's hopes lower. Detective Morgan did say he'd done a background check on all the staff.

"Did you fall asleep together?" she asks her.

"Yeah, but don't tell Donna. We're not meant to get into relationships here. There are a lot of rules when working at a summer camp. She thinks relationships between the staff will distract us from looking after the kids, but I love these guys! I would never let anything bad happen to them."

"Well someone has let something bad happen to Jenny." Madison feels guilty as soon as she says it, because Kat tears up, clearly concerned for the girl.

"Do you think she's going to be okay? None of us know what's happened to her, honestly. We talk about it all the time."

"And what's the most likely theory amongst the staff?" asks Nate, handing Kat a tissue.

"She's got to be in that creepy lake. There's no way someone came here and took her without any of us seeing it happen. Even if we hadn't noticed a stranger creeping around, Brody would've! That dog doesn't miss much, even when you think he's not around." She wipes her eyes. "I think Jenny's in the lake and the divers missed her. I saw a documentary about something similar once. There was this cute little eight-year-old girl in Canada who went kayaking on her own in the lake behind her house. Everyone assumed she was abducted or something, but it turned out her missing body was trapped underwater, under some real thick branches, so the divers never knew she was there until there was such a bad drought one summer that the water receded, exposing her remains."

Madison doesn't think that's likely in this situation, as she knows how thorough police divers are when looking for missing children. "I understand someone does a head count every evening to check everyone is accounted for. Is that right?"

"Yeah, we take it in turns."

"So who did it that night?" Grant had told them that the head count had been forgotten the night Jenny disappeared. She'd like to know who's responsible.

Kat goes back to shuffling papers. "I, er… I don't know. You'd have to ask Donna. I just know it wasn't my turn."

Madison wonders who she's covering for, but she could probably guess. "Well, if you think of anything that might be relevant to that night, please tell us."

Kat looks at Nate again. "Can I get your number? In case I remember anything?"

Madison tries not to laugh. She's clearly after a piece of Nate. She just hopes he's not dumb enough to give this girl his number.

"Sure. Here." He writes it down on a scrap of paper. "Whatever you tell us will be confidential."

Kat smiles up at him and fiddles with her necklaces. Madison's seen enough. She walks out of the cabin, shaking her head.

"What's the matter?" Nate asks, following her outside.

"She's too young for you. Didn't you learn that in priest school?"

He looks annoyed. "Don't you think it's a good idea to give the staff some way of contacting us in case they want to turn on one another? What if it *is* her boyfriend who took Jenny? She's unlikely to tell Detective Morgan, because she's already had plenty of opportunity to do that and hasn't, so it's better that she can contact one of us if she feels like confessing something."

His seriousness makes Madison feel like she's misjudged him. "Sorry. I just saw how she was looking at you and, well, I wouldn't be surprised if you were tempted."

She notices the dog is waiting for them. He's staring at Nate expectedly.

Nate strokes his head. "I'm more tempted to take Brody back to our cabin, to be honest."

She laughs, and his face softens. She's relieved he's not an asshole. It makes her wonder if she should actually confide in him instead of stringing him along under false pretenses.

Not yet. They still don't know each other well enough, and she can't risk losing her new job.

CHAPTER TWENTY-SEVEN

Esme is wringing her freezing hands with worry. She's been unable to warm them despite the hot air drifting in through the modern tri-fold doors. This house is unbearably quiet without Jenny stomping around and accidentally breaking things. She misses the noise.

Jenny would take any opportunity to spend time with her. Esme assumed it was because she was arguing with her mom a lot and needed to get away sometimes. She misses taking her shopping and trying on silly outfits together, and having afternoon tea at their favorite hotel. Jenny was like her little friend, always eager for attention, and so bright and funny. Grandchildren bring so much joy to a person's life that when they're no longer around, the world becomes a quiet, lonely place. To her, it feels as though life has muted its normal sounds and turned everything a pale shade of grey during this terrible time.

She looks around the white living room. All Jenny's belongings, normally spread around the house, are gone: her hair bands, nail polish, school books. Presumably they're all hidden away in her bedroom closet. It's almost as if she never existed. Grant likes the house tidy and would insist Jenny put her things away before bed each night, but it's never been this tidy. It looks like it's ready to be listed for sale.

She pulls the secondary cell phone out from her pocket. This one was bought just to liaise with the investigator. She doesn't know what made her do it, but something told her she shouldn't use her own. Maybe she was being paranoid.

She texted Nate Monroe for an update this morning but hasn't heard back from him, even though she knows he would have arrived in Shadow Falls a few hours ago. She expected to hear something to confirm he'd arrived and doesn't think she can last much longer in this perpetual state of worrying about where her beautiful granddaughter is.

Anna appears. She silently walks over to the couch and places a cup of coffee in front of Esme. "I've added a splash of brandy."

She's used the good china, which she rarely gets out, what with Jenny being so prone to breaking anything delicate. Esme would guess that's not the only reason why she's using it. It means nothing to keep your most precious things hidden away when you've lost a child. Everything is disposable now. Esme would give it all up to have her granddaughter back. What's the point of having money and nice things when a piece of your heart has been cut out? When a feeling of dread fills your entire body every time you think of what could have happened to her.

She looks up at her daughter-in-law and smiles weakly, trying to stay strong on the surface. "You know me so well."

Anna sits opposite her. "I know this is affecting your health, Esme. It's affecting all of us, but I can tell your anxiety is through the roof. I just wish there was something I could do for you. So does Grant." She pauses. "Don't you think you'd be better off back at home, so you have your own comforts around you? I know Beatrice is worried about you and wants to be there to help."

Esme doesn't think she could stand to be fussed over by her neighbor. Beatrice will gloat about her own grandchildren; she always has. It's been a stupid competition between them for years: who has the most grandchildren, who said their first words soonest, who took their first steps before anyone else. She shakes her head and sips her coffee. The brandy is strong.

"No. I'd feel useless there. I need to be here for any updates you get from the police. And I can update you on what the investigators find. Please don't shut me out, Anna. I'm family and I couldn't bear it." She starts crying, despite trying hard not to. She and Anna have never really connected in the way she always wanted to connect with her son's wife. They don't go shopping together, or on spa breaks. Their only mutual interest is Jenny, and now she's not here, they have nothing else to talk about. She wonders if Anna feels the tension between them as she does. Perhaps that's why they want her to go home.

"We won't shut you out. It's just that I'm not as hopeful as Grant." Anna takes her hands. "Esme, I have to be honest with you, though you're not going to like it. I don't think we'll see Jennifer again and I'm trying to prepare myself for the worst."

Esme looks at her, shocked. "How can you give up hope? It's only been two weeks! She could still be found." Her hands start shaking and she pulls them free from Anna's warm grip. Is she going to have to prepare herself for the worst now too?

Anna leans back. "I wish I had your optimism, Esme. I really do. But I don't think we'll be getting Jennifer back alive. I've seen this happen too many times to other families on the news. It never ends well." Her face crumples and she pushes her hands to her eyes.

It's Esme's turn to do the comforting. "No, don't say that!" She hugs Anna close. "There's always hope. Some children are found alive after ten years."

But Anna's shaking her head and sobbing. She's refusing to believe it. She really has given up all hope.

Esme feels like her heart is about to explode.

CHAPTER TWENTY-EIGHT

When Grant arrives home from work, he parks on the street, hesitating outside his own front gate. Once he presses that tiny button on his remote control, the gates will slide open and he'll be back to living his own worst nightmare.

He misses his daughter. He'd like nothing more than to open the front door and see Jenny having a meltdown about something stupid, like she's lost her cell phone, or her mom added vegetables to her dinner without asking. He would walk right up to her and hug her as tight as he could, making her understand how loved she is. He would tell her he's sorry that her parents didn't pay her more attention before she left for summer camp, how she deserved more patience and understanding from them. How she shouldn't have had to witness the worsening arguments between him and Anna. The tension must've been unbearable for his little girl. No one likes to see their parents hurting each other.

The thought that he'll never see Jenny again tears open his heart and makes his eyes ache with pressure. It feels like something in his brain is on the verge of exploding, and he can't help feeling that if that were to happen, it might be a massive relief in more ways than one. Putting on a brave face for his mother is hard. Men aren't supposed to show their true emotions; everyone looks to them for positivity and action. Everyone wants him to solve the problem.

But how do you solve a problem with no solution?

Everything's out of his hands. There's absolutely nothing he can do. He lets the tears come for the first time since that terrible night Jenny disappeared. He cries for Anna, for his daughter and for his mother. Life will never go back to the way it was, no matter what happens next.

CHAPTER TWENTY-NINE

Nate takes his car and drives into town, leaving Madison at the summer camp. She had some calls she wanted to make. He thought he'd go alone, but Brody jumped into the car as soon as he opened the driver's side. He tried to pull him out, but the dog growled at him.

"You better be house-trained, boy."

Brody barked at him, and Nate took him at his word.

As he drives out of the vast woods, he's relieved to get away for some alone time. He never sought an employee and Madison's already starting to rub him up the wrong way, what with her typical law-enforcement attitude and her digs about him and the girl in the office. He knows the best thing to do when he's annoyed is to get away from the situation. He's not the kind of guy who would explode at someone; he'd rather walk away and process his anger by himself. Maybe with the help of some coke.

Although his prison time couldn't have done him any good mentally, never mind physically, he feels he's come out relatively unscathed. Rex told him that one day, when the enormity of what happened to him finally hits home, he'll either implode or explode. Nate doesn't agree. Sure, he has moments when he wants to throw something at a wall or shoot himself in the head, but overall he's pretty steady, and he's certainly never been violent toward another person. It's just not him. He wonders if his measured personality has anything to do with the years spent in the Church growing up, devoting time to helping others. When you look outside of yourself it stops you taking yourself too seriously. There are other people going through worse than he did. Some of his fellow inmates are still in there. Somehow that seems worse than being executed.

Hunting Stacey's uncle keeps his mind occupied, stopping him from reflecting on his prison experience too much. He might be working on different cases in between, but that's only because he doesn't have any leads on Father Connor yet. Once he gets wind of his location, he'll be off, chasing him down before the lead goes cold. Just like when someone sent him an anonymous text telling him Father Connor was living in a mission in southern Brazil. It's just a shame Nate fell for a deliberate red herring, manufactured by Father Connor himself and designed to waste his time and money. He doesn't mind. He's used to playing the long game. He's waited before and he'll wait again. Because he knows it'll be all the sweeter when he finally locates the son of a bitch.

He pulls into the only gas station in Shadow Falls and fills up the car. An old woman comes out of the store and walks over to him. Brody barks in the front seat so Nate opens his door to let him out. He immediately runs off, behind the store. Shit. What if he doesn't come back?

"Fine-looking dog you've got there," says the woman. She's wearing grease-stained coveralls and is missing most of her teeth. Her mouth is caved in on itself, making her look like she's gurning.

"He's not mine, actually."

The woman raises her eyebrows. "Probably why he ran off. Can I clean your windshield for you? Top up your oil?"

Nate laughs. He's being upsold, even out here in the sticks. "No thanks. Everything's fine."

The woman gives the Jeep a look over. "Nice car. You must have some money. You connected to Camp Fearless?"

Nate finishes filling up the car and puts the gas hose back on its pump. He takes out two twenty-dollar bills, plus a ten for a tip, and hands them to her. "I'm just passing through. I heard there was a young girl missing from the camp. Did you know about that?"

She nods. "I sure did. The police asked me and my husband a ton of questions. They thought we might've seen an out-of-towner like you who could've abducted the poor thing. Thought he might have stopped to fill up on the way, I guess." She looks past him into his rear windows and he can't help but feel she's looking for the missing girl. "They also wanted to know if we had security cameras."

"Is that right? *Did* you see anyone?" He looks around for cameras and can see two. They look modern and out of place on the old gas station building.

She stares at him with suspicion in her eyes. "Are you with the police?"

She pronounces it *po-leece* and then spits on the ground. Nate smiles. "No. I'm not a fan of the police any more than you. Which is why I've been asked by the girl's family to do their job for them."

She suddenly holds her hand out. "I'm Jeanie-May. You'll want to come in and take a seat for what I've got to tell you."

"Nate." He shakes her hand and follows her into the store, looking around for Brody on the way. There's no sign of him.

"We only got cameras after the girl went missing. Didn't want a repeat occurrence and the cops said we were in a prime position to record any child abductor driving in or out of town. Not that they'll help the Lucas girl. Too late for her." Jeanie-May takes a seat behind the counter and pours them both a coffee from the oldest-looking coffee machine Nate has ever seen. The mug she hands him is dirty, but he doesn't want to be rude, so he takes a sip. It tastes fine.

"You know that camp has been going for fifteen years without incident," she says. "No kids have ever got hurt and it's done wonders for the businesses around here. We get families stopping by on their way in and out of town, when they're picking their kids up or dropping them off. We buy in extra snacks and magazines ready for them every summer. There's even rumors of a McDonald's being built nearby one day."

"Would that be a good thing?" asks Nate.

"Oh sure. Because that will bring other fast-food joints to town and then we'll finally grow. We've been too small for too long. We're forgotten out here in Shadow Falls and the name plays a big part in it. I keep telling the mayor we need to modernize. Change our name. I thought the summer camp would help, but it's taking a while."

Nate isn't really sure why she's telling him this and he doesn't want to waste his time, so he moves things along. "You've obviously lived here a long time and you must meet all sorts of locals and visitors in your line of work. Is there anyone around town you would suspect of abducting a child?"

She takes a deep breath and leans back in her seat. "There's a young man who works at the camp. Big mop of ginger hair. He has a brunette girlfriend who dresses like a hooker. But a cute one, you know; before the meth takes hold."

Nate assumes she's talking about Josh and Kat, but he's not met many of the other staff yet. Maybe there's more than one redhead with a hot brunette girlfriend.

"What about him?"

Just as she's about to open her mouth, an old man walks out from a room behind the counter. "Jeanie-May, what are you doing? I've told you before not to spread rumors." He looks at Nate and nods. "You take what she says with a pinch of salt, mister. She watches too many crime shows and gets reality mixed up with make-believe. It doesn't help that she suffers with that dementia."

Nate realizes Jeanie-May isn't as good a witness as he first thought. But whether she's fully aware of things around here or not, she must have picked up on something about Josh for her to mention him.

He puts his mug on the counter. "No problem at all. I should probably be going anyway. Thanks for the gas and the coffee." He turns to leave.

"Hey!" says Jeanie-May. "You didn't pay for your gas. Are you trying to rip us off or what?"

Nate knows he paid her but he doesn't argue. "My mistake." He pulls out another fifty bucks and hands it to her. "You folks take care."

He feels the man's eyes on his back as he walks out the door. The sunlight dazzles him before he puts his sunglasses on, and once his eyes adjust to the brightness, he's surprised to see Brody sitting next to the car, ready to go for another drive.

CHAPTER THIRTY

The office of Dr. Pamela Jarvis

Pamela stops at one small bourbon. The last thing she needs right now is people smelling liquor on her breath. She can't allow herself to fall apart under pressure, because today is a crucial day for her career and she has to remain professional. But she's fully aware it could be the last day she ever gets to work as a therapist.

There's a knock at her door, making her jump. Her nerves are shot. Before she can tell whoever it is to go away, the door opens and Stephen pops his head in. "The police keep calling. They want an update as soon as possible."

"Yes, I know that, Stephen. If you stop bothering me, I'll get through it a lot quicker."

He backs away and closes the door, leaving her feeling horrible. She can't worry about his feelings right now, though. She has to read on. There's so much to get through that she finds herself skim-reading some of the entries, like where her client talks about how difficult it is not to pick up her dead children's favorite foods at the grocery store by mistake, and how she has to cross the street if she sees the children's friends coming toward her.

Suddenly she notices a change in the handwriting. She flicks back through the journal, noticing that the everyday updates—about extended family, what her husband did at work, what the neighbors are up to—are all written neatly and with care. The more serious entries she's read so far, and the next unread passage, are barely legible; squeezed together and frantic. She can feel the strokes through the back of the page, as if the writer was pressing harder, desperately trying to get the words out quicker than her hand could keep up with her thoughts. Clearly the rushed, forced entries were the difficult days. Pamela takes a deep breath and reads on.

Next week is the one-year anniversary of Thomas and Susie's deaths, and I just feel numb. Summer has hit us and I think I prefer winter now. I never thought I'd ever feel that way. In winter I can stay in bed, claiming to be cold but really hiding from the world. I don't leave the house much anymore. Not unless I really have to. When I do go out, I prefer the cover of darkness, where no one can see me coming and going.

I'm pretty certain my husband is having sex with another woman, and I don't blame him. I'm certainly not available to him. The thought of his touch leaves me cold, inside and out, but I know he'll never leave me. We're bound together until the very end because of our shared grief. We created our beautiful children together and we buried them together. Nothing will ever change that horrifying truth. It's a macabre bond we'll always have.

I should stop writing. I'm having bad thoughts again. Maybe keeping this journal isn't good for me after all. Sometimes it's better to keep the words inside so as not to give them life. Because with life, they grow.

Pamela closes the journal and rubs her eyes. This is the first time a client's thoughts have made her want to cry. The awful realization hits her that she can't tell whether she's upset for her client or for what this journal means for her own fate.

CHAPTER THIRTY-ONE

Madison manages to speak to some of the camp counselors while Nate's out. She thinks she might have pissed him off with her comments about Kat. She's still getting used to relying on someone else and realizes she needs to be less of an asshole from now on. She can't afford to lose this job or his help.

In a way, things were easier in prison. She learned quickly that you really couldn't trust anyone, no matter how much you swapped stories about your family to pass the time, or how well you got on. Everyone inside was in survival mode and they would always choose saving their own skin over anyone else's. On the outside, it's different. You have to trust some people in order to survive, otherwise you'd spend your life alone in your house, in a self-imposed incarceration. If she wants to live again, she needs to trust someone like Nate. She just hopes her police instincts haven't dulled while she's been inside, as she would hate to find out she's put her faith in the wrong person.

She sits on the grass near the lake, watching the water gently lapping. Sunny days like these make it hard to believe anything bad could ever happen. She brushes some flies away and pulls out her phone. Once Nate left she had asked Kat to give her the phone number for the parents of Lizzie Buchanan, one of the girls who were swimming with Jenny on the night she disappeared. Madison knows it's important to hear what happened directly from someone who was there, but the parents collected both girls a couple of days after the disappearance, despite there being over a month left of camp. She doesn't blame them; she would do the same if Owen were staying here.

When a woman answers, Madison explains who she is and why she's calling. "The family have asked me to investigate, and I need to speak to your daughter to hear from her what happened that night."

After a brief hesitation, Lizzie's mother agrees. "She's already told the police what happened, so I don't know how much help talking to her will be. Hold on while I go get her."

Madison is relieved. She thought she might have a battle on her hands. She watches Becky, the girl from the cafeteria, walk past. She's alone and carrying some notebooks and pens. She gives Madison a wave as she passes.

"Hello?" says a tentative voice on the other end of the phone.

"Hi, Lizzie. My name's Madison. Did your mom explain what I'm calling about?"

"Yes."

"Great. Could you just explain to me what happened when you first got to the lake, before you all went swimming?"

There's silence for a few seconds, then, "She stole my candy and Jessie's bandanna."

Madison stands up. "Who did? Jenny?"

"Yeah. None of us went swimming. I did tell the policeman."

She realizes Morgan isn't being as transparent with them as he pretended. "So what happened then?"

"I guess we saw that Jenny was about to go swimming, so we followed her. We wanted our things back but she'd taken her backpack with her so we couldn't get them while she was gone from the cabin. She always carried it around with her and it was always full. I don't know what else she kept in there, but I was pretty sure she had our things because we couldn't find them."

"And what did you do when you caught up with her?"

"We just asked for our things back. She said she didn't have them and to leave her alone."

Madison thinks of Becky and the mean girls who were laughing at her in the cafeteria. It sounds like there's some bullying going on at this camp, but she can't tell which clique Jenny belonged to. For all she knows, Lizzie and her friend could have been falsely accusing Jenny of stealing to upset her. "Then what happened?"

"She turned her back on us and wouldn't say anything else. I think she was crying. So we left her alone and went back to the bunk. We thought she was sleeping outside that night so she didn't have to see us." Lizzie starts crying herself. "I'm sorry. I didn't know she would disappear. I hope she didn't hurt herself because of us."

Lizzie's mom comes back on the line. "I think that's enough. She's told you everything she knows, so please leave her alone." She ends the call.

Madison sighs. She hasn't really learned anything other than that none of the kids went swimming and there was a bit of an argument. Maybe Jenny went for a swim *after* the girls left and got into trouble. Or maybe she ran away after the argument, either to avoid the bullies or to hide the evidence. Or did she sleep here at the campfire, where she was exposed and vulnerable to being grabbed?

With all the different scenarios swimming around her head, Madison decides she needs to clear her thoughts. She takes a walk around the whole campsite, trying to figure out the layout and potential weak points in security.

The staff at Camp Fearless are pretty friendly overall, which surprises her. She expected them to be more defensive, even protective about the camp. This is how they earn their living, after all, and businesses don't like to be tarnished with a bad reputation. Especially one whose clients are children. She hasn't actually interviewed the staff—she has no power to; instead she's casually talked to everyone she's come across, to get a feel for how many employees there are and who may have something to hide. They all appear to know why she and Nate are here before she even tells them, but none of them raise the topic of the missing girl.

There are only ten staff on duty today, including Kat and Josh. The kitchen staff, all female, don't have much to say for themselves, but the sports counselors are mostly cocky young men who act pretty juvenile around each other. She wants to speak to them individually, but they're always surrounded by kids. One of them, a tall, lanky guy, refuses even to make eye contact with her, which is always a bad sign. She'll single him out at some point, whether he likes it or not.

She bumps into Josh.

"Hey," he says. "I'm free now, so let me show you where you'll be sleeping."

She follows him to one of the cabins at the far end of the campsite, near the thickest part of the woods. When she walks in, she's pleasantly surprised. It doesn't smell of socks, and it's almost bare inside. It's obviously been thoroughly cleaned in anticipation of summer's end. Josh acts the perfect host, explaining where the shower block is, asking if she needs any toiletries and then finding her some clean bedding. She's not impressed. If anything, it makes her even more suspicious of him. It's not unusual for a killer to insert themselves into an ongoing investigation into the disappearance of their victim. The more he talks to her, the more she dislikes him, which would seem irrational to anyone else, but if she told another cop how she felt about this guy, they'd understand.

She chooses a bed at the far end and sits down to remove her shoes.

As Josh is about to leave, she can't resist questioning him. "So, what do you think happened to Jennifer Lucas?"

He turns back, looking almost sad. The fluorescent lights in here highlight the dark circles under his eyes, and she realizes he appears exhausted. Maybe looking after other people's kids will do that to you. Then again, so would the pressure of hiding a dead body.

"I wish I knew," he says. "Pretty much everyone here thinks she drowned, because of the way she just vanished. But that doesn't explain why her towel and backpack are missing too."

"She could've accidentally slipped into the lake with them after she picked them up," she suggests. "Or one of the children could've stolen those items from the lakeside after she drowned, and now maybe they're too scared to come forward and admit it."

He leans against the doorway. Behind him, she can see that the sky is darkening fast. It's almost nine o'clock; the same time Jenny went missing. There's no sign of the temperature cooling down yet, and she's wondering whether it would be better to sleep next to the lake, to catch the cool breeze.

"It's unlikely. We've got a good bunch of kids here at the moment, no troublemakers or liars."

Madison laughs. "Don't all kids lie? I know I did as a kid."

He shakes his head. "Not about stuff like this. I mean, none of them liked Jenny all that much, but I'm pretty sure they wouldn't cover anything up."

She stands up. "What do you mean, none of them liked Jenny? Why not?"

Josh looks uneasy. He straightens up, crossing his arms. "Well, that's only my impression. I guess she struggled to make friends and was a little standoffish. She told a lot of lies, so the other kids didn't trust her, and… well, things had a way of disappearing when she was around."

Madison thinks about what he's implying. This changes everything coming from a member of staff. If Jenny wasn't liked by the other kids, could they have done something to her? So far, she and Nate, and even Detective Morgan, have suspected a member of staff could be involved. Failing that, maybe a dangerous drifter who was passing through town and taking his chance. None of them thought to suspect the kids. "So you're saying she was both unlikeable and a thief?"

They hear a dog bark outside, and Nate appears behind Josh in the doorway. "Who's an unlikeable thief?" he asks. He enters the cabin with their holdalls from the trunk, and Madison sees Brody run off behind him.

Josh shakes his head and moves to one side, letting Nate in. "Don't go jumping to conclusions. I was just telling your partner that Jenny struggled to fit in here. But that's not unusual; a lot of kids struggle being away from home for the first time. And let's face it, she was only here for a week, so she didn't have a chance to settle in properly. By the end of the summer, everyone's fast friends and they've forgotten all about their families. Jenny was clearly attached to her parents, because she didn't want to let go of her dad's hand when they first arrived."

Nate walks over to a bed opposite Madison's and drops his bag. "Were there tears from Jenny or her mom?"

Josh shakes his head. "Her mom didn't come. It was just Jenny and her dad. Normally mothers want to be there for a kid's first camp experience, but I understand some can find it too tough, and if they get upset, the kids get upset. Her dad kissed her on the head, gently pried her hand from his, and walked away without looking back. Probably to avoid a scene."

"How did Jenny react after her dad had left?"

"She watched him drive away, and then she stood there watching well after the car had gone. Kat had to lead her away in the end. She didn't cry, but she looked mad, and she had a bit of an attitude problem afterwards. Some kids are like that. If they're not looking forward to summer camp, they can act up because they feel like they're being deserted or betrayed."

"Why did you say things went missing while Jenny was here?" asks Madison.

Josh looks at his cell phone. "It was just candy and sodas, nothing valuable, and I have no proof. I'm just repeating what the kids told me. Look, I've got to go; I'm going to be late for a meeting with Donna." He pauses. "I don't have any evidence that Jenny was stealing things, but nothing's gone missing lately. That's all I mean."

He turns and walks out of the cabin, leaving Madison and Nate to share a look.

"What are you thinking?" asks Nate.

Madison sits back down on the bed. "Something doesn't add up. I don't know. I'm starting to think it's not the staff we should be looking into." She pauses and runs a hand through her hair. "I think the kids could've had something to do with Jenny's disappearance."

CHAPTER THIRTY-TWO

The following morning, Nate wakes before Madison. When he checks his cell phone for the time, he realizes they slept right through breakfast. Not ideal when they're on a case, but they drove through the night so it's unavoidable. They're no good to anyone exhausted. He wonders how he didn't hear the morning trumpeter Donna told him about.

He quietly gets out of bed, leaving Madison asleep under her thick comforter. When he returns from the shower block, where the water only reached lukewarm, he can hear her steady breathing as he gets dressed. She looks comfortable in her small single bed and he wonders if this is a step up from wherever she's been staying since her release. Watching her makes him feel guilty for getting a better outcome than she did. Hopefully this job will be a step on the ladder back to a normal life for her.

He needs to phone Esme Lucas to update her on what's happened so far. He wanted to call her last night, but he was exhausted by the long drive up here and skipping a night's sleep, so he turned in early.

Once dressed, he silently leaves the cabin and walks toward the campfire. There are logs arranged around a charred patch of grass and embers in the center. He spots a yellow police identification marker sticking out from one of the logs; a number 3. He assumes Morgan's team found something of interest here. So maybe Jenny fell asleep by the fire after all. He sits down and is instantly greeted by an enthusiastic Brody.

"Hey, boy. Have you had breakfast yet?"

Brody settles down on the grass in front of his feet, looking around and assessing the situation. He's alert to every sound. The birds are chirping loudly and there's a welcome chill in the air, with an ominous mist hanging over the lake while it's still shaded from the sun by the tall redwood trees. Nate's surprised when Brody ignores three rabbits hopping from one side of the camp to the other. He must be used to them.

He thinks about what Jenny might have experienced on her last night here. It would have been scary sleeping in the dark by herself, but then if she was starting to get into horror novels, maybe that's the experience she was after. He looks over his shoulder. The fire is pretty close to the woods. Could someone have been waiting for her to fall asleep before grabbing her? Or did one of the staff approach her and lure her away with them? That's more likely than a stranger, given how isolated the campsite is.

He strokes Brody's head whilst selecting Esme's number on his cell phone. The signal is hit-and-miss everywhere in the camp, but it's not too bad here.

She answers on the second ring. "Mr. Monroe, I'm so glad you've finally called."

"Sorry for the delay. The cell service out here isn't great and yesterday was a long day, what with the drive and all."

"I understand. I'm just relieved to hear from you. How are things up there?"

He thinks about it. There's not really much to update her on. "Well, the staff are friendly and helpful. No one's asked us to leave; in fact they're even putting us up free of charge, which is a good sign. And I met Detective Morgan yesterday."

"Really?" She sounds surprised. "You didn't tell him it was me who hired you, did you?"

He takes a deep breath. "I didn't really have a choice. But don't worry about him; he wants us to work together. Your granddaughter's disappearance is still very much an open case with the police department. They've run out of leads but they're looking into missing children from nearby towns to see if there's anything to link the cases."

She makes a strange groaning sound. "I hope he's not offended by me hiring an investigator. He might not try as hard to find Jenny."

Nate shakes his head, even though she can't see him. "No, I don't think that's true. If anything, it might make him work harder. He won't want us finding Jenny before him. Cops are very competitive."

"I'll take your word for it."

He thinks about what Josh told Madison last night and knows he has to raise it with Esme. "Mrs. Lucas, I'm sure you want me to be honest with you, no matter what I find out."

There's a hesitation before she replies. "Of course. What is it?"

"It's just that one of the staff here told us Jenny didn't make any friends during her short stay. He actually said the other kids weren't keen on her, as she was prone to telling lies. Does that sound like your granddaughter?"

The line is silent until he hears what sounds like a door closing. When Esme speaks, she's whispering. "Jenny is a lovely, intelligent girl. Other children can be jealous of her, because she's both pretty and smart. There's nothing she doesn't excel at—well, apart from sports—so she often gets picked on. That's what I was worried about when Grant told me they were sending her to summer camp. It's not a good fit for her, Mr. Monroe. I couldn't understand why they would put her through that."

Nate wonders how blinded she is by her love for her grand-daughter. Maybe Grant and Anna sent Jenny here to build some confidence and gain some life experience so she'd be better at interacting with her peers. He worries that Esme is ignoring the girl's true nature. The fact that one of the staff felt she was capable of stealing suggests she isn't as angelic as her grandmother is making out. Not that he'd ever say that to the woman, who is clearly suffering enough already.

"Does she have many school friends?" he asks. "Anyone that gets invited to her house?"

"Of course! She has one best friend called Jake. But he moved away a few months ago with his family. I'm not sure where they moved to; Anna would know."

"If you could get Jake's number, I'll speak to his parents. You never know, he could have some idea of whether Jenny was planning to run away."

"I'll ask Anna for it and send it to you."

"Great. And talking of Anna," he says, "how did she react to you hiring me?"

Suddenly Brody gets up and takes off in the direction of the cafeteria. Nate doesn't blame him; he's hungry too.

"She wasn't too keen at first, but she's come around to the idea. She keeps asking me if there are any updates yet. Grant was even less keen, probably because he feels he should be doing more. I actually think he should be searching those woods himself. He's relying on strangers too much. If I were younger, I'd be there with a group of my closest friends, people I could rely on to help me. The police are always tired and overworked; it would be easy for them to miss a vital clue. You hear about it on the news all the time."

"Is that what he did when Jenny first went missing? Did he help search the woods?"

"No, he wasn't allowed. He and Anna travelled up there, but they were told to stay away from the camp and deal directly with Trinity Creek PD, so they went straight to the police station instead. Anna has never actually seen the camp other than through its website. Grant only saw it briefly, when he dropped Jenny off."

Nate wonders why the police didn't let them visit the camp to collect their child's belongings. He'll ask Madison about that. "Do you know if Jenny had any social media accounts?"

"I don't think so. She liked to use the internet for her school-work, but I never saw her on anything like Facebook. I assume

Anna wouldn't have let her have an account. She's quite strict, and rightly so."

"Good." That means it's unlikely she was being groomed online and then tricked into meeting up with a sex offender.

"I just want to say that Detective Morgan has been respectful and polite," Esme continues. "It's only when he ran into a dead end that we stopped hearing from him. I know I'm supposed to let the man get on with his job, but it's been two weeks, Mr. Monroe! Jenny's been out there alone for fifteen nights now. How long are we supposed to wait to see her again?"

She starts sobbing, and Nate thinks that's a good place to leave things for now. Then he thinks of one last question he's not asked her yet.

"Mrs. Lucas? What do you think has happened to Jenny? What does your gut instinct tell you?"

There's a long pause while she finds a tissue and blows her nose. Nate doesn't think she's going to answer him at first. "I think she's still alive. I'd feel it if she wasn't, I know I would. I think someone from that camp has her tied up somewhere doing God knows what, and if you don't find her soon, I'll die of a broken heart. I just know it."

Nate feels for her. There's nothing he can say that will make her feel better. She just wants action. "I'll do my best."

He lets her hang up and runs a hand through his wet hair. He wonders again why he chose to do this job when he could easily retire and live a relaxing life by the ocean. But he knows why. Solving other people's problems and seeking justice for them makes him feel better about not getting justice for Stacey. At least, not yet. Her uncle's face pops into his head.

He remembers the look Father Connor gave him as he was being led out to the police cruiser all those years ago. He's still got to wipe the smirk off that asshole's face.

CHAPTER THIRTY-THREE

November 2015—Polunsky Unit, Livingston, Texas

Nate glances at the clock at exactly the same time the guard turns up to collect him. He's about to meet an important stranger, and for the first time in fifteen years, he feels a tiny spark of hope fluttering through his chest. He mentally quashes it before it can grow. It's best not to have hope where he is.

"Rise and shine, committer of crime," says Gus, the biggest asshole on the team of correctional officers. He opens Nate's cell door. "You're getting some time out of your own personal hell. Follow me, killer priest."

Nate has come to realize that the officers in this section are often more psychotic than the inmates. Gus likes to tell them all in minute detail what culinary delights he ate for dinner the night before, and brag about what his wife does to him in bed. Nate knows that much of it is lies, but he still hates him for it. Gus clearly gets off on the power he has over them.

Today, Nate doesn't answer back. He stays quiet as he follows Gus, glancing in at his fellow death row inmates as he passes their cells. They're all either asleep or listening to the radio, subdued into a non-existence. He doesn't know why the state drags out their deaths for so long. He's the only one here who stays physically active, but some days he doesn't know why he bothers. Exercising daily in his cell doesn't undo the damage of breathing in the same recycled air over and over and eating the crap they serve that is trying so hard to make him obese. He carefully reads every legal document he's given, just in case he finds something that will get his sentence overturned, but that's what every other guy in here does and it rarely happens. The system is stacked against them.

The last cell is empty. Fred Oslo was executed two nights ago. His belongings are piled into a corner, ready for the dumpster. Word on death row is that no one claimed his body, so he was buried out in Peckerwood Hill—the prison cemetery—with just a number on a stone to identify him and an "X" to show he was executed. Now that both of Nate's parents are dead—his dad died two years after he was convicted—there's no one to claim his body after execution. It's a bitter pill to swallow to think he'll be buried out there with serial killers and child rapists. His brother and sister gave up on him the night he was arrested and he's not seen or heard from them since. He sometimes wonders if they were relieved to have a reason not to stay in touch. They were never close.

Gus opens the door of the tired-looking meeting room and a woman glances up from behind the metal table. She smiles so widely anyone would think they already know each other.

Nate's handcuffs are secured to the table. This is the room where he meets his lawyer. It's the only reprieve he gets from his cell, apart from showers and minimal solo recreation time in a cage not much bigger than his cell.

"If you need me, ma'am, I'll be right outside. Just holler nice and loud," says Gus.

She gives him an icy stare. "I'll be fine."

Gus shakes his head on his way out and mumbles something like "ungrateful bitch" under his breath.

Nate inspects the woman in front of him. She's younger than he expected. Her hair is black and curly and she's wearing reading glasses.

"Thanks for your letter," he says.

She leans in and touches his hand; the first person to voluntarily do so in fifteen years. It awakens a part of him that yearns for human affection. Something he learned to ignore years ago. Her skin is warm and soft. Her nails aren't painted; instead they're bitten down to the quick.

"You're more than welcome, Nate. Can I call you Nate?"

He nods. She has a soft French accent, mixed with a Texas twang.

"As I said in my letter, I'm Kristen Devereaux and I lecture at the University of Texas school of law. Part of my teaching involves studying real trials in order to show my students where the attorneys and police may have gone wrong, or where the law wasn't followed precisely. As you can imagine, being based here in the state of Texas keeps us very busy."

Nate finds himself smiling at her joke. "I'll bet."

"Your case was given to me randomly, and my students and I felt something was wrong from the very beginning."

He lowers his head. Is someone finally going to do something about his wrongful conviction? He feels the build-up of years of emotion threatening to spill out, so he squeezes his eyes tight shut.

Kristen puts both her hands on top of his now. "I understand. I've been here before with other death row inmates. I can't promise you a happy ending, but my students and I believe we can fight for you. All we need is your permission."

Nate looks up at her and nods. "You have my permission to do whatever you've got to do. Just get me out of here." His shoulders sink. "Please."

CHAPTER THIRTY-FOUR

Madison and Nate grab lunch to go, because the cafeteria is full of loud, excitable kids. Plus, it's stuffy in there. The mixture of heat, sweat and food makes Madison feel sick. They sit on the grass by the lake, and Madison tells him she discovered Jenny didn't actually go swimming before she disappeared.

Nate considers it, then tells her about Esme's theory. "She didn't agree that Jenny was a liar, but she did admit she gets bullied at school because she's one of those smart and sensitive kids. When pressed about what she thinks has happened to her, she said it's got to be someone here who has her. She's convinced Jenny's still alive." He bites into a warm patty.

"Of course she is," says Madison, dipping into a bowl of pasta. "She's not going to want to believe the worst. Families of missing children never do. That makes it all the more difficult when you have to finally deliver the bad news. I forgot to ask Morgan if he checked Jenny's social media accounts. Maybe she agreed to meet up with someone she thought was around her age but he turned out to be an old fat guy."

"No," says Nate. "I asked Esme and she said Jenny wasn't on Facebook or anything like that. She said Anna was strict about that kind of stuff."

Madison rolls her eyes. "As if the grandmother would know!" She has to remember that Nate has no experience of kids and what they get up to. "Listen: just because they *think* she isn't online doesn't mean she's not got at least one account. Believe it or not, kids are great at keeping secrets." She sighs. "But I guess Morgan would have already checked that out. And it'll show up on her phone records when the data comes back."

They both watch as two young girls approach. They're holding hands and can't be more than ten years old. They could even be sisters, except for their differing hair color. They come close but don't speak; they just stare. It's kind of freaky.

"Hi, girls. How are you?" asks Madison.

They don't smile. The girl with long dark hair plucks up the courage to speak first. "Are you going to bring Jenny back?"

Madison looks at Nate, unsure how to respond, so he speaks up. "We're hoping to. Why? Do you miss her?"

The blonde girl shakes her head vigorously, but her friend drops her hand and says, "Don't be mean."

"Did you not like Jenny?" Nate asks the blonde girl.

"No. She used to scare me and make me cry."

"But you're a cry-baby," says the brunette. "Jenny was my friend. I liked her. I wish she'd taken me with her."

Madison wonders if these girls know something. "Do you know where she went?"

The brunette shakes her head. "No. But she said there were monsters in the woods. She said they tried to get in our cabins at night to eat us."

The blonde girl puts her hands over her ears. "Natalie, don't!"

Natalie rolls her eyes at her friend. "You're going against the camp motto; we're supposed to be *fearless*. Remember?" She turns back to Nate and Madison. "Jenny was just trying to scare us, I think. Do *you* know if there are monsters in the woods?"

"Oh honey," says Madison. "There aren't monsters anywhere. No one out here will hurt you."

The girl narrows her eyes like she's trying to figure out if she's being lied to. "How do you know? I've heard the whispering voices; we all have. There's something in the woods and it's got Jenny."

"No," says Nate. "What sounds like whispering voices is just the leaves of the trees rubbing together in the wind. There's nothing in the woods. The police have checked the whole area. There's nothing but squirrels, trees and birds. You're safe here."

Natalie shakes her head. She looks disappointed. Madison can't figure out if that's because she wants to see monsters or because she thinks Nate's lying to her.

"That's not what the voices say." She abruptly spins around and walks off, dragging her friend with her.

Nate looks at Madison and grins. "Kids just love me."

"Clearly." She looks after them. "It's starting to sound like Jenny could've been a bit of a troublemaker; trying to scare the younger kids with stories of monsters and whispering voices. Maybe she was being bullied herself and taking her anger out on them. Or maybe she was genuinely afraid of something."

All of a sudden Brody runs over to Nate, sniffing the second burger he's about to eat. He pulls it away from the dog.

"Don't be cruel, let him have it," says Madison.

"But I'm hungry!"

Brody sits, offers his paw and then barks. Nate rolls his eyes and holds out the burger. "Fine. Here you go." The patty is gone within seconds and Brody looks at him for more. "Sorry. That was the last one." He turns to Madison. "I'm glad I've already eaten the bacon."

The dog lies down next to him on the grass and all three of them watch the kids and counselors coming and going from the cafeteria and various cabins. The kids are quieter now they've eaten. They were pretty loud last night. Madison could hear them squealing in both delight and fear as they listened to ghost stories around the campfire. It sounded like Kat was doing some outlandish storytelling and she's surprised Donna lets her add to the kids' fear. But she also knows how much kids love ghost stories.

"Esme said the police told Grant and Anna not to come to the camp," says Nate. "Detective Morgan had them conduct all their meetings at the police station. Why would he do that?"

She places her empty bowl on the grass and swaps it for a mug of coffee, picking out a stray bug that's floating on top. "He would've wanted to preserve the crime scene. There are already too many people walking around here, contaminating it. If they'd found the girl dead somewhere, he would've needed to test every single item found here. The fewer people at the site, the quicker the elimination process."

"Is that a cop thing?" he asks.

She looks at him. "What?"

"The way you depersonalize the victim by referring to her as 'the girl' instead of using her actual name?"

She's annoyed. He's being judgmental. "Maybe we need to do that, what with the high volume of missing and deceased kids we have to deal with before returning home to our own after a sixteen-hour shift. Have you ever thought about that?"

He looks away from her and is quiet for a minute. "Would they have been given Jenny's belongings?"

She sighs. "No, probably not. Everything is evidence until someone's convicted."

She thinks about how hard it must have been for the family to be staying in town, just waiting for their daughter to be found. Unfortunately, she knows what it's like to have a missing child. To not know who the child is growing up with, or even whether they're still alive. The feeling of helplessness is almost unbearable. She suddenly feels a wave of sympathy for Grant and Anna. On top of losing their daughter, they're having to deal with the police asking intrusive questions and searching their home.

"I think it's time to look a little deeper into Josh," says Nate.

Madison looks surprised. "That's what I said yesterday."

"I know, but I thought his alibi checked out until I realized who his girlfriend was. I'm pretty sure she was snorting coke before we talked to her yesterday. She kept rubbing her nose."

She's surprised he noticed a detail like that, and then wonders if he's talking from experience. She nods. "It wouldn't surprise me. I don't know how a place like this can employ such young staff. They're barely older than children themselves. People are placing their precious kids in the care of precocious teenagers. I couldn't do it."

He takes a sip of his coffee and then looks over at her. "Do you have any idea where Owen is?"

She looks at him, feeling like she's been slapped in the face. "How do you know about Owen?"

"I told you I'd googled you after we first met."

"But he was just ten when I was arrested, and he was kept out of all the media reports. He was supposed to be anonymous."

"He nearly was. A couple of the reports mentioned you were a mother, but I read on a blog that you had a young son called Owen. No one knew what happened to him after you were convicted. Do you?"

She has her suspicions, but she's torn about confiding in him. If he's to help her, she knows she needs to tell him everything eventually, but working together is a test for him as much as it is for her. She reaches across him and pets Brody on the head. "All I know is that he was adopted by someone."

"Could he be living with his dad?"

She shakes her head. "No. His dad was a one-night stand who never found out I got pregnant. There's no one registered as Owen's father on his birth certificate, so child services couldn't have tracked him down."

"Are your parents still alive?"

She squirms, feeling like she wants to get up. "My mom died before I became a cop. My dad left us when I was a teenager."

"Sorry to hear that. Do you have siblings?"

She tenses. "Look, I don't know where Owen is. What's more important for me right now is to find out who framed me so my conviction can be overturned. Then we can track down my son. I can't be reunited with him while he thinks I killed someone. I want to clear my name first. Can you understand that?" She feels the prickle of tears in her eyes, and quickly rubs them away.

His face softens. "Of course." He stands up and Brody copies him. "In that case, we need to figure out what's going on here as fast as possible."

CHAPTER THIRTY-FIVE

Esme is torn. She desperately wants to ignore Detective Morgan's advice and drive up to Camp Fearless to search for Jenny herself. She knows Grant and Anna have agonized over the same course of action, but Anna doesn't want to anger the police in case they stop looking. From what Nate Monroe said, the police don't think that way, which strengthens her resolve. She opens the door to the spare bedroom, where she's been staying since Jenny disappeared, and walks downstairs, listening for voices.

Anna is sitting on the couch, reading a magazine. She's wrapped in her cashmere shawl again, despite the warm sunshine pouring through the windows. She doesn't even notice Esme arrive.

"Where's Grant?"

She looks up, dazed, and Esme wonders if she's been overdoing the sleeping pills. "He's taking a phone call outside."

Esme turns to the deck that overlooks the hills below as Grant walks back into the house.

"I need a coffee. Can I get you one, Mom?" he asks.

She shakes her head. "Sit down, Grant. We need to talk."

Like a robot, he does what she says. "That sounds serious."

Anna leans forward, worried. "Have you heard from the investigator? What did he say?"

Esme takes a deep breath. "He says everyone's cooperating with him, but he hasn't given me anything useful yet. I think it's time we drove up there again ourselves, this time to the camp."

Grant looks at her like she's gone mad. Anna glances away.

"Mom, there's nothing we can do up there. If Jenny ran away, she's more likely to eventually turn up here. She's a smart kid and she'll find a safe way of getting home."

Esme loses her cool. "You know as well as I do that she has *not* run away! She had no reason to! Children do not run away from happy homes. I need to do something. I can't sit here day after day thinking about it over and over. How can either of you?"

Anna speaks quietly. "We're in the same position as you, Esme. Only it's worse for us. You have your child with you; ours is missing." She looks up at her. "I haven't slept more than an hour since it happened. My hair's falling out, my skin is like sandpaper. Every time I have to get out of bed to face another day, I consider taking the whole pack of sleeping pills from my nightstand." She turns away and starts sobbing.

Esme, undeterred, looks at Grant. "You're her father. You should be doing more, otherwise you'll always regret it."

Grant stands up, his face reddening. "What would you have me do? Shadow the detective as he works? Knock on the door of every known sex offender in the area and ask if they'll show me their basement?"

Esme is shocked into sitting on the couch. "Is that really what you think has happened to her? You think she's with a pedophile?"

Grant yells now. "Of course she is! What other logical explanation is there? Some asshole has taken my daughter and is abusing her! And I don't know about you, Mom, but that's not something I can think about every day and still live. So I prefer to hope that she ran away and is on her way back to us. Which is why I stay here and try to carry on as normal."

Esme lowers her head. She can't bear to see either of them suffer like this, but they're just ghosts sharing a house while they live with the unknown. She'd rather be active. "I'll go on my own then."

"Mom, you're almost seventy!" he says. "You can't do an eleven-hour drive on your own. It's not safe."

She looks up at him, pleading with her eyes. "Then come with me. Please, Grant. Let's find Jenny."

Grant looks over at Anna.

She covers her face with her hands and lets out a strange groan that feels never-ending. Finally she looks up at them with red-rimmed eyes and slowly nods. "Let's end this one way or another."

CHAPTER THIRTY-SIX

Nate needs background information on a few people, so he leaves Madison questioning a group of boys while he phones his go-to guy. He doesn't know how Rex obtains his information and he'd never ask, to avoid the risk of being implicated in something illegal, but he gets it fast and it's usually reliable.

"How's it going upstate?" asks Rex, clearly chewing on something. The guy has a thing for candy. All his teeth are implants because he lost his own to tooth decay while he was in his twenties.

"It's nice up here; quiet and peaceful." Nate watches some kids playing a game of baseball while he talks. He doesn't recognize the male counselor who is enthusiastically coaching them. "But I don't have to tell you how idyllic locations are usually full of secrets, and Shadow Falls is no different."

"Oh yeah? You got a suspect yet?"

"We think we do, but we'll see."

"Who's we?" Rex suddenly sounds more alert, reminding Nate that he hasn't told him about Madison yet.

"My new employee. She needed a job so I thought I'd give her a try."

Rex laughs. "I can't believe you're branching out. What's her background? Want me to run a check on her?"

Nate cringes. He doesn't want Rex to know he's helping a former cop. Not until he has time to explain the circumstances anyway.

"Not on her, no. But I do need your help and I'm pressed for time, so that's a story for later." He's about to continue before Rex can put two and two together, but he doesn't get a chance.

"You're hiding something, aren't you? Your voice changed. I wasn't born yesterday, Nate. There's a reason you don't want to tell me. Which means you're doing something you're not happy with. Something your conscience isn't happy with."

Nate laughs. Rex can be overly dramatic. "I promise I'll tell you another time. For now, I have to focus on finding Jennifer Lucas. I need you to do a full background check on a guy named Josh—maybe Joshua—Sanders. He's a camp counselor here. The police have already ruled him out as a suspect, but his alibi is shady. I need his address and all the usual details. Check out his finances too."

"Okay, let me grab a pen. Josh Sanders. Got a date of birth?"

"Not yet, but I'll text you when I do."

"Okay. Anyone else?"

"Yeah, Donna Gleeson. She's the camp director. Look into her finances. You never know, she might have taken Jenny to blackmail the parents for money. They're obviously loaded and they're offering a twenty-five-thousand-dollar reward for information, so it's a potential motive."

"Have there been any demands for money?"

"Not yet, but I want to rule it out. I want to know why Jenny in particular was taken. This isn't a well-run, modern summer camp; in fact it's pretty basic, and the fees listed on their website are cheap. It's also almost seven hundred miles away from the Lucas home. So I'm wondering why her parents chose this camp over a more impressive version when they appear to be so well off. I'm also wondering if one of the staff saw Jenny as a potential ransom payout."

"Got it. That all?"

Nate thinks about the family. It's unlikely they're involved if the grandmother hired him to look into Jenny's disappearance, but you never can tell these days. Nothing shocks him anymore. "Do a criminal background check on the family: Anna Lucas, Grant Lucas and Esme Lucas. I don't have dates of birth, but I'll forward you a text with their address. I'd say the parents are in their late thirties and Grant's mother is probably in her late sixties or early seventies."

"Full financial check too?"

"Yeah." He knows Esme won't be happy when she sees on his invoice that she's paying for a background check to be done on her family, but she's hired him to do a job and that's what he's doing.

"While you're at it, look into Detective Ted Morgan from the Trinity Creek Police Department. See if there have been any internal investigations into him."

"Now you're talking!"

Nate can picture the smile on Rex's face. "That should keep you busy for a while."

"Yeah, while your new lady friend keeps *you* busy, no doubt."

"Cut it out, Rex. It's not like that."

"Whatever you say, buddy. And before you ask, no leads on Father Connor or Kristen yet. You'll be the first to know."

He *was* going to ask, because he can't help it. "Thanks, Rex."

Nate spots Madison outside their cabin, talking on her new cell phone. He wonders who she's still in touch with after her prison stay, and whether anyone she worked with stood by her. He can't shake the feeling that she's holding out on him. Trust comes hard to people who have been in their situation, but keeping secrets isn't going to help her in the long run.

Shielding his eyes from the sunshine, he spots Kat walking toward the office, holding the hand of a young girl. They're singing. As he approaches, she stops and smiles up at him. "Hey, Nate. Are you enjoying life at the camp?"

The girl lets go of her hand and runs ahead of her into the office.

"It's peaceful. You're not at full capacity, I take it?"

"No. A lot of kids have already left. It's not peaceful during orientation week, that's for sure! But Donna says the owners have decided to close camp early as we're running at a loss now. She's phoning the parents later to tell them to collect the kids at the end of next week. Some of them are really looking forward to going home."

He frowns. That gives them less time to find Jenny. Kat plays with the buttons on her shirt, and he wonders if it's a flirting tactic, to make his eyes drift there.

"Where's home for you?" he asks.

"Oh, I'm from here. Josh is too. We went to school together in the next town over. Shadow Falls isn't big enough for its own school yet."

"Have you been together long?"

"No." Her cheeks redden. "Only this summer. To be honest, he wasn't interested in me until recently. And we broke up after having a drunken argument at his birthday party last Saturday, but got back together the next day, when we were sober." She smiles. "I always said I'd get my claws into him in the end, and I was right."

Nate wonders why Josh would suddenly relent now, when he's known her forever. But then there can't be many women to choose from in a town as small as this, and Kat's certainly attractive, although still immature. "What will you do for work when the camp closes?"

She looks over at the cabin to see if anyone's missing her yet, then turns back to Nate. "Well, Josh is planning to move to Chicago to study business, but I'm hoping he'll stay in town with me. I want to move in with him."

Nate tries not to raise his eyebrows. He doubts Josh will give up a place at college to stay in a small town like this. Or maybe that's just a line he's fed her so their relationship doesn't last too long.

"But I'm starting to think he's just using me for the summer. You know, for sex."

Nate sighs. "I hope not, Kat. You seem like a nice girl."

She smiles. "I am! Before Josh, I never even touched alcohol or—" She stops.

"You wouldn't be the first girl to get into something they didn't want to because of a man."

She looks scared. "No, it's okay. He's a good guy. He makes me laugh. Anyway, I need to get back to work."

She spins around, so Nate steps in front of her and touches her arm lightly. "Kat? You want to help us find Jenny, don't you?"

Her eyes widen and she reminds him of a naïve schoolgirl. "Of course!"

"Do you think Josh might know what happened to her? It would really help if you were able to tell me anything at all. It doesn't have to be something that would get you in trouble. Just a clue of some sort. Something I can work with."

She looks over her shoulder to make sure no one's watching them. Brody is patrolling the camp and the baseball game appears to have finished so the kids are dispersing.

"To be honest with you, Nate," she whispers, "I don't know why he asked me to lie. I fell asleep, and when I woke up about an hour later, he was gone."

Nate thinks she's telling the truth this time. "Did you find out where he went?"

She shakes her head. "No. I fell back to sleep. He was with me when I woke up in the morning. I remember, because we had sex." She blushes hard. "He was rougher than usual, and he smelt of pot. I didn't enjoy it."

He feels for her, because she's clearly being used. "Was it Josh who should have taken the head count the night Jenny went missing?"

She looks at her feet and nods. "Detective Morgan already knows, but he thinks Josh forgot because we fell asleep. He did a background check on us both and found out Josh has a DUI from last summer. Josh was so pissed at him. He hates it when people snoop into his private business. Even I don't know that much about him, and I've known him forever."

So Josh was a suspect at one point. Nate assumes he would have been arrested by now if Morgan had found anything disturbing. "You can do better than him, you know."

She shrugs her shoulders. "Not around here. I'd have to move to the nearest city to meet someone else, but that costs money. Besides, my dad says I'm pretty much good for nothing, so I'd never get a job in the city."

Nate can tell she thinks about her situation a lot. Her father sounds like a regular asshole. "Has Josh got an opinion about what happened to Jenny?"

She glances toward the lake. "He's adamant she's down there. He won't even consider any other possibilities. But how could he know that?"

"He can't." *Unless he put her down there himself.* "Thanks, Kat. You've been really helpful."

She takes a step toward him. "Please don't tell him I said anything. He might break up with me."

Nate feels ashamed for being the same gender as Josh. "I won't say a word, I promise. But you are too good for him, Kat. Find yourself someone better, someone who doesn't ask you to lie for them."

Someone runs up behind Nate, grabs Kat and spins her around. It's Josh, right on cue. He kisses her lips and she giggles with delight. It's clear that Nate's advice is immediately disregarded.

"Who are you too good for?" he asks nonchalantly.

Nate resists the impulse to speak, as he doesn't trust what he'll say.

"This place," says Kat, her smile faltering. "Nate thinks they work us too hard here."

"You wouldn't be lying to me now, would you?" There's sudden menace in his voice. "You're not screwing our new friend here, are you, Kathryn?"

She looks at Nate with wide eyes before responding to Josh. "What? Of course not!"

"I'm just fucking with you." Josh turns to him. "I'd prefer it if you stayed away from my girlfriend." There's no smile now. "She's just a kid."

Nate glances at Kat. "How old are you?"

"Eighteen. Nineteen at Christmas."

He turns back to Josh. "Sounds like an adult to me. I think she can make her own decisions about who she talks to."

Josh takes a step closer. "You better watch yourself. One word from me and Donna will kick you off this camp, and then where will you be?"

"Well, actually, I'm a millionaire, so I'll just go and stay in the best hotel I can find. But don't worry, I'll still drop by to visit you all. I'm staying until I find Jennifer Lucas. Does that bother you, Josh?"

Josh looks like he wants to punch him. Instead, he grabs Kat by the wrist and drags her away, yelling over his shoulder, "Watch your back, man. Outsiders don't do well in Shadow Falls."

Nate watches them walk past the office and toward their cabin. Josh doesn't let go of her wrist the whole time, and when she looks back at Nate, she mouths, "Sorry."

Nate immediately messages Rex. Kat inadvertently revealed Josh's date of birth; last Saturday. He doesn't have a year, but the date could narrow it down. After what he's just witnessed, it's time to step things up a gear.

CHAPTER THIRTY-SEVEN

Madison has spent an hour on the computer in the camp's office, doing some online research into the town and its residents via news websites and court reports. Donna said she could use it as long as she didn't download porn or viruses.

"It's our only one and we can't afford to replace it."

Madison wonders whether the police took the computer away to check it for child abuse images. She would've done if she was Detective Morgan. According to Donna, everyone here has access to it; staff and kids. There are no passwords and no firewall—in other words, a recipe for disaster. Madison thought about telling her to set a password, but just then a young boy walked in. He was about Owen's age and was clearly homesick. He begged Donna to call his parents so he could go home. She remained firm and told him it was better to see out his final week and a half. Probably so she didn't have to refund any more money.

"I have a meeting with the cafeteria staff," she said, holding a folder and pen. "If the phone rings, just let it go to voicemail." She left Madison alone in the cabin.

Now Madison decides to see what she can find in the computer's internet search history. If no one has cleared the cache and cookies in a while, she might get lucky. She checks what Kat is doing; a quick look out the window shows she's helping a kid retrieve her tennis ball from the lake. Josh was with her, but now he's disappeared.

"Okay, let's see what's really happening in this place," she mutters. She opens the internet history page but it only brings up the last ten searches, and they're all hers. She googles how to expand the list. "Hmm, press control and H together." She does it. "Huh. Would you look at that."

A long list of searches is displayed, in time and date order. She scrolls down. It appears never-ending, and she can't believe her luck. She goes back to the top and starts scanning each website. There are the obvious sites you'd expect from a summer camp full of kids and teenagers: celebrity gossip, YouTube, social media, takeout menus, sports updates. Then she notices Jennifer Lucas's name. It looks like someone has been looking at the news reports. That's understandable. Kids would be worried and wanting to know what's happening, and the staff are probably keeping an eye out for negative press. She keeps going.

After twenty minutes, her eyes are blurring and she's thinking about stopping when something catches her attention. The words *pre-teen girls* have been typed into Google, but she can't tell what the user clicked next. Someone must have deleted the website but forgot about the Google search.

She doesn't try the same search herself—she's not a cop anymore and can't risk being accused of looking at that kind of thing—but she makes a note of the time and date and suddenly realizes it was the afternoon of Jennifer's disappearance. She pushes her hair back behind her ears and leans in to the screen as she keeps scrolling down to find any other unsavory searches. She's rewarded with *twelve-year-old girls*. It was googled just an hour before the other search.

She keeps scrolling for another twenty minutes, but there's nothing else. She needs to speak to Nate. She should probably call Detective Morgan immediately, but they don't know if he can be trusted yet. And she would assume he's already had this computer properly examined. But if that's the case, why is the history still intact? Why wasn't it wiped and proper firewalls put in place to stop anyone else searching for this stuff?

Kat walks back into the office. She's sweating from exertion but smiling.

"Kat? Who uses this computer the most?"

She looks surprised by the question. "Probably me and Donna. Plus, if someone can't get a signal on their cell phone, they'll pop in to search for something. And the kids will use it for YouTube. Why?"

Madison shakes her head. "No reason. Did Detective Morgan take it away as part of his investigation?"

Kat frowns. "No. He didn't take anything but Jenny's belongings. Why would he take our computer?"

Madison can't tell if she's really this naïve or whether she's playing dumb. "I don't know. Maybe Jenny was searching for somewhere to run away to before she left." She doesn't want to tell her it's because one of the staff members is looking at kiddie porn. If Kat gives anyone a heads-up, they'll have time to delete it, because Madison can't seize the computer.

Once again she's frustrated at the restrictions she faces now she's not a cop.

After Kat heads out to sort another problem for one of the kids, Madison's left alone to keep digging. Another fifteen minutes have passed when the door to the cabin opens and Nate appears.

"Are you ready to get out of here for a while?" he asks her.

She stands up. "Sure. But first, look at this."

He walks behind the desk and leans against her chair while she points out both searches on the screen.

"And check out the date. The same day Jenny vanished."

Nate turns pale. "Shit. Looks like you were right all along. This suggests she's been abducted and possibly raped."

"By someone she knows, too. Not an opportunist. Should we tell Morgan?"

He frowns. "Wouldn't he have seized this as part of his investigation?"

"He should have, but Kat says nothing was taken but Jenny's belongings."

"You're kidding?"

"I wish I was. It's becoming painfully clear that he has completely screwed this investigation up. He's out of his depth. So what do we do?" She feels excited to finally have a lead to work with.

"Follow me."

She closes the web browser and Nate leads her outside, where Brody is waiting. They both walk past him without stopping, and Madison can hear the sound of the dog panting as he follows them to the Jeep.

Nate looks up at the sky, which has turned alarmingly grey. "Looks like rain."

"Good, I'm ready for a break from the heat. It's too humid for me and the bugs are so annoying."

Nate agrees. "Yeah, I'm sick of being eaten alive. The humidity's making them worse." As he opens the car door, he looks at the dog. "Not this time, buddy."

Madison laughs. "He can't understand you."

But Brody barks at him and tries pawing the door behind the driver's seat. Nate pushes his paw away and checks for scratches. "Careful!"

Brody barks again.

"Maybe he's got cabin fever too," says Madison. "Poor thing probably never gets away from this place."

Nate relents and opens the back door. "Fine. Just don't destroy anything." Brody jumps in.

"Where are we going?" asks Madison.

Nate buckles himself in and checks his phone. She waits as he reads an email.

"I asked a friend to do a few background checks. First on that asshole Josh. Looks like we've got an address for him, so we're going to head there. He's working all day today, right?"

"Yeah, some of the kids told me there's a theatrical production planned and he's in charge of filming it for the parents. He'll probably be busy for a few hours."

Nate keeps reading the email. "Apparently Josh doesn't have any convictions apart from a DUI, and Rex hasn't been able to find anything else out about him apart from his work history."

"Who's Rex?" she asks.

"My go-to guy for background checks. He's a friend."

"Well, just because Josh doesn't have any other convictions doesn't mean he's clean. It only means he's never been caught."

"Exactly. I think it's worth checking his place out. I had an interesting run-in with him earlier and saw a different side to him. Plus, Kat told me he'd asked her to lie."

"What about?" she asks, feeling the old fire in her belly. She hasn't caught a bad guy in a hell of a long time.

"The night Jenny went missing. She did fall asleep with Josh next to her, but he was gone when she woke up an hour later."

"Bingo! I knew it was him." Madison smiles. This is starting to feel like being back on the force, and she loves it.

Nate's more cautious. "That doesn't automatically mean he had any involvement in Jenny's disappearance. He could've gone to hit on one of the other girls who works here."

Madison shakes her head. "Oh come on! He's hiding something, I'm sure of it. When we get to his house, are you just going to look around the outside?"

He turns to her and smiles. "You're definitely not a cop anymore, are you?"

"Of course not."

"Then no. I'm going in."

She laughs. "I'm starting to realize that being a PI might be more satisfying than policing. Less red tape to hold us back."

He smiles at her. "Less corruption, too."

She shakes her head at yet another dig as he drives them out of the camp.

CHAPTER THIRTY-EIGHT

The rain appears fast and hard, and Madison thinks she hears thunder rumbling in the distance somewhere. The humidity has finally broken. The afternoon turns dark and the car's windshield wipers struggle to keep up with the deluge.

As Nate drives, Madison thinks about the phone call she made earlier. It's been months since she called Stephanie, but she wanted her to know she'd finally found someone to help her find Owen, and she wanted to give Steph her new number. What she hadn't expected was to be shouted at.

"I've had people here looking for you; two men. Three times so far. They were threatening me, Madison."

Madison tried not to show her own alarm, to keep Steph calm. "Did they say much?"

"They asked if I've seen you since your release and whether I know where you are now. Obviously I said no to both, because that's the truth, but they didn't believe me. When's this going to stop, Madison? It's not fair that I have to put up with this kind of shit."

"Was it the same two men each time?"

"Yes. They're intimidating and you know I'm not easily scared. I'm seriously considering moving, because I can't live like this." Her voice broke.

Madison felt for her. She shouldn't have to live in fear. "I think that would be a good idea. You need to get out of Colorado."

"What? I meant move towns, not states! Why are they after you, Madison? What have you done?"

The accusation stung. Stephanie knows she hasn't done anything wrong. "I don't know who they are. Next time, I need you to take a photo of them or video them so I can see for myself. They won't like that. It might even put them off coming over again."

"If they won't like it, then I'm putting my life at risk. I would never ask you to do the same for me!"

"What do they look like?" she asked.

"Both white and big, possibly brothers. One's muscly, the other is just seriously overweight. I don't want to have to deal with them again."

Madison could tell she needed to take this seriously. "Move away as soon as possible. In the meantime, if they come back, don't open the door—just call the cops. Ask for Mike. He's trustworthy." Mike Bowers; her old sergeant. She thinks he can be trusted, but with the way the department treated her after her arrest, she can't be one hundred percent certain of anyone.

"Jesus. I can't believe what you've got me into, and we're not even together anymore."

"Steph, listen to me. If they wanted to hurt you, they would've done it by now. Next time they come, phone me and I'll speak to them while you wait for the cops to turn up."

"But then they'll know I've been in touch with you all along! That won't help anything."

Stephanie was right. "Okay, just call the cops then. I've met someone who's going to help me find Owen; an investigator. We'll be coming to Colorado as soon as we can, but I have to wait for him to finish work on another job first. I'll let you know as soon as we're on our way, I promise."

Steph sighed loudly down the phone. "I just hope you're not too late. I have a horrible feeling this isn't going to end well for either of us."

Madison can imagine her sitting in the living room they shared for five years, worrying herself sick. Her guilt makes her want to rush home to Colorado straight away, but she needs someone on her side and she has limited funds.

In order to secure his help, she misled Nate when she told him she suspected her police department of framing her. She knew that would appeal to him because of his distrust of cops, but actually, she suspects that someone closer to her was behind it.

She rests her head against the car's comfortable seat and watches the rain lash down.

Brody's panting over her shoulder is almost as loud as the rain. It's like he's gearing himself up for action.

When they reach the residential part of town, Nate appears taken aback to find it consists of only about thirty houses and a handful of stores. "How does anyone live in a town like this all their life?"

Madison looks at him. "Until you leave a town like this, it's all you know. Some people see somewhere better on TV and decide to take a risk and move away, but it's easier to stay within your comfort zone. If I hadn't been arrested, I'd still be in my small town, although it's bigger than this place."

"See, that surprises me. You seem more worldly than that."

"How do you think I got this way?" She experienced a lot in prison, mixing with people from all over the country. Her eyes were opened in more ways than one. "Ignorance can be bliss."

He looks at her. "You don't really mean that, do you?"

"Yeah, sometimes. I'd rather be living my old life, unaware of the world outside Colorado, than this shitty alternative."

She turns away and looks for Josh's house number through the rain.

The simple wooden houses here are spread far apart. You could come and go without your neighbors seeing you, which means you could hide a child without your neighbors knowing you'd even brought one home.

"It's that one there," she says, pointing. "The one with the red trailer out front."

Nate pulls over, but not right outside the house. For all they know, Josh could live with his mother. She's noticed Nate has good instincts; he would actually make a good cop. But he'd probably take offense if she told him that.

They both look around but can't see anyone nearby. The nearest house is in darkness. Presumably whoever lives there is at work, because although it's only late afternoon, the sky has turned so dark you'd need a light on in the house to see anything.

"Brody can have a look around," says Nate. "With his cadaver training he might pick up a scent. What about you? Are you coming?"

She releases her seat belt and can't help rolling her eyes at him. "Of course I'm coming. What do you expect me to do? Wait here in the car while you get yourself shot?"

He laughs, but she's not joking.

"I'm serious, Nate. You can't just turn up at someone's house unprepared. He could've seen us leaving the camp and be hot on our tail. Or he might have a roommate and could've phoned ahead to warn them we're coming. What if they're gun enthusiasts, or drug addicts? You have to be prepared to do battle every time you approach a suspect's property. Do you even have a weapon?"

He taps his head and smiles at her. "Just my mind."

Annoyingly, she finds herself laughing. "Oh shit. Then we're really in trouble."

CHAPTER THIRTY-NINE

The office of Dr. Pamela Jarvis

Feeling under pressure, Pamela takes an early lunch break. She tells Stephen she'll be back within the hour and asks him to find a specific report for her. She shuts down all his questions with a stern look before he even gets started.

When she returns, she expects the police to be standing outside her office door, but they haven't arrived yet. They're giving her time to read the whole journal and all her own notes, but that's not as easy as it sounds. Something that should take a morning to get through is taking much longer.

The fresh air has helped somewhat, along with three cigarettes smoked in quick succession. Getting her legs to walk her back to the office was difficult. Especially now that she's realizing this won't be her office for much longer. But she's a professional, and no matter what the outcome of this whole sorry affair, she must see it through to the end.

Stephen watches her walk into her office but he doesn't speak this time. She wonders if he can smell the tobacco trailing after her.

"Did you get the report I asked for?"

"Yes, it's on your desk. It's long. Shall I tell the police you need more time?"

She shakes her head. "No. I'll get through it. No interruptions."

She closes the door behind her and places her purse on one of the leather chairs. The journal taunts her. *Open me*, it says. She shakes her head, wondering if she'll end up a patient herself after all this.

Sitting at her desk, she resumes where she left off, removing her makeshift bookmark; a biro. The next entry is clearly rushed.

I thought I could do it. I really thought I could. But images of Susie and Thomas floating face down in our swimming pool keep flashing before me. Of course, everyone tells us we should move, that we shouldn't be living where the children died. But this is where we all lived together. This is where their spirits are. I've already lost their bodies; do I have to lose their souls too?

The attacks are getting worse. It's harder to hide them in summer, harder to cover up without people questioning me. If I told my therapist she'd probably assume I'm doing it to myself, but that's not me. I've never self-harmed. Part of me wants her to pull up my sleeves and see the bruises for herself. Would she believe me then? I want her to know, yet I can't tell her. The words are too big to come out of my mouth. I do enjoy visiting her, but only because it's time away from my awful life.

She looks at her watch a lot during our sessions. I feel squeezed in. I daren't go one minute over our allotted time. Some days I don't even get the full hour because she's so busy, her phone always ringing. Sometimes she sends messages while I'm talking. She probably thinks I can't tell, that I'm too self-absorbed, but I'm the opposite and she'd know that if she concentrated on what I'm saying. I think she's had enough of me. I don't blame her.

Is this ever going to end? I doubt it. If anyone ever reads these words, please help me.

Pamela pushes the journal away and rests her head on her folded arms, on top of her desk. Did she really come across as uninterested during their sessions? This entry is so damning that she feels panic building up inside her. She wants to call someone, to be told she's going to be all right, but no one would understand. Besides, this is all confidential: the journal entries, the client's details and the police investigation.

She thinks of her patient and how much she's suffered. Pamela has let her down, and for that reason she vows never to practice therapy again.

CHAPTER FORTY

Brody runs off as soon as he's released from the back seat. Nate told him no barking and so far he's complied. As the rain comes down, Nate pulls a raincoat from the trunk and slips it on, thinking again that Brody is wasted at the summer camp. He should be back on the force.

"Don't suppose you have a spare raincoat back there, do you?" asks Madison, rubbing her cold arms.

He pulls one out and her face lights up. "Great, thanks."

He waits for her to put it on. It's too big, but it should protect her from this heavy downpour at least.

She leans forward, noticing his collection of books in the trunk. "True crime? You read this stuff?"

"Yeah. I guess I'm trying to find some poor sucker who had it worse than me."

"But aren't they all convicted killers?"

He gives her a look. "So were we, remember? You know as well as I do that our judicial system doesn't always get it right. You'd be amazed how many of these guys denied being killers right up to the death chamber."

"But that's what real killers do: they deny everything."

He tries not to get wound up. "Think about it, Madison: the men and women who live on death row for decades and know they're being put to death have absolutely nothing to lose. Nothing. Especially in Texas. It's well known Texas doesn't do clemency. So how come so many people maintain their innocence right up until the bitter end?"

She looks dubious. "From experience, I know that some people don't admit their crimes because they don't want their families to know what they did. They want their mothers to be able to sleep at night."

He shakes his head and thinks of some of the guys he shared death row with. The ones who had no problem admitting their guilt. "Well, from *my* experience, the guilty ones don't even care about their own mothers."

She hesitates and pulls her hood up against the rain. "This isn't a discussion for right now. Where's the dog?"

He looks around, but Brody is nowhere to be seen. He quietly closes the trunk and they walk toward Josh's house. It's a one-story, with a lot of junk outside. Nate assumes it's a rental, what with Josh working part-time at the camp and planning to go off to college.

With the day growing ever darker under the heavy rain clouds, he's brought a flashlight from his car. He approaches a side door and shines the light inside. The kitchen. He tries the handle; it's locked.

Madison is checking above the door frame and under pots for a spare key. "Nothing."

They walk around the back of the property, lighting up each window as they go. Nate hears a car driving past, its wheels sloshing the rainwater. It sounds like it slows as it passes the house, but it doesn't stop so he carries on.

"There's nothing to suggest there's a child in there," he says over the rain. His hands are soaking wet and he can feel water seeping into his sneakers. He wasn't prepared for this weather.

Madison looks at him. "Of course there isn't. He's not stupid enough to leave kids' clothes lying around for us to find. Is there a basement?"

He ignores her condescending attitude and figures he'd be better off trying to learn from her experience instead. He looks around but can't see an outside entrance to a basement, though there is a small window under the kitchen, at ground level. "Looks like it."

He crouches and tries to pull the window open. It doesn't budge. The glass has been painted black, so he can't see through it, not even with a flashlight.

They walk to the other side of the house, where a rusting car is slowly fusing with the landscape. With tall grass and weeds growing around its wheels, it looks like it hasn't been moved in years. The trunk is stuck open at an angle. It's not hiding any bodies, but there is a family of rats bedding down under some damp cardboard in the far corner.

"Eww," says Madison.

Nate shines the flashlight in through the car's windows. It's completely empty, apart from some nasty-looking spiderwebs. Brody suddenly appears. His thick coat is soaking wet and he starts sniffing all around the car. Nate wishes he'd asked Esme for an item of clothing to give the dog a scent to work with.

Madison grabs his arm. "Listen."

He hears another car approaching, and this one stops with a damp skid right outside. He looks at her. "Shit."

"Get down!" She pulls his arm and they crouch behind the car. They hear running footsteps approach and then the front door slams shut.

"It's Josh," she says. "He must know we're here. Why don't you go and knock on the front door and keep him busy while I check out the back? Act casual. But keep a close eye on his hands at all times."

Nate doesn't want them to split up, but the reality is she's better trained for searching a property than he is. "Okay. Yell if you need me."

She laughs sarcastically, probably thinking that the idea of him protecting her is ridiculous. "Sure thing."

He walks to the front door, wondering whether Josh might appear with a gun. After a few seconds' hesitation, he knocks and then steps back slightly, out of the direct line of fire. Just in case.

Josh almost rips the door open in anger. "What the fuck are you doing here? Have you been in my house?"

Nate knows he has to calm Josh down, because if he calls the cops, it's them who will be in trouble. "No, of course not. I was just looking outside. Come on, man. It's my job to investigate. You won't be the only camp employee I pay a visit to."

Josh doesn't move to let him in. "You need a warrant to enter my house."

"Exactly. Which is why I haven't entered. Plus, I'm not a cop so I couldn't get a search warrant even if I wanted to. Anyway, I'm sure Detective Morgan has already searched the place."

Josh explodes. "What the fuck are you talking about? He hasn't been here. I'm not a suspect for anything."

Nate can't believe it. The police should've searched every house in this crappy town. It's not like it would have taken long. What have they been doing all this time?

"If you let me look around, I can rule you out as a suspect and let you get on with your day. I'll only be ten minutes."

Josh is shaking his head. "No way, man. You'll probably plant something on me. I know how the law works."

Nate can't fault his logic. "Again, I'm not a cop, so—"

"Get off my property! Next time I see you here, I'll shoot you without warning."

"You have a license for your weapon?"

"Yes, asshole! Now get out of here."

"You're only making yourself look suspicious, Josh. Can't you put yourself in the position of Jenny's parents? They just want to know where their daughter is. The more people I rule out, the closer I'll get to the truth of what happened that night. That will give her family closure. Can you imagine what it's like for them not knowing where she is?"

Josh doesn't even consider it. "I won't warn you again."

"Okay, fine. Whatever you say." Nate turns around. All Josh has done is incriminate himself further. There's no reason why a law-abiding citizen wouldn't let an investigator search their house when there's a child missing. Sure, they don't have to like it, but wouldn't an innocent person want to help?

He has to walk back to his car without Madison so that Josh doesn't know she's snooping around. He's sure she'll find a way to meet him down the block so he can pick her up, but where is Brody? When he reaches the road, he turns back to see if Josh is still watching him. He is. Nate really doesn't want to leave either of them here.

He wonders whether to keep walking.

CHAPTER FORTY-ONE

When Madison moves around to the other side of the rusty car, to stay hidden from Josh's view, she notices a wooden outbuilding at the far end of the back yard, under a large willow tree. Brody notices it too and starts sniffing around the door, then paws at it, trying to get it to open. The outbuilding is completely hidden from the road and is covered in creepers, almost disappearing into the landscape.

She can hear Josh yelling at Nate at the front of the house, so, knowing her time is limited, she runs over, puts her hands to the window and peers in. Inside, there's a small desk with four laptops stacked on it. The one on top is open and switched on, but she can't see what's on the screen because of the rain blurring her vision. She stands back, wondering how to open the door, then notices that Brody has managed to pull off one of the lower wooden slats with his claws and teeth.

"Good boy," she whispers. Getting soaked by the rain, she crouches down and pulls off two more slats. Brody tries to slip through ahead of her, but she pulls him back and squeezes in front of him. Her hands are wet and covered in mud, but it feels good to be back in action.

The navy raincoat she borrowed from Nate catches on a nail that's sticking out from the wall. "Shit." Knowing she has to be quick, she pulls the raincoat off. As she does, she looks up and realizes the interior walls are covered with weapons. On one wall alone she spots three handguns, a rifle, two machetes and what looks like an antique rifle similar to a Winchester. No matter what's on those computers, something's not right with Josh Sanders and there's no way on earth he should be working with children.

She crawls to the desk. There's no seat, so she kneels, dries her hands on her jeans and looks at the laptop screen. A screensaver of a naked woman disappears when she hits the space button.

Convinced the computer will ask for a password, she holds her breath. It doesn't. The desktop is open and ready for use. What a dumbass. She can't believe anyone would leave a laptop unsecured, especially someone who's clearly up to no good. Why else would he need four computers? She double-clicks on the internet icon, but a message says the computer isn't connected to a network. She looks desperately around the small shed but can't see anything that will connect it.

She stops to listen over the heavy rain and realizes she can't hear Josh's voice anymore. With Brody stationed by the hole in the door, she decides to risk her safety and keep checking out the laptop. It might be the only opportunity they get to catch this asshole and find Jenny. She clicks on "Documents" and fourteen folders appear. Chills run down her back as she realizes each folder is named after a different girl. She looks for Jennifer's name but it's not there, so she clicks on the first folder, which is named Kelly.

"Crap!" It wants a password. She tries the next one; same thing. They're all password-protected. But she's seen enough. She needs to get the police out here to seize these computers, because those folders can only contain something Josh wants to hide.

She looks out of the window as she fumbles for her cell phone in the discarded raincoat. She calls the police.

"Nine one one. What's your emergency?"

"I'm at a house in Shadow Falls that contains what I suspect is child abuse images. The suspect works at the summer camp where Jennifer Lucas went missing. He doesn't know I'm here but he's hostile, he has many weapons and I need backup immediately."

"Okay, ma'am. What's your location?"

She gives him Josh's house number and street name.

The emergency operator is typing fast. "I have two officers en route. Is the suspect armed right now?"

"I don't know. He's a Caucasian male, early twenties. Name of Josh Sanders."

"Copy that. And who are you?"

"My name's Madison."

"Which PD do you work with, ma'am?"

Madison hesitates for the first time. "I... well, I'm no longer serving. Get here fast." To avoid any further awkward questions, she ends the call. Brody is whining but she can't see anything outside the shed. She resists the urge to crawl out, but as Brody's whining gets louder, she wonders if Nate is in danger.

A loud gunshot rings out nearby, making her jump. She hopes to God it was just a warning shot. She looks at Brody and realizes they have to go and protect Nate.

"Let's go!"

She pulls her weapon and is about to follow the dog out when she hears the once-comforting sound of police sirens approaching. It makes her pause, because after everything that has happened to her, the sound of sirens now makes her want to flee.

CHAPTER FORTY-TWO

Madison's body is shaking with adrenaline. After explaining everything to the cops, she found Nate sitting on the couch in Josh's living room, grilling him about Jenny's whereabouts. But Josh remains adamant he had nothing to do with her disappearance.

A uniformed officer lets Detective Morgan enter. He rolls his eyes when he sees her and Nate. Then he notices Brody, who's sitting inches away from Josh, emitting a low growl and staring directly into his eyes. The dog barks when he looks up and sees Morgan.

"What the hell are you doing here?" Morgan addresses the dog, but Madison knows the question is intended for all three of them.

"Your job, by the looks of it," says Nate.

Morgan glares at him. "Listen, I know you hate cops, and thanks to a Google search of your name I know why, but don't take your issues out on me. I wasn't the one who put you in prison."

Madison's heart sinks. Morgan's done his digging. Donna must have given him Nate's last name. She looks across at him but she can't tell what he's thinking.

Morgan turns to Josh before Nate can respond. "Well, well, well. What else have you got hidden around here, Mr. Sanders? Jennifer Lucas, by any chance?"

"Fuck you. I've already said I want a lawyer."

"Spoken like a true criminal."

"I was framed by these guys," says Josh, nodding to Madison and Nate.

So much for waiting for legal representation.

"I got home from work and they were snooping around my house. I've never seen those laptops before in my life. I don't even own this house; it's leased. I'm being framed."

"All I want to know is where Jennifer Lucas is," says Morgan. "Did you take her?"

Josh is resolute. "No way, man! I'm not into kids, for God's sake! There's no way you can pin that on me."

"So where were you the night she vanished?" asks Madison. "Because your girlfriend has let slip you weren't with her all night."

Morgan looks as surprised as Josh to hear that.

Josh shakes his head. "I knew she couldn't keep her mouth shut." He looks up at them. "It's not how it sounds."

"Josh?" says Morgan. "You could do yourself a huge favor by being honest with us and telling me what you're hiding on your computers. My team will get access to them eventually, so we'll find out either way. But it'll look better for you in court if you cooperate. Are we going to find child abuse images on there?"

Josh shakes his head vigorously. "Of course not! I didn't have anything to do with Jenny's disappearance. If you ask me, she's in the lake."

"So what's in the folders?" asks Madison.

He looks at her but there's no defiance in his eyes, only embarrassment. "Just videos I took of various women."

She looks at Nate, who says, "Sex videos?"

Josh nods. "They didn't know I was filming them. And Kat didn't know I was screwing other women. That's where I was when I left her sleeping that night. One of the other counselors at the camp had been coming on to me for weeks. I decided to hook up with her."

Morgan shakes his head and mumbles, "What a waste of my time."

Madison's disappointed. She really thought Josh had taken Jennifer.

Morgan turns to the uniform. "Take him in, Officer. Get him all warm and cozy in interview room one. I'll be along when I'm ready to hear the sordid details of what's really going on at that summer camp."

"Yes, sir." The officer walks over to Josh and pulls him up. His hands are already cuffed behind him, so he needs help. As the officer marches him out of the house, Brody races ahead of them and jumps into the back of the police cruiser, tail wagging so hard anyone would think he was off for a trip to the beach.

"What's with that dog?" Morgan asks.

Nate stands and watches through the window.

"You don't know?" he says. "He's a former K9. His owner died in the line of duty."

Morgan looks thoughtful. "Maybe we could use him in our department."

Nate moves to the front door and calls him back. "Brody, come!"

The dog races back into the house, leaving room for the uniforms to push Josh into the car. Morgan removes his suit jacket and takes a seat on the worn-out couch next to Madison. He pulls out his notebook and pen. "Come on then. I guess you'd better tell me what happened here before I arrived."

Madison is surprised that he's asked her for the details. Maybe she could get him to trust her and let him in on the finer points of his unsuccessful investigation. She fills him in on finding the laptops.

He sighs. "Just because he's filmed a few girlfriends in the bedroom doesn't make him a child sex offender, but I'll see if the women in question want to press charges. The weapons will need looking into. If he doesn't have licenses, I could arrest him for that and then grill him further about Jennifer Lucas. Maybe he knows more than he's letting on. He's obviously untrustworthy, so he probably has some shady friends. But I don't think he took her."

"Why didn't you search his house?" asks Nate. "Surely all the camp staff are potential suspects?"

Morgan rubs his eyes. "I would have needed a search warrant, and for that I need probable cause; a reason to think he was involved in her disappearance. At the time, I had nothing. Unlike PIs, cops have to do things legally, otherwise we've got no chance of securing a conviction at trial."

"Well you need to seize the camp's office computer too," says Madison. "Because someone's been searching for pre-teen girls on that one, on the day Jennifer vanished."

He looks surprised. "You're kidding?"

"No. We won't be able to tell who it was, unfortunately, because everyone has access to it, but it might be worth checking the time and dates against the staff schedule to narrow down the list."

He raises his eyebrows and smiles at her. "We?"

She feels her face redden. She's getting carried away, but it can't be helped. This is what she's made for. "Okay, you. But I found it so I want to know what else you discover."

He nods. "Sure."

"Have you got the data back from Jenny's cell phone yet?"

"Yeah, there's nothing on it. No clues as to why she went missing. No social media accounts or strange messages. It's mostly just filled with selfies, a lot of them with her dad. None with friends, though, which is unusual for a girl of that age."

"It sounds like she struggled to make friends," says Madison. "In fact Josh told us the other kids accused her of stealing their stuff."

He nods. "Yeah, I heard the same thing. That's kids, though. I can't tell you how many teenage kleptomaniacs I arrested when I was in uniform." He closes his notebook before standing up. "Thanks for your help so far, but remember that this is still a police investigation, so I'm not at liberty to divulge anything to you."

"Will you at least be contacting Jennifer's grandmother to tell her what happened here?" asks Nate. "Because if you don't, I will."

Morgan looks annoyed. "Not unless I find something on those laptops that relates to her granddaughter. I'm not going to upset the family for no reason. Now just let me do my job. And remember, we have no evidence to suggest that Jennifer was abducted. She still might be at the bottom of the lake, or on the road having run away."

Morgan is clearly annoyed that Madison and Nate are doing a better job of investigating this case than he is. As they stand, he loosens his tie and crosses his arms. "I assume you've both given signed witness statements to my officers?"

They don't say anything.

"You're witnesses. You'll need to testify that you found those items, and explain what led you here in the first place. Otherwise Josh's lawyer could argue you planted them."

Madison looks at Nate. She knows there's no way he's going to get involved as a witness. That will mean too much involvement with the police.

"Let's see if there's anything incriminating on them first," he says. "We'll take it from there."

Morgan shakes his head. He looks around the living room. "I've got work to do here and I need you both to leave. I'll be in touch within the next few days for DNA samples."

Madison spins around to look at him. "What do you mean? I'm not giving you my DNA."

"Sorry, but you're standing in a potential crime scene. If I find any evidence that Josh was involved in Jennifer's disappearance, I'll need your DNA to rule out against any other DNA we find. I'm sure I don't need to tell you it's standard police procedure."

She turns to Nate and he calms her with just a look, then heads out the door. "Come on, Madison. Let the detective do his job."

Morgan watches them as they leave. Madison gets the impression he's about to start investigating them, but she can't understand why.

CHAPTER FORTY-THREE

Nate can feel Madison walking close to him as they head to his car. The rain has let up slightly, but it's still a pain in the ass. He wants a hot shower, a change of clothes and a line of coke to calm his nerves. But that'll have to wait.

"I'm not giving him a statement or my DNA," says Madison.

"I know. Neither am I. Not unless Josh could walk free without it."

She stops and pulls his arm, forcing him to stop. "Even then I won't do it." She looks determined.

"Are you saying you'd actually let him off the hook?"

She looks away, avoiding eye contact. "If it delays finding who framed me and reuniting me with my son, then yes. Convicting Josh is not my responsibility. If I was still a cop then of course I'd do it, but things are different now."

Nate doesn't know what to say. His opinion of her isn't improving any.

She must sense his disapproval. "I know it makes me sound callous, but I can't stay in this town, waiting around until the cops pull their shit together and go to trial. That could take a year. I can't keep putting other people first, Nate. Look where it's got me. No one ever puts me first! No one ever stands up for me! I'm left high and dry with no child and my career in tatters. I have nothing."

He touches her wet sleeve. "Listen, I completely understand why you feel that way. But you know better than me that guys like Josh Sanders should not be working with children. Regardless of what they find on his computers, and how old the women are, the guy's obsessed with weapons. A conviction would stop another summer camp employing him."

She looks at the ground, then turns back to the house, where Morgan is on his cell phone, watching them from the front window. "Goddammit." She slips into the passenger seat and slams her door shut.

Brody is waiting for the back door to be opened for him, but Nate can see he's dripping wet. "Shake off first."

The dog just stares at him.

Nate sighs. He walks to the trunk and retrieves a large towel from one of his holdalls. He approaches Brody slowly, in case he runs off, but the dog happily sits while Nate rubs him all over with the towel. He even licks Nate's ear as his paws are dried. His thick coat is hard to dry completely, but Nate gets what he can. When he opens the back door, the dog jumps in. Then he shakes himself off, all over the upholstery.

"Dog smell alert," he hears Madison mutter.

Nate gets in the front and slowly pulls away from Josh's street. The condensation from their wet clothes has steamed up the car windows, and Madison's right, it's quickly starting to smell in here, so he opens the windows for some air. "Let's not get hung up on any of that stuff yet—the statements, the potential court dates," he says. "The question now is, if Josh didn't take Jenny, then who did? He was our only suspect."

Madison leans forward and turns on the heating. He doesn't blame her; his wet hair is starting to chill him.

"I don't know if I even care anymore. I just want to go home and sort out my own problems."

He looks across at her and can't help feeling annoyed. "You asked me if I would hire you, Madison. Are you really going to quit at the first hurdle? Or was this all just a ploy to make sure I took your case? I mean, my God, did you give up this easy when you were a cop?"

She sighs and rubs her hands together. "Okay, okay, enough of the guilt trip. I'm allowed to have off days. Not everyone is as positive as you, you know."

He almost laughs. "Positive? Are you kidding me? Don't be fooled by my ability to focus on a job. You don't know what's going on in here." He taps his forehead. "Ever wonder why I choose to work when I don't have to?"

She looks at him. "Of course."

"Because it stops me reliving my sentence over and over. I'm just as angry and messed up inside as you, trust me. I'm just better at hiding it. I use all of this as a distraction. You'd benefit from doing the same."

He feels for Stacey's rosary beads around his neck, once again relieved that she left them hanging from his car's rear-view mirror just days before she was murdered. He had placed them around his neck to remind him to return them to her. He was wearing them when he entered the garage that night. Because he was arrested with them still around his neck, they were stored as his belongings until release.

Madison doesn't say anything. He hears Brody yawn loudly from the back seat.

"I'm not going back to the camp yet." He looks across at her. "Let's find some locals to ask their opinion of what's going on around here. That sound okay to you?"

She nods. "Sure."

He wonders if she'll see this case through to the end. He doesn't know whether he'd prefer her to leave so he can work on his own again.

CHAPTER FORTY-FOUR

June 2016—Polunsky Unit, Livingston, Texas

Nate opens his eyes and knows within seconds it's going to be a bad day. There was a time, about nine years ago, when he woke up like this every day for almost a year. He doesn't know how he got through that period, but he knows that because he did, he can get through the odd month or two of the black cloud pressing heavily down on him.

He turns onto his back. Looking up at the dirty low ceiling doesn't help his emotional state, but he finds that depression gnaws away at his muscles, making his whole body ache. His back and coccyx the most. He can't sit or lie in the same position for very long on days like this, making him restless. He used to think the aching was down to the beds they're made to sleep on: cheap, thin mattresses that don't disguise the metal ledge underneath. But now he knows better.

He tries to focus on anything other than the panic rising in his chest. It's trying to convince him he needs to run away from something, so he tries deep breathing. In for the count of five, hold for the count of five, out for the count of five. He repeats it for what seems like forever. He listens to the others waking up. Someone's crying. That's not unusual at this time of the morning. They all know about the mind-numbing repetition of every single day. Doing the same thing over and over will drive you insane. Wake up, use the toilet, exercise on the spot, eat whatever they feed you, behave, go to bed. Repeat. Repeat, repeat, repeat. Prison time is different to time on the outside. Individual days mean nothing; it's all about the years. And when every year is exactly the same, it's impossible to differentiate between them.

As he spirals, he hears Kristen's voice in his head.

"The professor in charge of our department is convinced we can get a new trial. There have been all kinds of previous internal investigations into Detective Diaz, and one of his convictions has already been overthrown. We're applying for a retrial. If they won't agree to that, we still have an application for clemency left."

He pictures her round, beautiful face looking at him with hope in her eyes. It's been eight months since she first came to meet with him, and she's visited him twice a month ever since. Those visits have changed his prison experience, but not for the better. He's been reminded of what he's missing. With no TVs allowed on Texas death row—only radios—it's hard to picture what's really going on outside this place. Kristen tells him about advances in technology, updates on politics, and what the kids are into these days. But most of all, she reminds him of Stacey. Of how amazing it is to have someone who cares about what happens to you. She holds his hand and fills him with warmth that he bitterly misses the minute she pulls away and has to leave. It's made him angrier at being inside.

Gus is extra cruel about Kristen because he's racist. Although he hates Nate, he's even harder on the black inmates.

Nate lets out a deep breath to the count of five. Kristen doesn't want him to give up on himself. She claims she's fallen for him and she wants him to take her on a date when he gets out. Nate doesn't know whether she's just saying that to give him hope and to keep him alive as long as possible. Whenever she mentions clemency, he mentally switches off. He has to, because the one thing he hears on death row more than anything else is: "Texas doesn't do clemency. Especially if you're innocent."

He feels something weighing heavy on his mind and his chest. The depression is taking hold now. He knows he won't get up today.

He won't eat and he'll barely make it to the toilet that's right next to his head. He just wants to cry. He wants to give up. He wants to revel in the unfairness of his sentence.

He hears Kristen again: "When you feel like that, you have to distract yourself. Picture our first date. Where are you going to take me, Nate? I'm not a cheap date by any means. I have French blood in me and I need to be impressed."

He can picture her smile; so positive and full of hope. She has full, kissable lips and her two front teeth slightly overlap. It's cute. He tries to think about where they'd go, but disruptive thoughts about the death chamber pop up every few minutes. If he ever got out of here, he'd find a way to take her to an expensive restaurant in Paris. That one thought gives him a tiny spark of motivation to do something with his time here. He should learn French in preparation, using books from the prison library. Then he could surprise her by ordering their meals in Paris.

He hears a door rattle. Gus appears. "Time to get up, killer priest. Breakfast is served." He pushes a bowl of beige food through the lockable hole in the bars and winks at him with a devilish grin as he moves on to the next inmate.

Nate turns to face the wall. He tries not to scream as loudly as his aching muscles.

CHAPTER FORTY-FIVE

Esme is sitting in the back of Grant's Lexus, clutching Jenny's school blazer. Grant and Anna are silent in the front seats. Every now and then Grant will switch the radio on to fill the eerie silence, but Anna will turn it off within minutes, claiming she needs to think.

On days like this, Esme feels like she's spending time with strangers. Jenny's disappearance has affected them all deeply and she worries they'll never find themselves again if they don't find her. She heard Grant and Anna arguing yet again last night, and thought she heard the sound of something smashing against a wall, but everything went silent afterwards so she couldn't be sure. Grant's not a violent person, so she doesn't think it was him. He raises his voice sometimes, but not usually to his family. He has the patience of a saint when it comes to Jenny. Of course, things could have been a little different when Esme wasn't there, but she doesn't want to think like that.

She hugs her arms round her waist and prays they don't split up. She doesn't think she could bear to see them any unhappier than they are now. She looks out the car window as they drive through California. They're hoping to reach Shadow Falls before sundown, but they're still hours away.

"Anyone hungry yet?" asks Grant.

They've been on the road for five hours. Esme could do with stretching her legs and using the restroom.

"No," says Anna.

"I'd like a break," says Esme. "I'm sure you could use a coffee." She places her hand on her son's shoulder and he touches it.

"Yeah, work's crazy at the moment, so I'm pretty tired. Maybe we should've waited until morning to do this."

Esme feels a small bolt of panic. She can't keep waiting any longer; it's best that they're on the road. It feels like they're doing something. "Let's stop for coffee. It will refresh us all."

"Sure," says Grant. "I'll pull in at the next rest stop."

Esme sits back in her seat and checks her cell phone for updates from Nate. She has a text.

Nothing to report yet. We've eliminated a potential suspect today, so making progress.

She wonders about the suspect. Did they work at the camp? Why were they a suspect? A sharp pain stabs her in the back, stopping her from taking a proper breath in. It passes within seconds and she almost immediately forgets it. She texts Nate back.

Thanks. Keep me updated.

She doesn't tell him they're on the way. She doesn't even know why, but she feels for some reason it would be better if he didn't know. She sighs. It's exhausting not knowing who she's supposed to trust. As she looks out of the window, watching the rugged, beautiful terrain that she's currently unable to appreciate, the stabbing pain returns. It's not dissimilar to the indigestion she's started suffering more of as she's aged. She searches for the chalky pills in her purse and remembers she finished the packet yesterday.

"Anna? Do you have any indigestion pills on you?"

"Check the glovebox," says Grant. "There's all kinds of stuff in the first aid kit."

Anna rummages through it, taking a while. Eventually she passes two pink pills over her shoulder. "Need some water to wash them down with?"

"I have some, thanks."

She takes them with water as Grant pulls into a truck stop.

They leave Anna in the car as they head inside the small diner. They both use the restroom and Esme is the first one to the counter. The smiling waitress asks what she can get for her.

"Two white coffees and one black, all to go. Thanks."

"Sure thing."

Esme reaches out her arm to pay the waitress, but a stabbing pain forces her to pull it back, close to her chest. She lets out a groan but can't tell where the pain came from. It feels like nerve damage.

"Ma'am? Are you okay?" asks the waitress. She temporarily stops chewing her gum.

Esme is bent over slightly and tries to straighten up. The pain has gone again. She tries to smile but fears it's more of a grimace. "Oh, just a little indigestion. Nothing a coffee won't fix."

The waitress eyes her warily, takes her money and then turns to start pouring the coffees into takeout cups. By the time she turns back with the drinks in her hands, Esme is on the ground.

CHAPTER FORTY-SIX

Anna is staring out of the car window at the other travelers coming and going, but she's not really seeing them. She's wondering what will happen at the start of the new semester at Jennifer's school in a few weeks. Will they have a special assembly to honor her memory? Will they pick a pointless colored ribbon to wear and plant a tree in memorial? Oh God, will she be invited to watch? She shakes her head and touches her throat at the thought of it. They probably won't do anything like that. Not if they never find her. Until then, Jennifer is technically alive. And until then, Anna might as well be dead.

Her cell phone rings. When she sees who's calling, she lets it go unanswered. They try again. She ignores it and clears the missed call notification. She can't deal with them today.

She sighs heavily, feeling anger swell in her chest. She doesn't want to be here. She wants to be at home with her family. She looks around the car for something to throw. Something to punch. Her pillow at home has taken several beatings since all this blew up. It's the only way she's been able to safely release her anger. Grant's constant need for tidiness means there's nothing in the car she can hurl. Instead she yells, "Shit!" as loudly and aggressively as she can. Then, for the first time in her life, she considers hurting herself. Maybe that will release some of the pain inside her. She tries to think what she could use to cut her arm, but just as she's reaching for her house keys, an ambulance appears with its lights flashing.

She spins around to see who's been hurt. There's no obvious accident scene, so she waits and watches the EMTs jump out of the vehicle. One of them races ahead into the diner, while the other grabs a large equipment bag. Anna's body tenses.

"Oh God."

She can't see anything through the diner's window because of the sunlight bouncing off it. She checks her phone, but there's nothing from Grant. Then her stomach dives. Has something happened to him? She tries not to panic as she watches and waits. A woman wearing a short red sundress walks out of the diner with her hand over her mouth. She pulls a cigarette from her purse and starts puffing away hard.

Anna's body has gone cold from the inside out. Something has happened to Grant. If that's true, where would that leave her? Childless and husbandless. She doesn't know if she can see Jennifer's disappearance through without her husband. She doesn't want to get out of the car, so she remains seated and tries to ignore whatever's happening in there. It's then that the woman looks over at her and starts approaching.

"No," Anna mutters. "Go away. I don't want to know."

When the woman reaches her open window, she puts a hand on the car door and throws the rest of her cigarette on the ground. "Are you Anna?"

She wants to say no. In the end, she can't even respond.

"Honey, something's happened. You need to get inside."

Anna whispers, "Just tell me."

The woman looks away, toward the diner. "I don't know their names, but the man told me to come and get you. I'll go with you if you want."

He's still alive. So it's Esme. Her body responds and she opens the car door. The woman moves out of her way and follows her to the diner's entrance. When Anna puts her hand on the door, she has to fight the urge to turn around, get in the car and drive away. She could stop whatever has happened by not knowing what it is. She could leave right now and live in ignorance somewhere new.

Somewhere she never had a daughter named Jennifer and a husband named Grant. Somewhere tragedy can't follow her.

Someone opens the diner's door from the inside; one of the EMTs. He stands to one side and she takes a step forward. Grant is on his knees, holding Esme's hands. Esme is flat on her back. Her eyes are staring at Anna but they're fixed, as if she's looking at something on the other side. The expression on her face is one of horror. Did she see her granddaughter as she passed? Did she see the truth of what happened?

Grant glances up. There are tears running down his cheeks. Anna has seen that look on his face too many times before.

He tries to say something, but she can't hear him. "What?" she whispers.

He tries again. "I said, you were right. We're cursed."

She can only watch as he breaks down and hugs his mother's lifeless body.

CHAPTER FORTY-SEVEN

Nate thinks about stopping at the local gas station to talk to Jeanie-May again, but is mindful that her husband might not approve. She may be suffering with dementia but she had Josh sized up perfectly, so she's not completely lost yet, although he can understand her husband being protective. Instead, he drives past and on toward the town's small shopping area. Turns out Main Street consists of just eight stores and a library.

"Wow, this place is almost as small as death row," he says.

Madison laughs, breaking the tension between them. "It's even smaller than my home town. I like it here. I like the forest and the remoteness. It's calm and relaxed and I bet it's beautiful in winter."

He looks at her as if she's out of her mind. "I'll take bustling Malibu over somewhere like this any day."

He parks outside the grocery store. "You stay here, Brody." He looks over his shoulder and realizes the dog is asleep on the back seat, obviously tired from their earlier exploits. He leaves both back windows rolled all the way down, hoping Brody would deter any potential car thieves. There's enough room for him to jump out if he feels too warm, but thanks to the earlier downpour, the weather has cooled right down.

"You know, he never got his reward for getting me into Josh's outbuilding," says Madison. "He tore that door apart for me."

Nate thinks about it. "You're right. What kind of reward do K9s get?"

She shrugs. "Probably something that's round and bounces, or maybe something meaty, but I'm just guessing."

Nate smiles. "Okay, I'll take care of it in here." He nods to the store. "Why don't you check out the other stores and see what you can find out?"

She nods and gets out of the car. Nate enters the grocery store. It's completely empty of customers apart from an old guy squeezing a few melons. Nate can't tell if he's judging their ripeness or having a good time, but he sure is focused.

He finds the small pet section and looks for a ball. There's only one. It's plastic, and when he squeezes it, it makes a high-pitched crying sound. He wonders whether that's too immature for a police dog, but there isn't much choice. He grabs some sandwiches and drinks for himself and Madison, then looks at the cooked meat section, settling on a pack of pre-cooked hot-dog sausages. He finds himself wondering again how different K9s are to pet dogs, and whether he's meant to treat Brody this way or be stricter. There must've been some rules in order to keep the dog focused on law enforcement work.

He walks over to the cashier, an older lady dressed in an ill-fitting maroon uniform. She's filing her nails when he places his goods on the decrepit conveyor belt.

"Did you manage to find everything you wanted today, sir?" she asks, looking him up and down.

Nate smiles. He didn't expect customer service in a place like this. She's wearing a name badge that says: *Hi! My name is Betty and I'm here to serve you.* There's another name under hers, crossed out. Presumably a former employee.

"I did, thanks."

She picks up the ball first. "Oh, you have a dog? I love dogs. I have four of the rascals." She names all four of them as she scans his items, then she tells him the breed and age of each dog and where she got them from. He doesn't mind listening. It's all part of building a rapport with the locals. He doesn't think Madison would be as patient.

"Dogs are just great, aren't they?" he says.

"What have you got?"

He's not the dog's owner but he decides to play along. "We think he's a husky mix, but we never met his parents. He's pretty handsome, though. Looks like a wolf."

She finishes scanning the last item and runs up the total. "A husky mix, you say? Hmm. My girl would probably like him. You ever offer him as a stud? Marmalade—the Rottweiler—is on heat right now and I know she'd love some action. She's a little overweight, so he'd have to be good at climbing."

Nate tries to think how a Rottweiler–husky puppy might look, but he can't get his head around the combination. "I don't know if he'd be able to perform on demand, to be honest."

She nods. "Yeah, men are a bit like that. They talk a good talk, but once someone demands something from them, they can't get it up." She winks at him.

He laughs. The old guy from the fruit section joins them, and Nate notices he didn't pick a melon in the end.

"What are you two laughing about?" he asks. He turns to Nate. "Bryan Goodfellow."

Nate shakes his hand. "Nate Monroe. Betty was just telling me about her dogs."

Bryan rolls his eyes. "Do you ever talk of anything else, Betty?"

She waves his comment away and ignores him. Clearly they know each other well.

"What brings you to our neck of the woods, Mr. Monroe?" asks Bryan.

Nate thinks about lying, but he'd guess old-timers like these two would see right through him, and he has nothing to hide. "I'm here looking for information about the young girl who went missing from Camp Fearless."

Bryan and Betty share a look. Bryan says, "You a cop?"

"No, an investigator hired by her family. They just want their daughter back."

Bryan chews the inside of his mouth for a minute, like he's thinking hard about whether to say something. "You know there's talk around town of Josh Sanders being involved. You met him yet?"

"Yeah. I've spent some time up at the camp. I happen to know for a fact that he doesn't have Jennifer Lucas, though. I can see why he was a good suspect, but he was busy doing something else that night."

Bryan looks at him. "I suppose you can't tell us *what* he was doing?"

"Afraid not. But I need another suspect. Did either of you notice anyone different in town the day before or after Jenny's disappearance?"

Betty laughs. "We don't get that many outsiders because we have no decent through road. The only time we see anyone new is when summer starts and the parents are dropping off their kids. Then again when they collect 'em at the end of the season."

Nate nods. That's about what he expected.

"Mr. Andrews, my boss, gave our security footage to the police," she continues. "They never did return those memory sticks, though. He had to buy a new stash and they're not cheap."

Nate's surprised that a place like this would have security cameras. He'd like to get a hold of that footage, but he knows Morgan won't want him to have it. "Do you know if the footage automatically backs up online, Betty?"

She nods. "Yeah."

"Do you know how to download it?"

"Well, sure. Mr. Andrews has written instructions in his office in case he ever needs to access it. His memory's not too great these days, so he writes everything down."

Nate doesn't expect to find anything in the footage, because the police would've acted on it by now, but he still needs to check it for his own peace of mind. "Do you think you could let me watch some of it?"

Betty looks at Bryan, who says, "Why not? If it might help find the poor child."

"Okay then." She looks at her watch. "We normally shut at eight, but I guess I could close up an hour early. It's not like anyone would notice."

Nate smiles, not believing his luck. "That would be great."

CHAPTER FORTY-EIGHT

Madison decides to start with the hair salon, where the two stylists take an instant dislike to her for no apparent reason. She can't help wondering when she lost her people skills. Maybe while she was in prison. All she did was ask whether anyone knew who the local pedophiles were. Turns out some people don't want to believe they have sex offenders in their midst. She wouldn't be surprised if either of them was married to one and covering up for them.

After receiving a frosty reception there, she decides to try the library. After all, librarians should be the font of all knowledge about a town, and they probably see a good mixture of locals on a regular basis. She crosses the road, pushes open the large oak door and walks into a musty-smelling building. There are few windows, making it dark, and she wonders if that's to preserve the books from the damaging effects of sunlight. At least it's cool and dry in here.

She walks up to the borrowing desk expecting to find a little old lady behind it, and is surprised when she sees a male sitting in front of a computer monitor. He looks up at her and smiles. He's a bit younger than her—early thirties, she'd guess—and is wearing the kind of glasses Clark Kent wears. He looks geeky but is attractive with it. She can't help thinking his good looks are wasted in a place like this.

"Hi, I'm Madison." She holds her hand out and the guy stands up to shake it.

"I'm Clark."

She laughs. "No way!"

He looks bemused. "Afraid so. What's so funny?"

"Sorry." She's embarrassed. "I was just thinking how your glasses made you look like Clark Kent."

He laughs. "If you say so. I don't turn into Superman, though, I'm afraid. Are you here for a particular book?"

She looks around to hide her red cheeks. "No, I'm actually here to figure out what happened to Jennifer Lucas." She turns back to him for his reaction. There is none.

"Do you have a badge?"

That's a strange question for him to ask right off the bat. Why did he not assume she was a friend of the family, or a reporter? "No, I'm not a cop. I'm an investigator. Jenny's family asked us to look into her disappearance because she's been gone for over two weeks now. We just want to give them some closure. I'm sure you understand."

He nods. "Of course. It must be terrible for them, but I really don't know how I can help you. I mean, I didn't know Jenny or her family. I gather they're not from around here."

She leans on the desk. "They're not. I just assumed that since librarians know everything about a place, you might be able to tell me what people are saying about her disappearance. Perhaps the finger of blame is being pointed in a particular direction that I could look into?"

He looks uncomfortable and removes his glasses. He's still attractive without them. "Of course people talk, but that's because everyone loves crime shows these days, so everyone wants to solve the case before the police."

She nods. "That's understandable. What about you? What do you think happened to her?"

He sits back down but maintains eye contact. "I haven't been following the case so I can't even guess. I just hope she's found alive. And if not, well, then I hope it was an accident and not something more sinister. If that camp closes, it's bad news for the town. We're already struggling to keep our heads above water financially."

She wonders why he stays here knowing that. What could possibly keep someone of his age in a town like Shadow Falls? She looks to his ring finger, but it's bare. He's not married but he could have a partner. Or maybe he's single. She thinks about all the single guys she's arrested in her career who turned out to be interested in kids. There weren't half as many of them as there were married men. "I assume the local police searched all the businesses and addresses around here when she first went missing?"

He thinks about it. "Well if they did, they didn't come here."

She's surprised. She's starting to believe Detective Morgan is incompetent. "No? Could it have happened on your day off?"

He laughs. "I don't get a day off. I run this place single-handed, and as I live upstairs, I work down here even when the library's not open."

"What do you work on?"

"I'm writing a book."

She raises her eyebrows. "Really? What about?"

He looks uncomfortable, but that's not unusual. She's seen famous authors squirm when asked the same question. For some reason, writers like to keep their cards close to their chest.

"If I knew that, it would be going a lot smoother."

She smiles. "Has this library got a kids' section?"

"Sure. Just over there." He points behind her left shoulder.

She can see a large display of paintings and drawings above some shelves of colorful books. "Mind if I take a look?"

"Not at all. You won't be able to borrow any books without a library card, though."

She walks over to the corner while he goes back to working at his computer. They only have a small selection of children's books. If Clark was into kids, he'd probably have a much bigger display, to entice children in. She sometimes hates that she thinks like a cop, because she's always considering everyone as a suspect. It can ruin potential relationships.

She looks closely at the paintings and can see that each one has a different name at the bottom. The fourth painting, of a black-caped figure looming over two small babies, is menacing. She wonders why Clark put it up. Surely it would scare the younger kids? Then she notices the name: Jenny. She tries not to gasp. Was this done by Jennifer Lucas? It's a common enough girl's name, but this is a really small town.

Not wanting Clark to know she's spotted it, she silently snaps a photo on her phone and casually walks toward the exit. "Thanks for your time."

He looks up from his computer. "No problem. Good luck with your search."

She walks out into the drizzle. She needs to find Nate.

CHAPTER FORTY-NINE

The only person Nate recognizes in the store's security footage is Donna Gleeson, the camp director. Betty and Bryan help name the other few patrons that day, all locals.

"You seen enough?" asks Betty.

He's about to say yes when he sees Donna accidentally drop some of her items and raise her hands in exasperation. She's clearly angry. "What happened there?"

Betty slips her glasses back on and squints at the computer monitor. "Oh, she was having a real bad day. She dropped a carton of milk and it went everywhere. She didn't even offer to help me clean it up. In fact she yelled at me instead."

"Why'd she yell at you?" asks Bryan.

"Because the milk went all over her shoes and she said they were ruined. She was a pain in the ass that day."

"Is she always like that?" asks Nate.

Betty stands up straight. "When she first moved here last year she was friendly enough, but the longer she's worked at that camp the angrier she's got. She never stops to pass the time of day with me anymore. She's just in and out, usually with a scowl on her face." She leans in to the computer again. "You know, I think it might have been that day that her credit card was rejected too."

Nate folds his arms. "Why was it declined?"

"Oh, we don't get told the reason—something to do with data protection—but if a card's declined, I'm instructed to cut it in half, and let me tell you, that didn't go down well at all."

Nate is intrigued. There might be something to Donna's strange behavior. "What happened?"

"Hit play and watch for yourself."

He does. "Is there any sound to go with this?"

"Nah, Mr. Andrews said that'd cost extra and he wouldn't need it."

Nate nods. That's fair enough. He'd bet nothing worth listening to usually happens in a town like this. He speeds through as Betty cleans up the milk while Donna waits at the checkout. She's looking at her cell phone. He slows down when Betty joins her to scan her items and take payment. They all watch as she tries her card. Donna quickly becomes agitated, and Nate can tell she's raised her voice just from her hand gestures. Then she picks up a basket and throws it across the checkout—not at Betty, just to the right of her.

"Shit," says Bryan. "That woman has issues."

"I know, right?" says Betty.

They watch as Donna storms out empty-handed.

"What did you do with her cut-up card?" asks Nate.

"Threw it in the trash."

"I don't suppose that trash is still here?"

Betty looks offended. "Of course not. I empty the trash into the dumpster at the end of every day. The dumpster gets emptied once a week. This was over two weeks ago."

Nate stands. "It was worth a try. Thanks for your help, both of you. I appreciate it."

Bryan looks at him. "You're not going to tell us what you're thinking?"

Nate laughs. "I think you already know. I need to look a little deeper into Donna's background and make sure she doesn't have any violent tendencies around kids."

Bryan turns to Betty and raises his eyebrows.

"But I'm sure she was just having a bad day. We all have them," says Nate. "And this is strictly confidential. I don't need the whole town thinking Donna took the missing girl. I just need to rule her out, that's all. It's a long stretch between someone having a bad day and hurting a child. You understand?"

Betty nods. Bryan touches his nose with his finger and winks. "We get what you're saying. No one will hear anything from me."

"No, but I might watch her a bit closer now," says Betty.

Nate thanks them again and walks back to the car, where Madison is waiting.

She looks up from her phone. "I've got something to show you."

CHAPTER FIFTY

Grant can't sit still. The small, uncomfortable hospital seats don't help. He doesn't know what he's supposed to do, but his body is fired up with adrenaline and he just wants to hit a wall. He needs to contain his feelings so as not to upset Anna further. He looks over at her, sitting next to his mother's bed. She doesn't look anything like the woman he married fourteen years ago. She's a ghost of her former self. She doesn't eat enough anymore. She also doesn't bother with make-up, and only combs her hair if she's leaving the house.

Part of him is glad to see how upset she is about his mother's death. He knows she never really bonded with Esme, never went the extra mile to let her in and become friends. There was a time when it almost happened, but then everything changed and Anna put a wall up and kept her distance emotionally. Unfortunately, that wall didn't just keep Esme out.

His mother tried her hardest to be there for them both during their worst times, but she wouldn't have understood what they were going through. Grant can't fully comprehend it himself. Just like he can't comprehend how three of them set out on this journey north and only two of them will arrive. He feels helpless. He wants to go back in time and insist his mom stay home instead. It was stress that killed her. The doctors won't say that because officially it was a cardiac arrest, but before Jenny disappeared she was happy and healthy, doting on her granddaughter. He can't believe he'll never speak to her again.

Anna catches him looking at her and offers him a weak smile. "I know what you're thinking, and I don't blame you."

He doesn't want to get into a fight. He sighs. "What am I thinking?"

"You're blaming me for this, aren't you?"

He shakes his head, but he can't go over there to comfort her. His mother is lying on the bed between them, dead for almost an hour. The staff keep coming in to ask if they're ready to say goodbye, but neither of them is yet. Does he blame Anna for this? If he's honest, partly. She should have been more concerned about how all this was going to affect someone of his mother's age. She should have been more caring. Instead she agreed with Esme that they should travel up to the summer camp.

"This is no one's fault," he says unconvincingly. He's not sure how much more he can put into this marriage. Now that his mom is gone, there's no one to disappoint if they get divorced. But then he thinks of the baby and looks at Anna again.

She doesn't have the expectant-mother glow that she had before. She pulls her cardigan tighter around her, always careful to hide her bump. She doesn't want anyone to know yet; she said it didn't seem right. He looks at his mother's grey face. He's glad she didn't know they were expecting a child. She would've wanted to celebrate it, despite Jenny being missing, but Anna isn't ready to acknowledge it publicly. She's terrified they'll lose the baby.

If they lose this one, then he'll take it as a sign from above that he wasn't meant to be a husband or a father.

CHAPTER FIFTY-ONE

As Nate drives them back toward the camp, the evening sun makes an appearance from behind the clouds and slowly begins to set. It's casting a red hue over the tall trees around them. The air feels warm again. There are a lot of puddles along the roadside, so he's expecting it to be muddy at the camp.

He can feel a headache forming behind his eyes. He's also a little shaky and doesn't think it's because he hasn't eaten in a while. A familiar feeling of dread is looming and he's powerless to do anything about it other than hope it doesn't take hold. He can't afford to let up on this case right now. To distract himself, he thinks about the painting Madison showed him on her phone, the one she thinks Jenny drew. "You know, that's a pretty disturbing picture. I'd be terrified if a kid of mine drew that."

Madison agrees. "It's creepy. Maybe her parents watch a lot of horror movies or something, and she was just painting what she saw on screen."

Nate thinks of Anna and Grant. They don't look like they're into horror movies, but how would he be able to tell, really?

"You don't think they're into some weird satanic shit, do you?" she asks.

He looks at her. "Seriously? They don't seem the type, and there was nothing to suggest that in their home."

"We only saw their living room and Jenny's bedroom. They'd probably keep that crazy shit for their own bedroom." She sighs. "No, I guess they don't seem the type. Maybe Jenny was acting out because she was being bullied. Or perhaps she's not the sweet, angelic little girl her dad and grandmother have made her out to be." She appears to think about it. "If Josh was telling the truth about the other kids not liking her because she was stealing from them, it's totally possible we're looking at this from the wrong angle."

Nate listens as she thinks out loud.

"Maybe she has some kind of issues that stop her bonding with her peers and they all got sick of putting up with her and pushed her in the lake, taking it a step too far. They probably didn't mean to kill her, just humiliate her. But if she was taken by surprise, she might have got into trouble and drowned."

"But the lake was searched," he says.

"It was, but maybe it's time to search it again." She sighs. "I don't know. I could be wrong. Maybe she did run away after all."

"But she comes from a good home."

"Doesn't matter. For all we know, Grant was abusing her. Or maybe he was too strict. There are a thousand reasons why kids run away from home, some of them reasonable, others not so much. Maybe she was just pissed at her parents and decided to teach them a lesson by disappearing. I mean, this painting is not what I'd expect from a happy twelve-year-old girl."

"We don't actually know that she's the same Jenny who painted it," he points out. "We're making assumptions. Would the camp staff even take the kids into town?"

"Sure. Kids get bored easily. A day trip to the library would pass some time. I expect the library has drawing classes or something." She turns to face him. "Did you notice how there were no missing child posters up anywhere in town?"

He shakes his head; he hadn't even thought of looking for posters.

"It's weird. Either they were all taken down by locals who didn't want reminding they have a potential abductor in their midst, or Morgan never arranged for any to go up. That would be unusual. Well, actually, it would be incompetent."

"You think Ted's not been effective in looking for her?"

Madison looks away. "It's hard to say without being on the inside. I'd give anything to be able to look through his investigation notes."

Nate can tell how much she misses being on the force. He finds himself rooting for her to get back there eventually. She's obviously made to be a cop; she asks questions and considers theories that he would never have thought of. It reassures him to know that not all cops are corrupt like Detective Blake Diaz.

He thinks about the footage of Donna's meltdown in the grocery store. "I can't help thinking Donna might be up to something after what I just learned." He tells Madison what happened.

"Sounds like she's got a short temper," she says. "Or maybe she was just on her period. God knows I could throw a shopping basket at someone on those days."

He daren't laugh. His cell phone pings and he glances at it quickly. He has a new email from Rex. He pulls over to the side of the road to read it while Madison eats one of the sandwiches he bought.

"Shit. Looks like Donna's bankrupt." He reads the short email, trying to concentrate despite the ache behind his eyes. "Rex says she owes four different credit cards a total of twenty grand, plus she defaulted on her home loan last year. Maybe that's why she took a live-in job at the camp." He opens his own sandwich and eats half of it, passing the other half to Brody, who's breathing down his neck in anticipation. "Do you think it's possible she might have taken Jenny to blackmail the parents out of some cash?"

Madison scrunches up her wrapper. "As far as we know, there haven't been any ransom requests."

He nods. "Not yet. Would there have been by now? Do you know of any kidnapping cases that have been about money?"

Madison thinks for a few minutes whilst sipping her bottled water. "I haven't worked any myself, but I'd assume the ransom request would come pretty quick. The more time someone holds a child, the more chance there is of it going wrong and them getting caught."

Nate thinks so too. "Maybe something happened to Jenny before Donna got a chance to ask for anything."

"You mean maybe she ran off?"

Nate nods. "Maybe she ran off, or maybe Donna accidentally killed her."

Her eyes open wide. "Oh shit. That's a possibility."

He starts the car. "Let's see if she'll answer some questions."

As soon as they arrive at Camp Fearless, Kat runs toward them with tears streaming down her face. Brody steps in between her and Nate, but she just dodges him.

"What have you done?" she yells, hitting Nate on the chest.

He holds her at arm's length while Brody barks at her. "Kat, your boyfriend's been screwing other women and recording them without their consent. Surely you can see *he's* the one in the wrong here, not us?"

"But he's all I've got! He's my only chance to get out of here and be someone." She collapses onto her knees and Nate crouches next to her on the wet grass. He looks up at Madison, but she's shaking her head in disgust. She clearly has no sympathy for the girl.

Donna joins them. "Is she right? Has Josh been arrested?"

Nate stands. "He has. But not in relation to Jennifer Lucas. Turns out Josh is a creep who has a thing for guns and filming women without their permission. Would you happen to know anything about that, Donna?"

She gasps as she takes a step back. "Me? Why would I know what he was up to in his spare time? He was a good employee, or so I thought. I manage almost twenty-five people; I can't be expected to know what they're all up to."

Nate is running out of patience. "I need to speak to you in private."

Madison pulls Kat up and leads her away, giving Nate a look of reproach for leaving her to deal with the girl. He ignores it. She needs to realize she's working for him now, and if he wants to take the lead, he will.

Donna looks terrified, and she walks quickly to the office, clutching her necklace. Once inside, she closes the door. Nate doesn't take the seat she offers him.

"What's going on around here?" she says. "First we lose a child, and now one of our counselors is a sex pest?"

"You can cut the innocent crap. Are you seriously telling me you had no idea Josh Sanders was a creep? Haven't you seen the way he treats Kat? I've been here just a few days and I've already witnessed it."

She sits behind her desk and opens a drawer. He's not surprised when she pulls out some vodka and takes a shot straight from the bottle. "These kids I employ are hard to keep track of, Mr. Monroe. They're all either screwing each other or fighting each other and I can't keep up. Just because Josh is a womanizer doesn't mean I should automatically suspect he's a criminal."

"But you should know what they're doing when they're here. Sounds like Josh was sleeping with several of your employees, plus someone's been searching for child abuse images on your computer. Isn't that your responsibility?"

Her eyes widen in shock. "What?"

"Madison found searches for underage girls on it. Know anything about that?" He's starting to sweat. It's not just grilling Donna in this hot office; his mood is changing.

"Are you sure you found child abuse images on there? Because I've done plenty of searches for how to entertain pre-teen girls, and activities for girls and boys. I suppose now, what with everything that's happened, I can see how those searches might be misinterpreted."

He doesn't know whether to believe her. "Why would you search for that?"

"Because it's hard work trying to keep all these kids entertained twenty-four seven! They all have different interests and temperaments. I have one young girl, Becky, who doesn't have any friends here yet, and I've been trying to find things to interest her."

Nate thinks she's telling the truth. "I guess we'll find out soon enough. Detective Morgan will be seizing your computer. Until then, I'd suggest you don't let anyone touch it."

"Trust me, Mr. Monroe, there is absolutely no opportunity for anyone to search for that kind of disgusting content on our computer. We monitor the users; Kat is present when the children use it, and my staff are rarely on it. You're barking up the wrong tree." She looks away and groans. "Oh my God. If Josh is charged with something, I'm going to be fired for hiring him, aren't I? We're going to be in the papers."

Nate's pissed. "Really? That's your only concern right now?" He's agitated and ready for an argument. "You make me sick. You hire people like Josh to work around the children in your care. Do you know how many unlicensed weapons he has at his house? What if he'd brought one to work with him and a kid got hold of it? And once your female staff realize he's filmed them having sex, they're going to want to press charges. So yeah, it's going to be all over the news. Meaning all eyes will be on you and this camp."

She looks shocked and takes another slug of vodka. Nate can see her putting two and two together. The media will expose her financial problems.

"So the question is, how are you going to survive, bankrupt and with no job?" he asks.

She looks down. "How do you know about that?"

"It's my job to check people's backgrounds. I know you don't have a penny to your name, other than your income here, which I'm guessing isn't much if the camp fees are anything to go by."

She takes a deep breath and holds back tears. "I only just get by. I get free food and housing here, but other than that, I don't have much."

"Is that why you chose Jenny?"

She looks up at him with panic in her eyes. "What?"

"Well, she clearly has wealthy parents, unlike most of the others. Did you google everyone's parents and think you'd hit the jackpot when you saw that Jenny is from a big house in Santa Barbara? I mean, it's not much of a stretch to assume they'd pay a good ransom to get their daughter back if she went missing."

Her eyes are wide open and her mouth moves, but nothing comes out. She wipes away her tears defiantly and a look of disgust settles over her face. "How dare you accuse me of something so heinous? I would never hurt a child. I need this job to survive and I wouldn't do anything to risk losing it."

"Not even for the twenty-five-thousand-dollar reward?"

She stands up. "You and your friend are no longer welcome at my camp. You need to leave immediately or I'll call the police."

Nate tries to read her. His gut tells him she's genuinely insulted and not hiding anything, but he can't be sure. He opens the door to her office and looks back. "If you know anything about what happened to that girl, you need to tell me or Detective Morgan as soon as possible, because the longer she's missing, the worse it's going to get for you. Especially now one of your employees has been arrested."

She reddens with anger. "Get out of my office."

He slams the door hard behind him.

CHAPTER FIFTY-TWO

Madison is on edge. Nate's driving them to a hotel, but his personality has taken a sudden nose-dive. After she'd dealt with Kat, she found him looking out over the lake, and when she asked how it had gone with Donna, he barely mumbled a response. When he turned to her, his eyes were red-rimmed and he looked hopeless.

She suggested they leave the camp and find somewhere else to stay tonight, and he agreed by just walking to his car. They left Brody at the campsite this time. Nate turned Madison down when she offered to drive, but his driving is erratic. He's been drifting off to the side of the road for no reason. She's worried he's having a stroke or something.

When they finally see a guest house, she's relieved. "This will have to do. Pull in, Nate."

He does what she says, again without communicating. When he switches the ignition off, he looks down at his hands.

"Nate, what's wrong? Are you feeling okay?"

He turns to her and the look in his eyes is one of despair. "This happens sometimes. I'm sorry. It's overwhelming."

Her heart goes out to him. She's seen this before, in prison. Nate's having a serious depressive episode. She knows it could end badly, so she gets out of the car and takes charge. "Wait here, I'll check us in."

She enters the guest house and is greeted by an empty check-in desk. She rings the handbell, and an older woman appears. Her hair is in a messy bun and her dentures are too big for her mouth, but she looks friendly.

"Good evening. I'm Mary."

"Hi, how are you? I need two rooms for tonight, please."

"Sure thing. That'll be a hundred and fifty dollars."

Madison hesitates. She'll need to use her own cash, as she can't ask Nate for money in his current state. She pulls her wallet out and hands the notes over. It hurts. Her wallet feels alarmingly light as she slides it back into her pocket.

"I'll need you to sign in, too."

Madison looks at the register and notices the page is yellowed with age. She's guessing they don't get many guests here. She signs in using just their first names.

"Here are your keys. The rooms are right next to each other with interconnecting doors. You're just in time for dinner, and breakfast is at seven. There are plenty of towels in the rooms, but if you need anything else, you just give me a holler."

"Thanks."

Madison turns to leave, but the woman wants to know more about her. "I've not seen you around before. Are you here to pick up your children from the summer camp?"

She turns back. "Er, no. Just having a break from work. My husband and I needed some down time."

Mary looks confused. "You're married but not sharing a room?"

She takes a deep breath. Since when did everyone have to act like a cop? "He snores. It's really bad." She offers a fake smile.

Mary makes a face to suggest she understands, and Madison heads back out to the car. Nate is standing by the side of the road. He looks like he's waiting to throw himself under the next heavy vehicle that passes. His rapid change in behavior is alarming.

She walks up to him and takes his arm. "Get our things from the trunk, then I'll lead the way."

He does what she says. She climbs the carpeted stairs to find their rooms, but there are only two doors on this floor, so it's easy. She opens the first one and lets Nate walk in ahead of her.

He drops their bags on the floor, slips his sneakers off and pulls his T-shirt over his head, revealing a toned torso and the rosary beads she glimpsed around his neck when she first met him. She can see they've been broken in several places, as if they've been pulled from his neck and then remorsefully fixed. Perhaps a sign of his wavering faith in God.

He closes the curtains, drops onto the bed and covers his face with his arm. "You should go. I'm not good company when I'm like this."

"I'll be the judge of that." She closes the door and enters the bathroom. She's looking for razor blades, or anything he could use to hang himself with. While in prison, she was unlucky enough to discover two of her cellmates hanging from their bunks. She hadn't expected it and beat herself up for not preventing it, so she's not going to let the same thing happen to Nate. He's been through so much to get here that he can't blow it all because of one bad day. But looking around, she can see a lot of items he could use to kill himself, and it's then that she knows she'll be staying in his room tonight.

Madison figures all she can do is keep Nate talking, but that's harder than she expected. He's buried himself under the comforter, in just his jeans, and keeps telling her to get out of his room.

As much as she'd love a night on her own in a comfortable, if somewhat flowery, hotel, she's not going to do that. She's sitting on the bed next to him, feet up and leaning her back against the headboard, with the TV on, hoping it will provide a distraction from whatever's going on in his head. "Tell me about how you got out."

He doesn't respond. He's eerily still and silent. She shakes his bare shoulder. "Nate? Tell me how you got off death row."

She hears his muffled voice under the cover. "Thought you googled me."

"I did, but I want to hear it from you. Who was Kristen?"

"For fuck's sake." He slides out of the bed and storms into the bathroom, slamming the door behind him.

She gives him a few minutes but listens to make sure he's just using the toilet or washing his face. Suddenly she hears him rifling through the drawers in there. He's looking for something.

She jumps off the bed and pushes the door open without knocking. He's got four lines of white powder lined up and is about to use a twenty-dollar bill to snort it. She pulls him away by his arm, but he pushes her into the bath. Her fall is softened by the shower curtain taking some of her weight, but she's still shocked. She scrambles out of the tub and slaps him hard across the face.

"Is this how you want to live?" she screams. "As a junkie? Is this what you waited all those years for: to waste what's left of your life?"

He doesn't react. His eyes don't even acknowledge that she's standing in front of him. He turns around and rolls up the twenty, so she squeezes between him and the coke and puts her hands on his shoulders. "Nate, you don't understand. I'm relying on you. You're literally all I have right now, and if you turn to drugs and end up OD'ing, I'm fucked."

He seems to hear her this time. With a patience that's clearly hard for him to manage, he takes her hands off him and leans in close. "Madison, it's you who doesn't understand. Coke helps me when I'm like this. Nothing else works. It brings me out of it. I can't explain it and I know how insane it sounds, but it's true. I need this to function. And you need to get out of my way."

His eyes are imploring her and she realizes he knows what he's doing. This isn't a random coke binge to numb his pain. He's obviously been using for a while now. She can't help but feel disappointed for him. When she first met him, she thought he was so put-together, so strong for dealing with life on death row. Now that she knows he needs a crutch, she doesn't respect him less; she just feels sorry for him. He'll never get off coke. Not while he's using it to repress his emotions.

She walks out of the bathroom, closing the door behind her.

CHAPTER FIFTY-THREE

Madison pulls her sweaty clothes off and slips into the bathtub. The hot water is instantly soothing but the tears still fall, from frustration more than anything else.

"How the fuck did I get here?" she mumbles, rubbing her eyes.

She expected to be back in Colorado by now, so it's difficult playing second fiddle to Nate when she has more pressing issues to attend to. She inhales the last of her cigarette before dropping the butt into the toilet next to the bath. Wetting a hand towel from the bundle in her room, she spreads it across her face, hoping the steam will fix the breakouts she's been prone to lately.

She thinks about Stephanie. She hopes she took her advice and spoke to Mike for reassurance. Madison is confident that Mike would agree to check in on Steph. He was one of the good guys in her police department. A sharp feeling of guilt washes over her for the situation her ex is in. She thinks she knows who's behind the heavies. And they're going to get the surprise of their life when she turns up in Lost Creek after all these years.

Nate's banging around in the adjacent bathroom and she wonders what he's up to. Working with him is hard because he wants to do everything his own way. She's used to having a uniformed partner to work with, someone on the same level as her, but it's clear Nate's controlling this investigation. It was good of him to take her on, but what's the point if she gets no say in anything? He should be using her police experience to help him find Jennifer Lucas.

Her thoughts turn to the girl's family. Something is bothering her. It's unusual for the family of a missing child to hire a PI. Especially for a grandparent to take the lead. Grant seemed in control of the household and didn't want to even consider the fact that his daughter might be dead. And Esme had gone ahead and hired investigators against his wishes, so there's a disconnect there. Anna seemed a little downtrodden and aloof. Perhaps Grant is domineering in that relationship. She was pretty quiet for a woman with a daughter missing. There were no emotional outbursts and no condemnation of the police investigation. She almost looked resigned to the fact that they'd never see Jenny again.

Removing the towel, Madison sighs. "Why do I even care?"

But she does care. Police work keeps her distracted from thinking about her son. About what kind of life he must have had without her.

She sits up. With damp hands she pulls another cigarette from its packet as she listens to Nate snorting coke on the other side of the wall.

CHAPTER FIFTY-FOUR

The long night passes achingly slowly for Nate. He's had time to dwell on a whole range of different regrets.

He knows he was out of line pushing Madison and he doesn't want to think about what would've happened if she'd bashed her head on the tiles going down. Rubbing his temples, he tries to stop thinking about it, because the shame is burning his face. He doesn't expect her to stick around now she knows he's not as perfect as she seemed to think. It's probably just as well, as he's not always easy to be with.

He spends most of the night thinking about Kristen, which just makes things worse. He's had to consume another four lines of coke to stop her face appearing every five minutes. Now he's on the inevitable come-down, which he's not ready for as it could mean the end of him when he's in this state. He's only just hung on overnight. As soon as the morning finally comes, he snorts one more line to help regulate his mood, then lies on the bed and lets it take effect. It makes him crave more, but he's learned to wait that feeling out until it passes. His body is buzzing with fake energy, but he ignores that too.

After thirty minutes, there's a knock at his door. He crosses the room and opens it. Madison looks nervous.

"Come on in." He moves to one side and searches for a clean T-shirt from his holdall.

"How are you this morning?" She doesn't step far into his room.

"Madison, I owe you an apology, and even that's not enough. I'm an asshole. I guess it's best you find that out sooner rather than later, but I'm still sorry for last night. If you want to part ways now, I'll understand. You have your own problems and I'll probably just make things worse."

She leans in and hugs him, which takes him by surprise. His face is sore from where she slapped him last night, and he was expecting the same thing again. Her hair smells of fruity shampoo and she's warm, but he's not good with hugs. He went so long without them that they feel strange, too intimate. He tries to pull away, but she keeps hold of him. It makes him feel panicked, but he contains it. He can smell cigarettes on her and realizes she's probably been smoking because of his behavior last night.

Finally she lets go. "Apology accepted." She smiles. "I don't warm to many people anymore, Nate, but I like you. I'm starting to care about you. But if you ever push me again, I'll shoot you."

He thinks she's joking, but she flashes her weapon. He hadn't realized she was armed.

"I won't." He pulls his T-shirt on. "But to make sure, don't get too close to me when I'm in that mood. It's like someone else takes over and all I can do is stand aside and watch the asshole ruin everything. He's not a good part of me and I haven't learnt how to contain him yet."

She nods as if she understands. Maybe she does. "Breakfast is being served. Come on."

Nate's stomach flips with the mention of food, making him slightly nauseous, but he follows her downstairs to a small room set out with tables and chairs. It reminds him of his grandmother's house, with dolls and paintings everywhere. There's a Jack Russell perched in the window, growling softly at each passing car.

Madison looks up at the petite woman who approaches them. So far, they're the only people in the room, and Nate wonders how many guests this place gets.

As the woman fills their cups with coffee, she asks, "Is this your husband?"

Madison quickly nods and Nate wonders what she's told her. "Yes, this is Nate. Nate, this is Mary."

"Nice place you have here," he says.

"I heard a bit of a commotion last night. Is everything okay?"

"Oh yeah, sorry." He smiles at her apologetically. "I'm such a klutz; I fell over in the bathroom. Nothing to worry about."

Mary looks horrified, like she's assessing whether they'll sue her.

"I didn't even bruise myself, so don't worry about it."

She looks relieved. "Two breakfasts coming right up."

They both pull out their cell phones and sit in silence. Nate sends Esme a quick update by text and says he'll call her later. He has the unenviable task of telling her they've been kicked off the camp because of the way he approached Donna's situation. She won't be happy and he doesn't blame her. Their leads have dried up and even he's not sure which direction to look in next.

He spots an email from Rex, which he reads whilst drinking his coffee.

The Lucas family are financially stable, with just the usual home loan and credit cards. But get this: I checked in with my contact in child services, and the girl—Jennifer—was adopted. Don't know if that changes anything, but thought I should let you know in case they haven't mentioned it. My contact couldn't get access to her full CPS record, so I don't know what her background is; who the biological parents were and why they gave her up. You'd have to ask the parents about that. Neither of them has any convictions.

He looks up. "Jenny's adopted."

Madison puts her phone down. She looks surprised. "Really? They never said."

"Is it relevant?"

She appears to think about it. "I guess not. It could mean they're infertile and they adopted because they wanted a child so badly. That can only be a good thing."

Nate thinks about the alternative. "What if her biological parents didn't want to give her up? What if she was taken off them by child services against their will? Maybe they were drug addicts, or the mother was really young. It could be that the parents wanted their daughter back."

She realizes what he's saying and starts nodding her head. "Maybe they've been looking for her, and when they finally found her, they took their opportunity."

"Summer camp would certainly be a good opportunity," says Nate. "No one there really knows what's going on. I mean, it's not exactly professional."

Mary places their cooked breakfasts in front of them and Nate can tell just by looking at his plate that all he'll be able to manage is the charred bacon, and only because it's just like the bacon they served in prison. He smiles up at her. "Thanks."

Madison eats fast and he wishes he had her appetite. He feels drained from the drugs and the depression, but he's glad it was a short episode this time. Sometimes they last weeks, so he knows he got off lightly. Maybe having Madison around helped. He forces himself to eat both rashers of bacon and is surprised when his appetite picks up. He eats the eggs next.

Just as he is about to speak, a woman walks into the room. He recognizes her, but because he wasn't expecting to see her here, it takes him a second to place her. Madison turns to see what he's looking at. The woman spots them and lowers her eyes.

"Mrs. Lucas?" says Nate, standing. "What are you doing up here?"

Anna reluctantly walks toward him. She tries to smile, but it looks pained. "Hi. We decided we needed to be here. It was too painful waiting at home for news." She breaks off and starts sobbing.

Nate leads her to their table and she takes a seat. They wait patiently while she composes herself.

"I can't believe I'm saying this, but Esme passed away on the drive up here." She looks at Nate. "The stress of it all killed her."

He and Madison share a look.

"I'm so sorry to hear that." Madison gets out of her chair and rubs Anna's back as she cries.

Nate is stunned, but he's also wondering where this leaves him. It was Esme who hired him, and against the parents' wishes. Is this where his involvement ends? Kristen's face flashes before him again. He wonders if his subconscious is telling him it's time to stop looking for other people's missing loved ones and start looking for his own.

CHAPTER FIFTY-FIVE

It's New Year. Nate's last year alive. His execution date is set for December 6, 2017. He'll be thirty-eight years old when he dies. Now that January has come, he can think of nothing else other than the death chamber at the Huntsville Unit. He's seen seven men go before him and he was deeply affected by all but one of their deaths. It's been difficult to defend his religion. The Bible says an eye for an eye, but Nate knows that even after what they've been convicted of, that way of thinking is too simplistic. He can't reconcile it with these men's lives.

He finds himself thinking about all the things he'll never do again: celebrate another Christmas, speak to a family member, spend time in the presence of children, laugh uncontrollably at something hilarious… The list is endless and overwhelming.

If he listened to Kristen, it would be easy to believe he would do all those things again. Some days he resents her for giving him false hope. Today is one of those days. As Gus leads him to the small interview room and shackles his hands to the table, he doesn't want to look at her. He's about to blow a fuse with all the anger inside him.

She reaches across the table and takes his hands. He tries to pull away, but he can't because of the cuffs.

She lets go and sits back. "Nate, what's the matter? Is it a bad day?"

He looks up at her enquiring face and shakes his head. "How many cases have you got right now?"

She looks confused. "What do you mean?"

"How many men are you trying to get out of prison? Because I know it's not just me."

He's taking a gamble, but Jordie, one of his death row neighbors, who has exhausted all his appeals and is set to be executed the week before Nate, told him she's probably visiting and falsely reassuring other prisoners, not just him. It made him feel catastrophically stupid. He'd naïvely assumed it was just him. It's hard to see the truth in here sometimes, because you become less sharp and more introspective.

She looks wary. "I visit four other men. They're in general population but still convicted of murder. They're all serving life without parole."

Nate shakes his head. He feels sick. "Do you feed them the same lines as me? Do you tell all of them that you want them to get out so they can take you to Paris?"

Tears well in her eyes but she ignores them defiantly. "No, Nate. My job involves teaching analytical skills to student lawyers. They choose cases where they think someone has been unlawfully convicted and I help them untangle the webs. My students visit the other guys more than I do. I always choose to visit you. I thought you knew what you mean to me. I can't fake that. I wouldn't. I'm not stupid; I know how dangerous it is to give anyone in here false hope."

He doesn't know whether to believe her. "I read a study in a law text that examined why women write to and sometimes marry men on death row. Do you know what it concluded?"

She looks down. "It doesn't matter what a bunch of academics with no life experience concluded. I only know how I feel."

He continues. "It concluded that women are drawn to men in prison, especially men serving long sentences, because it's a way of having a safe relationship. They get to speak to their man every day if he's in general pop. They always know where he is, that he can't cheat on them. And they do it knowing they'll never have to have sex with him. They have complete control over the relationship, unlike real-life relationships on the outside." He knows he's being an asshole, but it's hard to control it when he feels like this.

She wipes her eyes and opens a file, pulling out some paperwork. "I came to give you good news. The Texas Court of Criminal Appeals has agreed we can submit the hammer used to kill Stacey for new DNA testing. If they find someone else's blood on it, as we suspect they will, you could get a new trial."

Nate is floored. He wasn't expecting her to say that. "What?"

"We know your fingerprints were on the hammer because you were using it to fix up the house for Stacey's mom, but there's no reason for anyone else's blood to be on it apart from Stacey's. The court records show that the tests carried out by the prosecution at the time couldn't confirm who the secondary blood belonged to, so the prosecution poisoned the jury's minds with the thought that it had to be yours. I've read the transcripts; I know how they got away with whatever they wanted to during your trial. It's shocking, but now that DNA testing has advanced, we can hope to rule your blood out. Without that, there's no forensic evidence to prove you were the killer and therefore no reason to keep you locked up."

She pauses. "However, it is a reason to find Father Connor and get him tested to see if the blood matches. This is the first break we've had in your case and it's an important one. I've had someone completely exonerated by this judge before. They didn't even need a retrial."

She sits back in her chair and folds her arms. "So do you want me to keep pushing, or have you given up? Because I haven't, Nate. No matter what tricks your mind is playing on you."

Nate doesn't cry often, it's a red rag to a bull in here, but he holds his hands open and breaks down when Kristen encloses them with hers. They're not allowed to kiss or hug but he gains strength from her touch. For the first time in over a decade, he dares to hope that there's a way out of here that doesn't involve a coffin.

CHAPTER FIFTY-SIX

Anna leads the investigators to her room. She's staying on the floor above them and only arrived in Shadow Falls late last night. She had no idea they were staying here, but now she thinks about it, it is the only guest house or hotel she could find, so it should've been obvious.

She sits on her bed while Madison chooses the chair at the vanity and Nate Monroe stands. They're not going to like what she has to say.

"Now that Esme is no longer with us, Grant and I would like to settle your bill. We won't be needing your services anymore."

Nate doesn't look surprised. "Are you sure?"

"Yes. Grant has gone home to Santa Barbara to make arrangements for Esme's funeral. If he were here, he would tell you we both appreciate your efforts, but I expect Esme told you we weren't keen on the idea of a private investigator to begin with."

Nate nods. "I can understand why that might be uncomfortable for you, after having spent the last couple of weeks dealing with cops."

"It wasn't just that. I actually found Ted—Detective Morgan—to be friendly and professional, and we really believe he's doing whatever he can to find Jennifer. We didn't want to upset him and risk the relationship turning sour. I didn't see—in fact I still don't—how a private investigator can do any more than an entire police force. You'll have to excuse my ignorance; I'm not used to being in this situation."

Nate smiles sadly, not even attempting to justify his role, which she appreciates. She doesn't need a lecture about how investigators are better than the police. Madison is just staring at her.

"If you've learned anything you think will be helpful in our search for Jennifer, please let me know, but otherwise you're free to return home."

Nate appears to think about it. "There's something I learned today that we were discussing before you showed up."

Anna's stomach flutters. She doesn't know if she can handle any revelations after the last twenty-four hours. "What's that?"

"Am I right in thinking Jenny was adopted?"

She can't hide her despair; she stands up. How did they find out about that? They're going to assume she didn't love Jennifer because she's not her real mother.

"I'm sorry," Nate says, stepping forward. "I didn't mean to upset you."

She takes a deep breath and smiles weakly. "No, it's okay. It's just… well, we don't tell many people, because other mothers can be…" She pauses. "Other women can look down on you when they find out you're not someone's biological mother."

Madison shakes her head. "In my eyes you're better than a biological mother. It needs a lot of strength to take on someone else's child. I don't think people realize how much harder it can be to care for someone who has been taken away from their biological parents."

Anna looks at her but can't find any words. She's never had anyone say that to her before.

"It's actually a possible motive for Jenny's disappearance," says Nate.

She looks at him, shocked at what he's insinuating. "What?" she whispers.

"Well, if Jenny's biological parents decided they wanted their daughter back, they could've come to get her. If they managed to track her down and were waiting for the perfect time to grab her, summer camp would be that time."

She thinks about it. "I guess you're right."

"Do you know anything about her biological parents? Or about why she was taken into care in the first place?" asks Madison.

Anna thinks of the horrendous reports she'd had to read as part of the adoption process. Jennifer's file contained all the reasons she was taken away from her birth mother. It made her cry for weeks thinking what that poor baby had gone through.

She shakes her head. "I only know her parents didn't want her. I think they were too young or something. It doesn't matter to us, it never did. She's our child. No one else's."

"Of course," says Nate. "So what will you do now you're here?"

She thinks about what she and Grant agreed. "I'm going to check in with Detective Morgan for an update and then head home. Grant and I can't do anything useful up here." She pauses and then adds quietly, "Plus, we need to bury Esme. Grant has a family plot in Santa Barbara."

No one says anything for a while until she moves forward and holds out her hand. "Well, thank you for your time."

Nate shakes it first. "Can I get your contact details so I know where to send my invoice?"

She turns to the complimentary notepad by the bed and writes down her email address.

He takes it from her and glances at it. "Can I have your cell number too? In case any of the leads I'm chasing come up with something after we leave town."

She hesitates. She really doesn't want to have to speak to him again. She takes the piece of paper back and adds her number. She can hardly say no.

"Thanks," he says. Then, "I'm sorry for your predicament. Esme was clearly besotted with Jenny and I just wish we could've found her before she passed. I wish you luck for the future and I hope she's found soon."

Madison nods in agreement, but Anna notices she doesn't have the look of pity in her eyes that everyone else has.

She waits until they're gone before locking her door. Then she lies on the large bed and breaks down.

CHAPTER FIFTY-SEVEN

Nate and Madison go back to his room to talk about what just happened. Nate closes the door behind them. "Sad news about Esme," he says, walking to the nightstand. He plugs his phone in to charge.

"Stress is a killer," says Madison.

He's surprised and a little annoyed at her lack of compassion.

"So what now?" she says, hands on hips. "Colorado?"

He shakes his head. "No, Madison. We're not leaving."

"What? Why not? She's not going to keep paying us."

He sits on the bed and drinks some bottled water, trying to figure out if she's really as callous as she's coming across. "Don't you feel bad about Esme?"

She perches on the armchair by the window. "Of course I do. It's terrible what happened, and it couldn't have happened at a worse time. But we have no leads on the missing girl, Nate, and neither do the police. I don't see what else we can do if the family don't want us here. Unless your guy has told you something?"

He shakes his head again. "No. Rex looked into the family for me, but they seem clean. No bad debt or prior convictions."

"You know, if this were my investigation, I'd be interviewing them both separately at the police station. There's just something off about them."

He looks at her. "Like what?" Nate knows the police always suspect the immediate family before anyone else.

"I'm not sure yet. We've not spent enough time with them. But have you noticed how Anna only refers to her daughter as Jennifer, not Jenny or Jen?"

He hadn't. "Why's that important?"

"It's just so formal. Almost like she's distancing herself from the girl. I noticed it when we first met them and dismissed it as her being stressed. But she was calling her Jennifer just now too. It lacks any affection. When you have kids, you tend to shorten their names or use nicknames." She frowns. "I just think that if you're serious about finishing what we've started, we need to secure the trust of either Anna or Grant. We need to know what Jenny was really like, because I feel like we're getting mixed messages. The problem is, neither of them would be open to that. They seem to want to get rid of us as fast as possible now Esme's gone."

He nods. He doubts either of them had anything to do with their daughter's disappearance, but they could be covering for someone, perhaps another family member. "I didn't suspect they were involved, but now I'm starting to wonder if they know more than they're letting on."

"Because of what I've said?" she asks.

"Not just that. But for some reason they haven't told us they're expecting another child."

Madison's mouth opens in shock. "What? She's pregnant?"

He nods. "I'm surprised you didn't notice yourself."

She rolls her eyes. "Why? Because I'm a woman? Believe it or not, we don't all start lactating when we're around pregnant women, Nate."

He laughs, which relieves some tension. "Okay, fair enough. When we first visited them in Santa Barbara, she was wearing a thick cashmere wrap even though it was a hot day."

"I noticed that, but I thought it was just for comfort. Cashmere can feel like having arms around you. If she wasn't getting enough comfort from her husband, she might've been seeking it elsewhere."

"Maybe. But I saw a packet of pregnancy vitamins on her nightstand just now, so I naturally looked at her stomach, and although she's wearing a baggy shirt, I could see she had a bump underneath when she walked in front of the window. I'd say she's about five months gone."

Madison raises her eyebrows. "How did I not notice those vitamins?"

"Two reasons: first, they were behind something until she used the nightstand to write down her contact details; and second, you're too distracted by your own case. You're clearly ready to get out of here and it's stopping you from fully immersing yourself in this investigation."

She looks annoyed. "Don't be stupid."

"I'm being serious. I can tell you don't want to be here and I understand you want to find out who framed you as soon as possible, but to Esme, this job was just as serious."

"It's my ex." She sighs. "She's having problems with people looking for me. I'm worried they're going to hurt her."

He's glad she's finally opening up to him. "Would the local police help, or are they all untrustworthy?"

"There's probably one good guy she could rely on. I told her to call him if they come back and intimidate her, but I don't know if she will."

"Then you should give him the heads-up. And she needs to move house asap."

Madison nods and takes a deep breath. "I know, I know. She won't move, she's stubborn. And I've been putting off calling him because of everything that happened."

He stands up and walks over to her. "Madison? Come on. Aren't alarm bells ringing in your head right now? Your ex-girlfriend is at serious risk and you're not alerting anyone. You might not be a cop anymore, but you need to protect her. You know better than her in this instance. Get on the phone. Now."

She thinks about it, then nods and leaves the room.

CHAPTER FIFTY-EIGHT

The seriousness of her situation hits Madison when Nate spells out what she already knows. She's the experienced cop; she should be doing more to protect Stephanie. She walks into her room, cell phone already making the call.

Infuriatingly, it rings out and the cell provider's recorded message kicks in.

"Steph, it's me. I just want to check you're okay. You need to move out of town for a while whether you like it or not. I wouldn't say this if I wasn't seriously worried for your safety. You know me, I don't scare easy. Call me when you get this."

She follows it up with a text.

Call me asap.

As she sits on her bed, she can hear Nate's shower come on. He's giving her space to do what she needs to do. She checks the time—it's nine a.m. in her home town. Mike should be at work. She enters his cell number from memory. Some things are ingrained forever. He was her sergeant before she was promoted to detective, but she hasn't spoken to him for seven years. Will he even still use this number? Before she can think about his reaction too much, she hits the call button. He won't recognize her new number, so she'll be taking him by surprise.

After just two rings, he answers. "Detective Bowers."

Detective? She bristles. So while she was incarcerated, he was promoted. How nice for him. "Mike? It's me." She pauses. "Madison."

Silence. Just as she's about to hang up, he speaks. "Well fuck me sideways, Madison. I never thought I'd hear from you again. How are you?"

She lets out her breath, relieved that he's talking to her. "I'm not as bad as you probably think. I'm doing okay. How about you?"

She can hear him close a door. He's probably moved to an empty interview room to take the call in private. At least she hopes he has. The other alternative is that he's put her on loudspeaker for the whole department to listen. She just doesn't know how well she can trust him, so she's going to have to move slowly.

"I'm good," he says. "What are you doing now? Where are you?"

She's not going to tell him the answer to those questions. Not yet, anyway. "I'm not in Colorado, which is why I'm calling. I'm worried about Stephanie."

Mike knows Steph. Lost Creek is small, so everyone knows each other.

"Why? What's happened?"

The concern in his voice makes her feel better about calling him. "She's getting visitors at the house. Heavies. They're looking for me and they think she knows where I am, but she doesn't. Mike, I'm worried they're going to hurt her."

She hears him click a pen. "Who are they? Do we have names?"

"No. She described them as two tall white men, one verging on obesity, a typical heavy. They've visited her three times now, and each time they're a little harder to get rid of."

"Has she reported them to anyone?"

Madison almost laughs. "Are you kidding? After everything that happened to me? She doesn't trust the police, Mike. I'm sure you can understand that."

He doesn't reply.

"Would you do me a favor and stop by the house to check on her? I think it would reassure her to see you, and then she'll be more likely to call you if she needs help. I've told her to leave town for a while, but you know what she's like."

He grunts. "Sure do; she's stubborn like you. That's why you made a terrible couple."

Madison smiles to herself. They did make a terrible couple.

"Okay," he says. "I can do that."

"Thanks, I appreciate it." She feels the tension in her shoulders ease. "I know you don't owe me any favors, but it's nice to know not everyone's against me."

He sighs down the line. "I've never told you this, Madison, what with everything happening so fast after your arrest, but I'm sorry about what happened. Not everyone believed you were guilty."

She tries to hide her surprise. "I wish someone had spoken up and said that at the time. Especially to the press. I might have had a different outcome."

He doesn't reply, and she knows she has to hold back the old anger that's threatening to rise. She needs him while she can't be in Colorado herself.

"Do me one more favor and drop me a text to let me know when you've seen her, would you? Just to put my mind at rest. She might not tell me herself."

"Sure."

"Thanks." She almost hangs up, but finds herself saying, "Mike? Do you know where Owen is?"

He doesn't respond.

"Mike? I want to find my son. Have you heard anything about what happened to him after my incarceration?"

"What did CPS tell you?" He sounds wary, like he's choosing his words carefully.

"They said he was adopted by someone but they're not allowed to tell me who. Have you seen him since then?"

"No. I haven't. He's not here; I would've seen him. Just be thankful he was adopted and not put into a children's home. He got a better chance at life than those kids."

She wants to scream at him that Owen's best chance at life was with his mother, but Mike won't understand. He probably doesn't even care.

"Stay in touch," he says. "It's good to hear your voice."

"Maybe." She ends the call. Her hands are shaking. She just dived back into her old life and it was hard. If she's finding it difficult to do that over the phone, she can only imagine how much tougher it will be to go there in person.

CHAPTER FIFTY-NINE

The office of Dr. Pamela Jarvis

It's mid afternoon and Pamela has been told by her boss to hurry up. She keeps reading the journal, but she's mentally exhausted from thinking about all the possible repercussions of this inevitably being made public. She tries to focus on the words in front of her.

No one can see me standing on the beach, screaming into the waves. The waves that tempt me every night with their steady rise and fall. Several times I've walked in up to my chest and waited for the tide to pull me away, to take me to my babies. But it never did.

I've discovered something today and it's made my decision inevitable. I know what I'm going to do. For the first time since the accident, I feel a sense of peace. Something I never dared to hope would ever happen. The lightness that comes from knowing my pain will soon be over is elevating. I'm making plans; I'm actually looking forward to something. Then I remember it's not over yet and things could still go wrong.

My choice should be easy, but it's not. If it were just up to me it would be, but it's going to affect other people and they won't understand. As soon as I felt the familiar butterflies in my stomach, I knew there wasn't really a choice to make. I can't risk losing another child; I just couldn't bear it. I can't carry another child for nine months, love it for years until my abuser decides it's time for this baby to die too, because that would almost certainly happen. I just know it. The worst part would be not knowing when. Not knowing how many years I'd get with my child.

I worry about the new baby. Will he or she consume the turmoil I've been living in and be born evil, as some kind of punishment for what I'm about to do? I've decided it's a risk I have to take, as otherwise there will be no one left at the end of all this.

Pamela closes the journal before reaching the final few entries. It's time to put all this into some kind of context. She reaches for the report.

CHAPTER SIXTY

Nate's driving them to the camp, but he can tell Madison's not entirely happy with his decision to keep going with their investigation.

"What's the point?" she says. "It's not like we're welcome there. You said Donna told you to leave the premises, and Jenny's parents have fired us. I don't understand what good we can do when we're shut out of all possible angles. We could be on the road to Colorado instead."

He looks across at her. "Think about it for a second. Anna's pregnant. Neither she nor Grant told us about it. They also didn't tell us Jenny was adopted. What else are they hiding? I mean, why would you not tell anyone that?"

She turns away from him and they drive in silence for a few miles, watching the never-ending forest pass them. The heat is back today and there's not a single cloud in the sky to provide shade from the relentless sunshine. Nate's arms are burning just resting on his steering wheel, and it's still only mid morning. He turns the A/C up a notch.

"It's probably just superstition," says Madison. "She might have miscarried in the past. Not volunteering either of those things isn't a crime. It's actually none of our business."

He's not so sure. "It's bothering me. I wonder if Detective Morgan knows. He would probably come to the same conclusion as us and start looking for the biological parents. I think we should tell him, in case the Lucases didn't."

"So why are we headed to the camp?"

"Because when I called the police department earlier, I was told he's up there. Apparently he has a team searching the lake again. Maybe he's had a new lead."

She leans back in her seat. "You're not going to let this go until we find her, are you?"

He smiles across at her. "No. I like to finish what I start. Unless someone threatens to arrest me, in which case I'm outta here."

He drives a little faster.

Nate parks next to the detective's car, choosing a spot in the shade. He looks across at the lake. There's a team of divers bobbing up and down. A crowd of children is watching.

"Morgan should have instructed the counselors to move those kids away," says Madison. "If they're there when the divers pull Jenny's body from the water, they'll be traumatized for life."

They both get out of the car, and suddenly Brody appears. He seems pleased to see Nate and is practically throwing himself against him. Nate kneels down and gives the dog some attention.

"Hey, boy. Miss me?"

When he's satisfied, Brody runs off toward the lake, into some bushes on the edge of the water. Detective Morgan is standing there with his shades on, jacket off and sleeves rolled up. He watches Nate and Madison approach.

"It must be my lucky day," he says. "I thought the family asked you to back off."

Nate feels a hint of irritation. Anna must've called Morgan before they even left the guest house. "I wanted to tie up some loose ends before we go."

"You can't leave yet anyway," says Morgan. "I'm still waiting for your DNA samples and signed statements for the Josh Sanders investigation."

Madison laughs sarcastically. They all know it's not going to happen. "Did you interview Josh about what we found at his house?"

"I did. After consulting a lawyer, he gave us the password for those folders on his laptop." Morgan looks at them both. "It was as he'd said: adult women, consensual sex. We're still checking the other laptops, but he's not a suspect in Jennifer's disappearance."

Kat walks over to them. "Hey, Nate. Sorry for hitting you yesterday." She looks miserable. Probably still pining after her dick of a boyfriend.

"Forget about it. Where's everyone else? It seems pretty quiet around here."

She looks around. "Yeah, some of the other counselors have already left now they know we're closing next week. It always happens near the end of summer too. They move home ready for college or they get another job before anyone else can apply. It's depressing being one of the last staff standing."

Nate leans in and speaks quietly into her ear. "Why don't you get the kids away from here for a while? If the cops find Jenny in there, it's not going to be a pretty sight."

She looks at him, alarmed. "Good idea." She turns away and starts to round up the children. "Come on, everyone. It's time to clean your bunks and tidy camp ready for going home next week."

They groan in unison but follow her, a few of the boys looking back over their shoulders as they walk away.

Madison's watching them. "They might think they want to see what a real dead body looks like, but it's nothing like on TV. I've attended a drowning. The boy was in the water for three weeks and the smell made me sick. I couldn't eat without gagging for days. And I haven't eaten fish since."

Nate looks across at her. He's beginning to realize police officers have it tougher than he's ever considered.

Brody's watching the divers in the lake with interest, sniffing the air in front of him. Nate wonders if their movement in the water is releasing some kind of smell from a potential cadaver.

He turns to the detective. "Did you find anything related to Jenny Lucas in Josh's house?"

Morgan looks irritated, and not just because he's being eaten alive by bugs. "I think I've told you enough, Monroe. Your interest in this case needs to end."

"I thought you wanted us all to work together?"

He smiles. "Yeah, well. That was for Esme Lucas's sake, and unfortunately she's no longer with us. This is official police business and I'm under no obligation to share any more details with you than I would with a reporter."

So he knows about Esme too.

"Did you know Mrs. Lucas is pregnant?"

Morgan isn't able to hide his surprise. He looks at Nate and hesitates before responding. "Did she tell you that?"

"No. I figured it out for myself. Did you also know Jenny is adopted?"

His face gives away more surprise, but it's difficult to tell if it's a reaction to the news itself or to the fact that Nate has found out about it. He doesn't say anything.

"I just came here to let you know, in case it affects your investigation," Nate adds. "I'm sure you'll eventually put two and two together and realize she may have been taken by her biological parents, if they're still alive. Especially if they didn't voluntarily give her up in the first place."

"I've already checked them out," says Morgan. "They're not involved."

Nate can't tell if he's lying. He hears a car pulling up to the graveled parking lot and turns around at the same time as Madison. It's Anna Lucas. When she spots them, she doesn't get out of the car.

She doesn't move; she just stares. Nate turns to Morgan, who has gone a shade paler at the sight of her. He raises his hand in greeting.

At last Anna opens the car door and steps out. As she turns to lock it, Brody suddenly shoots past them and runs toward her, barking intensely. Before he reaches her, he sits and looks back over his shoulder at Nate. Nate doesn't know what the problem is.

"Get away from me!" shouts Anna with wide eyes. "Someone get him away from me, he bites!"

Before anyone can move, she starts walking around the car and away from the dog. Brody follows and jumps up at her. Both Morgan and Madison stare in shock as he grabs her arm in his jaws and starts pulling her down to the ground. It looks aggressive, but Nate knows police dogs are trained to keep hold of the arm. This isn't a random attack. Still, he runs over there as fast as he can.

"Brody, no! Cease! Stop!"

The dog immediately releases Anna's arm, leaving her on the ground, shaken. Although she's wearing a shirt, he can see blood starting to seep through the sleeve.

"Madison! Get her into the office," he yells. "See if they've got a first aid kit."

Madison runs up behind him and pulls Anna up from the grass. She leads her to the office while Nate holds onto Brody's collar. The dog is growling, but quietly and controlled. Nate doesn't like it.

"What the fuck was that?" says Morgan as he approaches. "I'm going to have that dog put down. He should *not* be around kids. Hell, he shouldn't be around anyone. He's dangerous!"

Nate doesn't disagree. He thinks Brody could be suffering with some kind of PTSD from his time on the force. He should not have reacted like that here. He wonders if it's because Anna's pregnant. He's heard of dogs acting aggressively around pregnant women.

Morgan is about to grab Brody, but the dog gives a warning growl that even Nate wants to back away from. "Let me take him for now," he says, opening the back door of his car. The dog whines when he realizes what's going on. "Come on, boy." Nate pats the back seat. "We'll just go for a ride."

"He's not going to listen to you. He's an animal. A dangerous one. I want him put to sleep."

Brody jumps onto the back seat, so Nate opens the windows and closes the door. Brody sits alert, looking toward the office cabin. Waiting.

CHAPTER SIXTY-ONE

Nate's leaning against his car, waiting for Madison to finish in the office, when one of the divers blows his whistle.

"We've got something!"

He and Morgan both spin around to face the lake. The sun is bouncing off the water, making Nate squint as he watches the divers. He wonders if this is it; if Jenny was down there all along, just as Josh predicted.

"What is it?" shouts Morgan.

"A number of bones," replies the diver. "All located in the same area."

Nate looks over at the detective. He's sweating and looks uneasy, pulling a tissue out to wipe his face.

"Copy that." Morgan sighs. "Bring them in."

While the divers do their work, Nate goes to check on Anna and Madison. He expected Morgan to do it, seeing as he has to deliver the bad news about remains being found, but the detective stays lakeside, shouting orders. Brody is still watching everyone. He's jumped out of the Jeep's window and is lying next to the car, out of the sun. He's more relaxed now, but he hasn't taken his eyes off the office. Nate has no idea what he's going to do with the dog. If he lets Morgan have his way, Brody will be toast.

As he walks into the office, both women look up at him. Donna's nowhere to be seen, and he wonders if she's just given up on this place like the rest of the staff. He can see that Anna has been crying, and Madison has managed to wrap her bleeding arm in a bandage.

"I've told her she needs to get checked out at the hospital," says Madison. "But she won't go."

Nate approaches them. "Mrs. Lucas, the dog could be carrying a disease that could harm your baby."

She looks up at him with shock and mistrust in her eyes. "What do you mean?"

"Well let's face it, he probably hasn't been vaccinated for a couple of years and he lives in a forest. He could've picked up anything from the wild animals around here."

"No, not that. I mean how did you know I was pregnant?"

He leans against the wall. "I saw your vitamins, and your bump. What are you, about five months?"

She looks down and cradles her injured arm to her chest. "Seven months. I should be showing more by now but I'm struggling to eat because of all the stress. This baby is going to be small."

Madison puts a hand on her shoulder. "That's understandable. I can't imagine what it's like to be pregnant when your child is missing. You can't do anything to protect Jenny right now, but you can protect your baby. Seriously, Anna, let us take you to the hospital. They'll probably just give you a few shots, clean up the wound and then you'll be good to go."

Anna suddenly clutches her stomach and winces in pain.

"What is it?" asks Nate.

"Oh my God, I feel like I'm being stabbed!"

Madison looks across at him and silently mouths, "Contractions?"

"Shit." He thinks about the remains being pulled from the lake. If Anna finds out, it could make her even more stressed, putting the baby in danger. As she leans forward on the chair, cradling her bump, he pulls Madison to one side and whispers into her ear. "They're pulling up bones from the lake right now."

Her eyes widen and she puts her hand to her mouth.

"She can't know. It won't help her and could make her condition worse," he says. "Take her car and get her to the nearest hospital.

You'll need to hustle her past before she realizes what the divers are doing."

Madison nods, but before she can move, the door to the cabin opens and Kat enters, looking tearful. She must know what they're doing out there. Before she can speak, Madison asks her where the nearest hospital is, just as Anna screams in pain.

"Oh my God, is she okay?"

"Kat, listen to me!" Madison says, trying to get her attention. "Can you come with us? You need to direct me to the hospital," she lowers her voice to a whisper, "or this woman could lose her baby."

Kat seems to understand that time is of the essence. "Sure, let's go." She holds the door open as Madison leads a wincing Anna outside.

Nate jogs ahead of them to grab Brody by his collar. Once the women are safely in Anna's car, he returns to Morgan. "Mrs. Lucas is having stomach pains, possible contractions, so Madison's taking her to the hospital. Don't tell her what they're doing." He nods to the divers, who are approaching the shore with a plastic tarp drifting behind them.

Morgan looks over at the women, who are slipping their seat belts on. He makes a move to approach them, but Nate steps in front of him. "Let them go. She can't lose another child."

The detective looks defeated, like everything that's happening is out of his control. As they watch the women drive away, Brody barks loudly.

CHAPTER SIXTY-TWO

Grant arrives home in Santa Barbara to an empty house. Of course it's empty: his mother is lying in a mortuary far from home, his daughter's dead in a ditch somewhere, and his wife has probably left him.

He throws his keys onto the table by the door and collapses on their white leather couch. His phone is constantly buzzing with messages and missed calls. He's numb to it all right now. He couldn't even begin to think about responding to work stuff, and he doesn't want to speak to his wife. Just thinking about Anna angers him. Without realizing what he's about to do, he thumps the glass coffee table in front of him with his fist. It cracks but doesn't shatter. He smiles wryly at the idea of them owning childproof safety glass.

He sits back, rubs his temples and tries hard not to scream. There's nothing left in his life that he cares about. He meant it when he told Anna that they're cursed. He just can't figure out whether it's him or her who brought them such bad luck.

An urge to be in Jenny's room overwhelms him. He wants to smell her pillow. He wants to sit amongst her childish belongings. With trembling legs—he hasn't eaten in twenty-four hours—he climbs the stairs. Jenny's door is closed. All kinds of images flash before his eyes as he looks at the door and imagines what's behind it. He reaches for the doorknob and slowly turns it. The blind is pulled down, blocking out the daylight. Jenny hated too much sunshine; she was sensitive to stuff like that. More than most kids. He knows she would have hated spending time outside at the summer camp.

He walks across to her small bed and sits down. He picks up a pillow and looks closely at it, trying to find anything of Jenny's; a stray hair from her head, maybe. But there's nothing. He holds it to his face and inhales. It smells of washing powder. Anna must've changed the sheets, because these covers are clean. His daughter hasn't been in them since she left for camp. Disappointment rises through his body and consumes him.

Racked with guilt, he realizes he has to read Anna's journal. He knows her therapist suggested she write down her feelings to help overcome her depression after the children died, but she's never invited him to read it. He knows where she keeps it because he spotted her through the bedroom window one day. She was opening the hatch to the swimming pool pump and he wondered what she was doing. When he realized she must be hiding her journal in there, he assumed she was writing to the children, pouring her heart out about missing them, so he didn't snoop.

But now, with nothing left to lose, he needs to know everything. Moving fast, before he can change his mind, he heads outside. The hatch to the pump is screwed on, but the two screws are easily loosened. The journal drops out in front of him. He sits on the ground and hesitates. Does he really want to know what Anna has been going through this last year? Her grief has been obvious to him, and this feels like prying. But he has unanswered questions.

As he starts to read through the pages of Anna's innermost thoughts, he's confronted with horrific answers, many of which he now realizes he would rather not have known about. More than once he gasps and stops reading, unable to continue through his sobs. This is worse than he ever expected. But one thing stands out: Jenny loved him. And Jenny needed him.

Once he has finished, he realizes with absolute certainty that it's all over for him and Anna. They can never recover from this. Not as a couple, and for him, not as an individual. His heart is broken. Numb, he stands up and enters the house, heading for his office. Finding an envelope big enough for the journal becomes a task in itself, making him angry enough to swipe everything else out of the way. He finally finds one and addresses it to Anna's therapist.

Then he grabs his handgun from the safe and leaves his house for the final time. After he drops the journal in at Dr. Jarvis's office, he'll be driving to Shadow Falls.

CHAPTER SIXTY-THREE

As Nate watches the divers bring bones and other unidentified objects to the shore, he keeps Brody subdued by stroking him. He can't understand why the dog went so crazy. He's more relaxed now and enjoying being petted. He drank a ton of water once the women had driven off, so maybe he was dehydrated, or hungry or something. Nate's considering whether to leave him be when he gets a call.

"Rex? How are you?"

"Hey, my man. How's things up there? Found the girl yet?"

Nate looks at the lake and takes a deep breath. "Possibly. Divers are pulling bones out of the lake as we speak."

"Holy shit. I'm sorry to hear that. I was hoping for a better outcome."

"Me too."

Rex clears his throat. "Do you know who might have put her there?"

"No. There are no obvious suspects and the family have fired me."

"No shit? What did you do to get fired?"

"Nothing. Esme Lucas passed away and her son and daughter-in-law no longer require my services. Said they don't want to upset the local police."

Rex sighs. "I'm sorry to hear about Esme. She seemed like a nice lady when I spoke to her."

"Yeah, it's sad that she didn't get to see her granddaughter come home."

Rex doesn't reply.

"What are you thinking?" asks Nate. Rex isn't often quiet.

"Well, this might be nothing, but I looked into that detective you told me about. Just confirm his name for me, would you?"

"Detective Ted Morgan, from Trinity Creek PD."

"Yep, yep. That's what I thought you said. Is he dark-haired, about five-ten, with brown eyes? Maybe mid thirties?"

Nate looks across at Morgan, who is examining the bones. That description fits him.

A coroner's van pulls up in the camp's parking lot, ready to transport the remains to the local mortuary.

"Yeah, that sounds about right."

"Hmm. How does he act around Jennifer's mother?"

Nate stands straight, pulling his hand away from Brody. He's taken aback by the question. "What do you mean?"

"Are they extra friendly? Seem like they know each other from before all this?"

Nate shakes his head. "No." Then he thinks about it. He realizes he's never actually seen them together. Brody attacked Anna before she reached them. Morgan didn't go inside to check on her. "Actually, I haven't witnessed them together. Why, Rex? What've you found?"

"Well, Ted's police record is clean as a whistle, so he's not obviously crooked, although we both know that could just mean he's not been caught doing anything."

Nate grunts in agreement.

"So I decided to look into his social media. He has a Facebook account that's completely locked down. But I also checked the social media pages of the Lucas family. Anna Lucas hasn't used her Facebook account for years, but she gets tagged in things all the time, so she came up on other people's pages. And one photo I found showed her from eight years ago—it was date-stamped—in a bar with a group of old college buddies. Looks like they had some kind of college reunion, because they're all wearing UCLA sweatshirts. Anyway, she's got her arms around a few girlfriends, and the last girlfriend has her arm around a guy. Ted Morgan. They were both tagged."

Nate's eyes widen and he looks back at Morgan. "They know each other from college?"

"It looks like it, unless they just happened to be in the same photo at the same time. That does happen. But they're both wearing college sweatshirts, and if it's a class reunion, it's likely they would've known of each other at least. Could've shared some classes."

"That's a good possibility."

Rex continues. "So I checked Anna's friend list, which she hasn't locked down, unlike Ted, and they're definitely Facebook friends. She ever mention to you that she knew him from way back?"

Nate thinks about his conversations with her. "No. All she said was that she didn't want an investigator looking into her daughter's disappearance because she was worried she'd upset the police. Maybe she didn't want to upset the police because they're friends and because of that Morgan would take offense at her not trusting him to find Jenny."

"Well you need to look into their relationship. Dig a little deeper. There's only so much I can do from behind a computer."

"Is he Facebook friends with Grant, too?"

"Negative. Grant isn't on social media. At least not using his real name."

Nate considers the practicalities of looking into these links. He's been fired, Anna isn't going to tell him anything if he asks outright, and it's not like he and Morgan get on. "I'll see what I can do."

"Maybe your new lady friend could be useful here. Maybe she could bond with Anna over lady things, secure her confidence, I don't know."

Nate laughs. "'Lady things'? You're so old-fashioned, Rex."

"Hey, that's what happens when you get old. I'm sixty-five this year, remember. It'll happen to you one day too."

"Leave it with me."

Nate ends the call and has absolutely no idea what to do next.

CHAPTER SIXTY-FOUR

At the hospital, Anna is attended to fast. Pregnant women always take priority, and for that Madison is relieved. Kat had to leave—she got a friend to pick her up—but Madison stays with Anna until a doctor pulls up a chair to do an internal examination. At that point she gives them some privacy.

Whilst waiting in the corridor outside, she buys a Coke from the vending machine and checks her cell phone. There's nothing from Mike yet, so he's probably not made it to Stephanie's house. It makes her feel uneasy. She'll feel better when she gets reassurance that he's spoken to Steph and made her see that she needs to get away for a while.

She wonders how long it'll be before she and Nate can leave this town, if it is Jenny's remains that have been found. The thought of going to Lost Creek makes her stomach roll, and she can't tell whether that's down to nerves or excitement. It can't be excitement. She hasn't been there since her trial ended, and nothing good will come out of stirring up the past. It's going to upset a lot of people.

The doctor comes out of Anna's room. He pulls his sleeves down. "Are you a family member?"

She nods yes, knowing the hospital won't tell her anything otherwise.

"Well, she needs complete bed rest. The baby's close to coming, but it's too soon. That little girl needs to stay in there as long as possible for the best chance of survival."

"Understood." So it's a girl. "Apart from that, is Anna looking okay?"

"She's clearly stressed; her blood pressure is way too high. What's going on in her life to cause that? Was it just the dog attack?"

Madison sighs. "I'm sure the dog didn't help, but her twelve-year-old daughter is missing. She's been gone for just over two weeks." She looks around to check she's not being listened to by anyone else. "It's actually possible that her daughter has just been found. I don't know for sure yet, as the remains need to be identified. That could take some time, as she was submerged in water."

The doctor's eyes widen. "I see. Well she can't know. Not yet, at least. She needs to lower her stress levels and stay in bed for as long as possible."

Madison thinks about the media. "In that case, we need to keep the TV off in her room. Tell the rest of the team who will be checking on her. Just pretend it's broken or something, okay?"

He realizes what she means. "I'll try. I guess we could hide the remote control. The set is pretty high on the wall, so she might not be able to reach it herself."

"Good. I'll do what I can. I need to get in touch with her husband. I'll let you know when he arrives."

The doctor nods, and then checks in on Anna again before he leaves. Madison follows him into her room.

"Mrs. Lucas, we'll get your husband here as soon as possible. I cannot reiterate strongly enough that you need complete bed rest if you want to keep your baby safe." He squeezes her arm. "She's relying on you, okay?"

Anna smiles weakly. "I understand. Thanks, Doctor."

"I'll get some food sent in. You need to eat more; I want a big baby come delivery day." He smiles, then he's off. Madison hopes he's going to brief his team.

She sits on the chair next to the bed. "Do you mind if I stay with you for a while?"

Anna shakes her head.

"How are you feeling?"

"Just tired. I've got to say, it's nice to rest and have people take care of me. It almost makes me forget what's going on in real life."

Madison feels for her. Although Anna's not been too friendly toward them, it's understandable that she would be wary. She's still got her doubts about her, though. There's something bothering her that she can't put her finger on. "Just try not to think about anything but your baby girl for now. Have you chosen a name yet?"

Anna's eyes light up for the first time since Madison met her. "I have lots of potentials, but Grant keeps vetoing them."

"Like what?"

She runs through a long list of names, and Madison is conscious that this could be helping her. The transformation in her personality is obvious. She's planning for life with a new baby, and when she's animated like this, you would never guess she has a missing child out there somewhere. This is the most she's ever opened up. When she stops talking, she sips the juice on her nightstand, and then a nurse enters with a tray of food.

"Here you go, sweetie. I just managed to get you some hot food before the kitchen closed. It's lasagna with a slice of garlic bread."

There's some fruit on the side too. Part of Madison relaxes knowing Anna will be taken care of while she's in here. The nurse checks the IV drip that's going into Anna's non-bandaged arm. As she lifts the sleeve of the hospital gown, Madison can see some nasty pink scars. She wonders if Anna's been self-harming, but looks away so she doesn't notice she spotted them.

"The doctor tells me you're to be caffeine-free for a while, to give your blood pressure a chance to drop," says the nurse. "If anyone brings you hot drinks, make sure you tell them."

Anna smiles. "Sure."

"What about you?" the nurse asks Madison. "Can I get you anything?"

"Actually, I need a coffee so I'll head to the cafeteria. You don't mind if I take a break, do you?" She touches Anna's shoulder.

Anna is wolfing her lasagna down. "No, of course not."

"Great."

They leave her to eat and Madison walks to the elevator. Her phone shows a text from Nate.

It's not Jenny. They're animal bones. How is Anna?

She's relieved that Jenny could still be alive, but also a little disappointed at the thought that they'll have to stay here longer to find her. That's if Anna finally opens up and helps them.

She texts back.

Doctor wants her de-stressed and on complete bed rest for as long as possible to help the baby. She's already relaxing in here. Should I stay?

In the cafeteria, she orders a cappuccino. As she looks out of the window at the parking lot below, she hears her phone buzz.

Stay with her for now. Apparently she knows Morgan from college. There's a link there so I'm going to quiz him about it. Call me if you need me.

Madison is shocked. Was that why Grant and Anna chose a summer camp in Shadow Falls: because they knew someone who lived here and he recommended it? Maybe he offered to keep an eye on Jenny for them.

She takes a seat as she slowly realizes that Detective Ted Morgan is now a potential suspect.

CHAPTER SIXTY-FIVE

Nate's trying to catch up with Morgan. The detective left Camp Fearless before he could quiz him about his relationship with Anna Lucas. When he spots Morgan's car pulled over at Jeanie-May's gas station, he pulls up alongside it and gets out.

When Morgan sees him, he rolls his eyes and looks like he's about to start his engine and drive away. Instead, he lowers the passenger window. "What now, Monroe? You know, you're really starting to get on my nerves."

Nate leans in. "Thought you'd like to know I've just heard from Madison. Mrs. Lucas needs complete bed rest, so she'll be staying in the hospital for a while."

Morgan nods. Is that relief Nate sees in his eyes? Concern for his friend? The detective's cell phone rings, and although he glances down at it, he ignores it and sighs loudly. Nate imagines he's feeling the pressure of the investigation going nowhere. He's probably getting his ass kicked by his chief of police back at the station. Especially if the chief knows there are two PIs on the case who appear to be doing a better job than his detective.

"Let me guess," says Nate. "You're taking some heat for not finding Jenny yet."

"It's none of your goddam business. Why haven't you left town yet, like Mrs. Lucas asked?"

"I like to see things through to the end. Can I ask you something?"

Morgan laughs and shakes his head. "You're going to anyway, right?" He looks to his left, away from Nate.

"How long were you and Mrs. Lucas in a relationship?"

Morgan snaps his head around so fast that he pulls a muscle in his neck, causing him to wince with the pain. "Motherfucker!" He massages his neck. "You're out of line now, Monroe. You need to leave this town and that family alone."

Nate realizes he's hit a raw nerve. He slowly shakes his head. "Sorry, I can't do that. I need to know someone's looking for that girl."

Morgan looks like he wants to get out of the car and punch him. His eyes narrow and the tone of his voice becomes threatening. "You might want to get out of here before I find something illegal in your car. I'm sure that wouldn't go down well in court, not with your history. You wouldn't want to go back inside, would you?"

Nate's smile fades as he considers what Morgan is implying.

"Hell, for all I know, *you* took the girl. Is that why you're so interested? Are you a sex offender, Nate? You into little girls? I mean, you were a priest in all but title. The media would love that, and I could sure make it look that way."

Nate shakes his head in disbelief. "I was right. I knew all cops were bad."

Morgan's smirk falters. He rubs his face and leans back against the headrest. "Jesus Christ. This case—this town—is sending me crazy."

Nate slowly returns to his car. As he drives away, he wonders if finding this missing girl is worth losing his freedom for.

CHAPTER SIXTY-SIX

Madison brings Anna a decaf coffee and sits in the armchair next to her bed. She's decided to try to gain Anna's trust, because she knows that's the only way they're going to find out what's going on.

It's so warm in the room that she has to remove the shirt she's wearing over her T-shirt. They're on the fifth floor of the building, so the windows don't open, and the air con must be busted.

"Have you tried calling your husband yet?" she asks.

Anna looks up at her. "Yes, but he's not answering. He's probably on his way up here. I've messaged him to say I'm in the hospital but that everything's okay."

"Good. I expect he'll arrive overnight." Madison checks her cell phone, wondering where Nate is. She doesn't mind babysitting Anna for now, but she doesn't want to be here for days on end.

A sound at the door makes them both look up, and a tall, slim woman enters the room. She's not wearing hospital scrubs or a white coat. They both look at her.

"So sorry to bother you at this difficult time, Mrs. Lucas, but I'm Ava Carter, a reporter from the local newspaper. We've heard about what happened today out at Camp Fearless. Would you like to give us a comment on the record?"

Madison's fuming. Anna didn't need to know about that until she's better.

Anna looks at her, confused. "What does she mean?"

Madison stands up and walks to the woman, pushing her out of the room. "You need to get out of here. You're not welcome."

The reporter tries to stand her ground. "I'm doing my job. Who are you anyway? A friend of the family? Here's my card if anyone wants to speak to us and get their side of the story out."

Madison pushes her harder.

"Hey! You can't do that."

Once outside the room, she leans in close. "You're putting her life at risk by stressing her out. You need to leave."

The reporter looks shocked. "Why? What's wrong with her? I heard it was just a dog bite."

Madison doesn't want the press finding out that Anna's pregnant. It would only add to their interest in the story of the missing girl. "It's none of your business. Are you going to leave, or do I need to find security to escort you out?"

The reporter glares at her for a few moments, then relents and walks away, annoyed. "Call me when you realize you have no control of the story."

Madison shakes her head in disgust and re-enters the room. Anna is trying to get out of bed.

"Whoa! Where do you think you're going?"

She collapses back, clutching her stomach. "Tell me what's going on! What's happening at the camp?"

Madison helps her get back into bed and pulls the blankets over her. "Nothing. The divers found some animal bones in the lake earlier. The press have obviously been tipped off by someone who works at the camp, but I promise you, it's not Jenny."

Anna tries to catch her breath and rests her head on the pillow. "It's going to revive interest in the story, isn't it? I'll never be able to get away from the news talking about Jennifer on repeat all day, every day."

"You know what they say, today's news is tomorrow's trash."

Anna relaxes a little, and pulls the blanket up to her chin. Neither of them speaks for a while.

"Can you put the TV on? I want to watch something to help me fall asleep."

Madison tenses. "Apparently it's broken; the doctor told me earlier. Sorry."

Anna looks at her. "Really?"

"Yes. But why would you want to watch what they're saying anyway? It's not going to do you any good. We know Jenny hasn't been found and we know stress could harm your baby. Just try to get some sleep."

"Why are you even here?" Anna's eyelids look like they're about to close. She's clearly exhausted.

"I didn't want to leave you alone. No one should be alone at a time like this. But as soon as your husband shows up, I'll leave if you want me to."

Anna doesn't answer. She closes her eyes and yawns. It makes Madison yawn too.

"Before you fall asleep, can I ask you something? You might not like it, but don't get worked up; it's just something I'm curious about."

Anna opens her eyes. She doesn't look concerned. "What's that?"

"If you're able to get pregnant, why did you adopt Jenny?"

Panic creeps into her eyes, but she doesn't look away. "You know, I ask myself that all the time." She thinks about it. "Ultimately, we wanted to help a child in need." Her voice becomes drowsy. "You hear of so many unwanted kids, and it's just devastating, you know? Grant earns a good wage and we had this big house for as many kids as we wanted. But now, in hindsight, I can see that we shouldn't have done it." Her eyes close again.

Madison leans in. "Why not? You love Jenny, I can see that."

Sleepily she says, "But everything was so perfect before. We were so happy. We didn't need another child. But I guess—"

Madison jumps in before she can stop herself. "*Another* child?"

Anna's eyes flutter awake. Her face suddenly changes. She looks grief-stricken, like she's suddenly remembering something. "I mean… well…" She stops, clearly unsure how to answer. "It's just… I'd miscarried a few times, so we assumed I couldn't carry a baby to full term. That's when we looked into adoption."

Her face is tense. Madison is certain she's hiding something, but she's not sure how to probe without upsetting her and raising her blood pressure again. She'll have to tread carefully.

"I know how devastating miscarriages are, trust me. If you're anything like me, you still see them as children. I get that."

Anna looks relieved, but Madison is just trying to keep her calm. If she's reading the subtext correctly, it sounds like the Lucases had another child they haven't told anyone about. She thinks about the painting from the library: a black figure looming over two small children. Are the children in the painting Jenny and her sibling? In which case, who is the black figure? Clearly someone Jenny was afraid of.

"You know, I really need to sleep," Anna says. "Do you mind leaving me alone for a while?"

Madison stands up, frustrated that she can't question her properly. She has to remember she's not a cop anymore, and she's lucky to even be here right now. Anna could have told her to leave and never come back the minute they got here. "No problem. I'll be close by if you need me."

Anna closes her eyes, and her breathing turns heavy before Madison even leaves the room.

CHAPTER SIXTY-SEVEN

Nate finds Madison on the fifth floor. She's sitting on a small plastic chair, leaning her head awkwardly against the wall. He assumes she's asleep until she opens her eyes and looks up at him.

"Hey," she says. "It's your turn to babysit."

He smiles at her disheveled appearance. "How about we get out of here?" He looks in on Anna. She's asleep. "She'll be okay here overnight. Let's head back to the guest house and get some food and sleep."

Madison looks relieved. "That's the best thing you've ever said to me."

As they walk out of the hospital, Nate wonders if Detective Morgan's checked on Anna yet. "Has anyone stopped by?"

She shakes her head. "Nope, no one. She called her husband but he didn't pick up. He'll probably be here by the time we get back tomorrow morning."

They walk to his car, and as she buckles herself in, Nate watches her glance behind her. "Brody!" The dog licks her face over the seat. She turns back to Nate. "What's he doing here?"

"If I didn't take him, Morgan was going to euthanize him. The son of a bitch would probably shoot the poor dog himself, given a chance."

"But he won't be allowed in the guest house, surely?"

He smiles as he drives away from the hospital. "He will if they don't know. I'll need you to distract Mary while I get him upstairs. Just for tonight. I'll find a no-kill shelter in the morning."

"A shelter?" She looks alarmed. "You do realize they all call themselves no-kill, but the majority still put the animals to sleep when they're full or low on donations?"

He considers it. "No way. They can't do that, can they?"

She rolls her eyes. "How can you be so naïve? Of course they do."

He glances in his rear-view mirror as he thinks about it. Brody is sitting up straight, panting and looking happy with himself. Nate sighs. He can't keep him—he doesn't live the kind of lifestyle a dog needs—so he has to find the right owner for him. Rex springs to mind. After a few miles he says, "I have a friend who lives on a ranch. He's managed to fill it with hundreds of rescue animals. I'm pretty sure he'd take Brody in."

"Where does he live?"

"San Diego."

"Shit, that means another delay in getting to Colorado. Can't we just take him with us for now?"

Nate looks at her. "How are we going to care for a dog while we're on the road?"

She smiles. "You've been doing pretty well already. Can't you see he's smitten with you?"

He checks the rear-view mirror. Brody is staring back at him, leaning his head to one side as if he knows they're discussing him. Then he barks.

"Jeez, how do I get myself into these situations? I guess he can come with us until I can get him to Rex."

"How does your friend afford to look after so many animals?" Madison asks. "Food alone would be expensive, never mind the vet's bills."

Nate looks across at her. "He's funded by wealthy schmucks who have nothing else to spend their money on."

It takes her a second to realize who he's talking about. "*You're* funding him?" She laughs. "That's sweet of you."

"Sweet, or stupid?"

After another ten minutes, he pulls up in front of the guest house and switches the engine off. "You better distract Mary for us."

Madison gets out of the car. "Piece of cake."

Once they've eaten dinner, they head to Nate's room. Mary was delighted when Nate asked for a doggy bag to take upstairs with him, obviously thinking her pot roast had been well received. He just hopes she doesn't find out how literal the request was. He opens the silver foil and places it on the floor in front of Brody, who starts by gently licking the grey meat to see what it is. Then he devours it, vegetables and all.

"Man, he's a noisy eater." Nate switches the TV on low. He sits on his bed and leans back against the headboard.

Madison takes the armchair by the window. After checking out the slow sunset, she turns to him. "Did you ask Morgan about his history with Anna?"

He pulls a face to suggest he did and it didn't go down well. "He didn't confirm or deny it."

"No?"

"No. Instead he threatened to frame me for something hideous and put me in jail if I didn't leave town."

She raises her eyebrows. "What the fuck?"

"The reaction of a guilty man."

"Sometimes I can see why you hate cops. But we're not all that way, I promise."

He doesn't respond.

"This is just getting weirder and weirder," she says. "I feel like the people who should want Jennifer Lucas found are the ones who are hiding something. Is that just me?"

He sighs and takes a sip of the coffee Mary made him. "I feel exactly the same way. I guess now we have to figure out what their relationship was. I mean, we can't assume they were lovers just because they went to the same university."

She sits back. "No. But that would explain why they don't want us to know."

Nate thinks about the implications of a romantic relationship. "What if they were lovers in college and she never told her husband? That would explain why they're being shady about it."

"But why would Grant care after all this time? He's married to her, and in this scenario, Anna obviously split up with Morgan at some point." Her face changes. "Holy crap. Unless they're having an affair now, and that's why Grant doesn't know about it."

He warms to the idea. The more he thinks about it, the more reasons he can find to explain their reluctance to tell anyone. "That could be it. You know, we could even jump one step further and consider whether Jenny was actually the result of their affair and not adopted."

She looks confused. "What do you mean? I thought we knew for sure she was adopted. Didn't your pal check with CPS?"

"Yeah, but maybe Grant had to adopt her because he wasn't the biological father, but Anna *is* the biological mother?"

Madison leans forward in her chair. "This is getting complicated. If Morgan's the biological father—and I think that's a big if—could that mean *he* took the girl? Maybe he thought Grant was an asshole; hell, maybe Grant *is* an asshole and Anna's been complaining that he beats them or something. That could make Morgan want to rescue his daughter. You know, to protect her. Maybe he and Anna agreed a plan to get Jenny away from Grant."

Nate's fully absorbed in this theory now. He gets off the bed and starts pacing the room. "That actually makes a lot of sense."

"You know what?" says Madison. "Wouldn't it be amazing if that's the case and Jennifer Lucas is actually still alive? It's been so easy to assume she was dead this whole time. I'd love to be right on this and get a happy ending to a missing child case for once."

Nate tries not to quash her hope, but they have to be realistic. "It would be great, but what are the chances of Morgan being able to live with his daughter in plain sight when everyone around here knows there's a twelve-year-old girl missing? He would have to leave town with her if that's what he's after."

She appears to think about it as Brody finishes his food. He's destroying the silver foil, so Nate picks it up. "You can't eat that, buddy." He throws it in the trash can and sits back on the bed. The dog rests on the rug.

They're both silent for almost five minutes, absorbed in possible theories, then Madison looks across at him. "You know what we have to do, don't you?"

"What?"

"We have to search Morgan's house."

The possibility of a police officer being involved in Jennifer's disappearance reinvigorates Nate. He smiles. He might not be getting paid for this job now that Esme's passed away, but there's something about catching bent cops that makes it all worthwhile.

CHAPTER SIXTY-EIGHT

Anna sleeps through the night; a whole eleven hours straight. As she slowly wakes up, she tries to think back to when she last had more than three hours' sleep, but it must have been a long time ago, because she can't remember. She rests her hands on her stomach and smiles at the curve of her bump. Is it just her imagination, or has it grown overnight? She laughs to herself. It can't have.

She sits up just as a nurse she hasn't met before enters.

"Morning, Mrs. Lucas!" says the nurse cheerily. "How do you feel today? You certainly had a good sleep. I came to check on you earlier and you were happily drooling away!"

Anna smiles and self-consciously wipes her mouth. "I feel amazing. Really refreshed. I'm hungry too, which is rare these days."

"Good. Breakfast will be along soon. I just need to check the dog bite isn't infected." The nurse unwraps the bandage on her arm. The cuts are leaking. "I know it looks nasty, but the liquid is clear, so that's a good sign. They should start drying up if we give them some air." She rubs some cream on them. "I'll leave the bandage off for today, but try not to touch the arm or wear anything over it until it's looking a bit drier, okay?"

Anna nods. The nurse checks the IV drip in her other arm. She takes her blood pressure and temperature, makes some notes and then leaves.

Anna is feeling optimistic, almost like today could be the start of something new. She realizes it's the first day of July and smiles at the thought of drawing a line under everything that's happened and using today as the start of her new life. Then she thinks of

Grant. A feeling of dread almost overwhelms her as she retrieves her cell phone from the nightstand.

She has three missed calls from an unknown number, but nothing from Grant. That's odd. Maybe he's about to turn up. Feeling uneasy, she tries calling him. She'd rather know where he is than wait for him to appear without warning. She lets the phone ring for longer than she would normally wait and is rewarded with a response.

"Anna?"

"Where are you, Grant?"

She can hear the sound of the car's engine in the background. He must be using hands-free.

"Grant? I'm in the hospital. Where are you?"

She hears a loud sigh. "I can't do it, Anna. I can't do it anymore."

Her chest suddenly tightens. "You can't do what? What are you talking about?"

"All this! It has to end! I read your journal."

Her heart sinks. She knows they can't survive as a couple now.

"I can't live like this anymore." He pauses. "I can't live with *you*, Anna. You won't see me again."

She grips the side of the bed with her spare hand. The positivity she woke up with vanishes in an instant. "Grant? What are you saying? Where are you? Come to the hospital, honey. I need you."

She hears sobbing and it makes her heart ache. "Grant? Don't you dare leave me this way. Don't make it all for nothing!"

He doesn't respond. She listens to the hum of the car's engine and the occasional gasping sob. Eventually he speaks again. "I'm going to be with Jenny."

She gasps. What does he mean? She's about to yell his name, but the call abruptly ends.

CHAPTER SIXTY-NINE

Breakfast is greasy but filling, and Nate manages to sneak some extra bacon up to his room afterwards for Brody. He isn't sure whether to take the dog with them to Detective Morgan's house. "What do you think?" he asks Madison.

She looks down at Brody, who's sitting next to the door, keen to get going. "Well, we can't leave him here. Mary would find him when she cleans our rooms."

He hadn't thought of that. "I guess that decides it then."

Just as they're about to leave, Nate's cell phone buzzes with a new email alert. When he sees who the sender is, his stomach flips with dread.

"I've got to read this."

"Okay, I'll just get a few things from my room and I'll be right back."

Nate sits on the bed, his legs suddenly weak.

I see you have a new lady friend. Yes, Nathaniel, I have eyes on you. First Stacey, then Kristen, and now a new woman. How long will it be before you get her killed too?

That's all it says. He stands up, knowing that's the confirmation he needs that Father Connor was involved in Kristen's disappearance. His adrenaline kicks up a gear and he feels the familiar craving for coke. He heads to the bathroom but doesn't pull out his stash. Instead he stares at himself in the mirror. He sees his twenty-one-year-old self looking back at him. Is this never going to end? He can't understand why Stacey's uncle won't leave him alone to live out the rest of his life in peace.

"What's the matter?" asks Madison, appearing behind him.

His fists are clenched and he feels like shit. He tries to concentrate on what he's about to do, but his mind is clouded by Father Connor's words.

"Oh shit. You're not using today, are you?" she says. "You can't turn up at a cop's house fully loaded, Nate. You could get us killed!"

He can't seem to speak. The words won't come out. He slides his phone across the vanity and she picks it up and reads the email.

"Is this the piece of shit who killed your fiancée?"

He nods.

She moves closer and puts a hand on his back. "Nate, you have to hold it together. You're letting him get to you, which is exactly what he wants."

"Why won't he leave me alone?" He spits the words out.

She reads the email again. "He likes the control he has over you. And he doesn't have eyes on you. He's just pretending he's got some paid knuckleheads clocking your every move, but it'll be *him* who's following you. His life is so shit, all he can do is track you around the country. And isn't he about seventy by now? Sure, he got away with murder, but now he's just some weak old man near the end of his pathetic life. You have your health, a good thirty years on him, plus a shit ton of money and your freedom. You win, Nate. Stop letting him control you."

He's taking deep breaths to calm down. If Madison wasn't here, he would've gone on a bender for sure. He knows she's right, but it's still galling that the guy can wind him up so badly. "He has his sister." He thinks of meek, deplorable Deborah, who lied about him under oath, despite her strong religious beliefs. He shakes his head. "It's the bit about him getting away with it that bothers me."

"I know. Trust me, I understand. But we'll get him in the end. Someone like that can't outsmart us."

He looks at her. Is she offering to help him? "I thought you wanted to go to Colorado?"

"Oh, we're going to Colorado. But let him follow us there." She smiles. "Let's wear him out, physically and financially. He's got no real power over you, and it's not like he's going to walk up to you in the street and shoot you dead. This is all just a game for him. So let him play by himself while you get on with your life. If you happen to cross paths eventually, then you'll get the chance to confront him."

He thinks about it and realizes that makes a lot of sense. He just wishes they could face each other man to man and end this today. He wants to confront Father Connor and find out what Stacey was going to tell him the night she died; what she had discovered. It has to be about her uncle. It has to explain why he killed her. But meeting man to man isn't how cowards work. Father Connor is biding his time. He probably wants to stage Nate's murder as a suicide, as that would make Nate appear to have committed the gravest sin. It might also suggest to the priest's supporters—of whom there are many—that Nate feels guilt for Stacey's death. But murdering him will be difficult while he has Madison travelling with him.

He stands up straight and relaxes his shoulders. "You're right. Let's ignore him for now." He doesn't feel as confident as he sounds, but he doesn't want her to see how badly the guy affects him.

Madison rubs his back. "Come on, Nate. You've got this."

He returns her smile, but inside he's sinking.

CHAPTER SEVENTY

Nate hasn't seen or heard from Kristen since her visit in January, and it's weighing heavy on his mind. Is it because of what he accused her of? Right now, he doesn't care if she's helping every inmate on death row, as long as she comes back to visit him. It's driving him crazy not knowing what's happening. His letters go unanswered, and he doesn't have a phone number for her. He tried calling the university where she works, but they wouldn't tell him anything. They were probably scared off by the recorded penitentiary message that precedes his few permitted calls.

Today he's been told his lawyer is visiting him. As Johnny, a new correctional officer, leads him to the interview room, he's secretly hoping to see Kristen there instead of Steve Freeman, his attorney.

Steve has a stupid grin on his face and Nate wants to strangle him with his cuffs. These last few months have been the toughest yet, because Kristen raised his hopes and has left him with nothing. That's worse than if he'd never met her. It's making Nate quick to anger.

Once he's chained to the table, the guard hovers. Nate turns and looks up at him. "I think you'll find that what's said between a man and his lawyer is confidential."

Johnny looks annoyed but jittery, like he's eager to hear what they're going to talk about.

Steve speaks up. "Come on, Johnny, you know the drill. Outside."

Johnny reluctantly leaves, but after he's closed the door, he keeps peeping in through the reinforced glass window.

Nate can't understand why he's so interested. He turns to his lawyer. "What's going on?"

"Well, Nate. I have the best news. Are you ready for this?"

Nate grits his teeth. "Stop dragging it out and just tell me, for Christ's sake!"

Steve's smile falters, but he continues. "As of now, legally but not technically, not yet anyway, you're a free man."

Nate's not in the mood for sick jokes. "If I wasn't chained to this table, I'd earn my place on death row by beating you to a pulp." He's surprised at his own reaction, but prison has taught him how to behave like an animal.

"No, Nate! I'm not shitting you. The judge overturned your conviction this morning. The blood on the hammer was re-tested and we know now that it's not yours. There is absolutely no forensic evidence to link you to Stacey's murder other than the cops finding you next to her body, and we have the neighbor's testimony that he saw you arrive just before the cops, meaning you didn't have enough time to get into an argument and kill her." He pauses, giving it time to sink in.

Nate's eyes sting. He daren't speak. The shock is numbing his mental reaction, but his body is way ahead of him. His face is wet within seconds. His hands start shaking and it spreads to his torso. He's overcome with trembling and he can't stop his teeth from chattering. "Tell me you're not lying to me?"

Steve gets up and claps him on the back. "You did it, Nate! You not only survived death row, but you managed to get out. Well, your friend Kristen and her college kids did it really. How do you feel, my man?"

Nate lowers his head into his shackled hands and starts sobbing. Images of Stacey dead on the floor overwhelm him. It's guilt. Guilt that he can feel happiness when Stacey is still dead. Steve sits back down.

"Now for the bad news. It'll take a while to get you out. God knows the Texas judicial system moves slowly, but you'll be moved to solitary eventually in order to keep you safe. It could take months, even years, but you have something to hold on to now. You've been exonerated and you will get out. Just hold on, okay?"

Months, years? How can that be fair? He's an innocent man but the state is going to keep him locked up for even longer while they sort out the admin? He tries not to let that ruin this moment. He's done seventeen years; he can do a few more months. But he can't help worrying they'll change their minds in the meantime. His freedom is so close, but he won't believe it until he walks out the front entrance of this hellhole.

Eventually he looks up. "Where's Kristen?"

Steve takes a deep breath. "I haven't been able to track her down. From what I can gather from speaking to the university, she stopped showing up for work in February." He pauses. "Her family notified the police that she was missing, but they've not found her. All her things are still at her house. It's not looking good."

Nate shakes his head. Why would she just vanish? Then Father Connor comes into his mind, and his body tenses. He wouldn't. Would he?

CHAPTER SEVENTY-ONE

Nate and Brody creep downstairs behind Madison and she gives them the all-clear when she's certain there's no one around, but Brody is excited by their covert operation and he barks.

Madison looks up at the guest house and spots Mary watching them from the parlor window. She looks unimpressed. "Shit. We've been rumbled." She gives Mary a wave that isn't returned.

"She's going to kick us out, isn't she?" asks Nate, getting into the car.

"Probably."

He turns to the dog. "You need to teach me your police code so I know how to instruct you in situations like this."

Brody seems to enjoy being spoken to. He barks and then leans in for a sloppy lick of Nate's face.

"Eugh, Brody! I'm going to smell of dog breath all day now. That's not exactly going to make me a babe magnet."

He notices the mess on the back seat.

"Have you seen the amount of fur this dog sheds?" he asks.

Madison has already spotted how much of Brody's fur is covering the upholstery, but she didn't want to get the dog into trouble so she kept it to herself. She laughs as she buckles her seat belt. "He can't help it."

Nate shakes his head and drives away from the guest house, heading to the address Rex gave them for Detective Morgan.

The sat nav tells her it's about twenty miles from Shadow Falls. While Nate drives, Madison compulsively checks her cell phone.

"Not heard back from your police contact yet?"

She looks at him and sighs. "No. I told him to let me know when he'd spoken to Stephanie, but there's been no word."

"Maybe he's just busy and hasn't had a chance to stop by yet."

She looks out of the window. "Maybe."

"If you're worried, why don't you call him back? Or call Stephanie?"

"I already tried her earlier, but she didn't reply. That's not unheard of, though. She doesn't like living in the past, and calls from me are just a reminder of everything that happened, so she tends to ignore them unless she needs something. I'd rather not call Mike again yet." She looks at Nate. "It was awkward. I knew it would be, but I felt uncomfortable talking to someone from back then. I don't even know if I can trust him."

Nate nods. He probably understands. "Well, hopefully we'll find Jennifer Lucas eating breakfast at Morgan's house and we can be out of here by lunchtime."

She laughs. "Wouldn't that be nice."

When they pull up on Morgan's street, Madison looks around to make sure no one's paying any attention to them. The houses are small and packed together. Trinity Creek is much bigger than Shadow Falls, but that just means it'll be harder to get into his house unnoticed.

"Look." She points out Morgan's house. A woman is coming out the front door and she has a young girl with her. "Oh my God, is that Jenny?"

Nate stares for a few seconds and then opens the photos he took on his phone of the family portraits at Jenny's house. Madison looks over his shoulder. Jenny is blonde and skinny. They both look up at the girl getting into the back of a red Ford while the woman holds the door open for her. She has black hair, jet black. Almost like it's dyed. But then Morgan's hair is mostly dark, with a few greys around the temples. The girl looks more athletic than Jenny, but Madison doesn't know how long ago the family portraits were taken. She could have had a growth spurt since then.

"It's hard to tell from this distance, and Jenny has blonde hair, not black," says Nate. "It's safer to assume it's not her until we know otherwise."

She nods. "That's got to be Morgan's wife. But if he's having an affair with Anna, and hiding his own child, his wife would have something to say, surely?"

Nate appears to think about it. "Maybe his wife can't have kids of her own and jumped at the chance of taking on Jenny?"

They both watch in silence as the woman drives away from the house. She doesn't pass them so they can't see much.

"Still want to go in?" asks Madison.

Nate starts the car and looks at her. "Not yet. Let's follow them instead."

She smiles. "You really should've been a cop."

To her delight, he gives her a look to suggest he's offended.

CHAPTER SEVENTY-TWO

The office of Dr. Pamela Jarvis

Pamela pushes the journal away and opens the report she asked Stephen to obtain for her. She reads the front page. It's stamped with *Child Protective Services* and *Confidential*. All she knows is that this report is about a baby called Jennie Scott, who was eighteen months old when child services discovered her. She takes a deep breath. Even after everything she's already read, she knows this is going to be the worst part.

She skips the photos and starts by reading about the reasons for Jennie's removal from her biological parents. Certain key phrases jump out at her.

Father unknown. Mom was an alcoholic and heavy smoker who frequently left the baby alone for long periods while she worked as a prostitute… Would bring multiple men home at the same time to maximize income, putting the baby at risk of abuse… On one occasion the fire department were called as Jennie had started a fire by knocking over one of Mom's candles. The smoke had woken Mom and she'd got them out of the apartment just in time. After they were moved to a new apartment, neighbors complained about the baby's long bouts of crying… Mother was heard through the walls screaming at Jennie, sometimes this would be followed by a "thud and then silence"… Jennie was placed in foster care on several occasions while Mom worked through her issues, but she always requested to have her back. This was granted when she showed sufficient improvement in her attitude, her addiction and her living conditions. But she had a pattern of skipping town and starting over with a new social worker, who would be unaware that she was already well known to child services in another state...

Finally, after a witness reported the baby being left home alone, CPS and the local police intervened, attending the address together. Jennie was found without a diaper, and her crib was badly soiled, suggesting she'd been alone for a number of days. She had signs of malnutrition and had been eating wallpaper she'd pulled off the walls from around her crib.

Pamela gulps back her anguish. She reaches for another bourbon, not caring now if her breath smells of liquor by the end of the day. No one should have to know that this stuff goes on in the world; that a parent can be so neglectful of their own child. And for what? So she can earn enough money to score drugs?

She leafs through the photos of the apartment Jennie and her mother shared. It's obvious her mom didn't put any of her earnings into looking after the home or taking care of her baby. Pamela usually has more sympathy than most for addicts—after all, she's qualified to know it's a horrible disease that isn't the fault of the addict—but there's no excuse for not putting your child before your cravings. That woman could've taken Jennie to CPS at any time. She could've left her with a friend or a neighbor while she was out.

She comes across a photo of Jennie in her crib on the day CPS found her. "Oh my God." She covers her mouth. The baby's hands are reaching out to the owner of the camera like she's asking to be picked up and hugged. Her eyes are red, desperate and needy. Her body is brown from the waist down. There are what look like cigarette burns all over her arms.

"That poor child," she mutters. "She was rescued from one horrific home to go to another."

She shakes her head as she forces herself to read on.

CHAPTER SEVENTY-THREE

Nate pulls up a few cars away from the house Morgan's wife has entered. It's nicer than the house she left, with a large, well-manicured front garden and a US flag flapping gently in the warm breeze. They didn't arrive in time to see the girl enter the house, but they can see Morgan's wife walking back to her car and waving at someone. An elderly woman is at the door waving back as she drives away.

"Now what?" asks Madison.

He turns to her. "Now we knock on the door and ask if we can borrow the phone."

"What? Why would she let us do that? It's not 1954!"

He smiles, realizing she's right. "Okay, what's your suggestion?"

"How about we say we're Jehovah's Witnesses? She's more likely to let us in. You can dazzle her with your knowledge of the Bible while I pretend to use the bathroom."

Nate thinks about the years he spent devoted to his faith. It hurts to recollect how different his life was before he fell in love with Stacey. "I don't think I could remember anything these days. I've not picked up a Bible in a long time."

Madison waves in dismissal. "She's old, she'll probably invite us in for a cup of tea and some cake no matter what we say."

He isn't so sure. "You can do the talking."

As they walk up the garden path, the front door opens and the elderly woman appears. The only problem is, she's holding a shotgun.

"Who are you and why are you on my property without permission?" she says, with a cigarette hanging out the side of her mouth.

Madison reacts fastest. "I'm sorry to bother you, ma'am, but we're just here to spread the good word of Jesus Christ, our Lord and Savior."

Nate looks at her in surprise. Where did she come up with that?

The woman scoffs. "There's no such thing as God. Get off my property before I shoot you and let you find that out for yourself."

They both walk back to the sidewalk, just outside her property line, but Nate doesn't want to leave. He needs to know whether that's Jenny in there. He turns back to face her.

"Ma'am? I'm going to come clean with you; we're colleagues of Ted Morgan. We just wanted to ask you a few questions."

She appears to consider it, even lowers her gun. "He's married to my daughter. I always thought she could do better, though."

Just then the young girl appears at the door. "What's going on, Grandma?"

Nate lifts his cell phone and snaps a photo as fast as possible. "What's your name?" he shouts.

The girl looks startled and the grandmother steps in front of her protectively. "What do you think you're doing? This is my granddaughter. Why are you here?"

"We're looking for the girl who went missing from Camp Fearless over in Shadow Falls," says Madison. "We thought your granddaughter could be her."

"What?" The old woman cackles with laughter. "This is Taylor. She's not the missing girl! Have you spoken to Ted about this?"

"Not yet, but we will," says Nate. "Taylor, is that correct? Your real name isn't Jennifer Lucas?"

The girl laughs, but she's nervous. "Of course not. I'm Taylor Morgan."

She certainly looks like she's telling the truth, which means they've got this all wrong. "I'm sorry to have bothered you both. We'll catch up with Ted as soon as possible, let him know what happened here. If you see him first, tell him Nate Monroe dropped by. He might swear a little, but there's no harm done."

The woman laughs. "This is the most entertainment I've had all week. Wait till I tell my girls at the shooting range."

She turns around and closes the door behind her. Nate feels stupid as he walks back to the car.

"It was worth a try," says Madison, sensing his mood. "Trust me, it's always worth a try. For every failed attempt there's a possible success, and that can mean the difference between life and death in cases like this."

Brody sniffs Nate's ear from the back seat. "I don't get it," Nate says. "If she's not Jenny, then what has Morgan's prior relationship with Anna got to do with Jenny's disappearance?"

"We still don't know for a fact they were even in a relationship. It could be they just knew each other at college and all this has been a coincidence. Although I'm with you. It would be some coincidence for Anna's daughter to go missing in the same town a former friend has jurisdiction over."

Nate looks at her. "I'm pretty sure Morgan won't tell us any-thing, and his mother-in-law is probably speaking to him right this minute. So our best bet is to drag it out of Anna and find out whether there's any link between them knowing each other and Jenny going missing."

Madison nods. "When she was falling asleep last night, she let out a bit more than she wanted, I think."

"Really? What did she say?"

"I thought she implied that she and Grant once had another child, but it could've been the drugs and the exhaustion confus-ing her. I asked her why they adopted when she can obviously get pregnant, and she said she had wanted to help a child in need but that it had been a mistake because they didn't need *another* child."

Nate can't think of any reason why they wouldn't have heard about the other child, if one existed. But then Anna and Grant kept the new baby a secret too. "This is getting weird."

"I agree. You'd think they'd want us to know everything in order to find their daughter."

He pulls his cell phone out and looks at the photo he took of Taylor.

Madison leans in. "It's hard to tell with kids, but she doesn't look like the portraits we saw."

He agrees. He starts a text to Rex.

"What are you doing?"

"Asking Rex to dig a little deeper. He needs to check whether the Lucases have any more kids, by searching birth records with the health department. You never know, maybe a child disappeared in mysterious circumstances. Jenny might not be the first."

She looks horrified at the suggestion. "God, I hope not."

He starts the car. "The fact that they're hiding things suggests one or both of them are guilty of something."

"I agree. We need to assume they're our best suspects at this point." Her face turns pale. "Oh my God."

"What?"

She looks at him slowly. "What if Esme's death wasn't natural?"

He swallows as he realizes where she's going with this.

She continues. "What if she found something and they had to kill her in order to silence her?"

He shakes his head. "No. I don't think that's plausible. They let Esme live with them, which they wouldn't do if they had something to hide, surely? Besides, anything suspicious about her death would show up during autopsy."

Madison runs her hand through her hair and leans back against the headrest. "You're right. This case is sending me crazy. I can't imagine either of them killing Esme."

Nate remembers something Esme told him when they first met her in Santa Barbara. "Jenny's best friend."

"What?" asks Madison.

"Esme said Jenny had a best friend but he'd moved away. She emailed me his mother's cell number."

Realizing where he's going with it, Madison says, "You think she'll know if they had more kids?"

He turns the engine off. "It's highly likely." He doesn't feel like he's the best person to talk to the woman at the moment. He's still distracted by Father Connor's email and he doesn't want to mess this up. He turns to Madison. "Why don't you call her? You've got more experience of speaking to a victim's friends and family than me."

Madison jumps at the chance and pulls out her phone. "Read out the number."

CHAPTER SEVENTY-FOUR

Anna's been sedated, so she's feeling sleepy. This morning's nurse caught her staggering along the corridor, and when she fought to be allowed to leave the hospital, she collapsed with more stomach pains. After a lot of fuss, she's been put under observation, so she'll never get out of here to find Grant now.

She's tired. Her hand strokes her bump as the baby kicks. It feels like she wants out too. Anna has decided to call her Esme, in memory of Grant's mother. He'll like that. She sent him a text to let him know, but he hasn't replied, which makes her wonder if she'll ever see him again. It doesn't really matter one way or another, because as long as she can keep this baby, she'll be happy. No one can hurt her now.

She thinks of everything they went through to adopt Jennifer. It was a long slog and there were several moments along the way when she doubted their decision. They already had two beautiful children: Susie and Thomas. Her life was filled with working at the school part-time, looking after the kids and keeping up with their busy schedules.

As a family unit, they were happy. Their friends asked them why they would adopt instead of trying for more of their own, but Anna had been adopted herself when she was six, and she was lucky enough to have been chosen by a wonderful family who'd given her everything she could ever have wished for. She wanted to give another child the same chance.

She remembered living in foster care during her early years. Her foster mother was a horrible woman who used to slap her every time she came in from the yard with dirt on her dress, or every time she couldn't finish her dinner. There was always a reason to slap her. When she'd told her social worker, he had just laughed and said she had an overactive imagination.

She felt she wanted to get a child out of foster care. After all, they could certainly afford it, and they had the room. Grant had taken some persuading, but when they first met Jennie Scott, as she was known then, he had bonded with her instantly. She seemed like a shy girl, with a pleasant manner. She was eager to please and gave them lots of drawings of them all together as a family. She was nine at the time, and therefore had little hope of being adopted until they came along. When Grant insisted she would fit well into their family, Anna agreed, and they renamed her Jennifer Lucas. Grant and Esme immediately referred to her as Jenny, but Anna never did. She found herself unable to abbreviate her name, like it was too familiar for the level of intimacy they shared.

There was something about Jennifer's eyes that unnerved her. Almost from the very beginning of their relationship, the girl looked at her slyly. A look reserved just for her. Esme loved the child instantly, of course, and doted on her. Anna wonders if that made the underlying friction between herself and Jennifer worse, because she was the only one to have reservations.

It took seven months for Jennifer to finally move in with them. By then, they were almost all bonded. Three-year-old Susie loved tying her new sister's hair up in scrunchies and clips, and Thomas, being just eighteen months old at that time, followed her around the house. Jennifer played gently with them and it all appeared to be working.

It took less than a year for things to take a turn for the worse, and Anna bitterly wishes she could go back in time and stop the adoption from ever happening. The more she thinks about it, the quicker the heart monitor next to her beeps.

Her cell phone rings. When she realizes who's calling, she hesitates and a blanket of dread envelops her.

"Ted?" she says, trying not to panic.

"What's going on? I'm taking heat from my boss for being incompetent, and those investigators have been at my mother-in-law's house to check if my daughter is Jenny! This is getting out of control."

"What?" she whispers. "Why are they investigating you?"

"Nate Monroe asked me if you and I had dated back in college, so he's found out something. I don't know how. I sure as hell didn't tell anyone."

"Neither did I," she says.

"Could it have been Grant? That guy hates me, so I wouldn't put it past him. Is he there?"

She doesn't reply.

"Anna? Where's Grant?"

"I don't know. I can't get hold of him. I think he's on his way up here, because he was driving last time I spoke to him. Ted, the investigators don't actually know anything; they're just speculating. Please stay calm."

"How can I stay calm? My job and my freedom are on the line. I did this for you! I should never have answered your phone call that day. I wish to God I'd never met you or your asshole husband." His voice sounds shaky and she hears him taking deep breaths to calm himself.

"Ted? I'm scared." Everything's unraveling.

"You're right to be scared," he snaps. "This whole situation is fucked up. I need to speak to Grant. If you see him before I do, get him to call me ASAP."

He ends the call before she can reply.

She tries to figure out how Nate and Madison learned about her relationship with Ted, and curses Esme for getting PIs involved.

She drops her phone on the bed and leans back, considering her options. It doesn't take her long to realize she has none. She has to see this out to the bitter end, with or without Ted and Grant's support.

CHAPTER SEVENTY-FIVE

The office of Dr. Pamela Jarvis

There's a knock at her door and Stephen sticks his head in. "The lieutenant will be here within the hour. He says the DA's office need the journal as soon as possible."

She nods. "I'll be ready. I've almost finished."

He closes the door behind him as she turns back to Jennie's CPS record. It would seem she was difficult to place, which is unusual, because babies always get adopted first. After being taken from her mother at nineteen months, she spent the next seven years in different foster homes, always being moved around, as if no one wanted her long-term. In her notes she was described as a whiny baby who never settled. At four she was playing with matches, and at five she cut her foster family's dog with a steak knife, claiming it was an accident. Trouble seemed to follow the girl.

The next page is a hospital report. It seems Jennie attempted suicide by slashing herself from elbow to wrist. Pamela checks the year and works out she was just eight at the time.

She turns the page to a statement written by one of Jennie's foster moms.

I kept expecting to wake up in the middle of the night with her standing over me, ready to slit my throat. We didn't bond at all, but she loved my husband. I couldn't understand why she hated me so much. I felt scared in my own home.

Her stomach leaps with dread. She turns to Anna Lucas's journal.

She loves Grant more than me. I feel afraid around her. I'm
scared she'll hurt me one day. She's so angelic around Grant.
That's why he doesn't believe me when I tell him how the girl
treats me. Instead he looks at me with pity, as if I'm going insane
and need taking care of. It infuriates me to the point that I don't
tell him about it anymore.

She thinks about it. Now she knows the girl's history before she
was adopted, she wonders if it's possible she was suffering from some
kind of attachment disorder. She flicks through her CPS file to the
last few pages and finds an envelope with a "sealed by the family
court" stamp across it, with a judge's name and a contact number
for his office. Pamela has come across these before, usually when
there's something that has been ordered to remain confidential
until the child turns eighteen, such as the biological parents' details,
the court transcripts if the child was removed from the parents, or
any juvenile record that is deemed sensitive. She's nervous that her
client would not have had access to anything sealed in this envelope
before she adopted Jennie Scott.

Knowing it will be read by the police anyway, she tears the
envelope open and finds a child therapist's report amongst the
paperwork. She briefly skims it.

In my opinion this girl suffers with reactive attachment disorder
and is extremely dangerous to any potential family she enters.
She needs intensive treatment before she is placed for adoption.
It's my recommendation that she remains in the care of CPS
until she has received successful treatment.

She wonders why the adoptive parents weren't told about this.
Could it have been sealed with the other paperwork by mistake?

Or by a well-meaning social worker who didn't want to put off a potential new family for Jennie? She'll never know. But the consequences have been catastrophic.

Although she's heard of RAD, she doesn't know much about it, so she turns to her laptop and searches for an explanation. She clicks on the first link:

> Reactive attachment disorder is a condition found in children who have not had the opportunity to bond with their primary caregivers before age five, usually as a result of gross neglect and abuse from the carer's side. The absence of love and warmth early on, in conjunction with harmful behavior from the primary caregivers, can cause severe harmful effects throughout the child's life.

The symptoms are listed: selective about who they positively interact with, control issues, anger management problems, limited sense of humor, aversion to physical affection, unhealthy relationship with one of the new primary caregivers if taken away from their own family, difficulty relating to others, manipulative or passive-aggressive tendencies.

Pamela has read enough. She closes the file and leans back in her seat. The mother was right all along. All those times she spoke about Jennifer hurting her, Pamela genuinely thought the girl was just physicalizing the pain she was experiencing from years of being passed around different foster homes. She also thought Anna was overreacting, as so many adoptive mothers do because they want their relationship with the new child to be perfect. She had no idea Jennifer was suffering from this disorder, but she should have figured it out after Anna told her she thought the child was evil.

She curses herself. Why didn't she pick up on that during their sessions and take it more seriously? She realizes she could have altered the outcome of this terrible situation. Her lack of action means this is professional negligence.

She looks at Anna's journal and notices there's only one passage left. She checks the date and realizes it was written the same week that Jennifer disappeared. Her hands start shaking.

CHAPTER SEVENTY-SIX

Madison calls the mother of Jennifer Lucas's best friend.

No one answers, so she leaves a message. "Hi, this is Madison Harper calling for Sian. I'm looking into the disappearance of Jennifer Lucas and I was hoping I could ask a few quick questions, as I believe your son was good friends with her. Call me back when you get this, it could be important. Thanks."

Nate starts the Jeep's engine and is about to drive to the hospital when Madison's phone rings.

She looks at him before answering. "That was quick. Hi, Madison Harper here."

"Hi, you just left me a message?" A tentative female voice.

"Yes. Thanks for returning my call so quickly."

She sounds shaky. "When I heard what it was about, I kind of figured I had no choice. Has Jenny not been found yet?"

"Afraid not. We're really struggling with leads, so we're looking into all possibilities at the moment."

"Oh. Poor Anna. I heard Esme passed away, is that right?"

Madison wonders where she heard that from so quickly. "Unfortunately, it is, yeah. It was Esme who hired me, actually."

Sian doesn't respond for a minute. "You're not with the police?"

"No, I'm a private investigator. Esme wanted a little extra reassurance, I think. But I'm working in conjunction with the police up here at the summer camp." She looks at Nate, who's trying to hear the other side of the conversation.

"What did you want to ask?" says Sian.

Madison doesn't want to give away the fact that she knows nothing about any other child Anna and Grant might have, so she has to bluff a little. "I want to know about the other children in the Lucas family."

Sian gasps.

When she doesn't respond, Madison asks, "Is there something wrong?"

When Sian speaks again, it's obvious she's crying. "I haven't thought about them for a while, that's all."

Madison is concerned at her reaction. This doesn't sound good. Gently, she prods. "Could you tell me what happened?"

"Why don't you just ask Anna?"

"I'm trying to minimize her suffering, as she has a lot to worry about right now. I'm sure you understand."

"Okay."

"I'm going to put you on loudspeaker so my colleague can listen in."

Sian sniffs. "Okay. Well, before they adopted Jenny, they already had two children: Susie, who attended the elementary school where Anna works, and Thomas. They both died in a terrible accident at their home about a year ago now."

Madison's heart sinks, but her mind is buzzing. Why on earth would the Lucases have kept that from them? Behind her, Brody sits up.

"It was awful, Ms. Harper. Anna and Grant fell apart and Jenny started acting up, which is totally understandable as she was only eleven herself and had just lost her younger siblings."

Madison puts the time frame together in her head: they lost their two youngest children in an accident a year ago, and now they've lost their only surviving child. What the hell is going on in that home?

"What was the cause of death?" asks Nate, leaning in.

Sian takes a deep breath. Her voice breaks as she tells them the children were both found in the pool.

He leans back in his seat and exhales loudly.

"That's terrible," says Madison. "I'm sorry to make you relive this, but the more we know, the higher the chance of finding Jenny. Can you tell me about her? For instance, did she have a good relationship with your son? I'm sorry, I don't know your son's name."

"Jake. They seemed to love each other. They became fast friends and Jenny was always inviting herself over to our house. I didn't really mind, as Jake had struggled to make friends up to that point. She was a nice girl, clearly intelligent and polite, but she was a little domineering. She'd boss Jake around. Sometimes things had a habit of going missing when she was around. I never said anything to Anna because I didn't want to accuse Jenny and ruin our relationship, especially as it was just a few toys and books. And I could tell there was some tension between the two of them, so I didn't want to make that any worse. But then things changed and… well, we had to move away."

Madison frowns, confused. "Why?"

"It's difficult to discuss without bringing up the feelings from that awful time." Sian sniffs back tears. "Jenny told Jake something so horrific that it still gives him nightmares. He refused to return to school and he started suffering with panic attacks. It was just awful to watch him deteriorate so fast."

Madison looks at Nate.

"Do you know what Jenny told him?" he asks.

"Yes, but I don't want to repeat it. I can't. If it's true, it will give me nightmares. I've tried hard to forget it, but I can't. Jake's only just starting to trust other kids again." She lowers her voice to a whisper. "Please don't make me repeat it."

Madison thinks of the worst thing Jenny could've told her friend, but she doesn't want to believe that a child of eleven would be capable of what she's thinking. "Does it have something to do with how the younger siblings got in the pool?"

Sian starts sobbing. "Yes."

Madison shakes her head and looks up at the car's ceiling. She's guessed, but she has to hear Sian say it in case she's wrong. "Sian, I'm thinking some pretty bad thoughts right now and I need you to tell me whether I'm right or not." She pauses. "Did Jenny claim she pushed her siblings into the pool?"

Sian sobs harder and they have to wait for her to stop. "Not only did she push them," she says. "She told Jake she held their heads underwater until they stopped kicking."

Goosebumps cover Madison's arms. That's fucked up. Nate is shaking his head in disbelief.

"Could this just have been Jenny's way of frightening your son, or do you think that's something she's actually capable of?" Madison presses. She knows kids make up all sorts of stories to scare each other. And it sounds like Jenny was messing with the younger girls at the camp too, telling them stories of monsters in the woods.

It takes Sian a while to compose herself. After several deep breaths she says, "The way that girl can look at you sometimes tells me there's something seriously wrong with her. She reminds me of those psychopaths you see on the true-crime documentaries. The ones who are analyzed by psychiatrists and found to be born evil. I think that's why Jake has been so affected by what she said: because he knows it could easily be true."

Madison leans back against the headrest and rubs her left temple. "Did you tell Anna what she'd said?"

"Of course not. How could I?"

Madison lets the woman go. She looks at Nate. "This changes everything."

CHAPTER SEVENTY-SEVEN

Anna is having a fitful sleep. The nurses keep waking her to check on the dog bite and take her blood pressure, and when she does manage to sleep, she dreams of her children. Her real children. She sits up and takes a sip of water. A quick glance at her phone tells her she has no missed calls or texts.

As she lies back on the bed, an image of the pool flashes in front of her eyes. Her therapist told her this happens because she's suffering with PTSD after being the one to find Susie and Thomas in the water.

She thinks of the first sign of trouble with Jennifer and remembers the time she claimed to feel ill one day so she didn't have to go to school. Anna took the day off work to be with her. She went into Jennifer's bedroom to take her something to eat around mid morning, but found her fully dressed and sitting drawing at her desk.

"How come you're up? You should be in bed." She reached for Jennifer's brow, but the girl pulled away.

"Get off me, bitch."

Anna was stunned. "What did you just say?"

"I said thanks for the food, Mommy." Jennifer smiled up at her.

It was the first time she had experienced one of Jennifer's mind games and it left her feeling like she was imagining things. Even now she can't believe how cunning and manipulative the girl was for someone of her age. She can't understand where she learned to be that way.

Over the following months, things slowly escalated: Jennifer would pull her hair while she was making dinner, hide things she needed for work, and then eventually hit her whenever they were alone. Anna told Grant, but he just wouldn't believe it. Jennifer was an absolute angel whenever he was around. She'd offer to help him with garden chores, tidy her things away as soon as he asked, and would even eat her vegetables when Grant was home for dinner, even though Anna knew she hated them. Inevitably she and Jennifer pulled him in opposite directions, leading to the breakdown of their marriage.

Grant refused to tell Esme what Anna had told him, so his mother didn't know what her granddaughter was capable of. It didn't matter; Esme wouldn't have believed her anyway. She was blinded by the love she had for her only remaining grandchild.

When she had nowhere left to turn, Anna told her therapist, Dr. Jarvis, but she was useless. She explained that Anna was afraid of losing another child, so she was subconsciously destroying their relationship in order to distance herself from the girl should the worst ever happen again. She even suggested she should temporarily take down photos of the other children in order for Jennifer to feel special, to help them bond. Anna resented her for that, but Grant thought it was a good idea. He confided in her that he was struggling to get over what had happened with constant reminders of them around. Because of that, she let him put all the photos of them into a special box. She knew Jennifer would love that. She finally had her father's full attention.

If her own husband and therapist wouldn't believe her, she knew no one would. No one would believe what Jennifer was capable of, and it was infuriating. She realized then that she was destined to live with this monster until she turned eighteen. Unless Jennifer killed her before then.

It was when Jennifer laughed about the children's accident that Anna began to violently hate her. She shivers under the thin hospital blanket as visions of their backyard float before her eyes. The children died on a sunny day in June while Anna was preparing for a BBQ at their house. She had invited all the kids' friends and their parents. Her three were playing on the grass near the swimming pool before everyone arrived, but the pool itself was fenced off and was always locked for their safety. She hadn't planned to unlock it until enough parents arrived to help her with lifeguard duties.

She had gone into the house to put a tray of food in the oven, having run out of space on the BBQ. Afterwards, she calculated it had taken her around ten minutes, as she needed a quick bathroom break on the way. By the time she got back out to the yard, she realized she couldn't hear the kids anymore. Susie had been singing when she left. She immediately turned to the pool and her worst nightmare was realized. The gate was wide open and both her beloved children were floating face down. She didn't hesitate; she jumped in after them fully clothed. She was screaming as she was faced with the agonizing decision of who to try to save.

She reached Thomas first. He was so small in her arms. She carried him to the pool's tiled surround and then went back for Susie, her thigh muscles unable to work fast enough against the weight of the water.

When she'd got them both out of the pool, she screamed for Jennifer to call 911, but that was when she realized the girl was nowhere to be seen. She looked back at the gate to see how it could have been opened and noticed the padlock was missing. The key to the padlock was discarded on the floor beneath the gate.

She tried CPR on Thomas first, but he wasn't responding so she had to leave him to attend to Susie. Susie's lips were already blue, but Anna tried breathing life into her anyway.

Grant had arranged to come home from work early to help her entertain everyone, but when he arrived there was a crowd outside on the driveway. He told her later that he'd let them all in behind him and then called her name as he walked through the house.

He found her lying between their children, holding their cold, lifeless hands.

She registered some screams from the other parents but blacked out soon after.

She shifts uncomfortably in the hospital bed as the tears fall. The heart monitor is beeping slowly and rhythmically.

Anna blames herself for not checking the padlock on the swimming pool gate before she went into the house. She blames herself for her children getting into the pool. That's a level of guilt that can destroy a person.

Her thoughts return to Jennifer. Just a couple of months ago, almost eleven months after the accident, she found the girl floating face down in the pool. Her heart stopped in her chest and she wanted to scream. But then Jennifer looked up at her. "I'm Thomas!" she said, giggling. When Anna didn't laugh at the cruel joke, Jennifer smiled and said, "Oh, wait. He was kicking when I held him down."

Anna ran from the house, not trusting herself. After a couple of hours, Grant eventually came looking for her and found her standing in the sea, the tide rising higher up her body with every passing minute.

"For God's sake, Anna! What are you doing?" He pulled her backwards, onto the sand. "Why did you leave Jenny alone? She could've hurt herself. She's just a kid!"

It was after that incident that she started researching Jennifer's personality traits, and finally came across a forum about children with RAD. The behaviors people were describing sounded just like her adopted daughter.

She was so relieved that she reached out to other women suffering the same things at home. Retrieving her cell phone now, she scrolls through the messages, deleting each one after reading it. She can't risk these being found. One woman suggested she set up some secret cameras in the house to capture what was happening, so she could show her husband and CPS. She couldn't fit cameras without Jennifer's knowledge—somehow she always knew Anna's every move—so she just had to use her cell phone. She set it up on so many occasions without Jennifer kicking off that she assumed she knew what she was up to. That was until one day when the girl went full psycho on her and hit her over the head with a vase as she was reading the newspaper at the dining table.

She touches the bump on her head. It never returned to normal. The vase didn't cause lasting damage, luckily, but it meant she had something to show Grant. He was devastated. He set up his own cameras, and each evening he'd watch what Jennifer was doing to her during the time between school letting out and him arriving home from work. That brought them back to each other. They shared the grief of knowing another child was lost to them.

Suddenly, she jumps. There's an unexpected knock on her door and Madison appears. Anna sits up, trying to focus on the here and now. Nate Monroe follows her into the room.

"Anna?" says Madison, taking her hand. "We need to ask you about something."

CHAPTER SEVENTY-EIGHT

Nate wonders how much more Anna Lucas can take. Losing two children in that way is unimaginable. She looks unsettled as they walk into her room, but eventually she smiles at Madison, who sits next to the bed. Nate chooses a seat near the door, not wanting to overcrowd her.

On the car ride over here, they discussed what involvement the parents could have had in Jenny's disappearance. Madison was adamant that if anyone killed her child, she'd want to kill them.

"Even if it was another child?" he asked.

"Anyone. I didn't say I *would* kill them, just that I'd want to. What if Grant found out what Jenny had told Jake? It would be easy to lash out in anger at that. Anyone is capable of killing someone when they're angry enough. I wouldn't put it past either of them."

"But what if it was *your* child who killed someone else's? What then?"

She hadn't even considered it. "He wouldn't do that. Owen was always a good child who knew right from wrong."

Nate held his tongue, but he wanted to say that all killers were someone's child once. He rubs his two-day-old stubble and wonders how this is going to go. He and Madison will never know what happened to Jenny if Anna or Grant don't tell them, because only two people, or possibly three if Detective Morgan is involved, know what happened. All he and Madison can do now is ask the person in front of them. Anna looks so frail and meek, he doesn't agree with Madison that she could be capable of murder. He could believe it of Grant, though.

Anna clearly knows why they're here. She takes a sip of water and looks directly at Nate. "My husband's gone AWOL. I'm afraid he may have harmed himself."

Nate wonders if Grant has left her to take the fall for this. "Hopefully he's just caught up in traffic," he says. "Mrs. Lucas, we've spoken to Jake's mom."

Panic flashes across her eyes. She looks at Madison, who says, "She told us about Susie and Thomas. I'm so sorry." Madison's voice breaks, and it's Anna who comforts her, rubbing her hand.

"Thank you. I appreciate that. They were beautiful children, full of fun and energy. We were lucky to have the time we got with them." She looks at Madison. "You have children, don't you?"

"Yes," says Madison, wiping her eyes. "A son. But he doesn't live with me. I haven't seen him for years, and although it's nothing like what you've gone through, the pain of not seeing him is unbearable some days."

Anna squeezes her hand. "Unfortunately, I know that pain. I don't know how any parent lives through this kind of thing, but I do think it's worse for mothers. When you grow a child inside you, you're bound to feel a deeper sense of emptiness and loss than anyone else in the family when that child is taken away from you. I hope you're reunited with him one day. I mean that."

Nate looks at Madison. Just because he doesn't have children doesn't mean he can't appreciate the loss the two women are feeling. Thoughts of Stacey threaten to cloud what he's here for, so he pushes them away. "Mrs. Lucas," he says. "Do you think Jenny killed your younger children?"

She looks at him with a blank expression. He can't see any shock there.

She nods slowly. "We believe so. You see, she hated me with a passion and she knew the best way to hurt me was to hurt my children. She was alone with them when it happened." She pauses.

"And two months ago, Grant found the padlock to the pool's safety gate in Jenny's closet."

Madison looks up at him. He knows that sounds pretty damning, but they should have told the authorities. There would've been an investigation. He's guessing they didn't do that.

"What did he do about it?" he asks.

Just then, Detective Morgan appears.

CHAPTER SEVENTY-NINE

"Anna? What's going on?"

Morgan looks at them all, and Madison can tell he's worried that Anna's confessing to something. Why would he be worried? Surely he should be as desperate for answers as she and Nate are?

On the ride over here, Nate convinced himself that Grant harmed Jenny, but her money is on Anna. The way she talks about Jenny isn't normal. There's no warmth in her voice, and Jake's mom confirmed there was tension between the pair. But Esme's description of Jenny is so different from what they've heard from other people. It's impossible to know the real Jennifer Lucas.

"It's okay, Ted," says Anna. "I'm just filling in a few gaps for them."

Madison watches him closely. His face is flushed and he's sweating. He walks to her bedside, the opposite side to where Madison is sitting. Anna takes his hand and smiles up at him. She looks exhausted. Almost like she's giving up. Holding the hand of the detective investigating your missing child isn't normal. That confirms it for Madison. They're having an affair. They must be.

Morgan turns to Nate. "I need you both to leave. You shouldn't be in here right now; you're not even related. Mrs. Lucas needs bed rest."

Nate shakes his head. "What's the matter, Ted? Are you worried she'll lose your baby?"

He stares back, open-mouthed. "What? What the hell are you talking about?"

"Well, you're holding the hand of a crime victim you supposedly don't know in a personal capacity. There's obviously something going on between you that you haven't told us about. I'm just wondering whether Grant has gone missing because he wasn't happy about your affair. Did he not feel like bringing up another man's baby? Or did you have to silence him?"

Morgan clenches his fists as Anna lets go of his hand.

"No, Mr. Monroe." She shakes her head. "You have it all wrong. Ted's an old friend of mine. We're not having an affair."

Madison asks, "Is the baby Grant's?"

"Of course she is! Grant and I love each other."

Morgan leans in to her ear, but they can all hear what he says. "Anna, I have to advise you not to say anything. If you want to speak, at least consult a lawyer first. Hell, at least speak to me first, in private."

She looks up at him and smiles. "It's okay, Ted. Really."

He grabs her wrist and tries to warn her with his eyes. "I'm not messing with you, Anna. You do *not* want to tell them anything."

"Let her go, Detective," says Madison, standing now.

"What are you trying to hide?" asks Nate.

Neither of them speaks. Anna looks unsure of herself now. She's deathly pale.

"At least tell us how you know each other," says Madison.

Morgan looks at her. "I don't know why you left law enforcement to team up with an ex-convict, but this is none of your goddam business, so stop interfering." He wipes sweat off his forehead. "You need to leave before I arrest you both."

Anna tries to calm him down. "Ted, it's not a secret." She turns to Madison. "We met at college. We shared a couple of the same classes and we did date for about a year, but only until I met Grant."

Her words clearly sting Morgan, because he looks bitter.

"So how come Jenny went missing in the same town your old flame works in?" says Nate. "I mean, Shadow Falls is a long way from Santa Barbara."

"It was an unhappy coincidence, Mr. Monroe," Anna says. "Coincidences do happen, no matter how much you'd like to believe they don't."

Morgan slowly exhales. "We hadn't spoken since we left college, so your little theory about us having an affair is way off the mark."

Madison can tell he's hiding something, but she can't figure out what.

CHAPTER EIGHTY

Anna knows what she has to do in order to get rid of this well-intentioned pair of strangers. She doesn't have any animosity toward them; she doesn't have the energy for that. The last twelve months has taken so much out of her that she just can't go on pretending any longer. They're too persistent.

Esme asked them to look for Jennifer, and they're trying to do that even when they know they won't be paid for it. She's realizing they won't give up until they find her, and she can help with that. Then she can move on. She can have her baby and forget any of this ever happened.

She thinks of Grant, and that's where her anger lies. He should be with her right now, dealing with this stress and protecting her, but he's taken the easy way out. She assumes he's killed himself. He's left her to deal with this alone.

She looks up at Ted. He's always loved her. That's why it was him she turned to when they needed help; she knew he'd do anything she asked. Part of her wonders if that's why she stayed in touch with him all these years. Just in case things didn't work out with Grant and she needed a backup. It's not like she's using him; she has genuine affection for him, just not the kind he wants from her.

She looks at Madison. "I'm going to be completely honest with you now."

Ted groans above her. "Anna, seriously, stop!"

She shakes her head slowly and then looks at her bed covers. "I know where Jennifer is."

CHAPTER EIGHTY-ONE

Madison moves closer to the bed, eager to hear what Anna has to say. If it's what she's expecting, she has to try to hide her contempt for this woman.

"Tell us everything." Part of her only wants to ask whether Jenny's alive or not, because she doesn't want to be interviewed by the police as a witness, and pulled further into this mess. She just wants to find Jenny and then leave. But professional curiosity and concern for the missing girl keep her here.

Morgan is pale and sweaty. He's stepped back, away from Anna. It's obvious that he's implicated in this somehow.

Anna looks down at her hands and speaks quietly. "When Grant found that padlock in Jennifer's room, it made the outcome inevitable. He showed me and I just about broke down. I couldn't handle it."

"Where was Jenny at this time?" Madison asks.

"She was at school. This was mid morning. Grant had taken the day off work because we'd planned to look for it. His attitude changed from the moment he found it; he shut down. He finally realized this young girl had manipulated him brilliantly, and that was a painful loss for him because he'd loved her more than I had. They'd bonded quickly, mainly because Jenny had made it happen that way. I believe that girl knew from the minute she met us that she would play us off against each other, because she wanted me out. She wanted Grant all to herself. You have to understand; she was clever."

Madison is suddenly overwhelmed with sadness. Anna just referred to Jenny in the past tense. She tries not to react to learning that Jennifer Lucas is undoubtedly dead and probably has been all along.

"I honestly believe she had a psychopathic personality. I researched her personality traits and learned she probably suffered with RAD—reactive attachment disorder. Have you heard of it?"

Madison nods. She doesn't give details, but she's come across it before whilst on the job. If this were her investigation, she'd want a professional to confirm that Jenny suffered from the condition. She wouldn't take the mother's word for it.

Anna describes in detail the symptoms and causes of RAD, and assuming she's telling the truth, Madison can understand the hell she was put through. It's still no excuse to harm a child, though.

"So the two of you plotted to kill her?" asks Nate when she's finished.

Madison knows that if they did, that's premeditated murder.

"Anna, you need a lawyer." Morgan steps in. "I'm not just saying that as your friend, but as a cop."

"No, Ted." She's defiant. "I want them to know. I want a fresh start for my baby." She looks back at Nate. "Grant decided to kill her. Did I go along with it? Yes, because I couldn't see an alternative. I tried telling staff at CPS about my doubts, but they didn't want to hear it. I told my therapist, but she thought I was the one with the problem, not Jennifer. It had taken so much just to get Grant to believe me! I had to secretly film Jennifer hurting me. When he saw the footage, he finally realized I was telling the truth."

"You could have shown CPS that video," says Nate.

Anna shakes her head and touches her bump. "No. No, Mr. Monroe. You have to understand: she killed our children. When I found out I was pregnant with this one, I almost terminated it because I just knew the baby would be at risk too. Once we found the padlock and knew for sure she'd killed Susie and Thomas, we realized we couldn't risk her killing our baby too." Tears start running down her face. "CPS work so slowly that even if they did finally agree to take her off us, they might have made us wait months or even years until they could place her somewhere else. She would've found out about the baby! Her bedroom would've been next to the nursery."

She looks at Madison like she's pleading with her to understand. "This was someone who deliberately made our lives a misery. Grant was so angry there was no reasoning with him. He was adamant that the only way not to inflict Jennifer on another family was to end her life. He said he'd make it quick and painless so she wouldn't know what was happening. Deep down I knew he wanted it over with fast because he felt so stupid for loving someone like that. He felt like he'd already lost another child because the girl he'd loved didn't really exist."

Morgan turns away and leans against the wall, covering his face.

Madison is struggling to remain composed. She wants to arrest Anna and Grant immediately, but of course she has no power over this fucked-up situation. Plus, there's no evidence. She doesn't think Anna would repeat this in a police interview.

"What about Esme?" she asks. "Did she know what you were plotting? Or did she find out afterwards and threaten to tell us? Because I wouldn't put it past either of you to kill her too."

Anna's face flickers with shock, then contempt. "We would never have hurt Esme. She died of a broken heart." A tear runs down her face. "She didn't know anything. That's why she fought so hard to find Jennifer. We asked her not to mention Susie and Thomas to you. She didn't understand, of course, but we explained it might take your focus off finding Jennifer because you'd assume we'd killed all three children. For what it's worth, that's my biggest regret over this terrible affair: that Esme suffered so much. But she would have suffered more if she was still alive to hear what Grant did."

"You mean what you both did," says Madison.

Anna lets the dig slide. "We knew we couldn't do it at home because the forensics would've incriminated us, so Grant came up with the idea of sending her to summer camp. That way he could sneak in at night, grab her and bury her out in the forest."

Madison covers her eyes with her hands and leans forward. She has to swallow her emotions and try to remain professional.

"I can almost understand your hatred for the girl," says Nate, "but you had other ways out. You didn't need to kill her."

Madison nods in agreement. She looks up. "Why use Camp Fearless? Why Shadow Falls?"

Morgan stays quiet.

"That was just random. Grant said we needed somewhere that didn't pay much attention to security, so he looked at the lower-priced camps. I didn't know Ted lived near here until he called to tell us of Jennifer's disappearance." Anna lowers her eyes.

Madison wonders if she's telling the truth. Could it really have been a coincidence? "So what did Grant do to her?" she asks, not wanting to know the answer.

Anna shakes her head. "I have no idea how he did it. I didn't come up here with him; I stayed at home. I couldn't ever hurt a child, not even that one. Grant took care of it."

Nate struggles to remain composed as he asks, "Where is Jenny's body?"

Anna rubs her eyes, but there are no tears. "In the Wildwood National Forest. Grant said he'd pushed her off a rock face into a large waterfall about ten miles from Camp Fearless." She looks at him with terror in her eyes. "Please don't bring her body back to me, Mr. Monroe. I couldn't bear it." She finally breaks down.

Madison looks away. She can't bring herself to comfort the woman.

CHAPTER EIGHTY-TWO

Morgan approaches Nate. The stress is showing on his face. "We need to talk."

Nate follows him out into the corridor. There are nurses everywhere so he keeps his voice low. "Are you going to call this in, or should I?"

Morgan's eyes look panicked. "Listen, we don't know anything for sure until we find her body. I'm going to drive up there, as I know the area better than you, but I'd like you both to come with me."

Nate is surprised. "Why? So we don't call your superiors and tell them how you're somehow involved in all this? I'm betting Anna confided in you at some point and that's why you weren't doing much detective work."

Ted leans back and raises his hands. "Whoa! I didn't know any of that. She never told me. When I had to phone the parents of the missing girl, I had no idea it was going to be Anna who answered until I heard her voice. I'd been given Grant's name as Jenny's contact, and thought it was just a coincidence that I knew a Grant Lucas."

"So why were you so keen on her not talking to us?"

"Because she's a friend, asshole, and I protect my friends. But if I had known her husband killed their daughter, I would've arrested him myself." He runs his hands through his hair. "I just wanted her to seek legal counsel so she didn't get tricked into admitting something she didn't mean. I mean, come on; she's exhausted, pregnant and emotional. It's easy to get confused in that state. She probably doesn't even know what she's saying."

Nate thinks about it, but he can tell Morgan clearly has feelings for her. "So, if we find Jenny's body out there, then what?"

"I'll excuse myself from the case and get a different detective from my department to arrest Anna. Then I'll search for the piece of shit she married. I know the guy and I'm guessing he's on the run. That means she'll take all the heat. The media are going to have a field day with this, and with the fact that I know her. I just want to try to control what I can to minimize everyone's suffering. You've got to understand that. We can't risk anything happening to that baby, because I genuinely don't think she'd survive losing a fourth child."

Nate is surprised when Morgan's eyes well up. The guy is still in love with her. He feels for him, but he's still wary. "Fine, I'll come with you, but Madison will stay here. Anna shouldn't be left alone in case Grant comes to silence her." He's about to walk back into the room when he adds, "Brody's outside, waiting by my car."

"No way. That dog's not coming with us."

"He's a trained cadaver dog; he's exactly what we need."

Morgan doesn't look so sure. "He's dangerous."

"I'll take care of him. You get us to the spot Anna described, and if Jenny's there, Brody will find her. If you'd rather go alone, I'll call your superiors right now."

He shakes his head. "Fine."

Nate walks back into Anna's room to tell Madison where he's going. He notices that Anna has taken her cardigan off. Her arm is scabbed over in places from where Brody bit her, but she's scratching her other arm, which has pink scars of its own.

"What's happening?" asks Madison, standing up.

He leads her into the corner of the room and lowers his voice. "We're taking Brody to go and find Jenny's body. If Anna's telling the truth, we can get the police out there when we locate her. I need you to stay here. Keep your phone charged, because I'll check in with you regularly by text, though I'm guessing the cell coverage is sporadic in the forest. If you don't hear from me for two hours straight, call the police and tell them everything."

She nods. "Why don't you just call the police now?"

He takes a deep breath. "Because I think there's more to this story than we've been told and I'm hoping to get more out of Morgan on the drive. If we let him go straight to his boss about this, he's going to twist it to protect Anna and blame everything on Grant. I also want to find out just how involved he was."

"How come you get to go? Why can't I? I'm way more qualified than you to handle the situation."

Nate sighs. He could do without this right now, and he doesn't need her reminding him he's probably out of his depth. "You're not a cop now, Madison. You're working for me and I need you to do what I say. If you don't think you can take orders, what we have won't work. Watching Anna is just as important as finding the girl. For all we know, Grant will turn up any minute and we can get both of them arrested at once. But not if you're not here. Okay?"

She nods reluctantly; he can tell she's unhappy.

"Are you armed?" she asks.

He's touched at her concern. He smiles. "I've got Brody."

She rolls her eyes. "Brody could be taking a crap while you get shot. Here." She discreetly pulls out her weapon. "Take this."

He pushes it away. The last thing he needs is Morgan accusing him of trying to shoot an officer; on top of that, the gun isn't registered to him and he doubts it's registered to Madison, so he could be up for a charge right there. He won't risk going back inside.

"Nate? You're going into a forest with a man who has a stake in how all this turns out. Take the goddam gun."

He shakes his head. He knows he needs to be careful around Morgan, but he'd rather be dead than spend another day in prison. "Thanks, but no." He touches her hand. "I'm doing this my way."

She stuffs the gun back in her waistband, under her shirt. "Well, I guess it was nice knowing you." She looks at the clock above Anna's bed and sighs. "If I don't hear from you regularly, I'm calling the police."

He nods and turns to the door, where Morgan is pacing back and forth. "Let's go."

CHAPTER EIGHTY-THREE

Madison's eyelids are growing heavy. She's struggling to stay awake, and when she looks over at the bed, it's clear that Anna is already asleep. She stands up and stretches her back. She's heard some screwed-up things in her time, both as a cop and as an inmate, but what Anna told them today might just top it all. She'll never understand how anyone could kill a child, especially one who was so dependent on them to protect her.

Even though she feels sick, her stomach's growling with hunger, so she leaves the room to head to the cafeteria in search of food. On the way, her phone buzzes with a text.

Still driving. Hitting some dense forest now so this might be the last contact for a while. Brody despises Morgan, so at least it's two against one.

She smiles. She's never been a dog person but Brody is growing on her. He's so eager to please and he's clearly besotted with Nate. She's not surprised. Nate's a special guy and she feels lucky to have met him. Once he's helped her get to the bottom of who ruined her life, she wants to help him find Father Connor. She'd like to get him some closure so he can move on and start living without thoughts of revenge holding him back.

As she sits in the half-empty cafeteria finishing off a stale cold chicken salad, her phone buzzes again. This time it's Stephanie.

Mike checked in on me but there's no need. I'm fine. Thanks for your concern. xx

Madison drops her plastic fork. Stephanie has never in her life added kisses to the end of a text. She always said they were passive-aggressive when other people used them. Could she have changed since they last saw each other? Madison doubts it. Her heart starts beating a little harder. She needs to call Steph, to hear her voice for herself.

As the phone rings, she moves away from anyone who can overhear her. There's no answer, so she immediately tries again. With each ring her dread builds, but she doesn't know why. Maybe Steph's out for the night and isn't taking calls. She tries the home number, which she knows off by heart since Stephanie still lives in the house they shared.

No reply.

She takes a deep breath. There's nothing she can do from here except reply to the text and wait for Steph to call back.

Call me asap.

If she hasn't heard anything by morning, she'll speak to Mike.

She ditches the last of the salad in the trash and heads to the restroom. It smells bad in here, of illness and medicine. She splashes water on her face and glances in the mirror. She looks tired and greasy; her forehead is shining with sweat. The air is so stale in this hospital. She'd love to go back to the guest house now and take another long, hot bath followed by eight hours' sleep.

She jumps when a nurse walks in and enters a stall.

She pulls her sleeves up to wash her hands, and is reminded of the scars she saw on Anna's other arm; the arm Brody didn't attack. Brody was pretty fired up when he saw Anna arrive at the summer camp. Could he have recognized her?

She turns the faucet off and rests her hands on the sink. No. He couldn't have. Anna said she never visited the camp. It was Grant who dropped Jenny off, and then it was Grant who came back to abduct her. Unless… Maybe Anna was in the car and didn't get out. Could she really have been present when Grant killed Jenny?

She realizes that all three of them have taken the word of someone who plotted with her husband to kill her own daughter. It was Anna who told them Grant had dealt with Jennifer. She thinks about the scars again. They weren't quite healed; they could easily have been made within the last month. And they look similar to the injury from Brody's attack on her other arm. Which would mean Anna did go to the camp at some point. But why would Brody have reacted to her?

She looks up at her reflection. Brody didn't just recognize Anna; he attacked her. They've not witnessed him do that to anyone else at the camp.

She suddenly realizes what it means. "It was *her*. Shit. It was her all along."

The nurse comes out of the stall to wash her hands. She looks at Madison in the mirror.

Madison is desperately trying to figure it out. "Brody was there that night. He tried to save Jenny from her mother!"

She realizes she's left Anna alone.

She ignores the nurse's questioning stare and dashes for the door. As she skids around the hospital corridors, trying to get back to Anna's room, she almost knocks a patient over.

"Sorry! Police business!"

When she gets there, the lights are off. She hopes that's just because a nurse has checked in on Anna and switched them off on the way out. She flips them on and glances at the bed. It's empty. She looks in the bathroom, but that's empty too. A quick glance at the spare armchair tells her Anna's belongings have gone.

"Shit!"

She thinks about Detective Morgan. He was pretty stressed when Anna was relaying what happened. Could he really be in on it?

Yes. Because he would be more likely to protect Anna than her husband.

Madison pulls out her cell phone and calls Nate. It goes straight to answerphone, which means they're so far into the woods there's limited service.

"Dammit!"

She sends him a text.

Brody had already attacked Anna earlier. She killed the girl. She's fled the hospital. Ted must be in on it. BE CAREFUL!

She hits send and prays Nate finds a signal in the forest before it's too late.

She runs through the hospital corridors. Anna couldn't have got far in her condition. But she's nowhere to be seen on this floor. She heads to the elevator, but it's too slow to arrive, so she swings open the stairwell doors and runs down the first flight. As she rounds the corner, she spots Anna—too late. She's holding a knife and lunges toward her.

Madison screams as the knife goes through her shoulder. The pain is sharp and intense. She loses her footing and slides down the stairs as blood rushes from the wound. She manages to push Anna against the wall as she passes, trying to stop her from running.

Anna falls onto her ass with a thud. Her expression changes from desperation to pain. She grabs her stomach and screams.

Madison's going dizzy. She can't get up; all she can do is watch as Anna panics.

"The baby's coming!"

Madison moves to help her, but blacks out at the foot of the stairs.

CHAPTER EIGHTY-FOUR

The office of Dr. Pamela Jarvis

Pamela hesitantly starts to read the last entry in Anna Lucas's journal, knowing this will be the final nail in her own coffin, career-wise at least.

I can't believe it's over. We reached a peak in this hell we were living and the only thing we could do was to kill Jennifer. Even Grant could see there was no other way out, but he was hesitant. Said he couldn't go through with it. Even after everything Jennifer had done, I think he still loved her, so he was conflicted.

When I found a summer camp near Ted, I knew it was a sign. He would be able to help us. He would be able to limit the investigation into her disappearance. I knew without a doubt that he would have my back.

Jennifer did not want to go away. I can't tell if she knew what we were planning, but sometimes she was like a mind-reader. She only agreed to go in the end because Grant said he would travel up there to collect her if she wanted to leave early. She trusted him and that's what Grant is struggling with now. On those days I remind him what Jennifer did to our children and I pull out their baby photos. It gives him renewed confidence in our decision.

Once Jennifer was at camp, our lives became lighter. I was able to relax for the first time in three years. I could read a book without waiting for something to hit me over the head. Grant and I even went out to dinner like a normal married couple.

But on the day he was due to drive up there, he couldn't do it. He couldn't even get out of bed. His mind shut his body down. He was weak when I needed him to be strong.

Desperate that she would end up coming home, I drove up there myself in a rental car I'd booked in a fake name online. I played loud music for the whole journey to block out my doubts and I only stopped for one break.

I didn't drive all the way up the long entrance to the camp; I stopped about three quarters of the way up so that no one would see me. I held a photo of my children as I approached the camp, and when I spotted some girls by the lake, I hid behind a tree. I could just make out Jennifer's thin, delicate frame in the fading light. The other girls had been teasing her, I could tell from her posture. Her hands were clenched like she was about to hit one of them. Then they ran off, leaving her alone.

The sun had almost disappeared, but I looked at the photo of my children and kissed them both. "This is for you."

I ran toward Jennifer and she seemed shocked to see me. "Daddy's here," I said. "We've come to take you home because he misses you so much."

She looked uncertain. "Where's the car?"

"Just down there." I pointed to my rental car, which was just visible in the dark, a way off. "Don't bother getting your things from the cabin; we'll have them sent home. We're going to stop for takeout on the way."

I could tell she was wondering why I was being nice, because by this point our relationship was non-existent, so I added, "I'd rather leave you here, but for some reason your dad misses you."

The look on her face—genuine love for her father—will never leave me. I almost backed out then. I suddenly realized she was just a child. Yes, she'd acted abhorrently, but deep down she had a child's emotions. She just wanted to be loved, and she *was* loved, by Grant. I had wanted to love her, I'd been open to it at the beginning, but she'd killed my babies. That's what made me go on: the crumpled photo in my hand. I had to be strong for them and the new baby.

"We have to be quick, otherwise someone will try to stop us," I said.

She picked up her things, slid her backpack on and started running to the car. I got there first, on shaky legs, and opened the back door for her. She jumped in without looking. When she realized Grant wasn't in the car, she looked up at me with confusion in her eyes. "Where's Daddy?"

I leaned in and wrapped rope around her, strapping her arms to her torso and her backpack to her back. I didn't have time to remove it first, I had to move fast. She kicked out at me, only just missing the baby, so I pushed her backwards in anger and she hit her head hard against the door. She stopped struggling, so I tied her legs together while she was passed out and closed the door on her. I ran around to the front of the car, but there was a large dog that had appeared from nowhere. He was growling at me. I tried slowly easing past him, but he lunged at me and grabbed my arm with his teeth. His mouth was like a vice and the pain was sharp. I couldn't risk being found, so I suppressed my screams and thumped him across the head until he let go. He looked stunned, but I could tell he was getting ready to lunge at me again. I managed to scramble into the car and shut the door, activating the child locks. I looked over at Jennifer; she was lying across the back seat, groaning quietly.

As I pulled away, the dog chased the car for over a mile. When he finally stopped, Jennifer said something I didn't quite catch. It made me freeze. "What?" I whispered.

"I didn't mean it," she said in a weak voice.

I didn't know if she was talking about killing my children, but it was such a typical response from a child that guilt consumed me. I pulled over, considering whether to back out.

"What do you mean?" I asked.

She turned her head to look at me. She had tears in her eyes. "I only pretended to hurt them. Thomas fell in and Susie tried to save him. They called for you, but you didn't come. I …" She started coughing. "I pretended I did it because you don't like me."

I couldn't believe what I was hearing. I leaned in close.

"But the padlock was in your closet," I whispered.

"I pretended." She started crying, but not the crocodile tears she used in front of Grant. "I didn't mean it, Mommy. If you let me go home, I'll be good, I promise."

Not wanting to believe her—convinced it was her final trick to torture me—I remained resolute and started the engine.

When we got deep into the forest, I cut the rope binding her legs and made her walk in front of me. By the time I found somewhere to bury her, I realized I couldn't do it. I couldn't stab a child. But I had to kill her. It was the only way my baby would be safe. So I pushed her off the waterfall and watched as she fell from a height into the rocky water. Even the biggest flashlight I could buy barely cut through the darkness of the night in the forest. I didn't see her emerge. She must have drowned quickly, either because her head hit a rock or because the rope around her arms prevented her from swimming to safety.

I knew no one would find her in there and assumed the wild animals would eat her remains if she washed up on the bank.

I can't believe I'm writing this.

I can't believe I've done this.

I'll never know if she was telling the truth and I'm more of a monster than I already thought.

I used the rental car to get back to a main road, then I drove north, eventually leaving the car in a covered ditch where it would be difficult for anyone to find because of the ground cover. I walked to the nearest gas station and phoned Ted, only telling him where I was and that I needed a ride.

Ted was pleased to see me, but he had a lot of questions. I told him everything; from the first time Jennifer showed her true colors to finding the padlock in her room. I didn't tell him about her final confession. He wouldn't help me if he took her word over mine. It all poured out of me and he placed me under arrest as soon as I'd finished. I'd kissed him and told him he was a good person, and how I felt that if I'd married him instead of Grant, none of this would ever have happened.

It took hours of talking, but eventually he agreed to drive me home and said he'd call me later with his decision. I knew he'd agree to cover up for me. It made me feel horrible, but after killing a twelve-year-old girl, there really wasn't much emotion left in me. I was exhausted, but my baby kicked a lot that night, trying to reassure me.

Grant and I never spoke about what had happened. He never asked any questions and I was glad. Ted didn't get in touch. I didn't hear from him until he turned up to give us the news that Jennifer had disappeared from the camp. I knew then that he had decided to protect me.

Even though we had visits from Ted and his team, and then the investigators, Grant reacted as if we knew nothing. I was surprised at his ability to pretend we weren't involved. I think he'd managed to convince himself we weren't. I never considered telling him about the look on Jennifer's face when she thought her father had come to rescue her from camp. Or that she might not have killed the children; that it could have been an accident after all. I knew that would break him, so I bore the brunt of that by myself. I've suffered. I must have looked like a grieving mother to most people. Unfortunately, I had learned that role well after the deaths of Susie and Thomas.

I'm not proud of what I've done and I think of Jennifer often—how could I not?—but could I really stand by and let her take a third child from me? I would only have found out whether or not she was telling the truth by letting her live alongside my new baby. That would have been a risk too far.

My therapist was right about one thing: keeping this journal was cathartic. It helped me to think things through logically. It helped me voice the feelings and thoughts I was having. I know I'll need to burn it eventually. For now, I need to keep it, so I never forget how it felt to live with Jennifer. How it felt to discover she killed our babies. Because if I ever forget that, I won't be able to live with what I did to her.

After Pamela closes the journal, it takes her a good five minutes to stop crying. She doesn't know if she'll ever get over the guilt of ignoring Anna's pleas about Jennifer. Both Anna and Jennifer were let down: by Pamela herself, by child services, by Jennie's real mother.

Her office door opens and the lieutenant she has only spoken to over the phone pops his head in. "Hi, Dr. Jarvis. Lieutenant Davis. Finished yet?"

She nods her head and wipes her eyes with her hands.

"Anything incriminating in there?" he asks.

She pours herself a triple shot of bourbon, downs it and turns back to face him. "Unfortunately, yes.'

CHAPTER EIGHTY-FIVE

Nate follows Morgan as they make their way through the forest toward the only waterfall he found on Google Maps that's anywhere near Camp Fearless.

The sun is setting fast behind the huge redwood trees. Nate can feel the temperature dropping too. It's eerily quiet out here, with none of the birdsong they get at the camp. It's as if all the woodland creatures have bedded down for the evening. Either that or they're hiding from those monsters in the woods the kids were talking about.

They each have a flashlight, and Brody's running ahead of them—nose down, tail high—with no sign of tiring. Nate's legs and back are starting to ache. Since prison, he's not used to hiking in this kind of terrain, but it's satisfying to hear Morgan struggling to catch his breath too.

"I thought cops were supposed to be fit," he shouts over his shoulder as he overtakes the detective.

Morgan doesn't reply. He suddenly stops. "You hear that?"

Nate stops to listen. It's the sound of running water. They could be near the waterfall Anna mentioned.

It spurs them on. Nate walks faster, following Brody. They come to a dense area of trees where the sun can't reach. It's much cooler and darker under here. As they come out the other side, into a clearing, Brody starts barking loudly.

Nate stops and glances back at Morgan, who looks like he'd rather be anywhere else than here. "This could be it. Are you ready?"

The detective nods.

Nate walks into the clearing and toward the waterfall. Visibility is poor, as the sun has completely disappeared behind the trees now. Brody is sitting next to a stack of large rocks. He's fully alert, looking over his shoulder at Nate. Nate's heart sinks as he realizes that the dog has found something and is now waiting for his reward. He made sure to bring the squeezy ball from the grocery store for this exact reason. As he approaches the rocks, his legs slow down. He doesn't want to see what Brody's found. He doesn't want to believe Anna's story because it's so disturbing.

He catches up to the dog and has to cover his nose and mouth with his arm.

Morgan turns away and dry-heaves.

Nate forces himself to look down at the ground. It's Grant Lucas. "He's dead. Looks like a self-inflicted gunshot wound." There are flies buzzing around Grant's head, laying their eggs in his flesh. Nate leans down to find the gun. He can just see the barrel sticking out from under Grant's chest. He must have shot himself whilst kneeling and then fallen forwards.

"Jesus," says Morgan, clearly shocked.

So Anna was telling the truth. Grant must have come back to see Jenny. He must have felt remorse.

Nate notices something to the right of Grant. It's a red sweater.

"That's what they said Jenny was wearing when she disappeared," says Morgan.

"You mean when your friend," Nate points to Grant, "abducted her." He can't resist the dig. He's not letting Morgan off the hook. He *was* friends with these people.

Brody comes over to him, pawing at his jeans and completely unaware of the implications of his find. It's safe to assume Jenny's remains are out here somewhere too. Nate pulls the ball from his pocket and the dog's eyes light up. He hasn't seen this one before. He sits back and barks excitedly. Nate smiles weakly and suddenly feels grateful to have him here. He throws the ball as far as he can, and Brody runs for it.

Nate shines his flashlight around Grant's body and spots a cell phone. He picks it up just as Morgan tries to grab it.

"Give that to me; it's evidence."

Nate holds it to his chest. "You can have it after I've had a look."

He turns it on and waits for a PIN request, but there isn't one. It opens to a video. "He can't have been dead long," he says. "There's still life in the battery."

Morgan tries to grab it again, so Nate calls Brody over. The dog notices instantly that the mood has changed. He sits between the two men, staring at the detective, but doesn't drop the ball from his mouth. He earned it so he obviously intends to keep it.

From Morgan's reaction, Nate is certain he's more involved in all this than he admitted. It doesn't surprise him. After all, Morgan's a cop. But it means he and Brody could be in danger.

He holds the phone up so they can both see it, and then hits play on the video. Grant Lucas's face appears. He doesn't look at all well.

CHAPTER EIGHTY-SIX

Nate's hand trembles as he tries to hold the cell phone steady. They watch in silence.

Grant looks directly into the lens. His eyes are bloodshot, exhausted. "By the time anyone finds this, I'll be dead." He waves a gun at the camera.

Morgan is shaking his head as he runs his hands through his hair. Nate glances over at him and realizes he looks like a desperate man. But why? What is he hiding? He checks on Brody, who's not letting the cop out of his sight.

He feels his phone buzz in his pocket and slowly pulls it out while Morgan is transfixed on Grant and what he'll reveal. He glances down and reads a text from Madison.

Brody had already attacked Anna earlier. She killed the girl. She's fled the hospital. Ted must be in on it. BE CAREFUL!

Shocked, he looks at Morgan, trying not to let his thoughts show on his face. Brody tried to protect Jenny from *Anna*. That's why he had such a strong reaction to her at the camp when he saw her again. And if it was Anna who killed Jenny, Morgan must've known about it. He must've helped her in some way. She said in the hospital that they hadn't spoken to each other since college, but Rex had told him about the class reunion photos on Facebook. They stayed in touch. They were closer than they wanted Nate to know.

Nate finds himself wishing he'd taken Madison's gun. He concentrates on the video while he thinks how best to react.

"I came here to find my daughter," says Grant. "But all I could find was this!" He holds up the red sweater.

Nate can see he's distraught. It's not easy to watch this.

"I just need the world to know that I loved Jenny as if she were my own blood. I didn't see the side of her that Anna talked about. I didn't believe her until she showed me the footage. I was devastated. That wasn't my experience of her at all." He pauses. "I didn't kill my daughter, but I went along with Anna's plan."

Nate takes a sideways glance at Morgan, but he's turned his flashlight off so his face is in darkness. Brody's still got eyes on him, though.

"Once I heard what Jenny had done to our beautiful children, I couldn't bear to look at her. She was a smart kid, and I think she knew what we were planning. She had something wrong with her that she couldn't control. It wasn't her fault; it was her biological mother who screwed her up. We should've tried harder to get help, but Anna convinced me that no one would believe us, and even if they did, we'd still be expected to live with Jenny because she was our responsibility until she was an adult." He pauses, rubbing his eyes. "And then I found Anna's journal and realized that Jenny hadn't killed our babies after all. She had only pretended to in order to get under Anna's skin. It really was just an accident. We made a devastating mistake."

"Wait. What?" Morgan takes a step back.

Nate is just as shocked as him. Anna told them the girl had killed the children and that was why they had felt it necessary to protect their unborn baby from her.

Grant sobs for a long time and Nate can feel his pain.

"Just know that I'm sorry. I'm sorry for not being a good enough dad to make Jenny better, for not being able to make her feel secure enough. That's why she pretended to kill her brother and sister, right? She thought we loved them more than her. It's all my fault. I should've spent more time with her. I should've helped her bond with Anna. Our family is broken." He looks into the lens. "Anna? You were wrong, honey. We're not cursed, we're just not good enough parents. If you love our baby, you'll give her up for adoption. Please don't make her grow up in prison." He wipes away the tears. "I wanted to tell Jenny I'm sorry, but I can't even do that because I can't find her. I *am* sorry, though. I'm sorry for every child out there who grows up unloved. Everyone who's had a shit parent who put themselves before their children. I put Jenny first until it was impossible to continue, but now that I know the truth, I just hope she can forgive me."

Grant disappears from view as he lowers the phone, and they both hear a loud gunshot. It makes Nate jump, and even Brody reacts by looking around for danger.

"Shit!" says Morgan with his hands behind his head.

The phone is dropped to the ground and Nate has to swallow the lump in his throat.

Morgan walks away.

Nate can barely see him now the sun has set. He pockets Grant's cell phone, and when he lifts his flashlight, he sees the gun in Morgan's hand.

CHAPTER EIGHTY-SEVEN

Madison wakes up in a hospital bed. A doctor and several nurses are working on her shoulder.

"Please stay still. I'm stitching you up," says the doctor.

"What happened?" asks a nurse.

She tries to clear the fog in her head, but she feels like she's going to vomit. "Anna." She suddenly remembers. When she woke in the stairwell, Anna was gone and Madison had managed to crawl to safety before blacking out again. She tries to sit up but the doctor pushes her back down.

"Not yet. I'm almost finished."

"I was stabbed by Anna Lucas. She's a patient here. She's pregnant. She can't get away. Her baby is at risk."

The doctor looks at the nurse and they don't appear to be convinced, so Madison retrieves her phone from her jeans pocket and calls Nate whilst still flat on her back.

It goes straight to voicemail. "Nate, call me when you get this. I need to know you're safe. I'm calling for backup."

Realizing there's only one thing she can do now to help Nate, she makes a call to the police.

"Nine one one, what's your emergency?"

As she tries to think how best to explain the whole sorry mess, she realizes she's going to sound like a wacko. "The body of missing school girl Jennifer Lucas is in the Wildwood National Forest, and Detective Ted Morgan from Trinity Creek PD might have helped put her there as he's a former lover of the girl's mother."

The hospital staff take a step back from her and listen, horrified.

"Ma'am, I'm going to need you to back up a little. What's your name?"

Madison is frustrated. "Listen to me! I'm a former cop and I have reason to believe Detective Ted Morgan is about to kill my colleague, Nate Monroe. I need you to get some backup out there asap. I have a rough location for the girl's body; are you ready to write it down?"

With no reaction, the dispatcher says flatly, "Go ahead, ma'am."

After Madison tells her the location, the dispatcher says, "Stay on the line while I radio all units. I'm going to need the whole story in just a minute."

Madison doesn't know if it's too late to save Nate. Before she can explain to the doctor, she passes out from the pain in her shoulder.

CHAPTER EIGHTY-EIGHT

Nate can see that Morgan is agitated and struggling to know what to do.

"Ted, you don't have to do this," he says. "Grant didn't implicate you, just Anna."

Morgan tries to control his breathing. He looks at Brody, who's clearly wound up, ready to pounce. If he does, Nate knows Morgan will have no qualms about shooting him.

The detective looks up. "He didn't implicate me because I didn't have anything to do with it."

"Okay, then tell me what happened. I'm assuming you wouldn't have actually helped her kill a child, because I'd like to believe you became a cop for a good reason."

"Of course I didn't help her kill anyone! How could you even think that?" He shakes his head. "I'm going back to the car. You need to walk ahead of me with your hands in the air. If that dog makes one wrong move, I'm shooting it."

Brody growls aggressively.

"I'm not turning my back on a bent cop and I'm not going anywhere until we find Jenny's body and you tell me what happened," says Nate. "If you weren't involved, you don't have anything to worry about. So why point a gun at me?"

Morgan thinks about it. Eventually he lowers his gun slightly.

"She called me. After it had already been done. I got a call completely out of the blue to say she needed a ride. I was shocked. I mean, I knew she lived in Santa Barbara so I couldn't understand why she was all the way up here in the middle of the night."

"So you went to her."

"Of course. She's a friend. I didn't know then what she'd done. It all came flooding out once I'd picked her up. She was sweaty and covered in dirt from the woods. She had all this stuff with her: shovel, flashlight... and a knife."

"What happened to all that?"

"Once she'd told me what she'd done, I was in shock. I actually arrested her." He looks down at the ground. "I drove her to a remote spot and told her to dump everything there. I didn't touch anything." He looks up. "But I was already in too deep by then. I had no choice but to keep her secret."

Nate shakes his head.

It angers Morgan. "You're judging me, Monroe, but what if someone you loved asked for your help? Wouldn't you be there?"

"Not if I was a cop. Not if it was my job to protect and serve."

He scoffs. "Yeah, right. Not even if it was your beloved Stacey who was asking?"

Nate takes a step forward in anger and Morgan raises his gun. "Stay back. I mean it, Monroe."

Brody drops his ball and barks viciously. Morgan backs away slightly. "I should have shot him the first time I laid eyes on him."

"So what now?" asks Nate. "How do we get out of this without killing each other?"

Morgan shakes his head. "I need time to think."

"Listen, the worst you'll be charged with is aiding and abetting. Unless you kill me. Then you'll get death row, if you're lucky."

Morgan's confused. "Why is that lucky?"

"Because life without parole is worse. You'll be in general population, and as a former cop, you'll be tortured in there. Death row's no vacation, but it has certain benefits over general pop. Want me to tell you about them?"

Morgan turns and vomits on the ground. The reality of his situation is clearly beginning to sink in.

Nate sees an opportunity to pounce. But a sound to his left stops him. The detective must have heard it too, as he looks up in the same direction as the noise.

Shivers run down Nate's body. There's someone in the woods.

CHAPTER EIGHTY-NINE

The sharp, cramping pains in her stomach have been getting worse with each day that passes. For the hundredth time, Jenny wishes she had rationed her candy better, but she couldn't possibly have known she would be lost for this long. Her backpack is completely empty of any food now, so she's using it as a pillow, with her swimming towel rolled up inside. At night, she has to use her towel as a blanket to keep warm, but not tonight. She doesn't have the energy to even retrieve it from her backpack.

She tries moving her right foot in a circle. As her stomach and energy levels have deteriorated, the pain in her ankle has improved. It twisted as her leg bashed a rock when she hit the water in the pool below. The impact, mixed with the water filling her lungs, momentarily dazed her, but somehow she didn't pass out. She eventually crawled out of the water, cold and shivering, and found a bush to hide behind. With her backpack getting soaked in the water, it loosened the rope around her arms, but she didn't untie it that first night. She was too stunned by what had happened. Upset that her mom hated her enough to try to kill her, she was paralyzed with fear and didn't sleep at all. It wasn't until the next day that she wriggled free.

She licks her dry lips and tries to ignore the hunger pains. Her death is being dragged out, and just when she thinks she won't wake up again, she always does. The fresh water from the waterfall has been invaluable in keeping her alive, but she panics every time she needs to hobble over to drink, convinced her mom will return to make sure she's dead. The survival skills Donna taught them at camp quickly became useful. She stayed out of the intense sunshine, finding shelter under the thick canopy of trees around her, and she's tried to stay put as much as possible.

The bugs mostly kept their distance on the first day, but when she started smelling sweaty, the mosquitoes buzzed around her day and night, sucking her blood and causing nasty, itchy bumps on her skin. That was when she started making sure to have a wash under the waterfall every day. But even worse were the creepy-crawlies, which would get into her ears and nose while she slept, and she's pretty sure she's seen snakes slithering under the fallen leaves around her. Staying alive was exhausting.

After the first week, the days and nights blurred into one, with nothing to distinguish between them. When she ran out of candy, she realized she would have to be brave and try to find a way out of here. She thought if she could find a highway, she could flag someone down and they could call the police for her. She could tell them what her mom had done in the hope that someone would believe her story. But when she tried to leave, she kept going around in circles, not just because her ankle was painful, but because the forest was so dense in places that she was unable to get through the thick underbrush. She had to turn back, exhausted.

After a whole day of walking, she ended back at the waterfall. With hunger kicking in after so much exertion, she desperately tried tasting a handful of small berries she couldn't identify. They immediately made her violently sick, stopping her from trying anything else as a potential food source. She was so ill she would have happily let death take her right then. There were a lot of tears that day, which made her thirsty, so she stayed close to the water while she thought about her mom and dad.

She misses her dad so much. Just thinking about him makes her cry again, but no tears fall because there's no fluid left in her. For days now she's been too weak to drink.

As she lies flat on her back, looking up at the stars through the small breaks in the lush canopy, she wonders again why her dad didn't come to save her. He must have wondered where she'd gone. She realizes it's time to accept the unbearable truth: he wanted her dead too. That means no one has ever really loved her. Not her first mom, her foster parents or her current parents. She knows it's her own fault. She tries to control her anger, but it springs up out of nowhere, and once she's angry, she has to release it on someone. After so many failed attempts at controlling herself, one day she took one of her foster mom's kitchen knives and sliced her arm badly. Everyone shouted at her. No one asked why she did it. No one ever helps her with her anger.

Her dad never makes her angry; she's always been able to relax around him. He's so patient with her, taking her fishing, helping her with school work. Grandma is nice, but she tries too hard, probably wishing Jenny were Susie. Jenny knows she misses Susie and Thomas and that she's just the replacement. But at least Grandma tries, unlike Mom.

From the minute she met her new mom, she knew she was mean like all the foster moms. She knew she wouldn't be patient enough. She was always too busy with the little kids. Her real children. So Jenny couldn't control her anger around her, despite trying hard. She wants a normal life so bad, but it never lasts. She feels like there's something wrong with her that means she's not supposed to be loved. She acts up to speed up the rejection, to get it over with.

She suddenly coughs, and it causes a searing pain in her chest. She's weakening. She knows she needs water, but she can't move today. She has no energy left. A strange feeling of calm has settled over her. It's like she doesn't care anymore what happens. Part of her knows she's going to die soon. She thinks of her biology books and knows her body will slowly disintegrate back into the earth.

"Earth to earth, ashes to ashes, dust to dust," she whispers.

Maybe the animals she hears at night will come and claim her bones.

She opens her eyes and realizes she's starting to fade. She doesn't have long left. Did she imagine the voices, or were they real? She listens. It's a man's voice, she's sure of it. She tries calling out, using all her remaining strength.

"Daddy?"

Her voice isn't loud enough. It's too late for her. She closes her eyes and drifts away.

CHAPTER NINETY

Nate hears the whisper of a voice and can see that Brody heard it too.

"Get her, boy!"

Brody zooms off ahead of him, running easily through the thick brush. When he starts barking, Nate's nerves jump. He doesn't want to get his hopes up, but he pushes through the foliage and shines his flashlight at the dog.

Brody is sitting alert, looking over his shoulder. Nate glances down as he reaches him.

"Oh my God."

He falls to his knees next to Jennifer Lucas. Somehow she survived her mother's attempted murder.

Morgan gasps behind him.

"Bring some water!" yells Nate. He leans his ear to her mouth and can feel her warm breath on his face. His hands are trembling as he shakes her gently by the shoulder. "Jenny?"

She doesn't react. They don't have much time.

"Jenny? Can you hear me? You're going to be okay, sweetie. You need to keep breathing, okay?"

Her eyes flutter open. It takes a minute for them to focus on him. "Where's my dad?"

Nate has to swallow the lump in his throat. He's overwhelmed to find Jenny alive, but he knows she'll be devastated when she finds out her father killed himself thinking she was dead. And he was so close to finding her. Then he thinks of Esme, who stopped at nothing to try and bring her granddaughter home. He can't be the one to break the news. "We're going to get you home, okay?"

She shakes her head and looks afraid. "Not home."

He understands her fear. "Not home. I meant somewhere safe."

She smiles slowly and closes her eyes again.

He hears multiple voices approaching and sees flashlights shining through the trees. He slowly stands as he realizes what's happening, and raises his hands above his head in surrender mode.

"What are you doing?" asks Morgan as he returns with cupped hands. He puts them to Jenny's mouth and lets the water wet her lips. She licks them but doesn't move.

Nate looks down at him. "I'm removing any ambiguity from this situation. You cops tend to shoot first and ask questions later."

A tall older guy in a suit approaches them and assesses the situation. "You stupid son of a bitch, Morgan."

Morgan looks up at him. "I didn't kill anyone, Chief. And we have time to save the girl. I had no idea she was still alive. The mother told me she was dead."

The chief leans in close as Nate watches. "Don't say a word to anyone," he says quietly. "We'll take care of you. The parents obviously went crazy and can't be trusted with their version of events. We have Anna Lucas. She attempted to run."

Nate burns with anger. They're going to protect Morgan, even though he helped Anna cover up what she'd done. Jenny could have been found sooner if he had acted like the professional he's supposed to be. Grant and Esme would still be alive.

The chief moves aside for the approaching ambulance crew, and the EMTs check Jenny over. When they're satisfied they can move her without causing any damage, they gently lift her onto a stretcher, put an oxygen mask on her face and carry her away.

Morgan rubs his face and then bends down to pick up his discarded weapon. The chief immediately takes it off him, but he doesn't cuff him and he doesn't ask for his badge. Instead he points his flashlight at Nate, who can barely contain his anger at the thought of Morgan getting off scot-free.

"I have to cuff you until we get you to the station and find out what happened here," he says.

Nate remains passive and silent. As the chief cuffs him, he never takes his eyes off Morgan, who looks away, clearly ashamed.

Maybe now he'll understand why Nate hates cops.

CHAPTER NINETY-ONE

Madison wakes to Nate looking down at her. She wipes her mouth.

"Oh my God, was I drooling?"

He laughs. "Just a little."

She's dressed, bandaged and ready to leave this hospital and this town. She didn't mean to fall asleep; it's the tablets they gave her for the pain making her drowsy. She's been sitting outside Anna's room for an hour, waiting for news from Nate. Standing, she notices he looks tired and disheveled. "What happened out there? Did you find Jenny? You look like shit, by the way."

He nods. "I feel like shit. I heard you got stabbed."

She shrugs. "It was just a kitchen knife. It didn't do too much damage, but it hurts like a bitch."

He smiles. "Where's Anna?"

Madison nods to the room behind her. "In there. She had her baby early, when she was trying to escape."

"I want to tell you both together what happened."

Madison gets goosebumps on her arms. She doesn't know if she wants to hear this.

A guy in a suit approaches them. "Hi, I'm Chief Hennessy. I take it you're the woman who called us about Mrs. Lucas?"

She nods.

Hennessy leads them past the two uniforms stationed at the door. Madison hangs back as he and Nate approach the bed.

Anna's sitting up, and despite everything, she looks happy. She has her baby next to her bed, with a nurse watching her closely. Madison wonders how long it will be before child services take the baby away, and whether Anna realizes that's what's going to happen. Just the thought of it makes her feel sick. After all, she's been there.

When Anna spots them all, her smile falters. "Who are you?"

"I'm Ted Morgan's boss, Chief Hennessy."

Her whole face drops. "Have you found Grant?"

He nods. "Yes. He's deceased. It looks like suicide. We have it on video."

Madison shakes her head. Even after everything she's done, she can't help feeling sorry for Anna. Hennessy's bedside manner could do with some work.

Nate obviously agrees, as he takes over. "Anna?"

Dazed, with tears running down her face, she turns to him. "Where was he?"

"He was in the forest. He'd gone there to look for Jenny. To apologize to her."

Anna looks down at the bed and rubs her hands together like she's cold. Madison is pleased to see she's affected by Grant's death, because it's been difficult to see the human behind what she did to her daughter.

"We found someone else," says Nate. "We found Jenny."

Anna raises her eyes and shakes her head. "I don't want anything to do with her remains. Someone else will have to bury her. Maybe Grant's family will take care of all that."

Madison closes her eyes against tears. She takes a deep breath. She's shocked at the callousness of Anna's reaction. How could she hate a child that much? She shivers and looks at Nate. It must have been awful for him to discover her. It's unlikely he's seen a dead child before, and she knows from experience that something like that is hard to forget. She'd be surprised if this doesn't trigger another depressive episode.

Nate shares a look with the chief, who nods, prompting him to go on. "Anna? Jenny's alive."

Madison takes a step back, as if pushed. "What?" She covers her mouth with her hands. She's never felt more relieved in her life. "Oh, thank God." Her reaction surprises her. She's always been so good at distancing herself from victims. But this case was different. It got to her.

Anna shouts, "What? Don't you dare say that! Tell me you don't mean it?" Her face has drained of all blood. Her shouting wakes the baby, who starts crying.

Chief Hennessy takes a step closer to the bed.

Nate continues. "Somehow she got out of the water in one piece and survived over two weeks alone in the woods."

"But there were so many rocks!" says Anna, clearly horrified.

"I guess she got lucky. Probably for the first time in her life."

Anna gulps, shaking her head. Madison feels like she might faint. She moves to the visitor armchair and sits down. This is amazing news.

Nate has one more revelation. "Jenny's here, Anna. She's on the floor above. She's going to be okay."

Anna screams and Madison's not prepared for it. It pierces her ears. She watches as Anna jumps out of the bed, pulling away from the machines she's wired to. Her baby cries louder; the nurse lifts her from the cot and takes her away.

Chief Hennessy has hold of Anna, and Madison steps in front of her to block the doorway just as the uniforms enter the room. She grabs her by the arms. "Leave her alone, Anna. She's just a child."

"She ruined my life!"

Madison wants to slap her. "You ruined your own life when you tried to kill her. That girl needed you and Grant, and you both failed her."

Anna's not listening. "My baby!" Her eyes frantically search the room, but the baby is no longer there. "You need to protect my baby from that girl!"

"Don't worry, your baby will be protected," says Madison, with unconcealed contempt. "She'll be protected from *you*."

Anna slumps onto the floor, defeated.

Chief Hennessy cuffs her. "Anna Lucas, I'm arresting you for child abduction and attempted murder. I suggest you hire a lawyer."

Nate takes Madison's hand and leads her out of the room as Anna sobs on the floor.

CHAPTER NINETY-TWO

When the prison guard cuts Nate's wristband and tells him he's free to go, Nate almost breaks down. Almost. He doesn't want to give the man the satisfaction. He was hoping Gus would be the one to free him, so he could look him in the eye as he did so, but Gus took the day off sick.

Nate picks up his brown paper bag of belongings and walks on shaking legs to the door. An officer he's never met holds it open, wishing him luck as he passes.

Nate stops to look at him. Is he being facetious? He looks into the man's eyes. No. He means it. That's the first time a guard has said anything positive to him in seventeen years. The first time he's been treated as an equal. He nods to the guy and then turns to the open doorway.

He worries that he's going to be grabbed and pulled back the minute he steps over the threshold, because that's what happens in his dreams: he's always taken straight back inside and told it was all a joke. Like the time Gus told him Kristen was waiting to speak to him, long after her disappearance, and escorted him to the interview room. Nate was burning with hope and relief, anxious to see her and find out what had happened to her. When he got in there, the room was empty. It was a cruel trick.

Now, the sunlight dazzles him and it takes a while for him to be able to see anything. The fresh air aggravates his lungs, making him cough. When he can open his eyes and look up, he sees the waiting press: hundreds of vultures in front of satellite vans wanting to know how he feels about being exonerated, and whether he'll sue the state of Texas for his wrongful conviction. He can hear crowds chanting something behind them. Probably a mixture of pro and anti capital punishment protesters.

He stops, not wanting to go over there. There are no walls or bars ahead of him, just an open landscape behind the crowds and an impossibly vast sky. He feels panicked, like he needs to find another way out, and even takes a step back toward the prison.

Suddenly he's almost floored as someone rushes up and hugs him so tight he can't breathe.

"It's over, Nate," Rex whispers into his ear. "The nightmare is over."

CHAPTER NINETY-THREE

Two days later, Madison is waiting to collect Nate from the jaws of law enforcement. He's had to give a written statement about what happened in the forest.

She smiles as she watches him walk out from behind the police station's front desk. Chief Hennessy escorts him.

"Thanks for your cooperation, Mr. Monroe," says the chief. He notices Brody, who is sitting patiently next to her. "That the dog from the summer camp? Morgan mentioned he needs putting down. Apparently he's aggressive."

"No, he's not," says Nate. "He just doesn't like child abductors and corrupt cops. Anyway, he's not mine."

"Well he might be now. I've spoken to the owners of Camp Fearless, who've told me they're shutting the place. They're hoping to let the bad press die down and then open it, rebranded, in a year or two. They don't want the dog, apparently. They say he never belonged to them. So if you don't claim him, he might not stand a chance."

Madison touches Nate's arm. She doesn't want to say it out loud, but she can tell Nate's picking up on her thoughts: they can't leave Brody with this bunch of assholes.

"We'll take him," he says.

The chief nods. "We'll be in touch about a court date."

Madison's smile falters. "What court date?"

Nate turns to her. "It's okay. I'm not being charged with anything. I may be called as a witness against Anna and Morgan, but hopefully not, as Grant's recorded confession and Morgan's testimony about his involvement should be enough to convict her."

"We have the mother's journal in our possession too," says the chief. "I understand it's pretty damning."

Madison is relieved. "What will happen to Jenny now?"

"She'll be under the protection of child services. They're best placed to take care of her."

Madison tries not to grimace. She hopes Jenny gets the psychological help she needs in order to move on from her ordeal, but the system is stacked against her.

"Has she been told about Grant and Esme yet?"

"No. Child services are flying in a specialist from New York to do everything properly. She needs the best of the best if she's ever to get a fresh start."

Madison popped in to see Jenny at the hospital yesterday. The girl obviously didn't know who she was, and Madison didn't go into detail; just said she was on the team of people trying to find her. She wanted to see for herself whether Jenny was as evil as Anna had made out, to try to understand Anna's thought process when planning to kill her daughter. What she found was an underweight, shy little girl who happily accepted her gifts of magazines and chocolate. Madison warmed to her, especially when Jenny hugged her to say thank you for not giving up on her. She had to leave then before she broke down. She didn't want to upset the girl.

After having met her, Madison believes in Esme's version of Jenny, and she prays child services will be more careful in their next choice of family.

"What about Morgan?" Nate asks Hennessy. "I assume he's at least fired."

"Of course. His wife bailed him out yesterday. He made a stupid decision based on his history with the mother. He's learned a terrible lesson, and he'll never serve as a cop again."

Nate shakes his head. "Stupid decision?"

Madison understands his anger. They all know that if Morgan wasn't a cop, he'd be sitting in a cell right now with no option of bail.

They're about to walk out of the station when Chief Hennessy holds out his hand to them. Madison automatically shakes it. She watches as Nate just looks at it. He's told her what Hennessy said to Morgan up in the forest; that he practically guaranteed he'd help Morgan get off as lightly as possible. That will bug the hell out of Nate. She doesn't think there's any chance he'll shake this man's hand.

She's right. Nate walks away. Over his shoulder he says, "You have my number."

Brody leads them out of the station. They walk to Nate's car, and after they buckle up, Madison checks her phone and sighs. No messages.

"What is it?" asks Nate.

She takes a deep breath. "I've not heard from Steph since she sent me a text with kisses at the end, which is out of character for her. She never uses kisses. It has me worried."

"Try calling her."

"I have, but she never picks up. I'm starting to worry. What if those men have got her?"

He thinks about it for a minute. "Let me try calling her using my phone. She might pick up if she doesn't think it's you."

She holds her phone out so he can see Stephanie's number. She hears the line ring about four times before it's picked up, but there's just silence. Nate puts it on loudspeaker.

"Stephanie?" he says.

After a few seconds, a man speaks. "Who is this?"

Nate looks at Madison. "My name's Nate. Is Stephanie there?"

More silence. Then, "Put Madison on the line."

Nate hands the phone over to her, confused.

Madison recognizes the voice. It's Mike. Somehow she knows what he's going to say. Her heart beats faster and she breaks out in a sweat. "Mike?" she says.

"Yeah. I've just had a call-out to Steph's house." He pauses. "It's bad, Madison."

Madison's arms go numb. She drops the phone and turns away. Nate picks it up off her lap. "What's happened?" he asks.

"I don't know who you are, but you need to get Madison here as soon as possible. Her ex-girlfriend is dead."

Nate reaches across and puts his hand on hers. "We'll be there as soon as we can." He ends the call.

"Madison? Did you hear that?"

She nods, her eyes filled with tears.

"I'm sorry."

His words can't comfort her. She needs action. He appears to sense this, because he drops her phone back into her lap and starts the car's engine. "I'm going to drive us straight to Colorado. Is that what you want?"

She's thinking of her son. Is he going to be next?

She looks at Nate as tears run down her cheeks. All she can do is nod.

A LETTER FROM WENDY

Dear Reader,

Thank you so much for giving the first book of my new series a try! I really hope you enjoyed it and that you're as excited as I am to find out what happens next to Madison and Nate. You can keep in touch with me and get updates about the series by signing up to my newsletter and by following me on social media.

www.bookouture.com/wendy-dranfield

You might be pleased to know Book 2 is on the way very soon. Both Madison and Nate have been through so much already in their lives and we have more to learn about them as the series progresses. I hope you'll stay on this journey with them.

If you enjoyed this book, please do leave a review, as this helps it to reach more readers.

Thank you!
Wendy x

🖥 wendydranfield.co.uk

🐦 WendyDranfield

f WendyDranfield1

ACKNOWLEDGMENTS

Thank you to Bookouture for believing in this new series as much as I do. Especially to Jessie Botterill, my editor, for providing such valuable and insightful feedback. Books are always made stronger with a skillful team of editors, and that is most definitely the case here.

Thanks also to my loyal readers who are always on my mind as I write. I try to make each book as thrilling as possible so you enjoy it as much as I do. I hope you enjoy this series and these characters as much as my last. There's even a dog in it for you!

And thank you to all the book bloggers who help share my books far and wide. I appreciate all your hard work and support.

Finally, thanks to my husband for always supporting my writing career and for being on hand to pop to the shops for chocolate on the dark days when it feels like I have no idea what I'm doing!

Printed in Great Britain
by Amazon